Carl Schurz

Life of Henry Clay

Vol. I

Carl Schurz

Life of Henry Clay
Vol. I

ISBN/EAN: 9783337061319

Printed in Europe, USA, Canada, Australia, Japan

Cover: Foto ©Raphael Reischuk / pixelio.de

More available books at **www.hansebooks.com**

American Statesmen

LIFE OF HENRY CLAY

BY

CARL SCHURZ

IN TWO VOLUMES

VOL. I.

BOSTON AND NEW YORK

HOUGHTON MIFFLIN COMPANY

The Riverside Press Cambridge

CONTENTS OF VOL. I.

HENRY CLAY.

CHAPTER I.

YOUTH.

FEW public characters in American history have been the subjects of more heated **controversy** than Henry Clay. There was no measure of detraction and obloquy to which, during his lifetime, his opponents would **not** resort, and there **seemed to be** no limit **to** the admiration **and** attachment of **his** friends. **While his enemies** denounced him as **a** pretender and selfish intriguer **in** politics and **an** abandoned profligate in private life, his supporters unhesitatingly placed him first among the sages of the period, and, **by way** of defense, sometimes even among its saints. The animosities against him have, naturally, long ago disappeared; but **even now, more** than thirty years after his death, we may hear old men, who knew him **in the days of** his strength, speak of him with an enthusiasm **and** affection so warm and fresh as to convince us that the recollection of having followed his leadership is among the dearest treasures of their memory. The remarkable fascination he exercised seems to **have**

reached even beyond his living existence. It is, therefore, not to be wondered at that his biographers, most of whom were his personal friends, should have given us an abundance of rhapsodic eulogy, instead of a clear account of what their hero thought on matters of public interest, of what he did and advised others to do, of his successes and his failures, and of the influence he exercised in shaping the development of this Republic. This, indeed, is not an easy task, for Henry Clay had, during the long period of his public life, covering nearly half a century, a larger share in national legislation than any other contemporary statesman, — not, indeed, as an originator of ideas and systems, but as an arranger of measures, and as a leader of political forces. His public life may therefore be said to be an important part of the national history.

Efforts have been made by enthusiastic admirers to find for him a noble ancestry in England, but with questionable success. We may content ourselves with saying that the greatness of his name rests entirely upon his own merit. The family from which he sprang emigrated from England not long after the establishment of the colony of Virginia, and settled on the southern side of the James River. His biographers, some of whom wrote under his own supervision, agree in the statement that Henry Clay was born on April 12, 1777, in Hanover County, Virginia, in a neighborhood called the "Slashes." His father, John

Clay, was a Baptist clergyman, of sterling character, of great dignity of deportment, much esteemed by all who knew him, and "remarkable for his fine voice and delivery." The pastor's flock consisted of poor people. A rock in South Anna River has long been pointed out as a spot "from which he used at times to address his congregation." Henry Clay's mother was a daughter of George Hudson, of Hanover County. She is said to have been a woman of exemplary qualities as a wife and a mother, and of much patriotic spirit.

The Reverend John Clay died in 1781, when Henry was only four years old, and there is a tradition in the family that, while the dead body was still lying in the house, Colonel Tarleton, commanding a cavalry force under Lord Cornwallis, passed through Hanover County on a raid, and left a handful of gold and silver on Mrs. Clay's table as a compensation for some property taken or destroyed by his soldiers; but that the spirited woman, as soon as Tarleton was gone, swept the money into her apron and threw it into the fireplace. It would have been in no sense improper, and more prudent, had she kept it, notwithstanding her patriotic indignation; for she was left a widow with seven children, and there was only a very small estate to support the family.

Under such circumstances Henry, the fifth of the seven children of the widow, received no better schooling than other poor boys of the neighborhood. The schoolhouse of the "Slashes" was a

small log-cabin with the hard earth for a floor, and
the schoolmaster an Englishman who passed under
the name of Peter Deacon, — a man of an uncertain past and somewhat given to hard drinking,
but possessing ability enough to teach the children
confided to him reading, writing, and elementary
arithmetic. When not at school Henry had to
work for the support of the family, and he was
often seen walking barefooted behind the plough,
or riding on a pony to Daricott's mill on the Pa-
munkey River, using a rope for a bridle and a bag
filled with wheat or corn or flour as a saddle.
Thus he earned the nickname of " the mill-boy of
the Slashes," which subsequently, in his campaigns
for the presidency, was thought to be worth a good
many votes.

A few years after her first husband's death, the
widow Clay married Captain Henry Watkins, a
resident of Richmond, who seems to have been a
worthy man and a good step-father to his wife's
children. To start young Henry in life Captain
Watkins placed him as a " boy behind the counter "
in the retail store kept by Richard Denny in the
city of Richmond. Henry, who was then fourteen
years old, devoted himself for about a year with
laudable diligence and fidelity to the duty of drawing molasses and measuring tape, giving his leisure
hours to the reading of such books as happened to
fall into his hands. But it occurred to Captain
Watkins that his step-son, the brightness and activity of whose mind were noticed by him as well as

others, might be found fit for a more promising career. He contrived through the influence of his friend Colonel Tinsley, a member of the House of Burgesses, to obtain for young Henry a place in the office of the Clerk of the High Court of Chancery, that clerk being Mr. Peter Tinsley, the Colonel's brother. There was really no vacancy, but the Colonel's patronizing zeal proved irresistible, and Henry was appointed as a supernumerary.

To Roland Thomas, the senior clerk of the office, who lived to see and admire Henry Clay in his greatness, we are indebted for an account of the impression produced by the lad as he appeared in his new surroundings. He was a rawboned, lank, awkward youth, with a countenance by no means handsome, yet not unpleasing. His garments, of gray "figinny" cloth, were home-made and ill-fitting, and his linen, which the good mother had starched for the occasion to unusual stiffness, made him look peculiarly strange and uncomfortable. With great uneasiness of manner he took his place at the desk where he was to begin copying papers, while his new companions could not refrain from tittering at his uncouth appearance and his blushing confusion. But they soon learned to respect and also to like him. It turned out that he could talk uncommonly well when he ventured to talk freely, and presently he proved himself the brightest and also the most studious young man among them. He continued to "read books" when the hours of work were over, while most of his com-

panions gave themselves up to the pleasures of the
town.

Then the fortunate accident arrived which is
so frequently found in the lives of young men of
uncommon quality and promise. He began to attract the attention of persons of superior merit.
George Wythe, the Chancellor of the High Court
of Chancery, who often had occasion to visit Peter
Tinsley's office, noticed the new-comer, and selected him from among the employees there to act
as an amanuensis in writing out and recording the
decisions of the court. This became young Clay's
principal occupation for four years, during which
his intercourse with the learned and venerable
judge grew constantly more intimate and elevating. As he had to write much from the Chancellor's dictation, the subject-matter of his writing,
which at first was a profound mystery to him,
gradually became a matter of intelligent interest.
The Chancellor, whose friendly feeling for the
bright youth grew warmer as their relations became more confidential, began to direct his reading, at first turning him to grammatical studies,
and then gradually opening to him a wider range
of legal and historical literature. But — what was
equally, if not more important — in the pauses of
their work and in hours of leisure, the Chancellor
conversed with his young secretary upon grave
subjects, and thus did much to direct his thoughts
and to form his principles.

Henry Clay could not have found a wiser and

nobler mentor. George Wythe was one of the most honorably distinguished men of a **period** abounding in great names. **Born in** 1726, he received his education at William and Mary College. **At** the age of thirty **he** devoted himself **to** the study and practice of the **law, and** rose quickly to eminence in **the** profession. **In** 1758 he represented the college in the House of Burgesses. In **1764 he drew** up **a** remonstrance against the Stamp **Act,** addressed to the British Parliament. As a member of the Congress of 1776 he was one **of the** signers of **the** Declaration **of** Independence. For ten years he taught jurisprudence at William and Mary. He aided **Jefferson** in revising **the** laws **of Virginia. In 1777 he** was appointed a Judge of the High Court **of Chancery, and** in 1786 **became** Chancellor. **He was a member of the** convention which framed **the federal** Constitution, **and one of its warmest advocates in the** Virginia **Convention** which ratified **it.** But he achieved **a** more peculiar distinction **by** practically demonstrating **the sincerity of his faith** in the humane philosophy **of** the **age. In his** lifetime **he** emancipated all **his slaves and made** a liberal provision for **their** subsistence. There were few **men in his day of** larger **information and experience, and scarcely** any of higher principle. **Nor was Henry Clay the only** one of **his** pupils who **afterward won a great name, for** Thomas Jefferson and John Marshall had been students of law in George Wythe's office.

When young Clay had served **four years as the**

Chancellor's amanuensis, his mind was made **up** that he would become a lawyer. He entered the office of Robert Brooke, **the** Attorney-General of Virginia, as a regular law **student,** spent about **a year** with him, and then obtained from the **judges of** the Court of Appeals a license to **practice the** profession. This was quick studying, **or** the license must have been cheap, unless we assume that **the** foundations **of** his legal **knowledge were** amply laid **in his intercourse with Chancellor Wythe.**

But **in** the mean **time he had** also **been introduced** in society. Richmond at that time possessed less than 5,000 inhabitants, but it was the most **important** city in the state, — the political capital as **well as** the social centre of Virginia. **The character** of Virginian society had become greatly changed during the Revolutionary War. The glories of Williamsburg, the colonial capital, with its "palace," **its** Raleigh **Tavern, its Apollo** Hall, its gay and magnificent gatherings **of the** planter magnates, **were** gone **never to** return. Many **of the** "first families" **had** become much reduced in **their** circumstances. Moreover, the system of **primogeniture** and entail had been abolished **by legal enactments** moved by Jefferson, **and thus** the legal foundation upon which alone a permanent landed aristocracy can maintain itself had disappeared. Although much **of the old** spirit still remained alive, yet the general current was decidedly democratic, and the distance between **the** blooded gentry

and less " well-born " people was materially lessened.
Thus the " mill-boy of the Slashes," having become
known as a young man of uncommon intellectual
brightness, high spirits, **and good** character, and
being, besides, well introduced through his friendship with Chancellor Wythe, found it possible to
come into friendly contact with persons of social
pretensions far above his own. He succeeded even
in organizing a " rhetorical society," or debating
club, among whose members there were **not** a few
young men who subsequently became distinguished.
It was on this field that he first achieved something
like leadership, while his quick intelligence and
his sympathetic qualities made **him** a favorite in
a much larger circle. According to all accounts
Henry Clay, at that **period of** his life, **was** un-
touched by vice **or** bad **habit, and** could in every
respect be esteemed as **an** irreproachable and very
promising young man.

But he soon discovered that all these things
would not give him a paying practice as an attorney in Richmond so quickly **as** he desired ; and as
his mother and step-father had removed **to** Kentucky in **1792, he** resolved to follow them **to the**
western wilds, **and** there to " grow up with **the**
country." **He was** in his twenty-first year when
he left Richmond, with his license **to** practice **as**
an attorney, but with little else, in his pocket.

This was the end of Henry Clay's regular schooling. Thenceforth he did not again in his life find
a period of leisure to be quietly and exclusively

devoted to study.   What he had learned was little
enough.   In Peter Deacon's schoolhouse he had received nothing but the first elementary instruction.
The year he spent behind the counter of Denny's
store could not have added much to **his stock** of
knowledge.   **In** Peter Tinsley's office he **had** cultivated a neat and regular handwriting, of **which**
a folio volume of Chancellor Wythe's decisions,
once **in** the possession of Jefferson, now in the
library of the Supreme Court of the United States,
gives ample testimony.   Under Chancellor Wythe's
guidance **he** had read Harris's Homer, Tooke's
Diversions of Purley, Bishop Lowth's Grammar,
Plutarch's Lives, some elementary law-books, and
a few works **on** history.   Further, the Chancellor's
conversation had undoubtedly been in a high degree instructive and morally elevating.   But all
these things did not constitute a well-ordered education.   His only more or less systematic training
he received during the short year he spent as a law
student **in the** office of Attorney-General Brooke,
and that **can** scarcely have gone far beyond **the**
elementary principles of law and the ordinary rou-
tine of practice in court.   **On** the whole, he had
depended upon the occasional gathering of miscel-
laneous information.   **He** could thus, at best, have
acquired only a slender equipment for the tasks
before him.   This, however, would have been of
comparatively slight importance had he, in learn-
ing what little he knew, cultivated thorough meth-
ods of inquiry, and the habit of reasoning out

questions, and of not being satisfied until the subject in hand was well understood in all its aspects. The habit he really had cultivated was that of rapidly skimming over the surface of the subjects of his study, in order to gather what knowledge was needed for immediate employment; and as his oratorical genius was developed early and well, he possessed the faculty of turning every bit of information to such advantage as to produce upon his hearers the impression that he possessed rich accumulations behind the actual display. Sometimes he may have thus satisfied and deceived even himself. This superficiality remained one of his weak points through life. No doubt he went on learning, but he learned rather from experience than from study; and though experience is a good school, yet it is apt to be irregular and fragmentary in its teachings.

Some of Henry Clay's biographers have expressed the opinion that the scantiness and irregularity of instruction he received, without the aid of academy or college, were calculated to quicken his self-reliance and thereby to become an element of strength in his character especially qualifying him for political leadership. It is quite possible that, had he in his youth acquired the inclination and faculty for methodical inquiry and thus the habit of examining both sides of every question with equal interest, he would have been less quick in forming final conclusions from first impressions, less easily persuaded of the absolute correctness of

his own opinions, less positive and commanding in
the promulgation of them, and less successful in inspiring his **followers** with a ready belief in his in-
fallibility.   But that he might have avoided grave
errors as a statesman had his early training been
such as to **form** his mind for more thorough thinking, and thus to lay a larger basis for his later development, **he** himself seemed now and then to feel.
It was with melancholy regret **that** he sometimes
spoke of his " neglected education, improved by
his own irregular efforts, without the benefit of
systematic instruction."

When **he** settled down **in** Kentucky his new
surroundings were by no means such as to remedy
this defect.   Active life in a new country stimu-
lates many energies, but it **is** not favorable to the
development of studious habits.   In this respect
Kentucky **was** far from forming **an** exception.

CHAPTER II.

THE KENTUCKY LAWYER.

AT the time when Henry Clay left Richmond to
seek his fortune in Kentucky, the valley of the
Ohio was the " Far West " of the country, attracting two distinct classes of adventurous and enter-
prising spirits. Only nine years before, in 1788,
the Ohio River had floated down the flat-boats carrying the pioneers who founded the first settlements on the northern bank at Marietta and on
the present site of Cincinnati ; but forthwith a
steady stream had poured in, which in twelve years
had swelled the population of the territory destined to become the State of Ohio to 45,000 souls.
They came mainly from New England, New York,
and Pennsylvania. Emigrants from the Slave
States, too, in considerable number, sought new
homes in the southern portion of the Northwest
Territory, but they formed only a minority. The
settlement of Kentucky was of an older date, and
its population of a different character. Daniel
Boone entered the "dark and bloody ground " in
1769, seven years before the colonies declared
themselves independent. Other hardy and intrepid spirits soon followed him, to dispute the

possession of the land with the Indians. **They** were hunters and pioneer farmers, not intent upon founding large industrial communities, but fond of the wild, adventurous, lonesome, unrestrained **life of** the frontiersman. **Ten years** after Daniel Boone's **first** settlement, Kentucky **was** said **to** contain **less than two** hundred white inhabitants. **But then immigration began to** flow **in** rapidly, so that in **1790, when** the **first** federal **census was taken,** Kentucky **had a** population **of 73,600,** — of whom 61,000 **were white. About one half of the** whites and **three fourths of the slaves had come** from Virginia, **the rest mostly from North** Carolina and Maryland, **with a sprinkling of Pennsyl-** vanians. At the period when **Henry Clay** arrived **in** Kentucky, **in** 1797, the population exceeded 18 0,000, about one fifth of whom were slaves, — the later immigrants having come from the same quarter as **the** earlier.

The original stock consisted of the hardiest race of **backwoodsmen. The forests** of Kentucky were literally wrested from **the Indians** by constant fighting. **The question** whether the aborigines had **any** right **to the soil seems to have** been **utterly** foreign **to** the pioneer's **mind. He wanted** the land, and to him it was a matter **of** course that **the** Indian must leave it. **The** first settlements planted **in** the virgin forest were fortified with stockades and block-houses, which the inmates, not **seldom for** months **at a time,** could not leave with- out danger of **falling into an Indian** ambush and being scalped. No part of the country has therefore more stories and traditions of perilous adventtures, bloody fights, and hairbreadth escapes. For a generation or more the hunting-shirt, leggins, and moccasins of deerskin more or less gaudily ornamented, and the long rifle, powder-horn, and hunting-knife formed the regular " outfit " of a very large proportion of the male Kentuckians. We are told of some of the old pioneers who, many years after populous towns had grown up on the sites of the old stockades, still continued the habit of walking about in their hunter's garb, with rifle and powder-horn, although the deer had become scarce and the Indian had long ago disappeared from the neighborhood. They were loath to make up their minds to the fact that the old wild life was over. Thus the reminiscences and the characteristic spirit and habits left behind by that wild life were still fresh among the people of Kentucky at the period of which we speak. They were an uncommonly sturdy race of men, most of them fully as fond of hunting, and perhaps also of fighting, as of farming; brave and generous, rough and reckless, hospitable and much given to boisterous carousals, full of a fierce love of independence, and of a keen taste for the confused and turbulent contests of frontier politics. Slavery exercised its peculiar despotic influence there as elsewhere, although the number of slaves in Kentucky was comparatively small. But among freemen a strongly democratic spirit prevailed. There was as yet little of that relation of superior and inferior **between** the large planter and the small tenant or farmer which had existed, and was still to some extent existing, in Virginia. As to the white population, society started on the plane of practical equality.

Where the city of Lexington now stands, **the** first block-house **was** built in April, 1775, by Robert Patterson, **" an early** and meritorious adventurer, much engaged in **the** defense of the country." A settlement soon formed under its protection, which was called Lexington, in honor of the Revolutionary battle then just fought in Massachusetts. The first settlers had **to** maintain themselves in many an Indian fight on that " finest garden spot in all Kentucky," as the Blue Grass region was justly called. In an early day it attracted " some people of culture " from Virginia, North Carolina, and Pennsylvania. In 1780 the first school was built **in** the fort, and the **same year** the Virginia legislature — for Kentucky was at that time still a part of Virginia — chartered **the** Transylvania Seminary **to** be established **there.** In 1787 Mr. Isaac Wilson, **of** the Philadelphia College, opened the " Lexington Grammar School," for the teaching of Latin, Greek, " and the **different** branches **of** science." The same year saw the organization of a " society for promoting useful knowledge," and the establishment of the first newspaper. A year later, in 1788, the ambition of social refinement wanted and got a dancing - school, and also the Transylvania Seminary was fairly ready to receive students : "Tuition five pounds a year, one half in cash, the other in property ; boarding nine pounds a year, in property, pork, corn, tobacco, etc." In ten years more the seminary, having absorbed the Kentucky Academy established by the Presbyterians, expanded into the "Transylvania University," with first an academical department, and the following year adding one of medicine and another of law. Thus Lexington, although still a small town, became what was then called "the literary and intellectual centre west of the Alleghanies," and a point of great attraction to people of means and of social wants and pretensions. It would, however, be a mistake to suppose that it was a quiet and sedate college town like those of New England. Many years later, in 1814, a young Massachusetts Yankee, Amos Kendall, who had drifted to Lexington in pursuit of profitable employment, and was then a private teacher in Henry Clay's family, wrote in his diary: "I have, I think, learned the way to be popular in Kentucky, but do not, as yet, put it in practice. Drink whiskey and talk loud, with the fullest confidence, and you will hardly fail of being called a clever fellow." This was not the only "way to be popular," but was certainly one of the ways. When the Lexington of 1797, the year of Clay's arrival there, is spoken of as a "literary and intellectual centre," the meaning is that it was an outpost of civilization still surrounded, and to a great extent permeated, by the spirit of border life. The hunter in his fringed buckskin suit, **with long** rifle and powder-horn, was still a familiar figure **on the streets of** the town. The boisterous hilar ity of the bar-room and the excitement of the card table accorded with the prevailing taste better than **a** lecture on ancient history; and a racing horse was to **a** large majority of Lexingtonians an object of far greater interest **than** a professor of Greek. But compared **with** other Western towns of the time, Lexington did possess an uncommon propor- tion of educated people; **and** there were circles wherein the social life displayed, together with the freedom of tone characteristic of a new country, **a** liberal dash of culture.

This was the place where **Henry Clay cast an-** chor in 1797. The society he found there was con- genial to him, and he was congenial to it. A young man of uncommon brightness of intellect, of fascinating address, without effort making the lit- tle he knew pass for **much** more, **of** high spirits, warm sympathies, **a** cheery nature, and sociable tastes, **he easily** became a favorite with the edu- cated as **a person of** striking ability, and with the many as **a** good companion, **who,** notwithstanding a certain distinguished air, enjoyed himself as they did. It was again as a speaker that he first made his mark. Shortly after his arrival at Lexington, **before he** had begun to practice law, he joined a debating club, in several meetings of which he par- ticipated only as a silent listener. One evening, when, after a long discussion, **the** vote upon the question before the society was about to be taken, he whispered to a friend, loudly enough to be overheard, that to him the debate did not seem to have exhausted the subject. Somebody remarked that Mr. Clay desired to speak, and he was called upon. Finding himself unexpectedly confronting the audience, he was struck with embarrassment, and, as he had done frequently in imaginary appeals in court, he began: "Gentlemen of the jury!" A titter running through the audience increased his embarrassment, and the awkward words came out once more. But then he gathered himself up; his nerves became steady, and he poured out a flow of reasoning so lucid, and at the same time so impassioned, that his hearers were overcome with astonishment. Some of his friends who had been present said, in later years, that they had never heard him make a better speech. This was, no doubt, an exaggeration of the first impression, but at any rate that speech stamped him at once as a remarkable man in the community, and laid open before him the road to success.

He had not come to Lexington with extravagant expectations. As an old man, looking back upon those days, he said: "I remember how comfortable I thought I should be if I could make one hundred pounds a year, Virginia money, and with what delight I received the first fifteen shillings fee." He approached with a certain awe the competition with what he called "a bar uncommonly distinguished by eminent members." But he did not find it difficult to make his way among them. His practice was, indeed, at first mostly in criminal cases, and many are the stories told of the marvelous effects produced by his eloquence upon the simple-minded Kentucky jurymen, and of the culprits saved by him from a well-merited fate. In one of those cases, — that of a Mrs. Phelps, a respectable farmer's wife, who in a fit of angry passion had killed her sister-in-law with a musket, — he used " temporary delirium " as a ground of defense, and thus became, if not the inventor, at least one of the earliest advocates, of that theory of emotional insanity which has served so much to confuse people's notions about the responsibility of criminals. But in the case of Mrs. Phelps the jury, with characteristic confusion of judgment, found that the accused was just insane enough not to be hung, but not insane enough to be let off without a term in jail.

There is one very curious exploit on record, exhibiting in a strong light Clay's remarkable power, not only as a speaker, but as an actor. A man named Willis was tried for a murder of peculiar atrocity. In the very teeth of the evidence, which seemed to be absolutely conclusive, Clay, defending him, succeeded in dividing the jury as to the nature of the crime committed. The jurors having been unable to agree, the public prosecutor moved for a new trial, which motion Clay did not oppose. But when, at the new trial, his turn came to address the jury, he argued that, whatever opinion the jury might form from the testimony as to the guilt of the accused, they could not now convict him, as he had already been once tried, and it was the law of the land that no man should be put twice in jeopardy of his life for the same offense. The court, having, of course, never heard that doctrine so applied, at once peremptorily forbade Clay to go on with such a line of argument. Whereupon the young attorney solemnly arose, and with an air of indignant astonishment declared that, if the court would not permit him to defend, in such manner as his duty commanded him to adopt, a man in the awful presence of death, he found himself forced to abandon the case. Then he gathered up his papers, bowed grandly, and stalked out of the room. The bench, whom Clay had impressed with the belief that he was profoundly convinced of being right in the position he had taken, and upon whom he had in such solemn tones thrown the responsibility for denying his rights to a man on trial for his life, was startled and confused. A messenger was dispatched to invite Clay in the name of the court to return and continue his argument. Clay graciously came back, and found it easy work to persuade the jury that the result of the first trial was equivalent to an acquittal, and that the prisoner, as under the law he could not be put in peril of life twice for the same offense, was clearly entitled to his discharge. The jury readily agreed upon a verdict of " not guilty."

It is said that no murderer defended by Henry

Clay ever was sentenced to death, and very early
in his professional career he acquired the reputation of being able to insure the life of any criminal intrusted to his care, whatever the degree of
guilt. That his success in saving murderers from
the gallows did not benefit the tone and character
of Kentucky society, Clay himself seemed to feel.
"Ah, Willis, poor fellow," he said once to the
man whose acquittal he had obtained by so audacious a dramatic coup, "I fear I have saved too
many like you, who ought to be hanged."

But he was equally successful in the opposite
direction when acting as public prosecutor. He
had frequently been asked to accept the office of
attorney for the commonwealth, but had always declined. At last he was prevailed upon to take it
temporarily, until he could obtain the appointment
of a friend, who, he thought, ought to have the
place. The first criminal case falling into his
hands was one of peculiar interest. A slave, who
was highly valued by his master on account of his
intelligence, industry, and self-respect, was, in the
absence of the owner, treated very unjustly and
harshly by an overseer, a white man. Once the
slave, defending himself against the blows aimed
at him, seized an axe and killed his assailant.
Clay, as public prosecutor, argued that, had the
deed been done by a free man, considering that it
was done in self-defense, it would have been justifiable homicide, or, at worst, manslaughter. But
having been done by a slave, who was in duty

bound to submit to chastisement, it was murder, and must be punished as such. It was so punished. The slave was hung; but his self-contained and heroic conduct in the presence of death extorted admiration from all who witnessed it; and this occurrence made so deep and painful an impression upon Clay himself that he resigned his place as soon as possible, and never failed to express his sorrow at the part he had played in this case whenever it was mentioned.

It was not long, however, that he remained confined to criminal cases. Soon he distinguished himself by the management of civil suits also, especially suits growing out of the peculiar land laws of Virginia and Kentucky. In this way he rapidly acquired a lucrative practice and a prominent place at the bar of his state. That with all his brilliant abilities he never worked his way into the front rank of the great lawyers of the country was due to his characteristic failing. He studied only for the occasion, as far as his immediate need went. His studies were never wide and profound. His time was too much occupied by other things, — not only by his political activity, which gradually grew more and more exacting, but also by pleasure. He was fond of company, and in that period of his life not always careful in selecting his comrades; a passion for cards grew upon him, so much so, indeed, that he never completely succeeded in overcoming it; and these tastes robbed him of the hours and of the temper of mind without which the calm gathering of thought required for the mastery of a science is not possible. Moreover, it is not improbable that his remarkable gift of speaking, which enabled him to make little tell for much, and to outshine men of vastly greater learning, deceived him as to the necessity for laborious study. The value of this faculty he appreciated well. He knew that oratory is an art, and in this art he trained himself with judgment and perseverance. For many years, as a young man, he made it a rule to read, if possible every day, in some historical or scientific book, and then to repeat what he had read in free, off-hand speech, "sometimes in a cornfield, at others in the forest, and not unfrequently in a distant barn with the horse and ox for auditors." Thus he cultivated that facility and affluence of phrase, that resonance of language, as well as that freedom of gesture, which, aided by a voice of rare power and musical beauty, gave his oratory, even to the days of declining old age, so peculiar a charm.

Only a year and a half after his arrival at Lexington, in April, 1799, he had achieved a position sufficiently respected and secure to ask for and to obtain the hand of Lucretia Hart, the daughter of a man of high character and prominent standing in the state. She was not a brilliant, but a very estimable woman, and a most devoted wife to him. She became the mother of eleven children. His prosperity increased rapidly; so that soon he was able to purchase Ashland, an estate of some six hundred acres, near Lexington, which afterward became famous as Henry Clay's home.

Together with the accumulation of worldly goods he laid up a valuable stock of popularity. Indeed, few men ever possessed in greater abundance and completeness those qualities which attract popular regard and affection. A tall stature; not a handsome face, but a pleasing, winning expression; a voice of which some of his contemporaries say that it was the finest musical instrument they ever heard; an eloquence always melodious and in turn majestic, fierce, playful, insinuating, irresistibly appealing to all the feelings of human nature, aided by a gesticulation at the same time natural, vivid, large, and powerful; a certain magnificent grandeur of bearing in public action, and an easy familiarity, a never failing natural courtesy in private, which, even in his intercourse with the lowliest, had nothing of haughty condescension in it; a noble generous heart making him always ready to volunteer his professional services to poor widows and orphans who needed aid, to slaves whom he thought entitled to their freedom, to free negroes who were in danger of being illegally returned to bondage, and to persons who were persecuted by the powerful and lawless, in serving whom he sometimes endangered his own safety; a cheery sympathetic nature, withal, of exuberant vitality, gay, spirited, always ready to enjoy, and always glad to see others enjoy themselves, — his very faults being those of what was considered good fellowship in his Kentuckian surroundings; a superior person, appearing, indeed, immensely superior at times, but making his neighbors feel that he was one of them, — such a man was born to be popular. It has frequently been said that later in life he cultivated his popularity by clever acting, and that his universal courtesy became somewhat artificial. If so, then he acted his own character as it originally was. It is an important fact that his popularity at home, among his neighbors, indeed in the whole state, constantly grew stronger as he grew older, and that the people of Kentucky clung to him with unbounded affection.

CHAPTER III.

BEGINNINGS IN POLITICS.

HENRY CLAY's first participation in politics was highly honorable to him. The people of Kentucky were dissatisfied with those clauses in their Constitution which provided for the election of the governor and of the state senators through the medium of electors. They voted that a convention be called to revise the fundamental law. This convention was to meet in 1799. Some public-spirited men thought this a favorable opportunity for an attempt to rid the state of slavery. An amendment to the Constitution was prepared providing for general emancipation, and among its advocates in the popular discussions which preceded the meeting of the convention, Clay was one of the most ardent. It was to this cause that he devoted his first essays as a writer for the press, and his first political speeches in popular assemblies. But the support which that cause found among the farmers and traders of Kentucky was discouragingly slender.

The philosophical anti-slavery movement which accompanied the American Revolution had by this time very nearly spent its force. In fact, its practical effects had been mainly confined to the **North,** where slavery was of little economic consequence, and where, moreover, the masses of the population **were** more accessible to the currents of opinion and sentiment prevailing among men of thought and culture. There slavery was abolished. Further, **by** the Ordinance of 1787, slavery **was** excluded **from the** territory **northwest** of the Ohio. But nothing was accomplished in the South except the passage of a law by the Virginia legislature in 1778, prohibiting the further introduction of slaves from abroad, and the repeal, in 1782, of the old colonial statute, which forbade the emancipation of slaves except for meritorious services. Maryland followed the example of Virginia, but then Virginia, ten years after the repeal, put a stop to individual emancipation by reënacting the old colonial statute. The convention framing the Constitution of **the** United States did nothing but open the way **for** the abolition of the slave-trade at some future time. On the whole, as soon as the philosophical anti-slavery movement threatened to become practical **in the** South, it stirred up a very determined opposition, **and** the reaction began. Indeed, the hostility to slavery **on** the part of some **of** the Southern Revolutionary leaders was never **of a** very practical kind. Very characteristic in **this** respect **was a** confession Patrick Henry made concerning the state **of his** own mind as **early as 1773,** in a letter to a Quaker : —

"Is it not amazing that, at a time when the rights of humanity are defined and understood with precision, in a country above all others fond of liberty, in such an age, we find men professing a religion the most humane, mild, meek, gentle, and generous, adopting a principle as repugnant to humanity as it is inconsistent with the Bible, and destructive of liberty? Every thinking, honest man rejects it in speculation, but how few in practice, from conscientious motives! Would any one believe that I am a master of slaves of my own purchase? I am drawn along by the general inconvenience of living without them. I will not, I cannot, justify it; however culpable my conduct, I will so far pay my *devoir* to virtue as to own the excellence and rectitude of her precepts, and lament my want of conformity to them."

This merely theoretical kind of anti‑slavery spirit lost all aggressive force, as those whose pecuniary interests and domestic habits were identified with slavery grew more defiant and exacting. In 1785 Washington complained in a letter to Lafayette that "petitions for the abolition of slavery, presented to the Virginia legislature, could scarcely obtain a hearing." While the prohibition of slavery northwest of the Ohio by the Ordinance of 1787 proceeded from Southern statesmen, the slave-holding interest kept all the land south of the Ohio firmly in its grasp.

At the period of the elections for the convention called to revise the Constitution of Kentucky, the philosophical anti-slavery spirit of the Revolution survived in that state only in a comparatively feeble flicker among the educated men who had come there from Virginia and Pennsylvania. It had never touched the rough pioneers of Kentucky with any force. The number of slaves held in the state was, indeed, small enough to render easy the gradual abolition of the system. But the Kentucky farmer could not understand why, if he had money to buy negroes, he should not have them to work for him in raising his crops of corn, and hemp, and tobacco, and in watching his cattle and swine in the forest. His opposition to emancipation in any form was, therefore, vehement and overwhelming. The cause so fervently advocated by Clay, following his own generous impulses, as well as the teachings of his noble mentor, Chancellor Wythe, and by a small band of men of the same way of thinking, was, therefore, desperate from the beginning. But they deserve the more credit for their courageous fidelity to their convictions. Clay was then a promising young man just attracting public attention. At the very start he boldly took the unpopular side, thus exposing himself to the displeasure of a power, which, in the South, was then already very strong, and threatened to become unforgiving and merciless. Nor did he ever express regret at this first venture in his public career. On the contrary, all his life he continued to look back upon it with pride. In a speech he delivered at Frankfort, the political capital of Kentucky, in 1829, he said : —

"More than thirty years ago, an attempt was made, in this commonwealth, to adopt a system of gradual emancipation, similar to that which the illustrious Franklin had mainly contributed to introduce in 1780, in the state founded by the benevolent Penn. And among the acts of my life which I look back to with most satisfaction is that of my having coöperated, with other zealous and intelligent friends, to procure the establishment of that system in this state. We were overpowered by numbers, but submitted to the decision of the majority with that grace which the minority in a republic should ever yield to that decision. I have, nevertheless, never ceased, and shall never cease, to regret a decision, the effects of which have been to place us in the rear of our neighbors, who are exempt from slavery, in the state of agriculture, the progress of manufactures, the advance of improvements, and the general progress of society."

His early advocacy of that cause no doubt displeased the people of Kentucky; but what helped him promptly to overcome that displeasure was the excitement caused by another topic of great public interest, on which he was in thorough accord with them, — the alien and sedition laws, that tremendous blunder of the Federalists in the last days of their power. The conduct of the French government toward the United States, and especially the corrupt attempts of its agents, revealed by the famous X Y Z correspondence, had greatly weakened that sympathy with the French Revolution which was one of the most efficacious means of agitation in the hands of the American Democrats.

The tide of popular sentiment **turned so** strongly **in favor of** the Federalists that they might easily, by prudent conduct, have attracted to themselves a large **portion of** the Republican rank and file, **thus severely crippling the** opposition to the administration of John Adams. But **to push an advantage too far is one of the most** dangerous **errors a** political **party can commit; and** this is what the Federalists **did in** giving themselves the appearance of trying **to** silence their opponents by the force of law. Nothing could have been better calculated not only **to** alarm **the** masses, **but** also **to repel** thinking **men** not blinded by party spirit, than an attempt **upon the** freedom **of** speech and **of** the press, wholly unwarranted **by** any urgency of public danger. The **result was as** might have **been** foreseen. The leaders of the opposition, with Jefferson at their head, were not slow **in** taking advantage **of** this stupendous **folly.** Their appeals **to** the democratic instincts of **the** people, **who** felt themselves threatened in their dearest rights, could not fail to **meet** with **an overwhelming** response. That response **was** especially strong west **of** the Alleghanies, **where** Federalism had **never** grown as an indigenous plant, **but existed only as an exotic. In** the young communities **of** Kentucky, **the** excitement was intense, and Clay, fresh from the Virginia school of democracy, threw himself into the current with all the fiery spirit **of** youth. **Of** the speeches he then delivered in **popular** gatherings, none are preserved even in outline. But **it**

is known that his resonant declamation produced
a prodigious impression upon his hearers, and that
after one of the large field meetings held **in the**
neighborhood of Lexington, **where** he had spoken
after George Nicholas, **a man noted** for his **elo**-
quence, he **and** Nicholas were put in **a carriage**
and drawn **by the people** through the streets **of the**
town amid great shouting and huzzaing.

It was not, however, until four years afterward,
in 1803, that he was elected to a seat in the legislature **of the** state, having been brought forward
as a candidate without his own solicitation. The
sessions in which he participated were not **marked**
by any discussions **or** enactments of **great importance; but Clay, who** had so **far been only the re-**
markable man of **Lexington and vicinity, soon was**
recognized **as** the remarkable man **of** the **state.**
In such debates **as occurred, he** measured swords
with the " big men " of the legislature who thus far
had been considered unsurpassed ; and the atten-
tion attracted by his eloquence was such that
the benches of the Senate became empty when he
spoke in the House.

At **this time, too, he** paid **his** first tribute **to**
what **is** euphoniously called the spirit of chivalry.
A Mr. Bush, **a** tavern-keeper at Frankfort, was
assaulted by one of the **magnates** of Kentucky,
Colonel Joseph **Hamilton** Daviess, then District
Attorney of the United States. The Colonel's influence was so powerful that no attorney at Frankfort
would institute an action against him for Mr. Bush.

Clay, seeing **a man in need** of help, **volunteered.**
In the argument on **the** preliminary question **he**
expressed his opinion **of** Daviess's conduct with
some freedom, whereupon the redoubtable Colonel
sent him **a** note informing him that he was not
in the habit of permitting **himself to be** spoken
of in that way and warning him to desist. Clay
promptly replied that he, **on** his part, permitted
nobody to dictate to him as to the performance of
his duty, and that he "held himself responsible,"
etc. The Colonel sent him a challenge, which Clay
without delay accepted. **The hostile** parties had
already arrived at the place agreed upon, when
common friends interposed **and** brought about an
accommodation.

He soon met Colonel Daviess again in connection with **an** affair **of** greater importance. In the
latter part of 1806, Aaron Burr passed through
Kentucky on his journey to the Southwest, enlist-
ing recruits and making other preparations for his
mysterious expedition, **the** object of which was
either to take possession of Mexico and to unite
with it the Western States of the Union, the whole
to be governed by him, or, according to other reports, to form a large settlement **on** the **Washita**
River. A newspaper published at Frankfort, the
"Western World," denounced **the** scheme as **a**
treasonable one, and on November 3d Colonel
Daviess, as District Attorney of the United States,
moved in court that Aaron Burr be compelled **to**
attend, in order to **answer** a charge of being en-

gaged in an unlawful enterprise designed to injure a power with which the United States were at peace. Burr applied to Henry **Clay** for professional aid. Colonel Daviess, the District Attorney, being a Federalist, the attempted prosecution of Burr was at **once** looked upon by the people as a stroke of partisan vindictiveness; popular sympathy, therefore, ran strongly on Burr's side. Clay, no doubt, was moved by a similar feeling; he, **too**, considered it something like a duty of hospitality to aid a distinguished man arraigned **on a** grave charge far away from his home, and **for** this reason he never accepted the fee offered to him by his client. Yet he had some misgivings as to Burr's schemes, and requested from him assurances of their **lawful** character. Burr was profuse in plausibilities, **and** Clay consented **to** appear for him. During the pendency of the proceedings, which finally resulted in Burr's discharge for want of proof, Clay was appointed to represent Kentucky in the Senate of the United States in the place of General Adair, who had resigned. Thereupon, feeling a greater weight of public **responsibility** upon him, he deemed **it** necessary to ask from **Burr a** statement in writing concerning the nature **of** his doings and intentions. This request did not seem to embarrass Burr in the least. **In a** letter addressed to Clay he said that he had no design, nor had he taken any measure, to promote the dissolution **of** the Union or the separation **of** any state from it; that **he had** no intention to meddle with the government or disturb the tranquillity of the United States ; that he had neither issued, nor signed, nor promised any commission to any one for any purpose ; that he did not own any **kind** of military stores, and **that** nobody else did by his authority ; that his views had been fully explained to several officers **of the government** and were approved by them ; that he believed his purposes were well understood by the administration, and **that they** were such as every man of honor and every good citizen must approve. " Considering the high station you now fill in **our** national councils," the letter concluded, " I have thought these explanations proper, as well to counteract the chimerical tales which malevolent persons have so industriously circulated, as to satisfy you that you have not espoused the cause **of** a man in any way unfriendly to the laws or the interests of the country."

Clay did not know the man he was dealing with. He knew only that Burr had been Vice-President of the United States ; that he was a prominent Republican ; that the Federalists hated him ; that the stories told about his schemes were almost too adventurous to be true. Burr's letter seemed to **be** straightforward, such **as** an innocent man would write. If the administration, at the head of which **stood** Jefferson himself, knew and approved of **Burr's** plans, they could **not** but **be** honorable. This is what Clay believed, and so he defended Burr faithfully and conscientiously. Nothing could be more absurd than the attempt made at the time, and repeated at a later period, to hold him in part responsible for Burr's schemes, the true nature of which he discovered only when he had his first interview with President Jefferson at Washington. Then his mortification was great. " It seems," he wrote to Thomas Hart, of Lexington, " that we have been much mistaken in Burr. When I left Kentucky, I believed him both an innocent and persecuted man. In the course of my journey to this place, still entertaining that opinion, I expressed myself without reserve, and it seems, owing to the freedom of my sentiments at Chillicothe, I have exposed myself to the strictures of some anonymous writer at that place. They give me no uneasiness, as I am sensible that all my friends and acquaintances know me incapable of entering into the views of Burr." The letter by which Burr had deceived him, he delivered into the President's hands. Nine years later he accidentally met Burr again in New York, where, after aimless wanderings abroad, the adventurer had stealthily returned. Burr advanced to salute him, but Clay refused his hand.

CHAPTER IV.

BEGINNINGS IN LEGISLATION.

CLAY took his seat in the Senate of the United States on December 29, 1806. When a man at so early an age is chosen for so high a place, a place, in fact, reserved for the seniors in politics, be it even to "serve out an unexpired term," it shows that he is considered by those who send him there a person forming an exception to ordinary rules. But it is a more remarkable circumstance that Clay, when he entered the Senate, was not yet constitutionally eligible to that body, and that this fact was not noticed at the time. According to the biographers whose dates were verified by him, he was born on April 12, 1777. On December 29, 1806, when he entered the Senate, he therefore lacked three months and seventeen days of the age of thirty years, which the Constitution prescribes as a condition of eligibility to the Senate of the United States. The records of the Senate show no trace of a question having been raised upon this ground when Clay was sworn. It does not seem to have occurred to any member of that body that the man who stood before them might not be old enough to be a Senator. In all prob-

ability Clay himself did not think **of it. He was**
sworn in **as a** matter **of** course, and, without the
bashful hesitation generally expected of young senators, **he** plunged at **once** into the current of **pro-**
ceedings as if he **had been** there all his life. On
the fourth day after **he** had taken his seat, we find
him offering **a** resolution concerning the circuit
courts of the United States; **a** few days later, another concerning **an** appropriation of land for the
improvement of the Ohio rapids; **then** another
touching Indian depredations; **and** another proposing an amendment to the federal Constitution
concerning the judicial power of **the** United States.
We find the young man on a variety **of** committees,
sometimes **as** chairman, charged with the consideration of important subjects, **and making** reports **to**
the Senate. **We** find him taking part in debate
with the utmost **freedom,** and on one occasion astonishing with a piece **of very** pungent sarcasm an
old Senator, who was accustomed to subdue with
lofty assumptions of superior wisdom such younger
colleagues as ventured to differ from him.

In one important respect Clay's first beginnings
in national legislation were characteristic of **the**
natural bent of his mind and the character of **his**
future statesmanship. His first speech was in **ad-**
vocacy of a bill providing for building a bridge
across the Potomac; **and** the measure to which
he mainly devoted himself during his first short
term in the Senate was an appropriation of land
" toward the opening of the canal proposed to be

cut at the rapids of the Ohio, on the Kentucky shore." This was in the line of the policy of "internal improvements." Those claim too much for Henry Clay who call him the inventor, the "father," of that policy. It was thought of by others before him, and all he did was to make himself, in this as in other cases, so prominent a champion, so influential and commanding a leader in the advocacy of it, that presently the policy itself began to pass as his own. In fact it was only his child by adoption, not by birth. But at the time of Clay's first appearance in the Senate there were two things giving that policy an especial impulse. One was a revenue beyond the current needs of the government, and the other was the material growth of the country.

It would be difficult to find in the history of the United States a period of more general contentment and cheerfulness of feeling than the first and the early part of the second term of Jefferson's presidency. Never before, since the establishment of the government, had the country been so free from any harassing foreign complications. The difference with Great Britain about the matter of impressments had not yet taken its threatening form, and the Indians, under the influence of humane treatment, were for a time leaving the frontier settlements in peace. The American people, also, for the first time became fully conscious of the fact that the government really belonged to them, and not to a limited circle of important gentlemen. Jefferson's conciliatory policy, proclaimed in the famous words, " We are all Republicans, we are all Federalists," produced the desired effect of withdrawing **from** the Federalist leaders a large portion of the rank **and file,** and of greatly mitigating the acerbity of party contests, which under the preceding administration had been immoderately **violent.** The Republican majority in Congress and in the country grew so large that the struggle of the minority against it ceased to be very exciting. **On** the other hand, the Federalists had left the machinery of the government on the whole in so good a condition that the party coming into power, although critically **disposed, found not** much to change. Those at the head of the **gov-** ernment professed to be **intent** upon carrying on public affairs in the **simplest and** most economical style. Under such circumstances the popular mind could give itself without restraint to the develop- ment of the country **in** the material **sense.** The disturbed state of Europe having thrown **a large** proportion **of** the carrying trade on the ocean **into the** hands of the American merchant marine, **the** foreign commerce of the seaboard cities expanded largely. Agriculture, too, was remarkably prosper- ous, cotton **was** rapidly becoming the great staple of the South, and other crops in increasing variety were greatly augmented by the breaking of virgin **soils.** Manufacturing industry began to take pos- session of the abundant water-powers of the coun- **try,** and to produce a constantly growing volume

and variety of articles. All these fields of activity
were enlivened by a cheerful spirit of enterprise.

But beyond all this new perspectives of territorial grandeur and national power had opened
themselves to the American people, which raised
their self-esteem and stimulated their ambition.
The United States had ceased to be a mere string
of settlements along the seaboard, with a few inland outposts. The " great West " had risen
above the horizon as a living reality. The idea
of a " boundless empire " belonging to the American people seized upon the popular imagination,
and everything connected with the country and its
government began to assume a larger aspect. The
young democracy felt its sap, and stretched its
limbs. By the Louisiana purchase the Mississippi
had become from an outer boundary an American
inland river from source to mouth, — the ramifica-
tion of the sea through American territory. The
acquisition of the whole of Florida was only a
question of time. The immense country beyond
the Mississippi was still a vast mystery, but steps
were taking to explore that grand national domain.
In the message sent to Congress at the opening of
the very session during which Henry Clay entered
the Senate, President Jefferson announced that
" the expedition of Messrs. Lewis and Clarke, for
exploring the river Missouri, and the best communication from that to the Pacific Ocean, had had
all the success which could have been expected,"
and that they had " traced the Missouri nearly to

its source, descended the Columbia to the Pacific Ocean, and ascertained with accuracy the geography of that interesting communication across OUR CONTINENT."

While only a few daring explorers and adventurous hunters penetrated the immense wilderness beyond the Mississippi, a steady stream of emigration from the Atlantic States, reinforced by new-comers from the old world, poured into the fertile region stretching from the Appalachian Mountains to the great river. They **found** their way either through Pennsylvania across the mountain ridges to Pittsburgh, and then by flat or keel boat down the Ohio, or through northern **New** York to the Great Lakes, and then on by water. The building of the famous Cumberland **Road** farther south had then only been just begun. Great were the difficulties and **hardships** of **the** journey. While the swift stage-coach reached Pittsburgh in six days from Philadelphia, the heavy carrier cart, or the emigrant wagon, had a jolt of three weeks to traverse the same distance. The roads were indescribable, and the traveler on the river found his course impeded **by** snags, sand-bars, and dangerous rap-**ids.** It was, therefore, not enough to have the great country ; it must be made accessible. Nothing could **have been** more natural than that, as **the** West hove in sight larger and richer, the cry for better means of communication between the East and the West should have grown louder and more incessant.

At the same time the commercial spirit of the East was busy, planning improved roads and waterways from the interior to the seaports, and from one part of the coast to the other. Canal projects in great variety, large and small, were discussed with great ardor. While some of these, like the New York and Erie Canal, which then as a scheme began to assume a definite shape, were designed to be taken in hand by single states, the general government was looked to for aid with regard to others. The consciousness of common interests grew rapidly among the people of different states and sections, and with it the feeling that the general government was the proper instrumentality by which those common interests should be served, and that it was its legitimate business to aid in making the different parts of this great common domain approachable and useful to the people.

This feeling was the source from which the policy of "internal improvements" sprang. There was scarcely any difference of opinion among the statesmen of the time on the question whether it was desirable that the general government should aid in the construction of roads and canals, and the improvement of navigable rivers. The only trouble in the minds of those who construed the Constitution strictly was, that they could not find in it any grant of power to appropriate public funds to such objects. But the objects themselves seemed to most of them so commendable that they suggested the submission to the state legislatures of an amendment to the Constitution expressly granting this power. This was the advice of Jefferson. While in his private correspondence he frequently expressed the apprehension that the appropriation of public money to such works as roads and canals, and the improvement of rivers, would lead to endless jobbery and all sorts of demoralizing practices, he found the current of popular sentiment in favor of these things too strong for his scruples. In his message of December, 1806, he therefore suggested the adoption of a constitutional amendment to enable Congress to apply the surplus revenue " to the great purposes of the public education, roads, rivers, canals, and such other objects of public improvement as may be thought proper," etc. " By these operations," he said, " new channels of communication will be opened between the states; the lines of separation will disappear; their interests will be identified, and their union cemented by new and indissoluble ties." This certainly looked to an extensive system of public works. No amendment to the Constitution was passed; but even Jefferson was found willing to employ now and then some convenient reason for doing without the expressed power; such as, in the case of the Cumberland Road, the consent of the states within which the work was to be executed.

Clay took up the advocacy of this policy with all his natural vigor. He was a Western man. He had witnessed the toil and trouble with which the

emigrant coming from the East worked his way to
the fertile western fields. The necessity of making the navigation of the Ohio safe and easy came
home to his neighbors and constituents. But **he**
did not confine his efforts to that one measure.
He earnestly supported **the** project of government
aid for the Chesapeake and Ohio Canal, which, in
the language of the report, was to serve " as the
basis of a vast **scheme** of interior navigation, con-
necting the waters of the Lakes with those of the
most southern states; " and if he was not, as some
of his biographers assert, the mover, — for as such
the annals of Congress name Senator Worthington,
from Ohio, — he was at least the zealous advocate
of a resolution, " that the Secretary of the Treasury be directed to prepare and report to the Senate at their next session, a plan for the application
of such means as are within the power of Congress,
to the purposes of opening roads and making canals, together with a statement of undertakings of
that nature, which, as objects of public improvement, may require and deserve the aid of government," etc., a direction to which Gallatin, then
Secretary of the Treasury, responded in an elaborate report. Thus Clay marched in large company, but ahead of a part of it; for while Jefferson and his immediate followers, admitting the
desirability of a large system **of** public improvements, asserted the necessity of a constitutional
amendment to give the government the appropriate power, Clay became the recognized leader of

those who insisted upon the existence of that power under the Constitution as it was.

The senatorial term, for a fraction of which Clay had been appointed, ended on March 4, 1807. He had enjoyed it heartily. " My reception in this place," he wrote to Colonel Hart on February 1st, " has been equal, nay, superior to my expectations. I have experienced the civility and attention of all I was desirous of obtaining. Those who are disposed to flatter me say that I have acquitted myself with great credit in several debates in the Senate. But after all that I have seen, Kentucky is still my favorite country. There amidst my dear family I shall find happiness in a degree to be met with nowhere else." We have, also, contemporaneous testimony, showing how others saw him at that period. William Plumer, a Senator from New Hampshire, a Federalist, wrote in his diary : —

" *December* 29, 1806. This day Henry Clay, the successor of John Adair, was qualified, and took his seat in the Senate. He is a young lawyer. His stature is tall and slender. I had much conversation with him, and it afforded me much pleasure. He is intelligent and appears frank and candid. His address is good, and his manners easy."

And later : —

" **Mr.** Clay is a young lawyer of considerable eminence. He came here as senator for this session only. His clients, who have suits depending in the Supreme Court, gave him a purse of three thousand dollars to attend to their suits here. He would not be a **candidate for the next** Congress, as it would materially **injure his business. On the second reading** of the bill to erect a bridge over the Potomac, Henry **Clay** made an eloquent and forcible speech against **the** postponement. He animadverted with great **severity on** Tracy's observations. As **a speaker** Clay is animated, **his** language **bold** and flowery. **He** is prompt **and** ready **at** reply, **but he** does not reason **with** the force **and** precision of Bayard."

And finally : —

"*February* 13. Henry Clay is **a man of** pleasure ; fond of amusements. **He is a great** favorite **with the** ladies ; is in all parties **of pleasure ; out almost every** evening **; reads but little ;** indeed, **he** said he meant **this** session should **be** a tour of pleasure. He is a man **of** talents ; is eloquent ; but not nice or accurate in his distinctions. He declaims more than he reasons. He is a gentlemanly and **pleasant** companion ; **a man** of honor and integrity."

The reports **of** Clay's speeches delivered at this session, **which** have been preserved, do not bear out Mr. Plumer's description of them. His oratory seldom was what might properly **be** called " flowery." While his appeals rose not unfrequently to somewhat lofty flights of rhetoric, he used figurative language sparingly. His speeches, occasional passages excepted, consisted of argumentative reasoning, which, in print, appears not seldom somewhat dry and heavy. But the dramatic fire of delivery peculiar to him gave that reasoning a vivacity to which the Senate, then a very small and

quiet body, was not accustomed, **and** which the
good Mr. Plumer probably considered too dashing
for the place and the occasion.

Clay had scarcely returned **to** Kentucky when
he citizens **of** his county sent him again **to the**
tate legislature as their representative, and he was
elected Speaker of the Assembly. The debates
which occurred gave him welcome opportunity **for**
taking position on the questions of the time. **The**
comfortable, calm, and joyous prosperity **of the**
country, which had prevailed under Jefferson's first
and at the beginning of his second administration,
had meanwhile been darkly overclouded by foreign
complications. The tremendous struggle between
Napoleonic France and the rest of Europe, led by
England, was raging **more** furiously than ever.
The profitable neutral **trade of** the American merchant marine was rudely interrupted by arbitrary
measures adopted by the belligerents to cripple
each other, **in utter** disregard of neutral rights.
The impressment and blockade policy of Great
Britain struck the American mind as particularly
offensive. **Of** this more hereafter. The old animosity **against** England, which had somewhat
cooled **during the** short period of repose and general cheerfulness, was fanned again into flame.
Especially in the South and West it burst out in
angry manifestations. In the Kentucky legislature
its explosion **was** highly characteristic of the lin-
gering backwoods spirit. **It** was moved that in no
court of Kentucky should any decision of a British

court, or any British elementary work **on law,** be read **as an** authority. The proposition was immensely popular among the members of the Assembly. More than four fifths of them declared **their** determination to **vote for it.** Clay was **as fiery a** patriot as any **of** them ; but he would not permit his state to make itself ridiculous by a puerile and barbarous demonstration. He was young **and** ambitious, **but he** would **not seek** popularity **by** joining, or even acquiescing, in a cry which offended his good sense. Without hesitation he left the Speaker's chair to arrest this absurd clamor. He began by moving as an amendment that the exclusion of British decisions and opinions from the courts of Kentucky should apply only to those which had been promulgated after July 4, 1776, as before that date the American colonies were a part of the British dominion, and Americans and English were virtually one nation, living substantially under the **same laws. Then** he launched into a splendid panegyric upon **the** English common law, and an impassioned attack upon the barbarous spirit which would " wantonly make wreck of a system fraught with the intellectual wealth of centuries." His speech was **not** reported, **but** it was described in the press of the time as one of extraordinary power and beauty, and it succeeded in saving for Kentucky the treasures **of** English jurisprudence.

Other demonstrations of patriotism **on** his part were not wanting. In December, 1808, when the

cloud had grown darker still, he introduced a series of resolutions expressing approval of the
embargo, denouncing the British Orders in Council
by which the rights of neutral ships were arbitra-
rily overruled, pledging to the general government
the active aid of Kentucky in anything it might
determine upon to resist British exactions, and declaring that President Jefferson was entitled to the
gratitude of the country " for the ability, uprightness, and intelligence which he had displayed in
the management both of our foreign relations and
domestic concerns."   This brought to his feet the
Federalist Humphrey Marshall, a man of ability and
standing, — he had been a Senator of the United
States, — but who was also noted for the bitterness
of his animosities and the violence of his temper.
Looking down upon Clay as a young upstart, he
opposed the resolutions with extraordinary viru-
lence, but commanded only his own vote against
them.

Clay then offered another resolution, recommending that the members of the legislature should
wear only such clothes as were the product of domestic manufacture.   The avowed object was the
encouragement of home industry, to the end of
making the country industrially independent of a
hated foreign power.   This was Henry Clay's first
effort in favor of a protective policy, evidently
designed to be a mere demonstration.   Humphrey
Marshall at once denounced the resolution as the
clap-trap of a demagogue.   A fierce altercation

followed, and **then** came the customary challenge and the " hostile encounter," in which both combatants were slightly wounded, whereupon the seconds interfered to prevent more serious mischief. Henry Clay may, therefore, be said to have fought and bled for the cause of protection when he **first** championed it, by **a** demonstration **in favor of** home manufactures as against those of **a foreign** enemy.

In the winter of 1809–10 Clay was again sent **to** the Senate of the United States to fill **an unexpired** term of two years, **Mr. Buckner Thurston** having resigned his seat. In April, 1810, he found an opportunity for expressing his opinions on the " encouragement of home industry " in **a more** tangible and elaborate form. To a bill appropriating money for procuring munitions of war and for other purposes, an amendment was moved instructing **the** Secretary **of the Navy to purchase** supplies of hemp, cordage, sail-cloth, etc., and to give preference to articles raised or manufactured **on** American soil. The discussion ranged over the general policy of encouraging home manufactures. Clay's line of argument was remarkable. A large conception of industrial development as the **result of a** systematic tariff policy was entirely foreign to his mind. He looked at the whole subject from **the** point of view of a Kentucky farmer, **who** found it most economical to clothe himself and his family **in** homespun, and who desired to secure **a sure** and profitable market for his hemp. Besides this, he thought it wise that the American people should, in case of war, not be dependent upon any foreign country for the things necessary to their sustenance and defense. "A judicious American farmer," said he, "in his household way manufactures whatever is requisite for his family. He squanders but little in the gewgaws of Europe. He presents, in epitome, what the nation ought to be *in extenso.* Their manufactories should bear the same proportion, and effect the same object in relation to the whole community, which the part of his household employed in domestic manufacturing bears to the whole family. It is certainly desirable that the exports of the country should continue to be the surplus production of tillage, and not become those of manufacturing establishments. But it is important to diminish our imports; to furnish ourselves with clothing, made by our own industry; and to cease to be dependent, for the very coats we wear, upon a foreign, and perhaps inimical, country. The nation that imports its clothing from abroad is but little less dependent than if it imported its bread."

He was especially anxious not to be understood as favoring a large development of manufacturing industries with a numerous population of operatives. Referring to the indigence and wretchedness which had been reported to prevail among the laboring people of Manchester and Birmingham, he said: "Were we to become the manufacturers of other countries, effects of the same kind might result. But if **we** limit **our** efforts by our own wants, the evils apprehended would be found to be chimerical." He had no doubt " that the domestic manufactories of the United States, **fostered by** government, **and** aided **by** household exertions, were fully competent to supply us with at least every necessary article of clothing." He **was,** therefore, " **in favor** of encouraging them, not to the extent to which they are carried **in** Europe, **but** to such an extent as will redeem **us entirely** from all dependence **on** foreign countries." And, aside from clothing, he did not forget to mention that " our maritime operations ought not to depend upon the casualties of foreign **supply ; "** that " with very little encouragement from government **he** believed we should not want a pound **of** Russia hemp ; " that " the increase of the article **in** Kentucky had been rapidly great," there having been but two rope manufactories in Kentucky **ten years** ago, and there being about twenty now, and **about** ten or fifteen of cotton-bagging.

Thus what he had **in view** at **that time was not** the building **up** of large industries by a protective system, **but** just **a little** manufacturing to **run** along with agriculture, enough **to keep** the people in clothes and the **navy** well supplied with hemp, and **so** to relieve the country of its dependence **on** foreign countries in case **of** war. For **this** home industry he wanted encouragement. **What** kind of encouragement? In his speech he briefly referred to two means **of** encouraging manufac-

tures : bounties, against which, as he was aware,
it was urged that the whole community was taxed
for the benefit of only a part of it; and protective duties, in opposition to which it was, as he
said, "alleged that you make the interest of one
part, the consumer, bend to the interest of the
other part, the manufacturer." He merely stated
these points, together with the "not always admitted" answer that "the sacrifice is only temporary, being ultimately compensated by the greater
abundance and superiority of the article produced
by the stimulus." He did not, however, commit
himself clearly in favor of either proposition. But
he thought of all "practical forms of encouragement," the one under discussion, providing merely
for a preference to be given to home products
in the purchase of naval supplies, whenever it
could be done without material detriment to the
service, was certainly innocent enough and should
escape opposition. He was also in favor of making
advances, under proper security, to manufacturers
undertaking government contracts, believing " that
this kind of assistance, bestowed with prudence,
will be productive of the best results."

A few days after Clay had made this speech,
Albert Gallatin, Secretary of the Treasury, presented to Congress a report on the manufacturing
industries of the United States, in which he showed
that several of them were already " adequate to
the consumption of the country," — among them
manufactures of wood, leather, and manufactures

of leather, soap, and candles, etc., — and that others were supplying either the greater, or at least a considerable, part of the consumption of the country, such as iron and manufactures of iron ; manufactures of cotton, wool, and flax ; hats, paper, several manufactures of hemp, gunpowder, window glass, several manufactures of lead, etc. Home industry was, therefore, practically not far from the point of development indicated by Clay as the goal to be reached. In response to the request of Congress, to suggest methods by which the manufacturing industries might be encouraged, Gallatin suggested that " occasional premiums might be beneficial ; " that " a general system of bounties was more applicable to articles exported than to those manufactured for home consumption ; " that prohibitory duties were " liable to the treble objection of destroying competition, of taxing the consumer, and of diverting capital and industry into channels generally less profitable than those which would have naturally been pursued by individual interest left to itself." A moderate increase of duties would be less dangerous, he thought ; but, if adopted, it should be continued during a certain period to avoid the injury to business arising from frequent change. But, he added, " since the comparative want of capital is the principal obstacle to the introduction and advancement of manufactures," and since the banks were not able to give sufficient assistance, " the United States might create a circulating stock bearing a low rate of interest, and lend it at par to manufacturers."

It will strike any reader conversant with the history of that period, that Clay's argument, if taken as a plea for protection, was far less decided in tone and strong in reasoning than many speeches which had been made in Congress on that side of the question before; and also that the methods of encouraging manufacturing industries suggested by him were, although less clearly stated, not materially different from those suggested by Gallatin, who was on principle a free trader.

This topic was, in fact, only one of a great variety of subjects to which he devoted his attention. He evidently endeavored to become not only a brilliant speaker, but a useful, working legislator. During the same session he made a report on a bill granting a right of preëmption to settlers on public land in certain cases, which was passed without amendment. Indian affairs, too, received his intelligent attention. A bill supplementary to "an Act to regulate trade and intercourse with the Indian tribes and to preserve peace on the frontier," was introduced by him and referred to a committee of which he was made chairman; and his report displayed sentiments as wise as they were humane. More conspicuous and important was the part he took during the session of 1810–11 in the debates on the occupation of West Florida, and on a bill to renew the charter of the Bank of the United States.

The West Florida case gave him his first introduction to the field of foreign affairs, and at once he struck the key-note of that national feeling which carried the American people into the War of 1812. Florida was at that time in the possession of Spain. The boundaries of Louisiana, as that territory had passed from France to the United States in 1803, were ill defined. According to a plausible construction the Louisiana purchase included that part of Florida to the west of the Perdido River, which was commonly called West Florida. But the United States had failed to occupy it, leaving the Spanish garrisons quietly in possession of their posts. Negotiations for the purchase of the whole of Florida from Spain had meanwhile been carried on, but without success. When Napoleon invaded Spain and that kingdom appeared doomed to fall into his hands, insurrectionary movements broke out in several of the Spanish American provinces. West Florida, too, was violently agitated. The revolutionists there, among whom were many persons of English and of American birth, set up an independent government and applied for recognition by the United States. There were rumors of British intrigues for the object of getting West Florida into the hands of England. The revolutionary excitement in the territory moreover threatened seriously to disturb the peace of the frontier. President Madison thought this an opportune moment to settle the boundary question. He issued a proclamation on October 27, 1810, asserting the claim of the United States to West Florida, the delay in the occupation of which "was not the result of any distrust of their title, but was occasioned by their conciliatory views," and announcing that "possession should be taken of the said erritory in the name and behalf of the United States." A bill was then introduced in the Senate December 18, 1810, providing that the Territory of Orleans, one of the two territories into which Louisiana was divided, "shall be deemed, and is hereby declared, to extend to the river Perdido," and that the laws in force in the Territory of Orleans should extend over the district in question.

The Federalists, who always had a deep-seated jealousy of the growing West, attacked the steps taken by President Madison as acts of spoliation perpetrated upon an unoffending and at the time helpless power, and their spokesmen in the Senate, Timothy Pickering of Massachusetts, and Horsey of Delaware, strenuously denied that the United States had any title to West Florida. Clay took up the gauntlet as the champion not merely of the administration, but of his country. For the first time in the Senate he put forth the fullness of his peculiar power. "Allow me, sir," said he, with severe irony, "to express my admiration at the more than Aristidean justice which, in a question of territorial title between the United States and a foreign nation, induces certain gentlemen to espouse the pretensions of the foreign nation. Doubtless, in any future negotiations, she will have too much magnanimity to avail herself of

these spontaneous **concessions in** her favor, made
on the floor of the Senate of the United States."
He then went into an elaborate historical examina-
tion of the question, giving evidence of much research, **and** set forth with great clearness and force
of statement. The case **he** made out for the
American claim was indeed plausible. **Accept-**
ing his patriotic assumptions, his defense of **the**
President's conduct seemed complete. The plea
that the Spanish government was sorely pressed
and helpless furnished him only an opportunity for
holding up his opponents **as the** sympathizers **of**
kings. "I shall leave the honorable gentleman
from Delaware," he exclaimed, "to mourn over the
fortunes of the fallen Charles. I have no **commis-**
eration for princes. My sympathies are reserved
for the great mass of mankind, and I own that the
people of Spain have them most sincerely." **But**
he had a still sharper arrow in **his quiver. Mr.**
Horsey had been **so** unfortunate as **to** speak **of the**
displeasure which the steps taken **by the President**
might give to Great **Britain. Clay turned upon**
him with **an** outburst which resounded **through the**
whole country : —

" **The gentleman reminds us that** Great Britain, the
ally of Spain, may **be** obliged, by her connection with
that **country,** to take **part** with her against **us, and to**
consider this measure **of the** President as **justifying an**
appeal to arms. Sir, **is the** time never **to** arrive, when
we may manage our own affairs **without the** fear **of**
insulting his Britannic majesty? **Is the rod of the**

British power to be forever suspended over our heads ? Does Congress put an embargo to shelter our rightful commerce against the piratical depredations committed upon it on the ocean ? We are immediately warned of the indignation of offended England. Is a law of non-intercourse proposed ? The whole navy of the haughty mistress of the seas is made to thunder into our ears. Does the President refuse to continue a correspondence with a minister who violates the decorum belonging to his diplomatic character, by giving and repeating a deliberate affront to the whole nation ? We are instantly menaced with the chastisement which English pride will not fail to inflict. Whether we assert our rights by sea, or attempt their maintenance by land, — whithersoever we turn ourselves, this phantom incessantly pursues us. Already it has too much influence on the councils of the nation. Mr. President, I most sincerely desire peace and amity with England ; I even prefer an adjustment of differences with her before one with any other nation. But if she persists in a denial of justice to us, or if she avails herself of the occupation of West Florida to commence war upon us, I trust and hope that all hearts will unite in a bold and vigorous vindication of our rights."

This was an appeal to that national pride which he himself of all the statesmen of his time felt most strongly, and therefore represented most effectively. Although he was the youngest man in the Senate, he had already acquired a position of leadership among the members of the Republican majority. He won it in his characteristic fashion ; that is to say, he straightway seized it, and in deference to his boldness and ability it was conceded

to him.   In the debate on the West Florida question he was decidedly the most conspicuous and
important figure; and when the veteran Timothy
Pickering, in a speech in reply to Clay, quoted a
document which years before had been communicated to the Senate in confidence, it was the young
Kentuckian who promptly stepped forward as the
leader of the majority, offering a resolution to censure Pickering for having committed a breach of
the rules, and the majority obediently followed.

From this debate he came forth the most striking embodiment of the rising spirit of Young
America.   But the manner in which he opposed
the re-charter of the Bank of the United States
was calculated to bring serious embarrassment
upon him in his subsequent career; for he furnished arguments to his bitterest enemy.   The first
Bank of the United States was chartered by Congress in 1791, the charter to run for twenty years.
Its establishment formed an important part of
Hamilton's scheme of national finance.   It was to
aid in the collection of the revenue; to secure to
the country a safe and uniform currency; to serve
as a trustworthy depository of public funds; to
facilitate the transmission of money from one part
of the country to another; to assist the govern
ment in making loans, funding bond issues, and
other financial operations.   These offices it had on
the whole so well performed that the Secretary of
the Treasury, Gallatin, although belonging to the
political school which had originally opposed the

Bank, strongly favored the renewal of its charter. He was especially anxious to preserve the powerful working force of this financial agency in view of necessities which the impending war with Great Britain would inevitably bring upon the government.

The opposition which the re-charter met in Congress sprang from a variety of sources. Although for twenty years the constitutionality of the charter had been practically recognized by every department of the government, the constitutional question was raised again. As the Bank had been organized while the Federalists were in power, and many of its officers and directors belonged to that party, its management was accused of political partiality in the distribution of its favors and accommodations. Some of its stock was owned by British subjects; hence the charge that its operations were conducted under too strong a foreign influence. All these things were used to inflame the popular mind, and the opponents of the Bank actually succeeded in creating so strong a current of feeling against it, that several state legislatures passed resolves calling upon members of Congress to refuse the renewal of the charter.

Gallatin, the ablest public financier of his time, and indeed one of the few great finance ministers in our history, ranking second only to Hamilton, knew the importance of the Bank as a fiscal ager of the government at that time too well not t make every honorable effort to sustain it. Without difficulty he refuted the charges with which it was assailed. But his very solicitude told against the measure he advocated. A very influential coterie, represented in the Cabinet by the Secretary of the Navy, Smith, and especially strong in the Senate, entertained a deadly hostility to the Secretary of the Treasury, and sought to drive him out of the administration by defeating everything he thought important to his success as a public financier. There is no reason to suspect that Clay was a party to this political intrigue. Nevertheless, he espoused the anti-Bank cause with the whole fervor of his nature. One reason was that the legislature of his state had instructed him to do so. But he did not rest his opposition upon that ground. He sincerely believed in many of the accusations that had been brought against the Bank; to his imagination it appeared as the embodiment of a great money power that might become dangerous to free institutions. But his principal objection was the unconstitutionality of the Bank, and this he urged with arguments drawn so deeply from his conception of the nature of the federal government, and in language so emphatic, as to make it seem impossible for him ever to escape from the principles then laid down.

"What is the nature of this government? (he said.) It is emphatically federal, vested with an aggregate of specified powers for general purposes, conceded by existing sovereignties, who have themselves retained what is not so conceded. It is said there are cases in which

it must act on implied powers. **This is not contro-
verted,** but the **implication must be necessary, and** *ob-
viously* flow from the enumerated **power with which it is
allied.** The power to **charter companies is not** specified
in the grant, and **I** contend it is **not** transferable **by
mere** implication. **It is one of** the most exalted attri-
butes of sovereignty. **In the** exercise of this gigantic
power we have **seen an** East India Company created,
which **is in itself a** sovereignty, which has subverted
empires and **set up** new dynasties, and has not only
made war, but **war** against its legitimate sovereign!
Under the influence of this power we have seen arise a
South Sea Company, and a Mississippi **Company,** that
distracted and convulsed all **Europe, and menaced a**
total overthrow of all **credit and confidence, and uni-**
versal bankruptcy ! Is it to **be imagined that a power**
so **vast** would have **been left by the wisdom of** the
Constitution to doubtful **inference?** In all **cases** where
incidental powers **are acted upon, the** principal and
incidental ought **to be congenial** with each other, and
partake of a common nature. The incidental power
ought to be strictly subordinate and limited **to** the end
proposed to be attained **by** the specific power. In other
words, under the name of accomplishing one object
which is specified, the **power** implied ought not **to be
made to embrace** other objects which are not **specified
in the Constitution.** If, then, **you** could establish a
bank to collect **and** distribute **the** revenue, it ought to
be expressly restricted to the **purpose of such** collection and distribution. **It is** mockery worse than usurpation to establish **it for a lawful** object, and then to
extend it to other objects which are not lawful. In de-
ducing the power to create corporations, such as I have

described it, from the power to collect taxes, the relation and condition of principal and incidental are prostrated and destroyed. The accessory is exalted above the principal."

The strictest of strict constructionists could not have put the matter more strongly. The reader should remember this argument, to compare it with the reasons given by Henry Clay a few years later for his vote in favor of chartering a new Bank of the United States, illustrating the change which was taking place not only in his, but also in other men's minds as to the constitutional functions of the government.

The bill to re-charter the Bank was defeated in the House of Representatives by a majority of one, and in the Senate by the casting vote of the Vice-President. It is not unfair to assume that, had Clay cast his vote in the Senate and also employed his influence with his friends in the House in favor of the bill, he would have saved it, and that, in this sense, his opposition made him responsible for its defeat.

CHAPTER V.

Upon the expiration of his term in the Senate, Henry Clay was elected a member of the national House of Representatives for the Lexington district, and took his seat on November 4, 1811. To him this was a welcome change. He " preferred the turbulence of the House to the solemn stillness of the Senate." Naturally it was a more congenial theatre of action to the fiery young statesman. The House was then much less under the domination of its committees than it is at present. It was not yet muzzled by rules permitting only now and then a free exchange of opinions. It still possessed the character of a debating body in the best sense of the phrase. The House of Representatives then was what the Senate afterwards became, — the platform to which the people looked for the most thorough discussion of their interests, and from which a statesman could most effectively impress his views upon the public mind. Moreover, it was in the House that the Young America of the time gathered in force to make their strength and spirit tell — the young Republicans who had grown somewhat impatient at the timidity and the over-anxious considerations of economy and peace **with** which the old statesmen of their own party, **in** their opinion, constantly hampered the national ambition **and** energy. Of **all** political elements this was **to** Clay the most congenial; **he** was **its** natural leader, and **no sooner had he appeared in the House than he was elected Speaker by a** very **large majority. It was well understood that the** duties **of** this position would not **exclude him from** participation in **debate.** On almost every occasion of importance he availed himself of the committee of the whole to proclaim his opinions, and for this the stirring events of the time furnished ample opportunity. It may be said without exaggeration that it was his leadership in the House which hastened the War of 1812.

Of the **events which figured as the immediate cause** of that war **only a short** summary can find room here. The profitable maritime **trade which** the great struggle between **France and** England had, from its beginning, thrown into the hands of American merchants, could be preserved only so long as the United **States** remained neutral **and** as their neutral rights were respected. President Jefferson earnestly endeavored to remain at peace with both belligerents, hoping that each would be anxious to propitiate, or at least not to offend this Republic, from fear of driving it into an active alliance with the other. In this he was disappointed. They both looked upon the United States as a *weak* neutral, whose interests could be injured, and whose feelings could be outraged, **with** impunity.

England **and** France sought **to** destroy **one an-**
other not only by arms, but by commercial restrictions. In 1804 Great Britain declared the French
coast from Ostend to the Seine in a state of blockade. In 1806 the blockade was extended from
the Elbe to Brest. **It thus** became in part a mere
" paper blockade." Napoleon answered **by** the
Berlin Decree **of** November **21,** 1806, establishing
the " continental system," designed to stop all trade
between Great Britain and the European continent.
Thereupon came from the British side the " Orders
in Council " of January 7 and November 11, 1807,
declaring the blockade of all places and ports **be-**
longing to France and her allies, from which the
British flag was excluded, also **all** their colonies ;
prohibiting all trade in the produce or manufactures of those countries and colonies, and making
subject to capture and condemnation all vessels
trading with and from them, and all merchandise
on board such vessels. The return shot on the
part of Napoleon was the Milan Decree of December **17,** 1807, declaring that every ship, of what-
ever nation, and whatever the nature of its cargo,
sailing from the ports of England or her colonies,
or of countries occupied by English troops, and
every ship which had made any voyage **to** England,
or paid **any** tax to that government, or submitted
to search by an English ship, **should be** lawful
prize.

Between these decrees and counter-decrees, which
were utterly unwarranted by international law, the

trade of neutrals was crushed as between two mill-
stones.   Indeed, these measures were purposely directed by the two great belligerents as much against
neutral trade as against one **another.**   Great Britain
would not let her maritime commerce slip out **of**
her grasp **to** build **up a** commercial rival sailing
under a neutral flag.   She would therefore permit
no trading at all except on condition that it should
go through her hands, **or** " through British ports
where **a** transit duty **was** levied for **the** British
treasury."   Napoleon, **on the** other hand, desired
to constrain **the** neutrals, especially the United
States, **to become** his active allies, **by** forcing upon
them the alternative : either allies or enemies.
There must be **no** neutrals, or if there were, they
must **have** no rights.   Thus American ships were
taken and condemned **by** both parties in great
numbers, and American maritime **trade was** suffering terribly.   But this was not all.   British men-
of-war stopped American vessels **on** the high **seas,**
and even **in** American waters, **to search them for**
British subjects **or for men they** chose to consider
as such, whom **they** pressed into the British naval
service.   A large number of these were Americans,
not a few of whom refused to serve under **the British** flag, **and** horrible stories were told of the **dun-
geons** into which they were thrown, and of **the**
cruelties they had to suffer.

The steps taken by **the** United States to protect
their neutral rights were those of **a** peace-loving
power not over-confident of its own strength.   Mad-

ison, President Jefferson's Secretary of State, made an appeal to the sense of right and fairness of the British government. That innocent effort having proved fruitless, commercial restrictions were resorted to, — first, the non-importation Act of 1806, prohibiting the importation of certain articles of British production. At the same time negotiation was tried, and a treaty was actually agreed upon by the American envoys, Monroe and Pinkney, and the British government; but as it contained no abandonment by Great Britain of the right of search for the purpose of impressment, President Jefferson did not submit it to the Senate. An attempt at further negotiation failed. In June, 1807, the British man-of-war Leopard fired into the United States frigate Chesapeake, and overhauled her for British deserters, some of whom claimed to be American citizens, an outrage which created intense excitement and indignation all over the country. An explanation was demanded, which it took four years to obtain. In the autumn of 1807, Jefferson called an extra session of Congress, and the famous embargo was resolved upon, forbidding the departure, unless by special direction of the President, of any American vessel from any port of the United States bound to any foreign country, — a very curious measure, intended to defend the foreign commerce of the country by killing that commerce at one blow. The effect was not, as had been hoped, to compel the belligerents by commercial inconvenience at once to respect the rights of neutrals; but on the other hand great dissatisfaction was created in the shipping towns of the United States; for most of the ship-owners and merchants would rather take what little chance of trade the restrictive measures of the belligerents still left them, than let their ships rot at the wharves and thus accept financial ruin from the hands of their own government.

The embargo would indeed have been proper enough as a measure preparatory for immediate war. But Jefferson was a man of peace by temperament as well as philosophy. His favorite gunboat policy appears like mere boyish dabbling in warlike contrivance. His nature shrank from the conflict of material forces. The very thought of war, with its brutal exigencies and sudden vicissitudes, distressed and bewildered his mind. His whole political philosophy contemplated lasting peace with the outside world. War, as a reign of force, was utterly hostile to the realization of his political ideals. When he saw that the comfortable repose and the general cheerfulness which prevailed during his first term were overclouded by foreign complications, and that the things he feared most were almost sure to come, he greeted the election of his successor, which took place in 1808, as a deliverance; and without waiting for Madison's inauguration, virtually dropped the reins of government, leaving all further responsibility to Congress and to the next President.

In February, 1809, Congress resolved to raise

the embargo, and to substitute **for it commercial** non-intercourse with England and France until the obnoxious orders and **decrees** should **be** withdrawn. A gleam **of** sunshine seemed to break through the clouds when, in April, a provisional arrangement, looking to the withdrawal of the **Orders in Council in case of** the reopening of commercial **intercourse, and** to an atonement for the **Chesapeake** outrage, was agreed **upon by** the Secretary of State and Mr. Erskine, the British Minister. President Madison at once issued a proclamation declaring commercial intercourse with Great Britain restored. But the ships had hardly left **their harbors, when** the general rejoicing was rudely interrupted. It turned out **that** Erskine, a well-meaning **and somewhat** enthusiastic young man, had gone **beyond** his instructions. He was sternly disavowed and recalled by the British government. A new Minister, Mr. Jackson, was sent in his place, who, in discussing the transactions **between** Erskine and the Secretary of State, made himself **so** offensive that further communication with him **was** declined. The situation was darker than **ever.** Non-intercourse with Great Britain was resumed; but a partial change of ministry **in** England — the Marquis of Wellesley succeeding Mr. Canning in the Foreign Office — seemed **to** open a new chance for negotiation. To aid this, Congress on May 1, 1810, passed an act providing that commercial non-intercourse with the belligerent pow**ers** should cease with the end of the session, only

armed ships being excluded from American ports;
and further, that, in case either of them should recall its obnoxious orders or decrees, the President
should announce the fact by proclamation, and if
the other did not do the same within three months,
the non-intercourse act should be revived against
that one, — a measure adopted only because Congress, in its helplessness, did not know what else
to do.

The conduct of France had meanwhile been no
less offensive than that of Great Britain.   On all
sorts of pretexts American ships were seized in the
harbors and waters controlled by French power.
A spirited remonstrance on the part of Armstrong,
the American Minister, was answered by the issue
of the Rambouillet Decree in May, 1810, ordering
the sale of American vessels and cargoes seized,
and directing like confiscation of all American
vessels entering any ports under the control of
France.   This decree was designed to stop the
surreptitious trade that was still being carried on
between England and the continent in American
bottoms.   When it failed in accomplishing that
end, Napoleon instructed his Minister of Foreign
Affairs, Champagny, to inform the American Minister that the Berlin and Milan Decrees were re-
voked, and would cease to have effect on November 1, 1810, if the English would revoke their Orders in Council, and recall their new principles of
blockade, or if the United States would " cause
their rights to be respected by the English," — in

the first place restore the non-intercourse act as to Great Britain. This declaration was made by Champagny to the American representative on August 5. The British government, being notified of this by the American Minister, declared on September 29, that Great Britain would recall the Orders in Council when the revocation of the French decrees should have actually taken effect, and the commerce of neutrals should have been restored. Thus France would effectually withdraw her decrees when Great Britain had withdrawn her Orders in Council; and Great Britain would withdraw her Orders in Council when France had effectually withdrawn her decrees.

Madison, however, leaning toward France, as was traditional with the Republican party, and glad to grasp even at the semblance of an advantage, chose to regard the withdrawal of the Berlin and Milan Decrees as actual and done in good faith, and announced it as a matter of fact on November 1, 1810. French armed ships were no longer excluded from American ports. On February 2, 1811, the non-importation act was revived as to Great Britain. In May the British Court of Admiralty delivered an opinion that no evidence existed of the withdrawal of the Berlin and Milan Decrees, which resulted in the condemnation of a number of American vessels and their cargoes. Additional irritation was caused by the capture, off Sandy Hook, of an American vessel bound to France, by some fresh cases of search and impressment, and by an encounter between the American frigate President and the British sloop Little Belt, which fired into one another, the British **vessel** suffering **most.**

But **was** American commerce safe in French **ports? By no means.** The French Council **of** Prize **had** continued **to** condemn American vessels, as if the Berlin and Milan Decrees were in undiminished force ; outrages on American ships by French men-of-war and privateers went **on as before,** and Napoleon refused reparation for the **con**fiscations under the Rambouillet Decree. **The pre**tended French **concession was, therefore, a mere farce.**

Truly, there were American grievances enough. Over nine hundred American ships **had been** seized by the British, and more than five hundred **and** fifty by the French. The number of American citizens impressed as British seamen, or kept in prison **if** they refused **to** serve, **was** reported to exceed **six** thousand, and it was estimated that there **were as many** more **of** whom no information had been obtained. The remonstrances of the American government had been treated with haughty disdain. **By both** belligerents the United **States** had been kicked and cuffed like a mere interloper among the nations of the earth, who had **no** rights entitled **to** respectful consideration. Their insolence seemed to **have** been increased by the irresolution **of the** American government, the distraction of counsel in Congress, and the division of sentiment among the people, resulting in a shifting, aimless policy, which made the attitude of the Republic appear weak, if not cowardly, in the eyes of the European powers.

Such was the situation of affairs when Henry Clay entered the House of Representatives and was made its Speaker. In his annual message Madison held fast to the fiction that France had withdrawn the offensive decrees, while at the same time he complained that the French government had not shown any intention to make reparation for the injuries inflicted, and he hinted at a revival of non-intercourse. But the sting of the message was directed against Great Britain, who had refused to withdraw the Orders in council, and continued to do things " not less derogatory to the dearest of our national rights than vexatious to our trade," virtually amounting to " war on our lawful commerce." Madison therefore advised that the United States be put " into an armor and attitude demanded by the crisis, and corresponding with the national spirit and expectations." This had a warlike sound, while, in fact, Madison was an exceedingly unwarlike man. He ardently wished, and still hoped to prevent, an armed conflict. To make him adopt a war policy required pushing.

But the young Republican leaders came to the front to interpret the " national spirit and expectation." They totally eclipsed the old chiefs by their dash and brilliancy. Foremost among them stood Henry Clay; then John C. Calhoun, William Lowndes, Felix Grundy, Langdon Cheves, and others. They believed that, if the American Republic was to maintain anything like the dignity of an independent **power, and** to preserve, **or rather** regain, **the respect of** mankind in any degree, — ay, its self-respect, — **it** must cease to submit to humiliation and contemptuous treatment; it must fight, — fight somebody **who** had wronged **or** insulted it.

The Republicans, having **always a** tender side for France, and **the fiction** of French concessions **being** accepted, **the theory** of **the war** party **was** that, **of** the two belligerents, England **had more insolently** maltreated **the** United States. Rumors **were spread** that an Indian **war** then going on, and resulting in the battle of Tippecanoe on November **7,** 1811, was owing **to** English intrigues. Adding **this to** the **old** Revolutionary reminiscences of British oppression, **it** was not unnatural that the national **wrath** should generally **turn against Great** Britain.

Madison **was all his life, even** in his youth, somewhat like **a timid** old **man.** He did not desire **war; neither did he venture to** resist the warlike current. **He was** quite willing to **have** Congress **make a** policy for him, and **to** follow its lead. In this respect **he could not** have found **a** man more willing to urge, **or drive,** or lead him, than Henry Clay, who **at** once **so** composed the important committees of the House as **to** put them under the con-**trol** of the war party. Then early **in** the session he took the floor in favor of putting at the disposal of the President a much larger army than the President himself had recommended. Every word of his speech breathed war. He spoke of war not as an uncertain event, but as something sure to come. As to the reason for it, he pointed out that "the real cause of British aggression was not to distress an enemy, but to destroy a rival." To that end, "not content with seizing upon all our property which falls within her rapacious grasp, the personal rights of our countrymen — rights which forever must be sacred — are trampled upon and violated" through the "impressment of our seamen." Was the question asked: "What are we to gain by war?" With ringing emphasis he replied: "What are we not to lose by peace? Commerce, character, a nation's best treasure, honor!" With such words of fire he stirred the House and the people. The character and result of the war, too, were predetermined in his imagination. It was to be an aggressive war, a war of glorious conquest. He saw the battalions of the Republic marching victoriously through Canada and laying siege to doomed Quebec. His dream was of a peace dictated at Halifax.

Not only the regular army was increased, but the President was authorized to accept and employ 50,000 volunteers. Then a bill was introduced providing for the building of ten new frigates, which gave Clay an opportunity for expressing his views as to what the American navy should be.

A large portion of **the** war party, Western and
Southern men, insisted upon confining the conflict
with England to operations on land. The navy
was not popular with them. They denounced **na-
vies** generally as curses to the countries which possessed them ; as very dangerous to popular liberty ;
as sources of endless expense without corresponding benefit ; **as** nurseries of debt, corruption, de-
moralization, **and ruin.** Especially in the war
then in prospect a navy would be absolutely use-
less, —— a curious prediction in the light of subsequent events. Cheves and Lowndes spoke with
ability **in favor of** a maritime armament, **but
Clay's** speech took a wider sweep. He easily disposed of the assertion that a navy was as danger-
ous to free institutions as a standing army, and
then laid down his theory upon which the naval
force of the United States should **be** organized.
It should **not be such " a force as would** be capa-
ble of contending with that **which any** other nation is able **to bring on the ocean, — a** force that,
boldly scouring every sea, would challenge to com-
bat the fleets **of** other powers, however great."
To build up so extensive an establishment, he admitted, **was** impossible at the **time,** and would probably never **be** desirable. The next species of naval
power, which, " without adventuring into distant
seas, and keeping generally on our coasts, would
be competent to beat off any squadron which might
be attempted to be permanently stationed in our
waters," he did **deem** desirable. Twelve ships of

the line and fifteen to twenty frigates, he thought, would be sufficient; and if the present state of the finances forbade so large an outlay, he was at least in favor of beginning the enlargement of the navy with such **an end in** view. But what he would absolutely insist upon was **the** building **up of** a force "competent to punish any single ship or small naval expedition" attempting to "endanger our coasting trade, to block up our harbors, **or** to lay under contribution our cities," such a **force** being "entirely within the compass of **our** means" **at the time.** "Because we cannot provide against every danger," he asked, "shall **we** provide against none?"

This was a sensible theory, **in its** main **prin**ciples applicable now as **well as then: to keep a** force not so expensive as **to** embarrass the country financially, not so large **as to** tempt the government into unnecessary quarrels, but sufficient **for doing** such duty of high police as might be **necessary** to protect our harbors and coasts against **casual attack** and annoyance, and to "show the flag," **and** serve as a sign of the national power in foreign parts, where American citizens or American property might occasionally need protection. With great adroitness Clay enlisted also the sympathies of the Western members **in behalf of** the navy, by showing them the importance of protecting the mouth of the Mississippi, the only outlet for the products of the Western country.

The war spirit in the country gradually rose, and

manifested itself noisily in **public** meetings, passing resolutions, and memorializing Congress. **It** was increased in intensity by **a** sensational " exposure," a batch **of** papers laid before Congress by the President **in** March, 1812. They had been sold to **the** government by John Henry, an Irish adventurer, and **disclosed a** confidential mission to **New England,** undertaken by Henry in 1809 at the **request of Sir** James Craig, **the** Governor of **Canada,** to encourage **a** disunion movement in the Eastern States. This **was the story.** Whatever its foundation, **it** was **believed,** and greatly increased popular **excitement. Yet the** administration seemed to be still halting, and **the war** party felt obliged **to** push **it** forward. Their programme was in the **first** place **a** short embargo of thirty days, upon which Clay, **as** their leader, **had** a conference with **the** President. Madison agreed to recommend an embargo of sixty **days to** Congress, **and this he** did in **a** confidential message **on** April **1.** The House passed **a corresponding** bill the same day; the Senate **the next day increased** the time of the embargo **to ninety** days, **which the House** accepted, and on **April 4** the bill **became a** law. The moderate Republicans and **the** Federalists had procured **the** extension of the time, still hoping for a pacific turn **of** negotiation. But Clay vehemently **declared** that the embargo meant war and nothing **but war.** When he was reminded of the danger of **such** a contest, and of the circumstance that the **conduct** of France furnished **cause** of war equally grave, he burst out in thundering appeals to American courage and honor. "Weak as we are," he exclaimed, "we could fight France too, if necessary, in a good cause, — the cause of honor and independence." We had complete proof, he added, "that Great Britain would do everything to destroy us. Resolution and spirit were our only security. War, after all, was not so terrible a thing. There was no terror in it except its novelty. Such gentlemen as chose to call these sentiments Quixotic, he pitied for their deficient sense of honor."

All over the country the embargo was understood as meaning an immediate preparation for war. In the South and the West and in Pennsylvania enthusiastic demonstrations expressed and further excited the popular feeling. It was a remarkable circumstance that the war spirit was strongest where the people were least touched in their immediate interests by the British Orders in Council and the impressment of seamen, while the population engaged in maritime commerce, who had suffered most and who feared a total annihilation of their trade by the war, were in favor of pacific measures, and under the lead of the Federalists violently denounced the measures of the government and the war party.

In May, 1812, President Madison was nominated for reëlection by the congressional caucus. It has been said that he was dragooned into the war policy by Clay and his followers with the threat that, unless he yielded to their views, another candidate for the presidency would be chosen. This Clay denied, and there **was no** evidence to discredit his denial. Madison was simply swept into the current by the impetuosity of Young America. He himself declared in 1827, in a letter to Wheaton, that " the immediate **impulse** " **to** the declaration of **war** was given by a letter from **Lord** Castlereagh **to** the British Minister at Washington, Forster, which was communicated **to** the President, and which stated " that the Orders in Council, to which **we had declared we would not** submit, would **not be** repealed without the repeal **of the** internal measures of **France.** With this formal notice **no** choice remained, **but** between war and **degradation."**

John Randolph made a last attempt to prevent **the** extreme **step.** Having **heard that** the President was preparing a message to Congress recommending a declaration **of** war, he tried **to** force a discussion **in** the House by offering **a** resolution, " that it **was** inexpedient to resort to war with Great Britain." He began **to** debate it on the spot. **Clay,** as Speaker, interrupted him, and put to the House the question whether it would proceed to the consideration of the resolution. The House **voted** in **the** negative, and Randolph was silenced. On **June 1 the** President's war message came. On **June 18 a bill in** accordance **with it,** which had passed both **Houses,** was signed by the President, who proclaimed hostilities the **next day.**

Thus Young America, led by Henry Clay, carried their point. But there was something disquieting in their victory. The majority they commanded in Congress was not so large as a majority for a declaration of war should be. In the House, Pennsylvania and the states south and west of it gave 62 votes for the war, and 32 against it; the states north and east of Pennsylvania gave 17 yeas and 17 nays, — in all 79 for and 49 against war. This showed a difference of sentiment according to geographical divisions. Not even all the Republicans were in favor of war. Thirteen Northern and two Southern Republicans voted against it. In the Senate the vote stood 19 to 13, and among the latter were six Republicans. So large a minority had an ugly look. It signified that there would be a peace party in the United States during the war. And indeed, those who called themselves the "friends of peace, liberty, and commerce" did make themselves felt in obstructing military preparations and subscriptions to the national loan. In some parts of New England this opposition assumed an almost seditious character.

Nor were the United States in any sense well prepared for a war with a first class power. The Republic was still comparatively weak in military resources. The population, including slaves, had not yet reached eight millions. Ohio, Kentucky, and Tennessee were the westernmost states. Indiana was still a territory, and part of it in the possession of Indian tribes. The battle of Tippecanoe had been fought the year before on its soil. The regular army had scarcely 10,000 effective men. Volunteer and militia levies had to be mainly depended upon, and to command these the number of experienced officers, aside from superannuated " Revolutionary veterans," was extremely small. The naval force consisted of a few old frigates and some smaller vessels. These were all the means at hand, when war was declared, to force Great Britain, through a rapid conquest of Canada, to respect the maritime rights of the United States.

All this looked unpromising enough. But Clay believed in the power of enthusiasm. His voice resounded through the land. His eloquence filled volunteer regiments and sent them off full of fighting spirit and hope of victory. From place to place he went, reassuring the doubters, arousing the sluggards, encouraging the patriots, — in one word, "firing the national heart." But, after all, his enthusiasm could not beat the enemy. His conquest of Canada turned out to be a much more serious affair than he had anticipated. Active operations began. The first attempt at invasion, made by General Hull on the Western frontier, resulted in the ignominious surrender of that commander, with his whole force, to the British, at Detroit. Other attempts on the Niagara River and on Lake Champlain ended but little less ingloriously. These failures were not only military disasters, but were calculated to bury in ridicule the advocates of the war with their glowing predictions of the taking of Quebec and the peace dictated at Halifax. Only the little navy did honor to the country. The American men-of-war gathered laurels in one encounter after another, to the astonishment of the world. It was a revelation to England as well as to the American people.

Meanwhile the situation was curiously changed by other events. Before the declaration of war was known in Europe, Napoleon tried to increase the excitement of the Americans against England, and to propitiate their feeling with regard to France, by causing to be exhibited to the American Minister a decree pretending to have been signed on April 28, 1810, but really manufactured for the occasion, to the effect that the Berlin and Milan Decrees should, as to the United States, be considered as having been of no force since November 1, 1810. On the other hand, in England the mercantile interest and the manufacturing population had at last become dissatisfied with the prohibition of the American trade. There had been a parliamentary inquiry into the effects of the Orders in Council, and the government, pressed by motions in Parliament for their repeal, had finally yielded and withdrawn the obnoxious measures on June 23, 1812, reserving the right to renew them, should the Americans persist in a policy hostile to British interests. But five days before, unknown to the British government, the United States had declared war. The Orders in Council had no doubt been considered the principal cause for that war.

Now Great Britain had shown herself ready to remove that cause. Nothing remained but the complaint about the impressment of American seamen. On that ground the war went on, — with what success at first, we have seen.

It is reported that Madison seriously contemplated making Clay commanding general of the forces in the field, and that Gallatin dissuaded him, saying: "But what shall we do without Clay in Congress?" Indeed, the next session showed how much he was needed there.

When Congress met in the fall of 1812 the general situation was dismal in the extreme. On land there had been nothing but defeat and humiliation. On the sea some splendid achievements, indeed, in duels between ship and ship, but no prospect of success in a struggle between navy and navy. England had not yet begun to put forth her colossal power. What was to happen when she should! With all this, the offered withdrawal of the Orders in Council stood as conclusive proof of the fact that, had the United States only waited a little longer with the declaration of war, the principal cause of complaint might have been peaceably removed. What an opportunity for an able opposition! Madison was indeed reëlected to the presidency in the fall of 1812, by an electoral vote of 128 against 89; but the opposition, especially bitter in New England, had no reason to be discouraged by that proportion.

Bills to increase the navy were swiftly passed,

almost without objection, for the Federalists themselves, especially those from the shipping states, desired a more efficient naval force. But on a bill **for** reinforcing the army the attack came. At first it was tame enough. The bill had already passed by a large majority to a third reading, when Josiah Quincy, of Massachusetts, the leader of the Federalists in the House, made an assault upon the **whole** war policy, **which in** brilliancy of diction and bitterness of spirit has hardly ever been excelled **in our** parliamentary history. He depicted the attempted invasion of Canada **as a** buccaneering expedition, **an act** of bloodthirsty cruelty against unoffending neighbors. **Its failure was** a disgrace, but "the disgrace of failure was terrestrial glory compared with the disgrace of the attempt." If an army were put into **the field** strong enough to acccomplish the conquest of **Canada,** it would also be strong enough to endanger the liberties of **the** American people. **In** view of the criminality **of** the attempt, he thanked **God** that the people of New England — referring to their vote against Madison in the preceding national election — **"had** done what they could **to** vindicate themselves and their children from the burden of this sin." This was not the way to obtain an **early** and honorable peace. "Those must be very young politicians," he exclaimed, his eye fixed on the youthful Speaker **of** the House, — "their pin-feathers not yet grown, **and,** however **they** may flutter **on** this floor, they are not yet fledged for any high **or** distant flight, who think that threats and appealing to **fear are the** ways of producing any disposition to negoti**ate in** Great Britain, or in any other nation which understands what it owes **to its own safety and** honor." **The** voluntary yielding of England with regard to the Orders in Council had shown how peace might have **been** secured. But **he was con**vinced that the administration did not want **peace.** The administration party had its origin **and** found its daily **food** in hatred of Great Britain. He **re**viewed the whole diplomatic history of the United States to show that Republican influence had always **been bent upon** forcing **a quarrel with** England, and that during Jefferson's and Madison's administrations **there** had been constant plotting against **peace** and friendship. This **review he** followed with a scathing exposure of the subserviency of the administration to the audacious and insulting duplicity of Bonaparte, and **the** shameful humiliation of the government in consequence of it. Finally, he declared that, while he would unite with any man for purposes of maritime and frontier defense, he would unite with no one nor with any body of men " for the conquest of any country, either **as a** means of carrying **on this war or for any other** purpose."

This savage attack struck deeply. It was fol**lowed** by several speeches **on** the same side, insisting that the quarrel between the United States and England had, after the revocation of the Orders in Council, been narrowed down to the impressment question, and that the United States would never have gone to war on that account alone.

Then Clay, the foremost of the young politicians whose "pin-feathers were not yet grown," took up the gauntlet. Quincy and his followers had made a mistake not unusually made under such circumstances. They had overshot the mark. The most serious danger of an opposition in time of war is to expose themselves to the suspicion of a lack of patriotism. This danger they did not avoid.

The report we have of Clay's speech, delivered on January 8 and 9, 1813, although not perfect, is sufficient to stamp this as one of his greatest performances. He did not find it difficult to defend Jefferson and Madison — who, indeed, had toiled enough to maintain peaceable relations with everybody — against the charge of having wantonly provoked a war with England. It was, he said, the interest, as well as the duty, of the administration to preserve peace. Nothing was left untried to that end. The defensive measures — non-importation and embargo — adopted to protect our maritime trade, were "sacrificed on the altar of conciliation." Any "indication of a return to the public law and the path of justice on the part of either belligerent was seized upon with avidity by the administration;" so the friendly disposition shown by Erskine. But — here the orator skillfully passed to the offensive — what was the conduct of the opposition meanwhile? When peaceful experiments were undergoing a trial, the opposition was "the champion of **war, the proud, the** spirited, the **sole repository of the** nation's honor, denouncing the administration as weak, feeble, pusillanimous," and incapable **of** being **kicked into war : —**

" When, however, foreign nations, perhaps **emboldened by the very** opposition here made, refuse to **listen to** amicable **appeals ; when, in** fact, war with one **of** them has become **a matter of** necessity, demanded **by** our independence **and our** sovereignty, behold **the** opposition veering round **and** becoming **the friends of** peace and commerce, telling of **the** calamities of war, the waste of **the** public treasury, the spilling of innocent blood — ' Gorgons, hydras, and chimeras dire.' Now **we see** them exhibiting the terrific form of the roaring king **of the forest ;** now the meekness and humility of the **lamb.** They are for war and no restrictions, **when the** administration is for peace. They are for **peace and** restrictions, when the administration is **for war. You** find them, sir, tacking with every gale, displaying the colors of every party and **of** all nations, steady only in one unalterable purpose, — to steer, if possible, into the haven of power."

Over the charge that the administration had been duped by France, a very sore point, he skipped nimbly, ridiculing the **idea of** French influence as **well as the** tremendous denunciations of Bona- **parte,** in which the opposition were fond **of** indulg- **ing.** With these denunciations he dexterously coupled an attack made by Quincy upon Jefferson; and then, to inflame the party spirit of wavering Republicans, he burst out in that famous eulogy

on Jefferson which has long figured in our school-
books : —

"Neither his retirement **from** public office, **nor** his
eminent services, nor his advanced age, can exempt this
patriot from **the coarse** assaults **of** party malevolence.
Sir, in 1801 he snatched from the rude hand of usurpation the violated Constitution of his country, and that is
his crime. He preserved that instrument in form, and
substance, and spirit, a precious inheritance for genera-
tions to come ; **and for** this he **can** never be forgiven.
How vain and impotent is party rage directed against
such a man ! He is not more elevated by his lofty resi-
dence upon the summit of his favorite mountain than
he is lifted, by the serenity of his mind, and the **consciousness** of a well-spent life, above **the** malignant **passions** and bitter feelings of the day."

Did the opposition **speak** of the danger to popular liberty arising from **a** large army ? They
were the same party that had tried **to** strangle
popular liberty with the alien and sedition laws.
Did the opposition, as Quincy had done, accuse
the Republican leaders of cabinet plots, presidential plots, and all manner of plots for the gratifica-
tion of personal ambition ? "I wish," he replied
with stinging force, "that another plot — a plot
that aims at the dismemberment of the Union —
had only the same imaginary existence." Then,
with a moderation of tone which made the arraign-
ment all the **more** impressive, he pointed at the
efforts made to alienate the minds of the people
of New England from the Union.

On the second day of his speech he discussed the causes of the war. " The war was declared," he said, " because Great Britain arrogated to herself the pretension of regulating our foreign commerce, under the delusive name of retaliatory Orders in Council; because she persisted in the practice of impressing American seamen ; because she had instigated the Indians to commit hostilities against us ; and because she refused indemnity for her past injuries upon our commerce. The war, in fact, was announced, on our part, to meet the war which she was waging on her part." Why not declare war against France, also, for the injuries she inflicted upon American commerce, and the outrageous duplicity of her conduct ? " I will concede to gentlemen," he said, " everything they ask about the injustice of France toward this country. I wish to God that our ability was equal to our disposition to make her feel the sense that we entertain of that injustice." But one war at a time was enough. Great Britain, he argued, demanded more than the repeal of the French decrees as to America ; she demanded their repeal as to Great Britain and her allies, also, before giving up the Orders in Council; and she gave them up only in consequence of an inquiry, reluctantly consented to by the ministry, into the effect of our non-importation law, or by reason of our warlike attitude, or both.

But now came the ticklish question : Were the Orders in Council the decisive cause of the war, and should their withdrawal end it? Does it follow, he answered, that what in the first instance would have prevented the war should also terminate it? By no means. The war of the Revolution was an example, begun for one object and prosecuted for another. He declared that he had always considered the impressment of American seamen as the most serious aggression, no matter upon what principle Great Britain defended her policy. "It is in vain," he said, "to set up the plea of necessity, and to allege that she cannot exist without the impressment of *her* seamen. The naked truth is, she comes, by her press-gangs, on board of our vessels, seizes *our* native as well as naturalized seamen, and drags them into her service. It is wrong that we should be held to prove the nationality of our seamen; it is the business of Great Britain to identify her subjects. The colors that float from the mast-head should be the credentials of our seamen." Then he put forth his whole melodramatic power, drawing tears from the eyes of his listeners.

"It is impossible that this country should ever abandon the gallant tars who have won for us such splendid trophies. Let me suppose that the genius of Columbia should visit one of them in his oppressor's prison, and attempt to reconcile him to his forlorn and wretched condition. She would say to him, in the language of gentlemen on the other side: 'Great Britain intends you no harm; she did not mean to impress you, but one of her own subjects. Having taken you by mistake, I will remonstrate and try to prevail upon her, by peaceable means, to release you ; but I cannot, my son, fight for you.'   If he did not consider this mockery, the poor tar would address her judgment and say : 'You owe me, my country, protection ; I owe you, in return, obedience.   I am not a British subject ; I am a native of Massachusetts, where lives my aged father, my wife, my children.   I have faithfully discharged my duty. Will you refuse to do yours?'   Appealing to her passions, he would continue : 'I lost this eye in fighting under Truxton with the Insurgente ; I got this scar before Tripoli ; I broke this leg on the Constitution, when the Guerrière struck.'   If she remained still unmoved, he would break out, in the accents of mingled distress and despair, —

> 'Hard, hard is my fate!   Once I freedom enjoyed,
> Was as happy, as happy could be!
> Oh, how hard is my fate, how galling these chains!'

"I will not imagine the dreadful catastrophe to which he would be driven by an abandonment of him to his oppressor.   It will not be, it cannot be, that his country will refuse him protection!   If there be any description of rights, which, more than any other, should unite all parties in all quarters of the Union, it is unquestionably the rights of the person.   No matter what his vocation, whether he seeks subsistence amid the dangers of the sea, or draws them from the bowels of the earth, or from the humblest occupations of mechanic life, wherever the sacred rights of an American freeman are assailed, all hearts ought to unite and every arm be braced to vindicate his cause."

After this, the objections to the invasion of Canada were easily disposed of.   Canada was simply a base of supplies and of operations for the British. Moreover, " what does a state of war present? The united energies of one people arrayed against the combined energies of another; a conflict in which each party aims to inflict all the injury it can, by sea and land, upon the territories, property, and citizens of another, subject only to the rules of mitigated war practiced by civilized nations." This was his final appeal: —

" The administration has erred in the steps to restore peace; but its error has not been in doing too little, but in betraying too great a solicitude for that event. An honorable peace is attainable only by an efficient war. My plan would be, to call out the ample resources of the country, give them a judicious direction, prosecute the war with the utmost vigor, strike wherever we can reach the enemy, at sea and on land, and negotiate the terms of a peace at Quebec or at Halifax. We are told that England is a proud and lofty nation, which, disdaining to wait for danger, meets it half way. Haughty as she is, we once triumphed over her, and, if we do not listen to the counsels of timidity and despair, we shall again prevail. In such a cause, with the aid of Providence, we must come out crowned with success. But if we fail, let us fail like men, lash ourselves to our gallant tars, and expire together in one common struggle, fighting for Free Trade and Seamen's Rights!"

This speech produced a profound impression in the House. What became known of it outside rang like a bugle-call all over the country. The increase of the army was voted by Congress. The

war spirit rose again with renewed ardor. But what news came **from** the front? In the West, General Winchester **was** overpowered at French-town on February 22. His command had to surrender and part of it was massacred. General Harrison found himself obliged **to** fall back. **On** the Niagara and the St. Lawrence, an expedition **was** pushed forward, which, on April 27, resulted in the temporary capture of York (now Toronto), but no lodgment **was effected.** While the navy had struck some splendid blows, the British gradually increased their force and made the superiority of their power tell. They strengthened their blockade of New York, of the Delaware, and the Chesapeake. British ships ascended the bays and the rivers, and landed parties to plunder and set fire to villages **on** the banks. Philadelphia, Baltimore, and Annapolis became alarmed for their safety. In Virginia, **a** slave **insurrection** was feared. The port **of** Charleston **was** strictly blockaded.

Every **day it** became clearer, too, that the Madison administration was ill-fitted for times of great exigency. **The** war and **navy** departments **were** wretchedly managed. There was incapacity above **and** below. **The** Treasury was in a state of exhaustion. By April 1, the requisitions of the war **and** navy departments must have gone unsatisfied had not Astor, Parish, **and** Girard, three rich foreigners, come to the assistance of the government. New England Federalism grew constantly more

threatening in its hostility to the **war** policy. **In**
addition to all this, tidings of evil import arrived
from Europe. Napoleon's disastrous retreat from
Moscow brought forth new **European** combinations
against him in aid of England. More and more
English ships and English veteran regiments might
then be spared from the European theatre of war,
to be hurled against **the** United States. The pros-
pect of dictating a peace at **Quebec or Halifax
grew** exceedingly dim.

Just **then a** ray of peace flashed from an unexpected **quarter.** When, late in **the summer of**
1812, the Emperor of Russia learned that the
United States had declared war against Great
Britain, **it struck him** as very inconvenient that his
ally, England, should be embarrassed by this outside affair while Napoleon was invading Russia,
and while a supreme effort seemed to be required
to prevent him from **bringing** all Europe **to his**
feet. Alexander resolved to offer himself as **a me-**
diator. His Chancellor, Romanzoff, on September
21, opened the matter **to** the American Minister
at St. Petersburg, John Quincy **Adams, as** well as
to the British envoy. **At** the same time, the **Rus-**
sian Minister **at** Washington, Daschkoff, was instructed to communicate to President Madison the
Emperor's wish. This he did **in** March, 1813,
a few days after Madison's second inauguration.
Madison received **the** proposition with exceeding
gladness. Without waiting **to** learn whether this
Russian **mediation was** acceptable to England, he

forthwith nominated as ministers, to act jointly with John Quincy Adams in negotiating a peace, Albert Gallatin, the Secretary of the Treasury, and Senator Bayard of Delaware, a patriotic Federalist, and a man of excellent abilities. They sailed for St. Petersburg early in May, and took instructions with them in which impressments and illegal blockades were designated as the chief causes of the war. With regard to the impressment question, the instructions said : " If this **encroachment** is not provided against, the United States have appealed to arms in **vain**. If your efforts to accomplish it should fail, all further negotiation will cease, and you will return home without delay."

The envoys reached St. Petersburg in July, and learned that Great Britain was not inclined to accept any mediation. The haughty mistress of the sea would not submit her principles of blockade and her claim to the right of impressment and search to the judgment of any third party. She preferred to treat with the United States directly ; and when the Russian offer of mediation was re**newed,** the British government sent a proposal of direct negotiation to Washington. This was promptly accepted, and the President appointed for that purpose **a** new commission, consisting of John Quincy Adams, Bayard, Clay, Jonathan Russell, then Minister of the United States to Sweden, and Gallatin.

Clay had again been elected Speaker, in May,

1813, when the new Congress met. He had again done all he could to " fire the national heart," this time by a resolution to inquire into certain acts of barbarous brutality committed by the British and their savage allies during the winter and spring. But when the President urged upon him a place in the peace commission, he accepted. His subsequent conduct permits the guess that his motive in accepting it was his anxious desire to prevent a humiliating peace. On January 14, 1814, he resigned the speakership of the House of Representatives, and soon afterward he set out on one of the strangest diplomatic missions of our time.

CHAPTER VI.

THE British government, when offering to negotiate directly with the United States, had designated London, or Gottenburg in Sweden, as the places where the negotiators might meet. Its purpose was to isolate the United States as much as possible. It desired to be left alone in dealing with the Americans, and to shut out all influences friendly to them. To this end, London and Gottenburg seemed to be convenient localities. Finally, however, it agreed that the peace commissioners should meet at Ghent, in the Netherlands. The American envoys had all arrived there on July 6, 1814. There were among them men so different in point of character and habits and ways of thinking, that to make them agree among themselves might have appeared almost as difficult as to make a satisfactory treaty with England. The principal clash was between Adams and Clay. John Quincy Adams was then forty-seven years old, with all his peculiarities fully matured, — a man of great ability, various knowledge, and large experience; of ardent patriotism, and high principles of honor and duty; brimful of courage, and a pugnacious spirit of contention ; precise in his ways ; stiff and cold in manners ; tenacious of his opinions ; irritable of temper ; inclined to be suspicious, and harsh in his judgments of others, and, in the Puritan spirit, also severe with himself ; one of the men who keep diaries, and in them regular accounts of their own as well as other people's doings. Two days after the commissioners had all arrived at Ghent, he wrote in his journal : —

"I dined again at the table d'hôte at one. The other gentlemen dined together at four. They sit after dinner, and drink bad wine and smoke cigars, which neither suits my habits nor my health, and absorbs time which I can ill spare. I find it impossible, even with the most rigorous economy of time, to do half the writing that I ought."

He had been a Federalist, but his patriotic soul had taken fire at the injuries and insults his country had suffered from Great Britain. For this reason he had broken with his party, exposed himself to the ill-will of his neighbors, and supported Jefferson's and Madison's administrations in their measures of resistance to British pretensions.

Clay was ten years younger than Adams, certainly no less enthusiastic an American patriot, nor less spirited, impulsive, and hot - tempered ; having already acquired something of that imperiousness of manner which, later in his career, was so much noticed ; quick in forming opinions, and impatient of opposition, but warm - hearted and genial ; no Puritan at all in his ways ; rather inclined to " sit after dinner," whether the wine was good or bad ; and, while willing to work, also bent on having his full share of the enjoyments of this world. " Just before rising," Adams wrote in his Diary one day, " I heard Mr. Clay's company retiring from his chamber. I had left him with Mr. Russell, Mr. Bentzon, and Mr. Todd, at cards. They parted as I was about to rise." John Quincy Adams played cards, too, but it was that solemn whist, which he sometimes went through with the conscientious sense of performing a diplomatic duty. No wonder the prim New Englander and the lordly Kentuckian, one the representative of eastern, the other of western, ways of thinking, when they had struck points of disagreement, would drift into discussions much more animated than was desirable for the task they had in common. Russell, a man of ordinary ability, was much under the influence of Clay, while Bayard, although not disposed to quarrel with anybody, showed not seldom a disposition to stick to his opinion, when it differed from those of his colleagues, with polite but stubborn firmness. " Each of us," wrote Mr. Adams, " takes a separate and distinct view of the subject - matter, and each naturally thinks his own view of it the most important." A commission so constituted would hardly have been fit to accomplish a task of extraordinary delicacy, had it not been for the conspicuous ability, the exquisite tact, the constant good-nature, the " playfulness of temper," as Mr. Adams expressed it, and the inexhaustible patience of Albert Gallatin, a man whose eminence among his contemporaries has probably never been appreciated as it deserves. Without in the least obtruding himself, he soon became the peacemaker, the moderating and guiding mind of the commission.

The British envoys, who arrived at Ghent on August 6, having permitted the Americans to wait for them one full month, were Lord Gambier, a vice-admiral, Henry Goulburn, Secretary in the colonial department, and Dr. William Adams, an admiralty lawyer, men not remarkable for ability or standing, but apparently somewhat inclined to be overbearing in conduct. Indeed, the advantage of position was altogether on their side.

Since the time when President Madison seized upon the Russian offer of mediation, in March, 1813, the fortunes of war had been vacillating. The Americans had made a successful expedition against Fort George, and the British had been repulsed at Sackett's Harbor. But the first great naval disaster then happened in the defeat of the Chesapeake by the Shannon off Boston Light. New naval successes, especially Perry's splendid victory on Lake Erie, September 10, 1813, relieved the gloom. General Harrison won in the fight of the Thames, in which Tecumseh was killed, on October 5. But a winter expedition led by Hampton and Wilkinson against Montreal failed; Fort Niagara was lost, Black Rock and Buffalo were burned, and great quantities of provisions and stores destroyed. These disasters were **scarcely** counterbalanced by General Jackson's success against the Creeks in the Southwest; but this and the recovery of Detroit were the only considerable advantages gained on land in 1813. The opening spring brought another failure of **an** expedition along the shore of Lake Champlain into Canada under Wilkinson. The blockade was **constantly** growing more rigid. Not a single American man-of-war was on the open sea. The successful fights at Chippewa and Lundy's Lane, and then the crowning disgrace of the capture of Washington, were still to come. Meanwhile the discontent with the war prevailing in New England, which was destined to culminate in the Hartford Convention, although apparently not spreading, continued to be active and to threaten rebellious outbreaks. **But the** most ominous events were the downfall of Napoleon, the conclusion of peace in Europe, and, in consequence, the liberation of the military, naval, and financial resources of Great Britain for a vigorous prosecution of the war in America. What had already happened was only child's play. The really serious business was now to come. The outlook appeared, therefore, extremely gloomy. While on his way to Ghent, Gallatin had spent **some** time in London, and had earnestly tried there to interest, in behalf of the United States, the Emperor of Russia, who was on a visit to his English **ally.** That effort, too, had failed. The United States were without an active **friend.**

Most of these things had become known, not only to the Americans, but **also to** the British commissioners. These gentlemen were, therefore, naturally inclined to treat the United States as **a** defeated enemy suing for **peace.** At the opening of the negotiation **the** British demanded **as a** *sine qua non* that a large territory in the United States, all the country **now** occupied by the states of Michigan, Illinois, and Wisconsin, the larger part of Indiana, and about one third of Ohio, should be set apart for the Indians, to constitute a sort of Indian sovereignty under British guaranty, not to be purchased from the Indians by the United States, and to serve as a " buffer," a perpetual protection of the British possessions against American ambition. They demanded also that the United States should relinquish the right of keeping any armed vessels on the Great Lakes ; and, in addition to all this, they asked for the cession of a piece of Maine in order to make a road from Halifax to Quebec, and for a formal renewal of the provision of the treaty of 1783 giving English subjects the right of navigating the Mississippi.

This **meant almost** a surrender of American independence. **It** was the extreme of humiliation. That such a proposition could be thought of was **a** most painful shock to the American envoys. All they could do was promptly **to** reject the *sine qua non,* and then think of going home. This they **did.** They not only thought of going home, but **they openly spoke of it. The** British commissioners received the impression, and reported it to their government, that the Americans were very much in earnest, and that what they really desired was not to make peace, but to put things in an aspect calculated to unite their people at home in favor of the war. Then something of decisive importance happened behind the scenes, which, no doubt, the Americans would have been glad to know. The leading statesmen in England were not at all anxious to break off negotiations, especially not upon points a final rupture on which might have " made the war popular in America." In fact, as Lord Liverpool wrote to Lord Castlereagh, they were apprehensive that then the war would be a long affair; that "some of their European allies would not be indisposed to favor the Americans," meaning especially the Emperor of Russia, and that this American business would "entail upon them prodigious expense." They did not desire to have it said that " the property tax was continued for the purpose of securing a better frontier for Canada." Besides, the state of the negotiations at the Vienna Congress was "unsatisfactory;" the situation of the interior of France was "alarming;" the English people were tired of war taxes. Was it not more prudent after all to let the Americans off without a cession of territory? The Duke of Wellington was consulted; he emphatically expressed himself against any territorial or other demand which would " afford the Americans a proper and creditable ground " for declining to make peace.

The British commissioners were instructed accordingly.

Of this the Americans were, of course, ignorant. Only Clay felt it intuitively. According to Mr. Adams's Diary, Clay had " an inconceivable idea that they will recede from the ground they have taken." That is to say, he had the instinct of the situation. The British dropped their *sine qua non;* they gave up a proposition which they made to treat on the basis of *uti possidetis*, each nation to hold what it possessed or occupied at the time of signing the treaty; they finally showed themselves willing to accept the American proposition of the *status ante bellum* as a basis for the final arrangement. But one thing they would not do: they would not listen to anything about stipulations touching principles of blockade, rights of neutrals, impressment and right of search, concerning which the Americans insisted upon submitting the draft of an article. This they declined so peremptorily that all further discussion seemed useless. What, then, became of " Free Trade and Seamen's Rights ? " What of the original instruction that the commissioners should break off forthwith and come home if they failed in obtaining a concession with regard to impressment? President Madison had in the mean time reconsidered the matter and sent further instructions authorizing them to treat on the basis of the *status ante bellum*, — substantially, to restore things to the state in which the war had found them. Not a proud thing to do, but better, he thought, than to go on with such a war.

When the British accepted this basis, and the Americans gave up their contention for definite stipulations concerning the principles of blockade and the impressment question, the peace was **virtually** assured. Only matters of detail **had to be** agreed upon, which, if both parties sincerely desired peace, would not be difficult. But confused and apparently interminable wrangles sprang up concerning the definition of the *status ante bellum*, mainly with regard to the British right to the navigation of the Mississippi and the American right to fish in British waters, which had been coupled together in the first treaty of peace, in 1783, between the United States and Great Britain. The British commissioners now insisted upon the British right to navigate the Mississippi, but proposed to put an end to the American right to the fisheries. **It is** needless to recount in detail the propositions and counter-propositions which passed between the **two** parties upon this point, as well as the furious altercations in the American commission between Clay and **Adams,** taxing **to** the utmost Gallatin's resources as a peacemaker; Clay insisting that a renewal of the right of the British to navigate the Mississippi, which had been conceded in the treaty of 1783, and again in Jay's treaty of 1794, when Spain held the whole of the right bank of the Mississippi, with part of the left, and the British dominions were erroneously sup>

posed to touch on the head-waters of the great river, would be giving them a privilege far more important than we should secure in return, as the fisheries were " a matter of trifling moment ; " and Adams maintaining with equal heat that the fisheries were a thing of great value, while the privilege to navigate the Mississippi enjoyed by the British under the treaty of 1783 had never led to any trouble or inconvenience. At last, after these long and angry discussions, after much sending of notes and replies, in which the American envoys displayed great skill in argument, and after repeated references of the disputed points by the British commissioners to the Foreign Office in London and long waiting for answers, the British government declared that it was willing to accept a treaty silent on both subjects, the fisheries as well as the navigation of the Mississippi. This declaration reached the American commissioners December 22, 1814, and with it the last obstacle to a final agreement was removed. It appeared that the British government had become fully as anxious for peace as the American. Clay adhered to his first impressions in this respect throughout the negotiation ; for ten days before, on December 12, when other members of the commission still suspected the British of seeking an occasion for breaking off, Adams wrote in his Diary: " Mr. Clay was so confident that the British government had resolved upon peace, that he said he would give himself as a hostage and a victim to be sacrificed if they broke off on these points." There is reason to believe that he would not have been sorry if they had broken off.

The treaty was signed on December 24, 1814. It may well be imagined that the American commissioners heaved a sigh of relief, all, at least, except Clay. For five weary months they had been fighting from point to point a foe who seemed to have all the advantages of strength and position, and all the while they had been in constant apprehension that any hour might bring more evil news to destroy the fruit of their anxious labors. With dignity but not without impatience they had borne the gruffness with which the English commissioners had frequently thought proper to emphasize the superiority of the power behind them. Like brave men they had gone through the dinners with their British colleagues, the ghastly humor of which during the first period of the negotiation consisted in cheerful conversations about the impossibility of agreeing, the short and fruitless visit of the American commissioners to Europe, their speedy return home, and so on. Then finally the altercations among themselves, which grew warmer as the negotiation proceeded, had made it appear doubtful more than once whether they would be able to present a united front upon all the important points. In these altercations Clay had appeared especially fretful, constantly dissatisfied, and ungovernable. Adams's Diary teems with significant remarks about Clay " waxing loud and warm ; " about his " great heat and anger ; " how " Mr. Clay lost his temper, as he generally does whenever the right of the British to navigate the Mississippi is discussed ; " how " Mr. Clay, who was determined to foresee no public misfortune in our affairs, bears them with less temper, now they have come, than any of us ; he rails at commerce and the people of Massachusetts, and tells us what wonders the people of Kentucky would do if they should be attacked ; " how " Mr. Clay is growing peevish and fractious," — and, recollecting himself, Adams contritely adds : " I too must not forget to keep guard on my temper." At the very last, just before separating, Adams and Clay quarreled about the custody of the papers, in language bordering upon the unparliamentary. But for the consummate tact and the authority of Gallatin the commission would not seldom have been in danger of breaking up in heated controversy.

The complaints about Clay's ill-tempered moods were undoubtedly well founded. Always somewhat inclined to be dictatorial and impatient of opposition, he had on this occasion especial reason for being ill at ease. He, more than any one else, had made the war. He had advised the invasion of Canada, and predicted an easy conquest. He had confidently spoken of dictating a peace at Quebec or Halifax. He had, after the withdrawal of the Orders in Council, insisted that the matter of impressment alone was sufficient reason for war. He had pledged the honor of the country for the maintenance **of the** cause of " Free Trade and Seamen's Rights."   Now to make a peace which **was** not only not dictated at Quebec or Halifax, but looked rather like a generous concession on the part **of a** victorious enemy ; **to** make peace **while** disgraceful defeats **of the** American arms, among them the capture **of the seat of** government and the burning **of** the Capitol, **were** still unavenged, and while, after **some** brilliant exploits, the American **navy** was virtually shut up in American harbors **by** British blockading squadrons ; **a peace** based **upon** the *status ante bellum*, without even an **allu**sion **to** the things that had been fought for, — **in one word, a peace,** which, whatever its merits and advantages, was certainly **not** a glorious peace, — **this** could not but **be** an almost unendurable thought to the man who, above all things, wanted to be **proud** of his country.

It is, therefore, **not** surprising that, during these five weary **months** of negotiation, Clay should **have** been constantly tormented by the perhaps half-unconscious desire **to** secure to **his** country another chance **to retrieve** its fortunes **and** restore its glory **on** the field **of** war, **and, to that end, to** break off negotiations on some point **that would rouse** and rally the American people. **Thus** we **find** that, **according to** Adams, **on** October 31, when complaint **was** made **of the delays of** the **British** government in **furnishing** passports for vessels to carry the despatches **of** the American **commissioners,** " Mr. Clay was **for** making a strong remonstrance on the subject, and for breaking off the negotiation upon that point, if they did not give us satisfaction." A passport arrived the same day, rendering the remonstrance unnecessary. When the negotiation had gone on for three months and it was perfectly well understood that the British would not listen at all to any proposition concerning impressment, Clay, who alone had pressed this subject, was again " so urgent to present an article " on impressment that Mr. Adams " acquiesced in his wishes ; " the article was presented and rejected by the British at once. Less than two weeks before the final agreement, discussing the question of the fisheries and the navigation of the Mississippi in the commission, Clay broke out, saying, " he was for a war three years longer ; he had no doubt three years more of war would make us a warlike people, and that then we should come out of the war with honor, — whereas at present, even upon the best terms we could possibly obtain, we shall have only a half-formed army, and half retrieve our military reputation." His agony grew as an agreement was approached, and culminated two days before the treaty was signed, when the British note on the fisheries and the navigation of the Mississippi had been received, which seemed to make the conclusion of the peace certain. " Mr. Clay came to my chamber " (writes Mr. Adams), " and on reading the British note manifested some chagrin. He still talked of breaking off the negotiation, but he did not exactly disclose the motive **of** his ill-humor, which was, however easily seen through.   In the evening we met, and **Mr.** Clay continued in his discontented humor. He was for taking time to deliberate upon the British note.   He was for meeting about it to-morrow morning.   He was sounding all round for support in making another stand **of** resistance at this stage of the business.   **At** last he turned **to me** and asked me whether **I** would not join **him** now and **break** off the negotiation.   **I told** him, No, there was nothing now **to break off on."**

Only then he gave **it up, and with a** heavy heart he consented to sign the treaty of peace.   The treaty provided that hostilities should cease immediately upon its ratification.   It further stipulated **for** a mutual restoration of territory (except some small disputed islands), of property, archives, etc. ; a mutual restoration of prisoners of war ; **a** commission to **settle** boundary questions, those questions, if the commission should disagree, **to be** submitted to some friendly government for arbitration ; cessation **of** Indian hostilities, each party to restore the **Indians** with whom they were still at war, to all **possessions** and rights they enjoyed in 1811 ; compensation for slaves abducted by British forces ; **a** promise by both governments to promote the entire abolition of the slave-trade ; but not a word to indicate what the British and the Americans had **been** fighting about.

Thus ended the war of 1812, on paper ; in reality, **it went on** until the news of the peace arrived in America. It stands as one of the most singular wars in history. It was begun on account of outrages committed upon the maritime commerce of the United States; but those parts of the country which had least to do with that maritime commerce, the South and West, were most in favor of the war, while those whose fortunes were on the sea most earnestly opposed it. Considering that the conduct of **Napoleon** toward the United States had been in some respects more **outrageous, certainly** more perfidious and insulting, than the conduct of **Great Britain,** it might be questioned whether the **war was not waged** against the wrong **party.** As a matter of fact the Orders in Council furnished **the** principal cause of the **war.** That principal cause happened to disappear at the same time that **the** war was declared. Hostilities were continued **on a secondary issue.** But when **peace was** made, neither the one nor the other **was by so much as a** single word alluded **to in** the treaty. To cap **the climax,** the principal battle of the war, the **battle of New Orleans, was fought after** the peace had **been signed,** but before it had become known **in** America. It is questionable whether such a peace would **have been** signed at all, had that battle happened at an earlier period. While the peace, **as to the United** States, **was not** one which a victorious power would make, the **closing triumph in** America had given **to the American arms a** prestige they had never possessed before.

Neither was the reception the treaty met with

in accord with the fears of the American, or **the**
hopes of the British commissioners. While the
leading statesmen of England congratulated one
another, as Lord Castlereagh, writing from Vienna,
expressed it in a letter to Lord Liverpool, upon
being " released from the millstone of **an American war,**" the war party in England, who wanted
to " punish " the impudence of the United States,
were deeply mortified. They would not admit
that the peace on the British side was an " honorable " one, since England had failed to " force her
principles on America," and had retired from the
contest **with** some defeats unavenged. In the
United States, on the other hand, where some of
the American envoys, especially Clay, had feared
their work would find very little favor, the news of
peace was received with transports of joy. To the
American people it came after the victory of **New**
Orleans ; and their national pride, relieved of the
terrible anxieties of the last two years, and elated
at the great closing triumph on the field of battle,
which seemed to wipe out all the shame of previous
defeats, was content not to look too closely at the
articles of the treaty. Indeed, the American commissioners received, for what they had done, the
praise of all their fellow-citizens who were unbi-
ased by party feeling, — praise, which, taking into
account the perplexities of their situation, they
well deserved. With no decisive victories on their
side to boast of, with no well-organized armies to
support their pretensions, with no national ships

on the high seas, with the capture of Washington, the burning of the Capitol, and the hurried flight of the President still a favorite theme of jest at the dinner-tables and in the clubs all over Europe, they had to confront the representatives of the haughtiest, and, in some respects, the strongest power on earth. If it was true that they had not succeeded in forcing the British formally to renounce the right of impressment and to accept just principles of blockade and of neutral rights, it was also true that the British had begun the negotiation with extravagant, humiliating, peremptory demands, presenting them in the most overbearing manner as *sine qua non;* that they had found themselves obliged to drop these one after another; that in the discussion about the fisheries and the navigation of the Mississippi, they had been dislodged from position after position, until finally they accepted a treaty which stood in strange contrast to their original attitude. The American commissioners had the satisfaction of hearing the Marquis of Wellesley declare in the House of Lords, that "in his opinion they had shown a most astonishing superiority over the British during the whole of the correspondence."

However reluctantly Clay had signed the peace, his proud patriotic heart became reconciled to it as the general effects of all that had been done disclosed themselves. These effects were indeed very great, and he had reason to be satisfied with them. The question has been much discussed, whether there was any statesmanship, any good sense, in making the war of 1812 at all. It is true that **it was** resolved upon without preparation, and that **it was** wretchedly managed. But if war is ever justified, there was ample provocation **for it. The legitimate** interests of the United **States** had been trampled upon by the belligerent powers, **as** if **entitled to no** respect. **The** American flag had **been** treated with a contempt scarcely conceivable now. **The** question was whether the American people should permit themselves **not** only **to be** robbed, and maltreated, and insulted, but also to be despised, — **all** this for the privilege of picking up the poor **crumbs** of trade which the great powers of Europe would still let them have. When a nation knowingly **and** willingly accepts the contempt of others, it is in danger **of** losing also its respect for itself. Against this the national pride of Young America rose in revolt. When insulted **too** grievously, **it** felt an irresistible impulse to strike. **It** struck **wildly**, to be sure, and received ugly blows in **return.** But it proved, after all, that this young democracy could **not** be trampled upon with **impunity, that it** felt an insult as keenly as older nations, **and that** it was capable **of** risking a fight with the **most** formidable **power** on earth in resenting **it. It** proved, too, that this most formidable power might find in the young **democracy** a very uncomfortable antagonist.

If the warlike impulse in this case was mere sentiment, as has been said, it was a statesmanlike sentiment. For the war of 1812, with all the losses in blood and treasure entailed by it, and in spite of the peace which ignored the declared causes of the war, transformed the American Republic in the estimation of the world from a feeble experimental curiosity into a power, — a real power, full of brains, and with visible claws and teeth. It made the American people, who had so far consisted of the peoples of so many little commonwealths, not seldom wondering whether they could profitably stay long together, a consciously united nation, with a common country, a great country, worth fighting for; and a common national destiny, nobody could say how great; and a common national pride, at that time filling every American heart brimful. The war had encountered the first practical disunion movement, and killed it by exposing it to the execration of the true American feeling; killed it so dead, at least on its field of action, in New England, that a similar aspiration has never arisen there again. The war put an end to the last remnant of colonial feeling; for from that time forward there was no longer any French party or any English party in the United States; it was thenceforth all American as against the world. A war that had such results was not fought in vain.

Clay might, therefore, well say, as he did say a year later in a debate in the House of Representatives : —

"I gave a vote for the declaration of war. I exerted

all the **little influence** and talent **I** could command to make **the war. The war** was made. It is terminated. **And** I declare, **with** perfect sincerity, **if** it had been permitted **to me** to **lift** the **veil of** futurity, and to foresee **the precise** series **of** events which has occurred, my vote **would have been** unchanged. We had **been** insulted, **and** outraged, **and** spoliated **upou** by **almost all** Europe, — by Great Britain, by France, Spain, **Denmark,** Naples, and, **to cap** the climax, by the little contemptible power **of** Algiers. **We had** submitted too long and too much. We had become the scorn **of** foreign powers, and the derision of our **own** citizens. What have we gained by the war ? Let any man look at the degraded condition of this country before the war, the scorn of the universe, the contempt of ourselves ; and tell me if we have gained nothing by the **war ?** What is our situation now ? Respectability and character abroad, security and confidence at home."

All this **was true ; but** he was very far from foreseeing such happy results at the time when he put his name to the treaty of peace. To him it seemed then a "damned bad treaty," and his mind was restless with dark forebodings as to its effect upon the character of his country and his own standing as a public man.

But the **sojourn in Ghent** was after all by **no** means all gloom to his buoyant nature. He had found things **to** enjoy. The American commissioners were most hospitably received by the authorities and the polite burghers of Ghent. Public and private entertainments in their honor crowded one another, and they enjoyed **them.** Even Mr.

Adams enjoyed them, **he,** however, **not** without characteristic remorse, for thus he castigates **him-**self in his Diary: " There are several particulars **in my** present mode **of** life **in which there is too** much relaxation **of** self-discipline. **I have** this month frequented too much the theatre and other public amusements; indulged **too** much convivial-ity, and taken too little exercise. The consequence is that I am growing corpulent, and that industry **becomes** irksome **to me. May I be** cautious not to fall into any habit **of** indolence or dissipation!" Clay's temperament, no doubt, enabled him to bear such pleasures with more fortitude and less appre-hension of dire consequences. There was no twinge of self-reproach in his mind, and later **in** life **he** often spoke **of** the days of Ghent with great **satis-**faction. He would certainly **have** enjoyed them still more, had **he at the time looked** farther into the future.

The diplomatic business **at** Ghent completed, Clay, in conjunction with Adams and Gallatin, was instructed to go to London for the purpose of negotiating a treaty of commerce. **He did not, however,** make haste to present himself **in Eng-land, for there was** still a feeling weighing upon his mind, as if, after the many defeats in America and the to him unsatisfactory peace, he would not like to be in the land of a triumphant enemy. So he lingered in Paris. But as soon as he heard of the battle of New Orleans, **he** was ready to start. " Now," said he to the bearer of the news, " now

I can go to England without mortification." While in Paris he was introduced to the polite society of the French capital. A clever saying is reported of him in a conversation with Madame de Staël: "I have been in England," said she, "and have been battling for your cause there. They were so much enraged against you that at one time they thought seriously of sending the Duke of Wellington to lead their armies against you." "I am very sorry," replied Mr. Clay, " that they did not send the duke." "And why?" "Because if he had beaten us, we should but have been in the condition of Europe, without disgrace. But if we had been so fortunate as to defeat him, we should have greatly added to the renown of our arms."

He arrived in London in March and went to work with Gallatin to open the negotiation intrusted to them. Mr. Adams did not follow them until May. They met again, as British commissioners, Goulburn and Dr. Adams. Mr. Robinson, afterwards Lord Goderich and Earl Ripon, then Vice-President of the Board of Trade, were substituted for Lord Gambier. The negotiation lasted three months ; it was friendly in character, but resulted in very little. The British government declined to open the questions of impressment, blockade, trade with enemies' colonies in time of war, West Indian and Canadian trade ; nothing of value was obtained save some advantages in the commerce with the East Indies, and a provision abolishing discriminating duties.

Clay arrived in the United States again in September, 1815, and was duly received and feasted by his friends and admirers. The people of the Lexington district in Kentucky had in the mean time reëlected him to the national House of Representatives.

CHAPTER VII.

BEFORE Clay left Lexington to take his seat in Congress, he received a letter from the Secretary of State, James Monroe, offering him the mission to Russia. He declined it. He was evidently resolved to remain in Congress while Madison was President, for when, less than a year later, in August, 1816, Madison invited him to a place in his cabinet as Secretary of War, his answer was still a refusal.

On the first day of the session, December 4, 1815, Clay was again elected Speaker. In both Houses the Republicans had strong majorities; in the Senate twenty-two against fourteen Federalists, and in the House of Representatives one hundred and seventeen against sixty-five. But the Federalists, as a party contending for power, were weaker even than these numbers indicated. There is no heavier burden for a political party to bear, than to have appeared unpatriotic in time of war. The Federal party went down under this load at a period when its principles were, one after another, unconsciously adopted by its victorious opponents.

The Republicanism left behind by the war of

1812 was no longer the Republicanism of frugal economy, simple, unpretentious, narrowly circumscribed government, and peace and friendship with all the world, which the famous triumvirate, Jefferson, Madison, and Gallatin, had set out with in 1801, and which was the political ideal of bucolic democracy. The rough jostle with the strong powers of the external world had made sad havoc of the idyl. Instead of the least possible government there had been, even before the war, while Jefferson himself was President, during that painful struggle under the oppressive practices of the European belligerents, enormous stretches of power, such as the laws enforcing the embargo, which equaled, if not outstripped, anything the Federalists had ever done. Instead of frugal economy and regular debt paying, there had been enormous war expenses with new taxes and heavy loans. Instead of unbroken peace and general friendship, there had been a long and bloody war with the nearest of kin. Now, with that war finished, there was a large public debt, a frightfully disordered currency, a heavy budget of yearly expenditures, and a people awakened to new wants and new ambitions, for the satisfaction of which they looked, more than ever before, to the government. The old triumvirate of leaders were indeed still alive ; but Jefferson was sitting in his lofty Monticello, the sage of the period, giving forth oracular sounds, many of them very wise, always respectfully received, but apt to be minded only when what he said corresponded with the wishes of his listeners; Gallatin, having witnessed and sagaciously recognized the break‹ down of his favorite theory of government, was serving the Republic as a diplomatic representa‌ive abroad; Madison was still President, but, having never been a strong leader of men for his own purposes, he could offer but feeble resistance to the new tendencies. A new school of Republican leaders had pressed forward into the places of these retired veterans, — new leaders, who would speak with pity of a government "going on in the old imbecile method, contributing nothing by its measures to the honor and reputation of the country;" who wanted a conduct of public affairs "on an enlarged policy;" who thought that revenues might be raised, not only to provide for the absolute wants of the government, but, beyond that, for the advancement of the public benefit.

Of this new Republican school Clay and Calhoun were the foremost champions. Clay boldly put forth its programme in a speech made in committee of the whole on January 29, 1816, on a bill reported by Lowndes, to reduce the direct taxes imposed during the war. After having defended, with great force, the war of 1812 as a just and necessary war, and the peace of Ghent as an honorable peace, he enumerated the reasons why he deemed no great reduction of taxes advisable. Our relations with Spain, he said, were unsatisfactory; there would be more wars with Great Britain; and the United States might have to aid the Spanish

South American colonies in their struggle for independence. It was necessary, therefore, to maintain a respectable military establishment, to augment the navy, and to provide for coast defenses. Furthermore he would, " as earnestly, commence the great work, too long delayed, of internal improvement. He desired to see a chain of turnpike roads and canals from Passamaquoddy Bay to New Orleans, and other similar roads intersecting the mountains, to facilitate intercourse between all parts of the country, and to bind and connect us together." He would also " effectually protect our manufactories, — not so much for the manufactories themselves, as for the general interest. We should thus have our wants supplied, when foreign resources are cut off; and we should also lay the basis of a system of taxation to be resorted to when the revenue from imports is stopped by war." Provision for the contingency of war was a prominent consideration in all this; Clay's political ideas had not yet come down to the peace footing. Calhoun followed him with a vigorous speech of similar tenor. These arguments prevailed, and the direct tax was in part retained.

Then the tariff was taken in hand. The embargo, the non-intercourse, and the war, while dealing the shipping interest a terrible blow, had, by excluding foreign products, served as a powerful stimulus to manufacturing industry. But after the war the country was flooded by a tremendous importation of English goods. American industry, artificially developed by an abnormal state of things, was now to be artificially sustained against that competition. Tariff duties were resorted to for **that** avowed purpose, and a scheme was proposed by Dallas, the Secretary of the Treasury. **He** arranged the articles subject to duty in three classes: 1. Those of which the home supply was sufficient to satisfy the demand; they were to bear the highest duty, thirty-five per cent. ad valorem. 2. Those of which the domestic supply was only partially sufficient to satisfy the demand, comprising cotton and woolen goods, as well as iron and most of its coarser products, distilled spirits, etc.; these were to bear twenty per cent. And 3, **those of** which **the** home production was small, or nothing; **these were to** bear **a** simple revenue tax.

Most of the Federalists opposed this protective policy, while the Republican protectionists, illustrating the remarkable mutation of things, quoted against them Hamilton's famous report on manufactures. Webster and most of the New England men opposed it, because it would injure the shipping interest. **John** Randolph, independent **of** party, opposed **it, because it would** benefit the Northern States at the expense of the South. Calhoun, Lowndes, and their Southern followers supported it, not only as a means of national defense, but also in order to **help the** cotton interest, since England at that time levied a discriminating duty on raw materials to the disadvantage of cotton raised in America, and since the coarser cotton fabrics imported into the United States were mostly made of India cotton. The principal argument urged by Clay and generally accepted by the Republicans was, that certain manufacturing industries must be built up and sustained for the safety of the country in time of war. Thus the tariff of 1816 was enacted, embodying substantially the scheme proposed by Dallas.

So far Clay had, as to definite measures of public concern, preserved a plausible consistency with the principles and measures advocated by him before the war of 1812. But he should not be spared the ordeal brought on by direct self-contradiction. The war had thrown the currency into great disorder. Upon the expiration of the charter of the United States Bank, the renewal of which Clay had helped to defeat, the notes of that institution were withdrawn, and the notes of state banks took their place. These banks multiplied very rapidly. In the years 1811, 1812, and 1813 one hundred and twenty of them went into operation, many with insufficient capital. The Secretary of the Treasury endeavored in vain to bring the banks into prudent coöperation. They began to refuse one another's bills. In 1814 specie payments were suspended. Reckless paper issues produced a corresponding inflation of prices. Under such circumstances Dallas finally saw no other way to restore order in the currency than by the promptest possible return to specie payments, and to this end he proposed the establishment of a specie-paying national bank, virtually a revival of the old Bank of the United States.

The Republican majority of 1816 was ready to return to Hamilton's plan of a financial agency, which the Republicans of 1811 had denounced and rejected ; and they were **ready,** too, to enlarge that plan in all the features formerly objected to. But how could Clay support such a scheme? We shall see.

On January 8, 1816, Calhoun reported to the House of Representatives a bill providing that a Bank of the United States **should** be chartered for twenty years, with a capital of $35,000,000, divided into 350,000 shares, Congress **to** have the power to authorize an increase of the capital to $50,000,000 ; 70,000 shares, amounting to $7,000,000, to be subscribed and paid for by the United States, and 280,000 shares to be taken by individuals, companies, or corporations ; the government to appoint five of the twenty-five directors ; the bank to be authorized to establish branches, to have the deposits of the public money, subject to the discretion **of** the Secretary **of** the Treasury, and to pay to the government $1,500,000 in three instalments, as a bonus for its charter. **This** was substantially Hamilton's National Bank of 1791, only on **a** larger scale. It was exactly the thing which, five years before, Clay had found so utterly unconstitutional, and in its very nature so dangerous, that he could under no circumstances consent to a pro**longation of its** existence.

Again the two parties found themselves reversed in position : the Federalists were now opposing the bank, — some of them, like Webster, because the capital was too large; while the Republicans, with some exceptions, were favoring it as a necessity. But how did Clay perform his somersault? He made a speech which his contemporary friends praised as very able. It was not reported, but he reproduced its main propositions in an address subsequently delivered before his constituents for the purpose of defending himself against that charge which has such terrors for public men, — the charge of inconsistency. This was his argument: In 1811 the legislature of his state had instructed him to oppose the re-chartering of the bank, while now the people of his district, as far as he had been able to ascertain their minds by conversation with them, were in favor of a new bank. Secondly, the old bank had abused its powers for political purposes, while the new bank would be deterred from doing so by the fate of its predecessor. This was making an audacious draft upon the credulity of his audience. Thirdly, the bank had been unconstitutional in 1811, but it was constitutional in 1816, owing to a change of circumstances. We remember that magnificent passage in Clay's speech of 1811 in which he arrayed in parade the monster corporations of history, arguing that so tremendous a power as the authority to charter such companies could not possibly have been given to the federal government by mere inference and implication ; that, if **the Constitution** did not grant **that** power in so many words, **directly**, specifically, unmistakably, it was not granted **at all.** What did he say now ?

" The Constitution contained powers delegated and prohibitory, powers expressed and constructive. It vests in Congress all powers necessary to give effect to the enumerated powers. The powers that may be so necessary are deducible **by** construction. They are not defined in **the** Constitution. They are in **their nature undefinable. With regard** to **the degree of** necessity various **rules** have **been, at** different **times, laid** down ; but perhaps, at last, **there is no** other than **a sound and** honest judgment, exercised **under** the control **which** belongs to the Constitution and the people. **It is manifest that** this necessity **may not** be perceived at **one time under** one state **of things,** while it **is perceived at** another time under **a** different state of things. The Constitution, it is true, never changes ; it is always the same ; but the force of circumstances and the lights of experience may evolve, to the fallible persons charged with its administration, the fitness and necessity of a particular exercise of constructive power to-day, which they did not see at a former period."

And how did he apply **this** constitutional theory to the **pending** case ? In 1811, he said, the bank did not seem to him necessary, because it was supported mainly upon the ground " that it was indispensable to the Treasury operations," which, in his opinion, could have been sufficiently aided by the state banks then existing. Therefore the re-chartering of the United States Bank would have been, in his view, at that time unconstitutional. But now he beheld specie payments suspended. He saw about three hundred banking institutions which had lost the public confidence in a greater or less degree, and which were exercising what had always and everywhere been considered " one of the highest attributes of sovereignty," namely, the " regulation of the current medium of the country." They were no longer capable of aiding, but were really obstructing, the operations of the Treasury. To renew specie payments and to prevent further disaster and distress a national bank now appeared to him " not only necessary, but indispensably necessary." Under these circumstances, therefore, he considered the chartering of a national bank constitutional. " He preferred," he added, "to the suggestions of the pride of opinion the evident interests of the community, and determined to throw himself upon their candor and justice. Had he in 1811 foreseen what now existed, and no objection had lain against the renewal of the charter other than that derived from the Constitution, he should have voted for the renewal."

This was virtually a confession that he had seriously mistaken the situation of things in 1811, when, against Gallatin's judgment, he had helped in disarranging the fiscal machinery of the government on the eve of a war. But it was a confession, too, that he had thrown overboard that constitutional theory according to which such things as the power of chartering corporations, not being among the specifically granted powers, could **not** be an implied power. He had familiarized himself with larger views **of** governmental function, **as** the Republic had grown in dimensions, **in** strength, and in the reach of **its** interests. Indeed, the **reasoning** with which he justified his change of position in 1816 stopped **but** little, if **at** all, short of the assertion that whatever may be considered necessary, or even eminently desirable, to help the country over a temporary embarrassment, may also be considered constitutional. Clay, who **seldom, if** ever, reasoned out **a** point in all its logical **bearings, would** not have admitted that **as a** general proposition. **But** he evidently **inclined** to the most latitudinarian construction. His constitutional principles had become prodigiously elastic according to the requirements of the occasion. In this respect **he was not peculiar. Most** of our public men have been inclined to interpret the Constitution according to their purposes. This tendency **was** especially strong among **the young** Republicans of that period; and **there it was all the more remarkable as their party had in its de-**sign and beginning been **a** living protest **against** the strong government theory favored by the Federalists. There was, however, this difference left between them and their old antagonists: the Federalists believed that government, in order to **be** good, or even tolerable, must **be** strong enough to restrain the disorderly **tendencies of** democracy; while the young Republicans rejected the theory of strong government in that sense, but believed that it must have large powers in order to do the things which they thought it should do for the development of a great nation.

At the next session of Congress, in February 1817, Calhoun took the lead in advocating a bill to set apart and pledge the bonus of the national bank and the share of the United States in its dividends, as a permanent fund for "constructing roads and canals and improving the navigation of watercourses, in order to facilitate, promote, and give security to internal commerce among the several states, and to render more easy and less expensive the means and provisions for the common defense." In his speech Calhoun pronounced himself strongly in favor of a latitudinarian construction of constitutional powers, and a liberal exercise of them for the purpose of binding the people of this vast country more closely together, and of preventing "the greatest of all calamities, next to the loss of liberty, and even that in its consequence — disunion." Clay thanked him for "the able and luminous view which he had submitted to the committee of the whole," and vigorously urged the setting apart of a fund to be used at a future time when the specific objects to be accomplished should have been more clearly ascertained and fixed. This contemplated the accumulation of funds in the Treasury with the expectation that suitable objects would be found for which to spend them, — a dangerous practice in a democratic government. "Congress," he said, "could at some future day examine into the constitutionality of the question, and if it had the power, it could exercise it; if it had not, the Constitution, there could be no doubt, would be so amended as to confer it." At any rate, he wished to have the fund set apart. Clay himself did not doubt that Congress had the constitutional power to use that fund, and possibly he thought that, if only the money were provided to be spent, Congress would easily come to the same conclusion.

The bill passed both houses, but old-school Republicanism once more stemmed the tide. President Madison, who himself had formerly expressed opinions favorable to internal improvements, vetoed it on strictly constitutional grounds, much to the astonishment and disgust of the young Republican statesmen. It was his last act.

Clay had in the mean time, by way of episode, gone through the experience of flagging popularity. It was not on account of his constitutional doctrines, or any other great question of state, but by reason of a matter to which he had probably given but little thought. At the previous session he had voted for a bill to increase the pay of members of Congress from a *per diem* of six dollars to a fixed salary of $1,500 a year, the law to apply to the Congress then in session. He supported it on the ground that he had never been able to make both ends meet at Washington. "The rate of compensation," he said, "ought to be such at least as that ruin should not attend a long service in Congress." Such arguments prevailed, and the bill passed both houses. But many of Clay's constituents thought differently. To the Kentucky farmers a yearly income of $1,500 for a few months' sitting on cushioned chairs in the Capitol looked monstrously extravagant. They were sure men could be found who would do the business for less money. When the election of members of Congress came on, Clay was fortunate enough to force the candidate opposing him into a "joint debate," in which, as that gentleman had been "against the war," Clay made short work of him. But he himself had an arduous canvass. It was then that his meeting with the old hunter occurred, which furnished material for a school-book anecdote. The old hunter, who had always voted for Clay, was now resolved to vote against him on account of the back-pay bill. "My friend," said Clay, "have you a good rifle?" "Yes." "Did it ever flash?" "Yes, but only once." "What did you do with the rifle when it flashed,—throw it away?" "No, I picked the flint, tried again, and brought down the game." "Have I ever flashed, except upon the compensation bill?" "No." "Well, will you throw me away?" "No, Mr. Clay; I will pick the flint and try you again." Clay was tried again, but only by a majority of some six or seven hundred votes. At the next session of Congress he voted for the repeal of the compensation act, avowedly on the ground of its unpopularity; but **he** favored the raising of **the** *per diem.* The pay of members of Congress was fixed at eight dollars per day. This was the only time **that** his home constituency threatened to fail him.

James Monroe was elected President in 1816 with little **opposition. He** received 183 electoral votes; **while his** competitor, Rufus King, the candidate of **the Federalists,** had only 34. **Monroe** was inaugurated **March 4,** 1817, and the famous " era of good feeling " set in, — that is to say, with the disappearance **of** the Federal party as a national organization, the great organized contests of the old parties for power ceased, to make room for the smaller contests of personal ambitions. But these infused fully as much bitterness into the era of good feeling as the differences on important questions **of** public policy had infused into great party struggles. Until **then the** Presidents of the United States had been men of note in the American Revolution. Monroe was the last **of the** Revolutionary generation and of the " Virginia dynasty." It was taken for granted that he **would** have his **two** terms, and that then the competition for **the** presidency would be open to **a new** class of men. As Madison **had** been Jefferson's Secretary of State before he became President, and Monroe had **been** Madison's, the secretaryship of state was looked upon as the stepping-stone **to the** presidency. Those who expected to be candidates for the highest place in the future, therefore, coveted **it** with peculiar solicitude.

One of them was Henry Clay. Among the citizens of the United States he could find none, to whom the succession to Mr. Monroe, as he believed, belonged more rightfully than to himself. Thus he started on the career of a candidate for the presidency, and that career began with a disappointment. Monroe selected for the secretaryship John Quincy Adams, a most excellent selection, although Clay very decidedly did not think so. Monroe also signified his appreciation of Clay's merits by offering him the war department, and then the mission to England. But Clay declined both places, on the ground, as Mr. Adams reports, " that he was satisfied with the situation which he held, and could render more service to the public in it than in the other situations offered him." This was true enough; but it is also probable that he was then already resolved to stand as a candidate for the presidency after Monroe's second term, although Adams had been designated as heir-apparent; and, moreover, his disappointment had so affected his personal feelings toward Monroe and Adams, as to make unsuitable his acceptance of a place among the President's confidential advisers. This supposition is borne out by his subsequent conduct.

The fifteenth Congress met on December 1, 1817, and Clay was on the same day reëlected Speaker of the House of Representatives by an almost unanimous vote, — 140 to 7. An opportunity for an open disagreement between Clay and the administration was not long in appearing. In his first message to Congress, Monroe, referring to the passage at the preceding session of the act concerning a fund for internal improvements, which Madison vetoed, deemed it proper to **make** known his sentiments **on that** subject beforehand, **so** that there should be no uncertainty **as to** his prospective action in case such a bill were passed again. **He declared it to be** his " settled conviction " that Congress did not possess the right of constructing roads and canals. " It is not contained in **any** of the specified powers granted to Congress; nor can I consider it incidental to, or a necessary means, viewed on the most liberal scale, for carrying into effect any **of** the powers specifically granted." He then suggested, as Jefferson and Madison had done, the adoption of **a** constitutional amendment **to** give to Congress **the** right in question.

This spontaneous declaration by the President **of** what he intended to **do** in certain contingencies was taken as something like a challenge, and the challenge was promptly accepted. Calhoun, next **to Clay** the foremost champion of internal improvements, having gone into the Cabinet as Secretary **of War,** Tucker **of** Virginia reported on December 15, from a select committee, a resolution equivalent to that which Madison had vetoed. Against it Monroe's constitutional objections were marshaled in debate. Clay **took up** the gauntlet and **made** two speeches, in which he disclosed his views of policy, as well as his constitutional principles, more pointedly than he had ever done before. He maintained that the Constitution did give the general government the power to construct roads and canals, and that the consent of the states, which had been thought necessary in the case of the Cumberland Road, was not required at all. He spoke as a western man, as a representative of a new country and a pioneer population, needing means of communication, channels of commerce and intelligence, as the breath of life. He spoke as a citizen of the Union, looking forward to a great destiny. Was the Constitution, he asked, giving Congress the power to establish post-offices and post-roads, and to regulate commerce between the states, made for the benefit of the Atlantic margin of the country only? Was the Constitution made only for the few millions then inhabiting this continent? No! " Every man," he exclaimed, " who looks at the Constitution in the spirit to entitle him to the character of a statesman, must elevate his views to the height which this nation is destined to reach in the rank of nations. We are not legislating for this moment only, or for the present generation, or for the present populated limits of the United States; but our acts must embrace a wider scope, — reaching northwestward to the Pacific, and southwardly to the river Del Norte. Imagine this extent of territory covered with sixty, or seventy, or an hundred millions of people. The powers which exist in this government now will exist then; **and** those which **will** exist then exist now."

"**What** was the object **of the** Convention," he asked, "in framing the Constitution? **The lead- ing** object was UNION. Union, then, peace external **and** internal, and commerce, but more particularly union and peace, the great objects of the framers of the Constitution, should be kept steadily in view in the interpretation of any clause of it; and where it is susceptible of various interpretations, that construction should be preferred which tends to promote the objects of the framers of the Constitution, to the consolidation of the Union." **This he emphasized** with still greater force. "**I am a** friend, **a true friend,** to **state** rights, but not in all **cases as** they are asserted. We should equally avoid **that** subtile process of argument which dissipates into air the powers **of** the government, and that spirit of encroachment which would snatch from the states powers not delegated to the general government. We shall then escape both the dangers I have noticed, — that of relapsing into the alarming weakness of the Confederation, which **was** described as a mere rope of sand; and also that other, perhaps not the greatest, danger, consolidation. No man deprecates more than **I** do the idea of consolidation; yet between separation and consolidation, painful as would be the alternative, I should greatly prefer the latter."

Here was the well-spring from which Henry

Clay **drew** his political inspirations, — a grand conception of the future destiny of the American Republic, and of a government adapted to the fulfillment of that great destiny; an ardent love for the Union, as the ark of liberty and national grandeur, **a Union** to be maintained at any price; an imaginative enthusiasm which infused its patriotic glow into his political opinions, but which was also apt to carry him beyond the limits of existing things and conditions, and not seldom unfitted him for the formation of a clear and well-balanced judgment of facts and interests. But this enthusiastic conception of national grandeur, this lofty Unionism constantly appearing as the inspiration **of his** public conduct, gave to his policies, as they stood forth in the glow of his eloquence, a peculiarly potent charm.

The result of this debate was the passage, not of the resolution reported by Tucker, but of a substitute declaring that " Congress has power, under the Constitution, to appropriate money for the construction of post-roads, military and other roads, **and of** canals, and for the improvement of watercourses." Other resolutions, asserting the power of Congress not only to appropriate money for such roads and canals, but to construct them, failed by small majorities, so that Clay carried his **point** only in part.

That Clay would continue to assert the power of Congress to construct internal improvements, President Monroe's message notwithstanding, everybody expected. But when he interspersed that advocacy with keen criticism of Monroe's attitude concerning that subject, — criticism which had **a** strong flavor of bitterness in it, — the **effect was** not to his advantage. The unfriendly tone of his remarks was generally attributed to **his** disappointment in the matter of the secretaryship of state. Not many men like to see personal resentments carried into the discussion of public interests ; and in this case, to make the matter worse, the demonstrations of resentment were, in the shape of oratorical flings, darted at a President who was by no means a great man, rather a man of moderate parts, but who was regarded as inoffensive **and** well-meaning, and as honestly busying himself about his presidential duties, — one of those respectable mediocrities in high public station, with whom people are apt to sympathize in their troubles, especially when unnecessarily attacked and humiliated by persons of greatly superior ability.

But the disappointment of the aspirant for the presidency was so little under his control that he permitted it to appear even in another of his great endeavors, which, in order to succeed, required particularly prudent management. This was his effort in behalf of the Spanish American colonies, which had risen against the mother country, and were struggling to achieve their independence.

It has been said by Clay's opponents that **his** zeal for the cause of the **South American patriots** was wholly owing to his desire to annoy the Monroe administration. This is clearly an unjust charge, for he had loudly proclaimed his ardent sympathies with the South American insurgents while Madison was still President. We remember that in his speech on the direct taxes in January, 1816, he seriously put the question whether the United States would not have openly " to take part with the patriots of South America." So on January 24, 1817, before Monroe's inauguration, he had stoutly opposed a bill " more effectually to preserve the neutral relations of the United States," intended to stop the fitting out of armed cruisers in American ports ; he had opposed the bill on the ground that it might be advantageous to old Spain in the South American struggle. All this had sprung naturally from his emotional enthusiasm. He was therefore, although imprudent in his propositions, yet only true to himself, when, under Monroe's administration, he continued to demand that the neutrality law of 1817 be repealed ; that our neutrality be so arranged as to be as advantageous as possible to the insurgent colonies ; and finally that the United States send a minister to the " United Provinces of Rio de la Plata," thereby formally recognizing that revolutionized colony as an independent state. This he proposed in March, 1818. Three commissioners had been appointed by the President to go to South America for the purpose of looking into the condition of things ; and, to cover the necessary expenses, the

President asked for an appropriation. Clay strenuously opposed this on the ground that the commissioners had been appointed without the advice and consent of the Senate. He moved instead an appropriation for a regular minister to be sent there.

The speech with which he supported this proposition was in his grandest style. South America had set his imagination on fire. In gorgeous colors he drew a picture of "the vast region in which we behold the most sublime and interesting objects of creation; **the** loftiest mountains, the most majestic rivers in the world; the richest mines of the precious metals, the choicest productions of the earth; we behold there a spectacle still more interesting and sublime, — the glorious spectacle of eighteen millions of people struggling to burst their chains and to be free." **A** burning description followed of their degradation and sufferings, and of the terrible cruelties inflicted upon them by their relentless oppressors. **In** his imagination they were a people of high mental and moral qualities, notwithstanding their ignorance and their subserviency to the influence of **the** church. He was sure that, "Spanish America being once independent, whatever may be the form of the governments established in its several parts, these governments will be animated by an American feeling, and guided by an American **policy.**" He affirmed that they **had** established and **for years** maintained an independent government on the river La Plata, and that, as the United States always recognized *de facto* governments, it was a duty to recognize this. He demanded it in the name of a just neutrality. As the United States had received a minister sent by Spain, so they were "bound" to receive a minister of the La Plata republic if they meant to be neutral. "If the royal belligerent is represented and heard at our government, the republican belligerent ought also to be heard." All this, he thought, could be done without any danger of war. Spain herself was too much crippled in her resources to make war on the United States, and no other power would do so.

It was a brilliant display of oratorical splendors, but the House resisted the fascination. In the discussion which followed, much of the halo, with which Clay's poetic fancy had surrounded the South American people and their struggle, was dissipated by sober statements of fact. Neither was it difficult to show that Clay was much in error in his views of true neutrality, and that neutrality between two belligerents did by no means always require equal diplomatic relations with them. Finally, the contemptuous flings at the President and the Secretary of State, with which Clay seasoned his speech, displeased a large part of the House. It was well known that Monroe and Adams were not at all unfriendly to the insurgent colonies; only they wanted to be sure of the fact that the new government had the necessary element of stability to justify recognition; they hoped to obtain the coöperation of England in that recognition ; they desired to avoid the embarrassment which a hasty recognition would cause in the negotiations between the United States and Spain concerning the cession of Florida; and finally, they wanted to be first assured that the public opinion of the country would sustain them in so important a step.

The motion was defeated by a vote of 115 against 45. But Monroe was terribly disturbed at Clay's hostile attitude, so much so indeed that, two or three days after Clay's great speech, Adams wrote in his Diary : —

"The subject which seems to absorb all the faculties of his (Monroe's) mind is the violent systematic opposition that Clay is raising against his administration. . . . Mr. Monroe added, if Mr. Clay had taken the ground that the Executive had gone as far as he could go with propriety towards the acknowledgment of the South Americans, that he was well disposed to go further, if such were the feeling of the nation and of Congress, and had made his motion with that view, to ascertain the real sentiments of Congress, it might have been in perfect harmony with the Executive. But between that and the angry, acrimonious course pursued by Mr. Clay, there was a wide difference."

Monroe was perfectly right. Clay would have served better the cause he had at heart had he maintained friendly relations with the administration. But that strange disturber of impulses and motives, of perceptions and conclusions — the aspiration to the presidency — clouded his discernment.

In the second session of the fifteenth Congress a debate took place which was destined to be of far greater consequence to Clay's political fortunes than anything that had gone before. It was the first clash between Henry Clay and Andrew Jackson. This is the story. The Floridas were still in the possession of Spain. They served as a place of refuge for runaway slaves, and a base of operations for raiding Indians. Spain was bound by treaty to prevent hostile excursions on the part of the savages, but too weak or too negligent to do so. There were frequent collisions between whites and Indians on the border, one party being as often the aggressor as the other. General Gaines sent soldiers against the Indians, and an Indian war began. In December, 1817, General Jackson took command. He received authority to pursue the Indians, but, as the administration understood it, he was to respect Spanish rights. This was Jackson's famous Seminole war. He enlisted volunteers in Tennessee by his own proclamation, without waiting for the President to call upon the governor for a levy of militia in the legal, regular way. He broke into Florida in March, 1818, took the Spanish fort of St. Mark's, hung Indian chiefs who had been captured by stratagem; ordered a Scotchman and an Englishman, Arbuthnot and Ambrister, whom he had found with the Indians, to be tried by court-martial for having instigated the savages to hostilities ; and when, on **very** insufficient evidence, **they** were found guilty, he had them **promptly** executed, after having changed **the** sentence in Ambrister's case from mere flogging to **the** penalty **of** death **by** shooting ; **he took** Pensacola on his **way** home, deposed **the** Spanish governor, appointed **a** new one, left a garrison there, and conducted himself throughout as a victorious general with absolute power in a conquered country, like **a** Roman proconsul in a subjugated province.

When the news arrived in Washington, the President and **the** Cabinet were astonished **and** perplexed. Except Adams, who was always inclined to take **the** highest ground **for** his country against **any** foreign power, they all agreed **that General** Jackson had gone far beyond his instructions and done lawless things. Calhoun, the Secretary of War, thought **that** the General should promptly be held to a severe account. But they shrunk from affronting the "hero of New Orleans." The administration finally concluded to **restore to** the Spaniards possession of the forts taken **by** General Jackson, and to affirm that the capture of those places by Jackson and his conduct generally **were** justified, on the principle of self-defense, by the hostile attitude of the Spanish governors, thus denying that any warlike step had been taken against Spain, while **at** the same time making a case against her officers.

On January 16, 1819, **the** House of Representatives began the discussion of **a** resolution reported

by its military committee, " disapproving the proceedings in the trial of Arbuthnot and Ambrister," to which three further resolutions were added, declaring the seizure of **Pensacola** and Fort Barrancas to have been contrary to the Constitution of the United States, and calling for appropriate legislation. A debate of three weeks followed, in which Clay was the most prominent figure on the anti-Jackson side. He had no personal feeling against General Jackson. On the contrary he was sincerely and profoundly grateful to the man who, after all the disgraceful failures of the war of **1812**, had so brilliantly restored the lustre of the American arms, and enabled him to " go to England without mortification." But as a friend of constitutional government he felt that he could not possibly approve of the General's lawless conduct in Florida. There is no reason to attribute the position he took to any but conscientious motives. But he was an aspirant to the presidency, and known to be such, while Jackson, too, was beginning to be whispered about as a possible candidate for that honor. Would not a frank expression of his views on Jackson's conduct appear like an attempt to injure a dreaded rival? It dawned upon him that his unnecessary flings at the Monroe administration had subjected his motives to suspicion, and thus, while attacking, he felt himself on the defensive. He began with an almost painful effort to retrieve the ground which he feared that he had lost in the confidence of the House and the country : —

"In rising to address you, sir, I must be allowed to say, that all inferences, drawn from the course which it will be my painful duty to take in this discussion, of unfriendliness either to the **chief** magistrate of the country, **or to** the illustrious military chieftain **whose** operations are under investigation, will be wholly unfounded. Toward that distinguished captain who shed **so much** glory on our **country, whose** renown constitutes **so** great a portion of **its** moral property, I never had, I never **can** have, any other feelings than those of the most profound respect and of the utmost kindness. I know **the motives** which have been, and will again be, attributed **to** me in regard to the other exalted personage alluded to. They have been and they will be **unfounded.** I have **no** interest other than that of seeing the concerns of my country well **and** happily **administered.** Rather than throw obstructions in the way of the President, I would precede him and pick **out those, if I** could, which might **jostle** him in his progress. I may **be** again reluctantly compelled **to** differ **from** him, but **I** will with the utmost sincerity assure the committee **that** I **have** formed no resolution, come under no engagements, **and** that I never will form any resolution, **or** contract any engagements, for systematic opposition **to his** administration, or **to** that of any other chief magistrate."

This might have **been** sufficient to disarm suspicion, had he not been believed to have an eye **toward** the presidency.

He arraigned General Jackson's conduct with dignity and a certain degree of moderation. He emphatically acquitted him of " any intention to violate the laws of his country, or the obligations of humanity." He declared himself **far from** wishing to intimate that "General Jackson cherished **any** design inimical **to** the liberties of the people." He believed the General's " intentions **to be pure and** patriotic." But he denounced the hanging of Indian chiefs without trial, " under color of retaliation," **as** utterly unjustifiable and disgraceful. He admitted retaliation as justifiable only when " calculated to produce an effect in the war," but never on the motive of mere vengeance. As to Arbuthnot **and** Ambrister, whether they were innocent **or guilty,** he utterly rejected the argument by which Jackson tried to justify their execution, namely, " that it **is an** established principle of the law of nations, that any individual of a nation, making war against the citizens of any other nation, they being at peace, forfeits his allegiance, and becomes an outlaw **and a pirate."** He maintained that, " whatever **may be the** character of individuals making **private war, the** principle is totally erroneous when applied to such individuals associated **with a power,** whether Indian **or** civilized, capable of maintaining the relations of peace or war." He showed that Jackson's doctrine would make every foreign subject serving in **an** American army **an** outlaw and a pirate ; he might have cited **La Fayette and** Steuben. This was the moral he drew : —

" However guilty **these** men **were,** they should not have **been** condemned **or** executed without the authority of **law.** I **will not** dwell on the effect of these precedents in foreign countries, but I shall not pass unnoticed their dangerous influence **in our own.** Bad examples are generally set in the case of bad men, and often remote from the central government. It was in the provinces that were laid the seeds **of** the ambitious projects which overturned the liberties of Rome."

He affirmed that Jackson, going far beyond the **spirit** of his instructions, had not only **assumed,** by **an** unauthorized construction of his own, **to** determine what Spain was bound by treaty to do, **but** had **" also assumed** the power, belonging **to** Congress alone, **of** determining what should **be** the effect and consequence of her breach **of** engagement;" **that then he** had seized the **Spanish** forts and thus usurped the power of making **war,** which the Constitution **had** "expressly **and** exclusively" vested **in** Congress, " to guard **our** country against precisely that species of rashness **which** has been manifested **in** Florida." A glowing peroration followed, protesting against " the alarming doctrine **of** unlimited discretion in our military command**ers,"** and pointing **out** how **other** free nations, from antiquity **down, had lost** their liberties, **and how we might** lose ours. **" Are** former services," **he exclaimed, "** however eminent, to preclude even inquiry **into** recent conduct? **Is** there to be **no** limit, no prudential bounds **to the** national gratitude? I hope gentlemen **will** deliberately survey **the awful** isthmus on **which we** stand. They **may** bear down all opposition ; they may even vote the **General** the public thanks; they **may carry** him triumphantly through this House. But if they do so, it will be a triumph of the principle of **insubordination**, a triumph of the military over the civil authority, a triumph over the powers of this House, a triumph over the Constitution of the land. And I pray most devoutly to Heaven that it may not prove, in its ultimate effects and consequences, **a** triumph over the liberties of the people."

It was a fine speech and much admired; brilliant in diction; statesmanlike in reasoning; **full** of stirring appeals; also undoubtedly right in its general drift of argument. But it had some very weak points. Clay had again gone a little beyond what the occasion required; he had attacked, aside from Jackson's conduct in Florida, certain Indian treaties which Jackson had made, and this attack **was** based upon an imperfect knowledge of facts. Such flaws were exposed, and thus the impression was created that he had been rather quick in making his assault without having taken the trouble of thoroughly studying his case. In fact, he had not exactly measured the power which in this instance **he** had to deal with. It was the popularity of **a** victorious soldier.

A military "hero" has an immense advantage over ordinary mortals, especially in a country where the military hero is a rare character. The achievements of statesmen usually remain subject to differences of opinion. A victory on the field of battle won for the country is a title to public gratitude, seldom to be questioned by anybody.

It is a matter of common pride. It lives in the imagination of the people. That imagination is apt to attribute to the hero of such a victory an abundance of other good qualities. His failings are judged with leniency. To many it appears almost sacrilegious to think that **a man who has** rendered his country service so valuable in the crisis of **war** should ever be able to act upon any but the most patriotic motives. It will require **an** extraordinary degree of wrong-doing **on** his part to make suspicion and criticism with regard to him acceptable to the popular mind; and even then he is apt to be easily forgiven.

General Jackson enjoyed this advantage in the highest degree. He had given the American people a brilliant victory when **it was most** needed to soothe the popular pride. Would he disgrace and endanger the Republic after having so magnificently fought for it? To convince the people, and to make Congress declare, that **he** had done **so,** would have required a very calm and careful presentation of the case, moving from point to point **of** the allegation, and proving every position with evidence **so** conclusive as to extort a verdict of guilty from ever so unwilling a jury. **Even then** the result would not have been certain. But any argument not absolutely irrefutable; any arraignment having in it the smallest flaw; any appeal proceeding in the slightest degree upon a mere assumption of fact, was sure to be drowned by a cry far more powerful than any oratorical declamation,

— the battle of New Orleans. So it was in this instance. The hero of New Orleans could not have intended, he could not have done, **any** wrong. **At** any rate, he had **full absolution for** what he had done, perhaps also for what **he** might **do in the** future, and the resolutions disapproving **his con-** duct were voted down by heavy majorities.

Thus was Henry Clay defeated **in** his **first en-** counter with Andrew **Jackson.** The **great duel** had begun which **was to embitter** the best part of Clay's life. **His war of** 1812 **had put** the military hero into **his** way, and a military hero, too, **of** the most exasperating kind; a hero who would not be conciliated **by** a mere recognition **of** his good in- tentions; who demanded absolute compliance with his will, and who treated any **one** finding fault with him as little better **than** " an outlaw **and a** pirate;" a hero who not **seldom** made **Clay** al- most despair of the Republic. The case was in- deed not as desperate as Clay sometimes feared. Victorious generals begin to become really danger- ous to republican institutions when a large portion **of** the people are tired of popular liberty. **It is** true, however, **that** their peculiarly privileged posi- tion before the popular mind may put those in- stitutions **at** all times to temporary strain, and fa- cilitate the establishment **of** precedents prolific of **evil.**

For the present General Jackson, " vindicated " **by** the House of Representatives, was received **wherever** he went with great enthusiasm, and **was** "thought **of** in connection with the presidency," not only as a hero, but as a persecuted hero. At the same time Clay's star seemed to be somewhat obscured. The impression that his disappointment with regard to the secretaryship of state had led him to make a factious opposition to the administration, **had** lowered **him in** the estimation of many men. This impression had become so general as to make his reasons for permitting now **and then** an administration measure to pass unchallenged a matter of gossiping speculation. A striking instance of this is found in Mr. Adams's **Diary, where Mr.** Middleton, of South Carolina, **is** introduced as telling the story, that Clay neglected to oppose a certain bill because "the last fortnight of the session Clay spent almost every night at the card table, and one night Poindexter had won of him eight thousand dollars. This discomposed **him** to such a degree that he paid no attention to the business of the House the remainder of the session. Before it closed, however, he had won back from Poindexter all that he had lost, except about nine hundred dollars." Whether this story in all its details was true or not, certain it is that Clay at that period spent far more time at the card table than was good for his reputation. Indeed, Nathan Sargent says in his recollections ("Public Men and Events"): "When a candidate for the presidency, Mr. Clay was denounced as **a** gambler. He was no more a gambler than was almost every Southern and Southwestern gentleman

of that day. Play was a passion with them; **it** was a social enjoyment; they loved its excitement, and they played whenever and wherever they met; not **for the** purpose **of** winning money of one **another,** which is the gambler's motive, but for the pleasure it gave **them.** They bet high **as a** matter of pride and **to** give interest **to** the game." But Clay himself felt **that** his habits in that respect had been unfavorably noticed. Soon afterwards, in a speech in the House, **he** referred by **way of** illustration to games of chance, as "an amusement which in early life he had sometimes indulged **in,** but which years and experience had determined him to renounce." To a man of Clay's standing before **the** country there was a keen self-humiliation in a remark like this, and **he would** hardly have made it, had he not thought something like a promise of better conduct urgently called **for.** The promise referred, **however,** only to "games of chance," for whist seemed to maintain an almost irresistible charm over him, except **in his own** house **at Ashland, where no card** playing was allowed.

Clay's political standing **was** so much shaken that about the time of the opening of the sixteenth Congress, in December, 1819, several members of the House went to President Monroe to consult with him as to whether it would be advisable to displace Clay as Speaker. Adams says **in** his Diary that Monroe advised against it, partly because such a movement would increase Clay's importance, partly because **Clay's** course had injured his own influence more than that of the administration, and partly because, as there was no western **man in the Cabinet,** it was a matter of pride with **that** part **of** the country to have a western man in **the** Speaker's chair, and **there** was no western man **of** sufficient eminence to be put in competition with Clay. "In all this," wrote Adams, "I think the President has acted and spoken wisely." **It was** indeed wisely spoken, for, had **a** contest been made, **it** would after all have appeared that most of the members of the House, although they voted against Clay time and again in his opposition to the administration, were proud **of** the lustre his brilliant abilities shed upon the House, believed in his patriotism, and liked the gay, spirited, dashing Kentuckian as a man. **So he was, on the** first day of the session, December **6, 1819,** reëlected Speaker virtually without opposition.

Before long he was **up in** arms against **the administration** again. After long and arduous negotiation, Mr. Adams had, **in** February, 1819, concluded a treaty with the Spanish Minister. which provided for the cession of the whole of Florida to this Republic, fixed **the** southwestern boundary **line** of the United States along the Sabine River (thus excluding Texas), expunged the claims of Spanish subjects against the United States, and provided that the United States, as a compensation for the cession of Florida, should undertake to set. tle the claims of American citizens against Spain to an amount not exceeding $5,000,000. The treaty was unanimously approved by the Senate; but the King of Spain, faithlessly it was thought, withheld his ratification of it, which ratification should have taken place within six months. This conduct produced an irritating effect in the United States. Many were in favor of treating the whole matter again as an open one. The proposition to take forcible possession of Florida was freely discussed and widely approved, and a bill to that effect was introduced in Congress. Then the news arrived that the Spanish government had sent a new minister. Under these circumstances Monroe addressed a special message to Congress, on March 27, 1820, mentioning the friendly interest taken in the matter by the great powers of Europe, — England, Russia, and France; expressing the hope that, in response to their solicitations, the King of Spain would soon ratify the treaty, and suggesting that Congress for the time being should postpone action on the matter.

This brought Clay to his feet. He took the ground that, as the King of Spain had not ratified it within the prescribed time, the whole treaty had fallen, and that it ought not to be renewed, mainly because it had, by accepting the Sabine as the southwestern boundary line, instead of insisting upon the Rio Grande del Norte, surrendered to Spain a large and valuable territory belonging to the United States, namely Texas. It had indeed been a disputed question whether the limits of

Louisiana **did not embrace** Texas. If so, Texas **belonged by** purchase to the United States ; if not, **it was** considered part **of the** Spanish American territory. Adams, in making his treaty, had **only** reluctantly **given up the line of the Rio Grande del** Norte, and accepted that **of the Sabine ; he** might have carried his point, had not Monroe, with the **concurrence** of the rest of the Cabinet, desired **the** Sabine **as a** boundary for peculiar reasons. **In a** letter to General Jackson he said : " Having long known the repugnance with which the eastern portion of our Union have seen its aggrandizement **to the** West **and South, I** have been decidedly of opinion **that** we ought to **be** content with Florida for the present." It was, therefore, in deference to **what** Monroe understood to be northeastern sentiment that Texas was given up, and it was the abandonment of Texas which Clay put forward as a decisive reason for not renewing **the** Spanish treaty.

He introduced **two** resolutions **in the** House : **one** asserting that no treaty making **a** cession of territory was valid without the concurrence of Congress ; and the other, substantially, that **the** cession **of** Florida to the United States was not an " adequate equivalent " for the " transfer " of Texas by **the** United States to Spain. In support of these resolutions **he** made **a** fiery speech, fiercely castigating the administration for truckling to foreign powers, and extolling the value of Texas, which he stoutly assumed to belong to the United States under the Louisiana purchase. Texas was, in his opinion, much more valuable than Florida. Even if the treaty were not renewed, Florida would surely drop into our lap at last, but Texas might escape us. Lowndes answered, as to the first resolution, that, if the principle asserted by Clay were admitted in its whole breadth, the treaty-making power under the Constitution (the President and the Senate) would no longer have authority to make a treaty for a boundary rectification, which almost always involved a cession of territory on one side or the other ; and, as to the second resolution, that Texas had always been considered by the United States as a debatable territory, and it had been given up as such, not as a territory clearly belonging to this Republic.

Clay's resolutions failed. The King of Spain finally ratified the treaty, the Senate reaffirmed it by all except four votes, and it was proclaimed by Monroe, February 22, 1821. But Clay had made his mark as maintaining the right of the United States to Texas. How little could he then foresee what a fateful part the acquisition of Texas was to play twenty-four years later in his public career!

The miscarriage of his opposition to the Spanish treaty did not deter him from renewing his efforts for the South American colonies. On May 20, 1820, he spoke to a resolution he had moved, declaring it expedient to provide outfits and salaries for a minister or ministers to be sent to " any of the governments in South America which have established and are maintaining their independence of Spain." His attacks became more virulent. For instance: "If Lord Castlereagh says we may recognize, we **do**; if not, we do not. A single expression of the British Minister to the present Secretary of State, then **our** minister abroad, **I am ashamed to** say, has moulded the policy of our **government** toward South America." In the **same** speech he furnished a picture of the character of the South American people and their future relations with the people of the United States, as his imagination painted it. "That country has now a population of eighteen millions. The same activity in the principle of population would exist in **that country as** here. Twenty-five years hence, it **might be** estimated at thirty-six millions; fifty years hence at seventy-two. We have now **a** population of ten millions. From the character of our population we must always take the lead **in commerce** and manufactures. Imagine the vast power of the **two** countries, **and the value of** the intercourse between them, when we shall have a population **of** forty, and they of seventy millions!" The fifty years **are** over, and we have **had** ample opportunity to appreciate this forecast. As to their political capabilities, too, he entertained glowing expectations. "**Some** gentlemen," he said, "had intimated that the people of the South were unfit for freedom. In some **particulars,** he ventured to say, the people of South America were in advance **of us.** Grenada, Venezuela, and Buenos Ayres had all emancipated their slaves; — [recollecting himself] he did not say that we ought to do so, or that they ought to have done so under different circumstances, but he rejoiced that the circumstances were such as to permit them to do it."

His resolution passed by 80 yeas to 75 nays, but the administration, which was then still occupied with the Spanish treaty, did not stir. Clay returned to the charge in February, 1821, when he moved directly an appropriation for the sending of a minister or ministers to South America, which was defeated by a small majority, owing probably to the arrival at that time of the ratification of the Spanish treaty by the king. But, nothing daunted, he was up again shortly afterwards with a resolution " that the House of Representatives participates with the people of the United States in the deep interest which they feel for the Spanish provinces of South America, which are struggling to establish their liberty and independence, and that it will give its constitutional support to the President of the United States whenever he may deem it expedient to recognize the sovereignty and independence of any of the said provinces." This resolution, being mainly a declaration of mere sentiment, passed, the first clause by 134 yeas to 12 nays, and the second by 87 to 68. A committee was appointed, at the head of which was Clay himself, to present this resolution to the President. Still the administration would not move until a year later, when the ability of the South American republics to maintain **their** independence was as a matter of fact beyond reasonable doubt. On March **8,** 1822, Monroe sent a message to Congress recommending the recognition of the independent South American governments, which was promptly responded **to.**

Clay's efforts in behalf **of** this cause **gave him great renown in** South America. **Some of his** speeches were translated into Spanish and **read at the head** of the revolutionary armies. **His name was a** household word among the patriots. In the **United** States, **too,** his fervid appeals in **behalf of an** oppressed people **fighting for** their liberty awakened the memories **of** the North American war for independence, and **called** forth strong emotions of sympathy. There **is no** doubt **that** those **appeals** were on his part not **a mere** manœuvre of **opposition,** but came straight **from his generous** impulses. The idea of the whole **American continent** being occupied by a great family of **republics** naturally flattered his imagination. That imagination supplied the struggling brethren with all the excellent qualities **he** desired them to **possess, and his** chivalrous nature **was** impatient **to** rush to **their** aid. **This** tendency **was** reinforced by his general **aptness to** take a somewhat superficial **view** of things, and, as **is** often **the** case with **men of the** oratorical temperament, to persuade himself with **the gorgeous flow of** his **own** rhetoric. That his **own thoughts** appear **to him originally** in the seductive garb of sonorous phrase, is a source of serious danger to the oratorical statesman. The influence which his embittered feeling towards the administration had on Clay's conduct, was simply to make him more inaccessible to the prudential reasons which the administration had for its dilatory policy. There was indeed a fundamental difference of views between them. The administration had the Spanish treaty much at heart, and would not permit the recognition of the Spanish American republics to complicate that transaction. Clay wanted his country to possess all it could obtain, and as he thought that Florida would some time drop into the lap of the United States in any event, and as the Spanish treaty relinquished the claim to Texas, it was from his point of view the correct thing to hasten the recognition of the South American republics and thereby to defeat the Spanish treaty.

There was also a great difference of opinion as to the character of the South American revolution. Adams gives in his Diary an account of an interview between him and Clay in March, 1821, at which an interesting conversation took place.

"I regretted (he wrote) the difference between his [Clay's] views and those of the administration upon South American affairs. That the final issue of their present struggle would be their entire independence of Spain I had never doubted. That it was our true policy and duty to take no part in the contest was equally clear. The principle of neutrality in *all* foreign wars was, in my opinion, fundamental to the continuance of

our liberties and our Union. So far as they were con‑
tending for independence I wished well to their cause ;
but I had seen, and yet see, no prospect that they would
establish free **or** liberal institutions of government.
They **are not likely to promote** the spirit **either of** free‑
dom or order by their example. They **have** not the
first elements **of free** or good government. Arbitrary
power, military **and** ecclesiastical, **was stamped** upon
their education, **upon their** habits, **and** upon **all** their in‑
stitutions. **Civil** dissension **was** infused into all their
seminal principles. War **and** mutual destruction was
in every **member of their** organization, moral, political,
and physical. **I had** little **expectation of any** beneficial
result to this country from **any** future connection with
them, political or commercial. We should derive no
improvement to our own institutions **by any communion
with** theirs. **Nor** was there any appearance of any dis‑
position in them to take any political lesson from us.
As to the commercial connection, there **was no** basis for
much traffic between us. They want none of our pro‑
ductions, and **we** could afford to purchase **very few of**
theirs. Of these opinions, both his and mine, **time** must
be the **test.**"

This kind of reasoning appeared painfully cold
by the side of Clay's glowing periods. **But** it must
be confessed **that** Adams's prognostications **have
in the** main stood **the test** of **time** far better than
Clay's. It seems that Clay then did not command
sufficient information **to** answer such arguments,
for we find it recorded **that** when Adams had fin‑
ished **his** lecture, Clay " **did** not pursue the discus‑
sion." Neither would he, at that **moment,** have

believed the prediction, if anybody had made it, that only four years later he and Adams, as members of the same administration, would bear a common responsibility and suffer the same reproach for a common policy friendly to the Spanish American republics.

At any rate a popular vein had been struck by his speeches in behalf of a foreign people. But he strengthened his reputation and political standing more substantially by his efforts to avert a danger which threatened the disruption of his own country.

CHAPTER VIII.

THE MISSOURI COMPROMISE.

On March 6, 1818, a petition was presented in the House of Representatives praying that Missouri be admitted as a state. A bill authorizing the people of Missouri to form a state government was taken up in the House on February 13, 1819, and Tallmadge of New York moved as an amendment, that the further introduction of slavery should be prohibited, and that all children born within the said state should be free at the age of twenty-five years. Thus began the struggle on the slavery question in connection with the admission of Missouri, which lasted, intermittently, until March, 1821.

No sooner had the debate on Tallmadge's proposition begun than it became clear that the philosophical anti-slavery sentiment of the revolutionary period had entirely ceased to have any influence upon current thought in the South. The abolition of the foreign slave-trade had not, as had been hoped, prepared the way for the abolition of slavery or weakened the slave interest in any sense. On the contrary, slavery had been immensely strengthened by an economic development making it more profitable than it ever had been before. The invention of the cotton gin by Eli Whitney in 1793 had made the culture of cotton a very productive source of wealth. In 1800 the exportation of cotton from the United States was 19,000,000 pounds, valued at $5,700,000. In 1820 the value of the cotton export was nearly $20,000,000, almost all of it the product of slave labor. The value of slaves may be said to have at least trebled in twenty years. The breeding of slaves became a profitable industry. Under such circumstances the slave-holders arrived at the conclusion that slavery was by no means so wicked and hurtful an institution as their revolutionary fathers had thought it to be. The anti-slavery professions of the revolutionary time became to them an awkward reminiscence, which they would have been glad to wipe from their own and other people's memories.

On the other hand, in the Northern States there was no such change of feeling. Slavery was still, in the nature of things, believed to be a wrong and a sore. The change of sentiment in the South had not yet produced its reflex in the North. The slavery question had not become a subject of difference of opinion and of controversy among the Northern people. As they had abolished slavery in their states, so they took it for granted that it ought to disappear, and would disappear in time, everywhere else. Slavery had indeed, now and then, asserted itself in the discussions of Congress as a distinct interest, but not in such a way as to arouse much alarm in the Free States. The amendment to the Missouri bill, providing for a restriction with regard to slavery, came therefore in a perfectly natural way from that Northern sentiment which remained still faithful to the traditions of the revolutionary period. And it was a great surprise to most Northern people that so natural a proposition should be so fiercely resisted on the part of the South. It was the sudden revelation of a change of feeling in the South which the North had not observed in its progress. " The discussion of this Missouri question has betrayed the secret of their souls," wrote John Quincy Adams. The slave-holders watched with apprehension the steady growth of the Free States in population, wealth, and power. In 1790 the population of the two sections had been nearly even. In 1820 there was a difference of over 600,000 in favor of the North in a total of less than ten millions. In 1790 the representation of the two sections in Congress had been about evenly balanced. In 1820 the census promised to give the North a preponderance of more than thirty votes in the House of Representatives. As the slave-holders had no longer the ultimate extinction, but now the perpetuation, of slavery in view, the question of sectional power became one of first importance to them, and with it the necessity of having more Slave States for the purpose of maintaining the political equilibrium at least in the Senate. A struggle for more Slave States was to them a struggle for life. This was the true significance of the Missouri question.

The debate was the prototype **of all the slavery** debates which followed in the forty **years to the** breaking **out of the** civil war. (1) One side offered the constitutional argument that any restriction as to slavery in the admission of a new state would nullify one of the most essential attributes of state sovereignty and break the " Federal compact (2) the moral argument that negro slavery was the most beneficial condition for the colored race in this country, and for the white race too, so long as the two races must live together ; **and** the economic (3) argument that negro slavery was necessary to the material prosperity of the Southern States, as white men could not work in the cotton and rice fields. The other side offered (1) the constitutional argument that slavery was not directly recognized by the Constitution itself; (2) that the power of the general government to exclude slavery from the territories had always been recognized, and that, in admitting a new state, conditions of admission could be imposed upon it; (3) the moral argument that slavery was a great wrong in itself, and that in its effects it demoralized the whites together with the blacks ; and the economic argument that, wherever it went, it degraded labor, paralyzed enterprise and progress, and greatly injured the general interest.

No debate on slavery had ever **so stirred the**

passions to the point of open defiance. The dissolution of the Union, civil war, and streams of blood were freely threatened **by Southern men,** while some anti-slavery men declared themselves ready to accept **all** these calamities rather than the spread **of** slavery over the territories yet **free from it.** Neither was the excitement confined **to the halls of** Congress. **As** the reports **of the** speeches made there went over **the** land, the people were **profoundly** astonished and alarmed. The presence of a great danger, and a danger, too, springing **from** an inherent antagonism in the institutions of the country, suddenly flashed upon their minds. They experienced something like **a first** violent shock of earthquake, making **them** feel that the ground under their very feet was **at** the mercy of volcanic forces. It is true, wise **men had foretold** something like this, but actual experience was far more impressive than the mere prediction had been. Resolutions earnestly demanding **the** exclusion **of** slavery from Missouri **were** passed by one after another of the Northern legislatures except those of New England, where, however, the same **sentiment** found vigorous expression **in numerous memorials** from cities and towns. **Of** the slave-holding states, one, **Delaware, spoke** through a unanimous resolve of its legislature in the same sense ; and even in Baltimore a public meeting protested against the extension of **slavery.** But beyond these points no anti-slavery sentiment made itself heard **in the** South. **The** legislatures of Virginia and

Kentucky pronounced loudly for the admission of Missouri with slavery, and the Maryland legislature joined them. Public sentiment in the other Slave States spoke out with equal emphasis. Thus the country found itself divided geographically upon a question of vital importance.

On February 16, 1819, the House of Representatives adopted the amendment restricting slavery, and thus passed the Missouri bill. But the Senate, eleven days afterwards, struck out the antislavery provision and sent the bill back to the House. A bill was then passed organizing the Territory of Arkansas, an amendment moved by Taylor of New York prohibiting the further introduction of slavery there having been voted down. Clay had opposed that amendment in a speech and thrown the casting vote of the Speaker adversely to it on a motion to reconsider. Thus slavery was virtually fastened on Arkansas. But the Missouri bill failed in the fifteenth Congress. The popular excitement steadily increased.

The sixteenth Congress met in December, 1819. In the Senate the admission of Missouri with slavery was coupled with the admission of Maine, on the balance-of-power principle that one free state and one slave state should always be admitted at the same time. An amendment was moved absolutely prohibiting slavery in Missouri, but it was voted down. Then Mr. Thomas, a Senator from Illinois, on January 18, 1820, proposed that no restriction as to slavery be imposed upon Missouri in framing a state constitution, **but** that in **all the rest** of the country ceded by France to the United States north of 36° 30′, this being the southern boundary line of Missouri, there should be neither slavery nor involuntary **servitude.** **This was** the essence **of** the famous Missouri Compromise, and after long and acrimonious debates and several **more votes** in the House for restriction and in the Senate against it, this compromise was adopted. By **it** the slave power obtained the present tangible **object it contended for ; free labor won a** contingent advantage in the future. The South was strongly bound together by a material interest ; it obeyed a common impulse and **an** intolerant will, presenting a solid and determined front. The Northern anti-slavery men were held together, not by a well understood common interest, but by a sentiment ; and as this sentiment was stronger or weaker in different **individuals,** they would stand firm **or** yield **to the** entreaties or threats of the Southern men. Thus the bargain was accomplished.

Clay has been **widely** credited **with being the** " father " of the Missouri Compromise. As **to the** main features of the measure this credit he did not deserve. So far he had taken a prominent but not an originating part in the transaction. His leadership in disposing of the Missouri question belonged to a later stage of the proceeding. But the part he had so far taken appeared to be little in accord with his **early anti-slavery** professions. The **speeches he made in the** course of these debates, among them **one of** four hours, have **never** been reported. But some of the things he said we can gather from the speeches of those who replied to him. Thus we find that he **most** strenuously **opposed the exclusion** of slavery from Missouri, and any interference with it ; we find him asserting that Congress had no right whatever to prescribe conditions to newly organized states in any **way** restricting their " sovereign rights ; " we find him sneering at the advocates of slavery-restriction as afflicted with " negrophobia ; " we find him pathetically, **in** the name of humanity, excusing the extension **of** slavery as apt to improve the condition of the negro, and advancing the argument that the evils of slavery might be cured by spreading it ; we find him provoking **a reply** like the following from Taylor of New York : —

" It [labor] is considered low and unfit for freemen. I cannot better illustrate this truth than by referring to a remark of the honorable gentleman from Kentucky [**Mr.** Clay]. I have often admired the liberality of his sentiments. **He** is governed by no vulgar prejudices ; **yet** with what abhorrence did he speak **of** the **performance, by your** wives and daughters, of those domestic offices **which** he was pleased **to** call **servile !** What comparison did he **make** of the " black slaves " of Kentucky and **the** " white slaves " **of** the North; **and** how instantly **did he** strike **a balance** in favor **of** the condition of **the former !** If such opinions and expressions, **even in** the ardor of debate, **can fall from that** honorable gentleman, what **ideas do you** suppose **are** entertained of laboring **men by the majority of slave-holders ! "**

We find him arguing that the provision of the Constitution, " The citizens of each state shall be entitled to all the privileges and immunities of citizens in the several states," would be violated by the restriction to be imposed on Missouri as to slavery.

The compromise as proposed he supported heartily, and when the bill embodying it had passed we find him resorting to a very sharp and questionable trick to save it from further interference. The bill passed on March 2. On the morning of March 3, John Randolph, having voted with the majority, offered a motion that the vote be reconsidered. Clay, as Speaker, promptly ruled the motion out of order " until the ordinary business of the morning, as prescribed by the rules of the House, should be disposed of." The House went on receiving and referring petitions. When petitions were called for from the members from Virginia, Randolph moved " that the House retain in their possession the Missouri bill until the period should arrive when, according to the rules of the House, a motion to reconsider should be in order." Speaker Clay " declared this motion out of order for the reason assigned on the first application of Mr. Randolph on this day." When the morning business was at last disposed of, Randolph " moved the House now to reconsider their vote of yesterday." Then Speaker Clay — so the record runs — " having ascertained the fact, stated to the House that the proceedings of the House on

that bill yesterday had been communicated to the
Senate by the clerk, and that, the bill not being
in possession of the House, the motion to reconsider could not be entertained." The bill had
been hurried up to the Senate while Speaker Clay
was ruling Randolph's motions out of order. It is
certain that a mere hint by the Speaker to the clerk
would have kept the bill in the House. It is also
probable, if not certain, that the first motion by
Randolph, being heard by the clerk, would have
had the same effect, had not that official received
a hint from the Speaker, that he desired the bill
to be hurried off, out of Randolph's reach. The
history of the House probably records no sharper
trick.

Thus it is clear that Clay, who at the beginning
of his public life had risked all his political prospects by advocating emancipation in Kentucky,
now not only favored a compromise admitting a
new slave state — some of the sincerest anti-slavery men did that — but in doing so used some of
the very arguments characteristic of those who had
worked themselves up to a belief in slavery as a
blessing and endeavored to strengthen and perpetuate its rule.

Were these his real sentiments? Clay's conduct with regard to the slavery question appears
singularly inconsistent. It is impossible to believe
that his condemnations of the system of slavery,
and his professions of hope that it would be extinguished, were insincere. His feelings in this re-

spect would occasionally burst out in an unpre-
meditated, unstudied, and unguarded way, as when,
at this same period, while the Missouri struggle was
going **on in all** its fury, he complimented the new
South American republics for having emancipated
their slaves. But the same **man** would advocate
"with great force," and "in a speech of consider-
able length," a bill **to** facilitate the catching of
"fugitives from justice, and persons escaping from
the service of their masters." He would in the
Missouri struggle "go with his section" in doing
what could be done at the time to secure the foot-
hold of slavery in new states, and thus to facilitate the growth of its power. It is a remarkable
circumstance **at** the same time that none of the
speeches he made on the pro-slavery side, although
they were mentioned in the record of the debates,
were reported, even in short outline. Did he suppress them? Did he dislike to see such arguments
in print coupled with his name? We do not know.
We shall find more such puzzles in his career.

At the close of the session in May, 1820, Clay
announced to the House that he found himself
obliged to retire from public **life** for some time.
He had formed that resolution **on** account of the
embarrassed condition of his private affairs. He
had lost a large sum of money by indorsing the
obligations of a friend, and there was a rumor also,
whether true or not, that he had suffered heavily
at play. At any rate, his necessities must have
been pressing, for he strenuously urged with the

President and the Secretary of State an old claim for a " half-outfit," $4,500, due him as a commissioner of the United States in negotiating a commercial convention with Great Britain in 1815. He returned to Kentucky with the hope of repairing his fortunes by industrious application to his legal practice; and at the meeting of the sixteenth Congress for its second session, in November, 1820, a letter from him was read to the House, in which, " owing to imperious circumstances," he resigned the office of Speaker, as he would not be able to attend until after the Christmas holidays. In fact he did not reach Washington until January 16, 1821. Then his services were urgently in demand.

The " Missouri question," which in the previous session seemed to have been put to rest by the compromise, had risen again in a new, unexpected, and threatening form. The bill passed at the last session had authorized the people of Missouri to make a state constitution without any restriction as to slavery. The formal admission of the state was now to follow. But the Constitution with which Missouri presented herself to Congress not only recognized slavery as existing there; it provided also that it should be the duty of the legislature to pass such laws as would be necessary to prevent free negroes or mulattoes from coming into or settling in the state. This was more than those Northern men who accepted the compromise of the last session had bargained for. Not a few of them, at heart profoundly dissatisfied with what

had **been** done, and whose scruples had been revived and strengthened by their contact with the
popular feeling at home, were ready to seize upon
this obnoxious clause in the state Constitution, to
reopen the whole question. A good many Southern men, **too,** disliked the compromise, **on** account
of the exclusion of slavery from the territory north
of 36° **30′.** The most prudent among them were
willing **to yield a point** on the questioned constitu-
tional clause, rather than put in jeopardy the solid
advantage of the admission of Missouri as a slave
state. But the bulk of them **were** for insisting
upon the reception of the state without further condition. A few Southern extremists still thought
of upsetting the 36° 30′ restriction. In the Senate,
Eaton **of** Tennessee offered **to** the resolution ad-
mitting Missouri an amendment providing " that
nothing herein contained **shall be** so construed **as**
to give **the** assent of Congress to any provision **of**
the Constitution **of** Missouri, if any there be, that
contravenes the **clause in the** Constitution **of** the
United States that ' the citizens of each state shall
be entitled **to all** the privileges and immunities of
citizens **in the** several **states,**" — the point being
that, as free **persons** of color were citizens in some
states, **for** example, Massachusetts, Vermont, and
New Hampshire, the proposed Constitution of Mis-
souri deprived them in that state of the privileges
granted them by the federal Constitution. After
long and acrimonious debates, the **resolution with**
this amendment passed the Senate, **on December
12, 1820, by a** majority of eight.

In the House the struggle raged at the same time. On November 23, Lowndes of South Carolina re. ported a resolution to admit Missouri, taking the ground that, as Congress at the last session had authorized the people of Missouri to form a state constitution, Missouri had thereby been invested with all the rights and attributes of a state, and all those who in good faith respected the acts of the government would now vote for the formal admission of Missouri as a matter of course. This was vigorously combated by John Sergeant of Pennsylvania, a staunch opponent of slavery, and a man of fine ability and high character, whom we shall meet again in political companionship with Clay under interesting circumstances. He stoutly maintained that Congress, when authorizing the people of Missouri to form a constitution, had not parted with the power of looking into that constitution to see whether it conformed to the prescribed conditions. The debate then ranged again over the whole slavery question, growing hotter as it went on, and finally the resolution admitting Missouri was, on December 13, rejected by a majority of fourteen. The excitement which followed was intense. When the vote was announced, Lowndes rose and solemnly called upon the House to take measures for the preservation of peace in Missouri. The apprehension that the fate of the Union trembled in the balance was again freely expressed. Six weeks later, on January 24, a resolution offered by Eustis of Massachusetts, to admit Missouri on condition that she expunge **from her** Constitution the provision discriminating against free persons of color, was taken **up for** consideration. It was voted down by 146 **yeas to 6** nays. When the vote had been **announced,** there **was** a pause in the proceedings. The deadlock seemed complete. **A** feeling of help-lessness appeared **to** pervade the House. It was then that **Clay, who** had arrived **a week** before, took the matter in hand. Breaking the silence **which** prevailed, **he** rose and said that, if **no** other gentleman made any **motion on the** subject, "he should **on the day** after to-morrow move to go into committee **of the** whole **to** take **into** considera-tion the resolution from the Senate on the subject of Missouri."

He did so on January 29. **He** declared himself **ready** to vote for the senate resolution **even** with the proviso it contained, although he did not deem that proviso necessary. The speeches he delivered on this occasion were again left unreported, but their arguments appear in the replies they called forth. Admitting that the clause in the Missouri Constitution respecting free persons of color **was** incompatible with the Constitution of the United States, this circumstance could not, he argued, **be an objection to the** admission of Missouri **as a** state of the Union, because the legislators of Mis-souri would **be** bound **by** their oaths to support the **federal** Constitution, **and would,** therefore, never make any law obnoxious **to it.** The weakness of this argument did not escape the **attention of his** audience. But, he said, if the Missouri legislature should enact any law in pursuance of the obnoxious clause in their Constitution, it would be declared void by the courts of the United States. However, he added, a limitation or restriction upon the power of the legislature of Missouri might be imposed by adding to the senate resolution a provision, that no law should be enacted, under the obnoxious clause of the state Constitution, affecting the rights of citizens of other states. Thus he argued on both sides of the question, trying to conciliate the good-will of all, at the same time addressing to them the most fervid appeals to unite in a spirit of harmony, in order to save the country from this dangerous quarrel which threatened the disruption of the Union. But the peacemaker had a complicated task before him. In order to unite, he had to convince or move men who pursued the most different objects, ranging from the absolute exclusion of new slave states to the unconditional admission of them. There were not a few also who thought of postponing the whole subject to the meeting of the next Congress. Several amendments to the senate resolution were moved, but all were voted down. Nothing was found on which a majority could be united. The perplexity and excitement increased. Then, as a last expedient, Clay moved to refer the senate resolution to a special committee of thirteen members. This was agreed to, and Clay was put at the head of the committee.

On February 10 he brought in a report, which was rather **an** appeal than an argument. " Your committee believe that all must ardently unite in wishing an amicable termination of **a** question, **which,** if **it be** longer kept open, cannot fail **to** produce, and possibly **to** perpetuate, prejudices and animosities among a people to whom the conservation of their moral ties should be even dearer, **if** possible, than that of their political bond." **The** committee then proposed a resolution to admit Missouri into the Union " **on** an equal footing with the original states **in** all respects whatever, upon the fundamental condition that the said state shall never pass any law preventing any description **of** persons from coming to and settling **in the said** state who now are, or hereafter may become, citizens of any of the states of this Union." This was to satisfy the Northern people. **The resolution** provided further that, as soon as the Missouri legislature should, by solemn public act, have declared the assent of the state **to** this fundamental condition, the President should by proclamation announce the fact, whereupon the admission **of the** state should be considered complete. **This was to** prevent further trouble in Congress. Finally the resolution declared that nothing contained in **it** should " be construed **to** take from the said state of Missouri, when admitted into this Union, the exercise **of** any right or power which can now be constitutionally exercised by any **of** the original states." This was to conciliate the extreme state-sovereignty men. " Thus consulting the opinions of both sides of the House," he said in opening the debate, " in that spirit of compromise which is occasionally necessary to the existence of all societies, he hoped it would receive the countenance of the House." He concluded by " earnestly invoking the spirit of harmony and kindred feeling to preside over the deliberations of the House on the subject." But this appeal still failed. After a heated debate the resolution was voted down in committee of the whole by a majority of nine, in the House by a majority of three, and upon reconsideration by a majority of six. Among the yeas there were but few Northern, among the nays only four Southern votes, and these were extremists of the John Randolph type. This was on February 13. There were not many days of the session left. The situation became more and more critical and threatening.

On February 14 the electoral vote was to be counted, Monroe having in the preceding autumn been reëlected President. The people of Missouri had chosen electors. The question occurred, should their votes be counted? Some Southern members hotly maintained that Missouri was of right a state. Northern men asserted with equal warmth that she was only a territory, having no right to take part in a presidential election. The Missouri quarrel threatened to invade, and perhaps to break up in disorder, the joint convention of the two Houses sitting to count the electoral vote.

The danger was averted by skillful management.
Clay reported, from the joint committee to which
the matter had been referred, a resolution "that,
if any objection be made to the votes of Missouri,
and the counting or omitting **to** count which shall
not essentially change the result of the election, —
in that case they shall be reported by the President
of the Senate in **the following manner :** Were
the votes of Missouri to be counted, the result
would be, for **A. B.** for President of the United
States, —— votes; **if not** counted, for A. B. as
President of the United States, —— votes; but in
either case A. **B.** is elected **President:** and in the
same manner for Vice-President." This resolution
was adopted and served its purpose. Fortunately
the three electoral votes **of** Missouri were **of** no
practical importance, Monroe having received all
the votes but one, and Tompkins, for Vice-President, a very large majority.

But as **soon** as Missouri was reached in the
electoral count, objection was made by a Northern
member to the counting of **her** votes, on the
ground that **she** was not a state of the Union.
The Senate then withdrew, and the House having
been called to order, Floyd of Virginia moved **a**
resolution that Missouri was a state of the Union,
and that her vote should be counted. He thought
he had **now** forced the issue, so that **it** could
not be avoided. "Let us know," he exclaimed
in closing his speech, "whether Missouri be **a**
state of the Union or not. Sir, we cannot take

another step without hurling **this** government into **the gulf** of destruction. For **one, I** say I have gone as far as I can go in the **way of** compromise; and **if** there **is** to **be a** compromise beyond that **point, it must be at the** edge of the **sword."** After some more speaking in **a** similar vein, mainly by **John** Randolph, Clay rose **to** pour oil **on the** troubled waters. He calmly reminded the House **of the** fact that **a** resolution **had** been adopted covering the treatment of the **vote of** Missouri, **to** bridge over the very difficulty now presenting it- self. **He** therefore moved that Floyd's resolution be laid **on** the table, which was done by **a** large majority. The Senate then was invited to return, **and** the counting of the electoral vote proceeded to **the end.** When the result **was to** be announced, Randolph and Floyd tried once more to interpose, but were ruled out of **order; the** President of the Senate finished his announcement, and the act of vote-counting was happily concluded.

But after all this, the Missouri question seemed **to be no nearer** its solution. **As the** end of the session approached, the excitement rose and spread. **Some attempts** were made **in** the Senate and **the House to** find **a** basis **of** agreement, but without avail. Then, **as a last resort,** Clay moved **the** ap- pointment of **a** committee, together with a similar committee **to** be appointed by the Senate, **to** con- sider and report " whether **it** be expedient **or not to** make provision for the admission of Missouri **into** the Union, **and for** the execution **of the laws** of the United States within Missouri ; and if not, whether any other and what provision, adapted to her condition, ought to be made by law." This was adopted by 101 yeas to 55 nays. The committee was to consist of twenty-three members, the number of the states then in the Union. Although it was to be elected by ballot, Clay was by tacit consent permitted to draw up a list to be voted for. The Senate elected a committee of seven to join the twenty-three of the House. On February 28 Clay reported a resolution, the same in effect as that which he had previously reported from his committee of thirteen, and in introducing it he said that the committee on the part of the Senate was unanimously in its favor, and that on the part of the House nearly so. After a short debate the resolution was adopted by 86 yeas to 82 nays. The bulk of the Northern vote went against it ; of the Southerners, only a few extreme men under Randolph's lead. The resolution passed the Senate likewise. Missouri promptly complied with the fundamental condition, and thus the struggle which had so violently agitated Congress and the country came to an end.

It was generally admitted that this final accommodation was mainly due to Clay's zeal, perseverance, skill, and the moving warmth of his personal appeals. He did not confine himself to speeches addressed to the House, but he went from man to man, expostulating, beseeching, persuading, in his most winning way. Even his opponents in debate acknowledged, involuntarily sometimes, **the** impressive sincerity of **his anxious** entreaties. What helped him in gaining over the number of **votes** necessary **to form a** majority **was the grow-ing fear that this** quarrel would break **up** the ruling party, and lead **to the** forming of new divisions. His success added greatly to his reputation **and** gave new strength to **his** influence. Adams wrote in his journal that one of " the greatest results of this conflict of three sessions " was **" to** bring **into** full display the talents and resources and influence **of** Mr. Clay." In newspapers and speeches he was praised as " the great pacificator."

As a measure of temporary pacification the com-**promise** could not indeed have been more success-ful. Only a short time before its accomplishment the aged Jefferson, from his retreat at Monticello, had sent forth a cry of alarm in a private letter, which soon became public : " The Missouri question is the most portentous one that ever threatened the Union. In the gloomiest moments of the Revolutionary War I never had any apprehension equal to that I feel from this source." No sooner had the **compromise** passed than the excitement **and** anxiety subsided. With that singular careless-ness, that elasticity of temper, which is character-istic of the American, the danger, **of** which the shock of earthquake had warned him, **was** forgot-ten. The public mind turned **at** once to things of more hopeful interest, and the Union seemed safer **than ever.**

The American people have since become painfully aware that this was a delusion; and the question has often been asked whether, in view of what came afterwards, those who accommodated the Missouri quarrel really did a good service to their country. It is an interesting question. The compromise had in fact settled only two points: the admission of Missouri as a slave state; and the recognition of the right of slavery to go, if the settlers there wanted it, into the territory belonging to the Louisiana purchase south of 36° 30'. It was practically so recognized in the newly organized territory of Arkansas. So far, the compromise directly and substantially strengthened the slave interest. On the other hand, the slave interest had, in order to secure these advantages, been compelled to acquiesce in two constitutional doctrines: that Congress had the power to exclude slavery from the territories of the United States, and that the admission of new states could be made subject to conditions. But these points, especially the first one, were yielded only for the occasion, and might be withdrawn when the interests of slavery should demand that the territory north of 36° 30' be opened to its invasion, as actually happened some thirty-four years later in the case of Kansas.

The compromise had another sinister feature. The anti-slavery sentiment in the North, invoked by the Missouri controversy, was no doubt strong and sincere. The South threatened the dissolution of the Union; and, frightened by that threat, a sufficient number of Northern men were found willing to acquiesce, substantially, in the demands of the South. Thus the slave power learned the weak spot in the anti-slavery armor. It was likely to avail itself of that knowledge, to carry further points by similar threats, and to familiarize itself more and more with the idea that the dissolution of the Union would really be a royal remedy for all its complaints.

Would it not have been better statesmanship, then, to force the Missouri question to a straight issue at any risk, rather than compromise it?

It was certain that the final struggle between slavery and free labor would ultimately come, and also that then, as slavery was an institution utterly abhorrent to the spirit of modern civilization, it would at last be overcome by that spirit and perish. The danger was that in its struggle for life slavery might destroy the Union and free institutions in America. The question, therefore, which the statesmanship of the time had to consider was, which would be the safer policy, — to resist the demands of the South at any risk, or to tide over the difficulty until it might be fought out under more favorable circumstances?

Had the anti-slavery men in Congress, by unyielding firmness, prevented the admission of Missouri as a slave state, thus shutting out all prospect of slavery extension, and had the South then submitted, without attempting the dissolution of the Union, the probability is that the slave power would have lost hope, that emancipation movements would have sprung up with renewed strength, and that slavery would have gradually declined and died. But would the South in 1820 have submitted without attempting dissolution? There is good reason to believe that it would not. The Union feeling had indeed been greatly strengthened by the war of 1812, but it had not grown strong enough in the South to command the self-sacrifice of an interest which at that time was elated by the anticipation of great wealth and power. In New England all there was of anti-Union sentiment had been crushed, but not so in the South. The dissolution of the Union was not then, in the popular imagination, such a monstrous thing as it is now. The Union was still, in some respects, regarded as an experiment; and when a great material interest found itself placed at a disadvantage in the Union, it was apt to conclude that the experiment had failed. To speculate upon the advisability of dissolving the Union did not then appear to the popular mind politically treasonable and morally heinous.

That the dissolution of the Union was freely discussed among the Southern members of the Sixteenth Congress is certain. James Barbour of Virginia, a man of very high character, was reported to be canvassing the free-state members as to the practicability of a convention of the states to dissolve the Union, and to make arrangements for distributing its assets and liabilities. At one period during the Missouri struggle, the Southern members seriously contemplated withdrawing from Congress in a body; and John Randolph, although he had not been for some time on speaking terms with Clay, one evening approached him, saying: " Mr. Speaker, I wish you would leave the chair. I will follow you to Kentucky, or anywhere else in the world." "That is a very serious proposition," answered Clay, " which we have not now time to discuss. But if you will come into the Speaker's room to-morrow morning, before the House assembles, we will discuss it together." They met. Clay strongly advised against anything like secession, and in favor of a compromise, while Randolph was for immediate and decisive action. The slave-holders, he said, had the right on their side; matters must come to an extremity, and there could be no more suitable occasion to bring them to that issue.

The secession of the Southern delegations from Congress did indeed not come to pass; it was prevented by the compromise. But Clay himself, when the excitement was at its height, gloomily expressed his apprehension that in a few years the Union would be divided into three confederations, — a Southern, an Eastern, and a Western.

While thus the thought of dissolving the Union occurred readily to the Southern mind, the thought of maintaining the government and preserving the Union by means of force hardly occurred to anybody. It seemed to be taken for granted on all sides that, if the Southern States insisted upon cutting loose from the Union, nothing could be done but to let them go. It is true there was talk enough about swords and blood ; but the wars were expected to turn upon questions of boundary and the like, after dissolution, not upon the right of states to go out. Even such a man as John Quincy Adams, not only an anti-slavery man but a statesman always inclining to strong measures, approved of the compromise as " all that could be effected under the present Constitution, and from extreme unwillingness to put the Union at hazard ;" and then wrote in addition: " But perhaps it would have been a wiser as well as a bolder course to have persisted in the restriction upon Missouri, till it should have terminated in a convention of the states to revise and amend the Constitution. This would have produced a new Union of thirteen or fourteen states unpolluted with slavery, with a great and glorious object to effect, — namely, that of rallying to their standard the other states by the universal emancipation of their slaves. If the Union must be dissolved, slavery is precisely the question upon which it ought to break." Thus even this patriotic statesman thought rather of separating in order to meet again in a purer condition of existence — a remarkably fantastic plan — than of denying the right of secession, and of maintaining by a vigorous exertion of power the government of which he was a leading member, and the Union of which his father had been one of the principal founders. It must be admitted also that, while the North was superior to the South in population and means at that period, yet the disproportion was not yet large enough to make the maintenance of the Union by force a promising task.

An attempt by the South, or by the larger part of it, to dissolve the Union would therefore, at that time, have been likely to succeed. There would probably have been no armed collision about the dissolution itself, but a prospect of complicated quarrels and wars afterwards about the property formerly held in common, and perhaps about other matters of disagreement. A reunion might possibly have followed after a sad experience of separation. But that result would have had to be evolved from long and confused conflicts, and the future would at best have been dark and uncertain. Even in the event of reunion, the fatal principle of secession at will, once recognized, would have passed into the new arrangement.

In view of all this, it seemed good statesmanship to hold the Union together by a compromise, and to adjourn the final and decisive struggle on the slavery question to a time when the Union feeling should be strong and determined enough to maintain the integrity of the Republic, if necessary, by force of arms, and when the Free States should be so superior in men and means to the slave-holding section as to make the result certain.

That this train of reasoning was Clay's conscious motive in doing what he did will not be asserted. It is more likely that he simply followed his instinct as a devoted friend of the Union, leaving for the moment all other interests out of view. Although he had not originated the main part of the compromise, having exercised decisive influence only at the close of the controversy, yet, by common consent, he carried off the honors of the occasion. As the peculiar brilliancy of the abilities he possessed, his involuntary showiness, made him always the most conspicuous figure whenever he appeared in a parliamentary contest, so he had impressed himself in this instance upon the popular mind as the leading actor in the drama. He retired, therefore, to private life with a larger stock of popularity than he had ever possessed. What he had lost by the appearance of captiousness in his opposition to Monroe's administration was now amply retrieved by the great patriotic service rendered in bringing a very dangerous controversy to what was considered a happy conclusion. It is interesting to hear the judgment passed upon him at that period by another public man of high distinction. After a visit he had received from Clay, John Quincy Adams delivered himself in his Diary as follows : —

"Clay is an eloquent man, with very popular manners and great political management. He is, like almost all the eminent men of this country, only half educated. His school has been the world, and in that he is proficient. His morals, public and private, are loose, but he has all the virtues indispensable to a popular man. As he is the first distinguished man that the Western country has presented as a statesman to the Union, they are profoundly proud of him. Clay's temper is impetuous and his ambition impatient. He has long since marked me as the principal rival in his way, and has taken no more pains to disguise his hostility than was necessary for decorum, and to avoid shocking the public opinion. His future fortunes and mine are in wiser hands than ours. I have never even defensively repelled his attacks. Clay has large and liberal views of public affairs, and that sort of generosity which attaches individuals to his person. As President of the Union, his administration would be a perpetual succession of intrigue and management with the legislature. It would also be sectional in its spirit, and sacrifice all interests to those of the Western country and the slave-holders. But his principles relative to internal improvements would produce results honorable and useful to the nation."

This was not the judgment of a friend, but of a man always inclined to be censorious, and, when stung by conflicts of opinion, uncharitable. It was the judgment, too, of a rival in the race for the presidency, — a rival careful to admit to himself the strong qualities of the adversary, while dwelling with some satisfaction upon his weak points. When speaking of Clay's " loose " public morals, Adams can have meant only the apparently factious opposition to Monroe's administration, and his resort to tricky expedients in carrying his points in the House.　He cannot have meant anything like the use of official power and opportunities for private pecuniary advantage, for in this respect Clay's character was and remained above reproach.　No species of corruption stained his name.　Neither could Clay be justly charged with a sectional spirit.　His feelings were, on the contrary, as largely and thoroughly national as those of any statesman of his time.　Although he had at first spoken the language of the slave-holder in the Missouri debate, it could certainly not be said that he was willing to " sacrifice all interests to those of the slave-holders."　He would have stood by the Union against them at all hazards, and his tariff and internal improvement policy soon became obnoxious to them.　But, barring these points, Adams's judgment was not far astray.　In the course of this narration we shall find more opinions of Adams on Clay, expressed at a time when the two men had learned to understand each other better.

When Clay left Washington, his professional prospects were very promising.　The Bank of the United States engaged him, upon liberal terms, as its standing counsel in Ohio and Kentucky.　He expected his practice to retrieve his fortunes in three or four years, and to enable him then to return to the service of the country.

CHAPTER IX.

CLAY'S retirement was not of long duration. The people of Kentucky were then passing through the last stages of a confused excitement caused by a popular delusion that riches can be created and happiness acquired by a plentiful issue of paper money and an artificial inflation of prices. The consequence was what it always is. The more plenty the paper money became, the more people ran into debt. They then sought "relief" by legislative contrivances in favor of debtors, which caused a political division into the "relief" and the "anti-relief" parties. The "relief measures" came before the highest state court, which declared them unconstitutional; whereupon the court was abolished and a new one created, and this brought forth the "old court" and the "new court" parties in Kentucky. The whole story is told with admirable clearness in Professor Sumner's biography of Andrew Jackson. In these fierce controversies, Clay took position as an advocate of good sense, honesty, and sound principles of finance, sometimes against a current of popular feeling which seemed to be overwhelming. He made enemies in that way from whom he was to hear in later years; but, on the whole, his popularity weathered the storm. Without opposition, he was elected to represent his faithful Lexington district in the House of Representatives of the eighteenth Congress, which met on the first Monday in December, 1823. During his absence from the House there had been contest enough about the speakership. But as soon as he appeared again, an overwhelming majority of the members gathered around him, and he was elected Speaker by 139 to 42, the minority voting for Philip P. Barbour of Virginia, who had been Speaker during the seventeenth Congress.

This was the session preceding the presidential election of 1824, and Clay was a confessed candidate for the succession to Monroe. His friends in Kentucky — or, as many would have it, the people of Kentucky — were warm and loud in their advocacy of his "claims." His achievement as "the great pacificator" had much increased his popularity in other states. His conduct in the House was likely to have some effect upon his chances, and to be observed with extraordinary interest. The first thing he did was to take the unpopular side of a question appealing in an unusual degree to patriotic emotion and human sympathy. He opposed a bill granting a pension to the mother of Commodore Perry, the hero of Lake Erie. The death of her illustrious son had left the old matron in needy circumstances. The debate ran largely

upon the great services rendered to the country by
Commodore Perry in the days of great public danger and distress; and, by way of contrast, on the
sorrows and cares of the bereft mother.   The eloquence expended upon these points had been formidable, threatening with the contempt of the American people those who dared to "go back to their
constituents" to tell them "that they had turned
from their door, in the evening of a long life, the
aged and venerable mother of the gallant Perry,
and doomed her to the charity of the world."   It
looked like a serious matter for any presidential
candidate who naturally desired to be popular with
people of tender sensibilities and patriotic feelings,
and who had also to look after the soldier and sailor
vote.   Of this aspect of the case, however, Clay did
not seem to think.   He calmly argued that this
case, however great the sympathy it deserved, did
not fall within the principles of the pension laws,
since Commodore Perry had not died of injuries
received in the service; that the principle of the
law had already been overstepped in granting a
pension to his widow and children; that there must
be a limit to gratitude at the public expense for
military and naval service; that he saw no reason
why the services of the warrior should be held in so
much higher esteem than the sometimes even more
valuable services of the civil officer of the Republic, and so on.   His apprehension concerning the
superiority in popular favor of military glory over
civil merit, he was to find strikingly confirmed by

his own experience. Evidently this candidate for the presidency still had opinions of his own and courage to express them. It was not by the small tricks of the demagogue, but rather by a strong advocacy of the policies he believed in, that he hoped to commend himself to the confidence of the people. So we find him soon engaged in a hot debate on internal improvements.

In May, 1822, Monroe had vetoed a bill to establish tollgates on the Cumberland Road, and on the same occasion submitted to Congress an elaborate statement supporting his belief that the practical execution of works of internal improvement by the general government was unwarranted by the Constitution, admitting however the power of Congress under the Constitution to grant and appropriate money in aid of works of internal improvement to be executed by others. In January, 1824, a bill was reported authorizing the President to cause the necessary surveys, plans, and estimates to be made for such a system of roads and canals as he might deem of national importance in a postal, commercial, or military point of view. For this purpose the bill proposed an appropriation of $30,000. The debate turned mainly on the point of constitutional power, and in his most dashing style Clay attacked Monroe's constitutional doctrines, stopping but little short of ridicule, and pronounced himself again in favor of the most liberal construction of the fundamental law. In the power " to establish " post roads, he easily found the power to build roads and to keep them in repair. The power to " regulate commerce among the several states " had to his mind little meaning, if it did not imply " authority to foster " inter - state commerce, " to promote it, to bestow on it facilities similar to those which had been conceded to our foreign trade." To him, this involved unquestionably the power to build canals. " All the powers of this government," he argued, " should be interpreted in reference to its first, its best, its greatest object, the Union of these states. And is not that Union best invigorated by an intimate social and commercial connection between all the parts of the confederacy?" He described the unsatisfied needs of the great West in stirring terms, and then opened once more that glorious perspective of the great ocean-bound Republic which his ardent mind was so fond of contemplating. "Sir," he exclaimed, "it is a subject of peculiar delight to me to look forward to the proud and happy period, distant as it may be, when circulation and association between the Atlantic and the Pacific and the Mexican Gulf shall be as free and perfect as they are at this moment in England, and in any other, the most highly improved country on the globe. Sir, a new world has come into being since the Constitution was adopted. Are the narrow, limited necessities of the old thirteen States, indeed of parts only of the old thirteen States as they existed at the formation of the Constitution, forever to remain a rule of its interpretation? Are we to forget the wants of our country? Are we to neglect and refuse the redemption of that vast wilderness which once stretched unbroken beyond the Alleghany? I hope **for better** and nobler things ! "

These were captivating appeals, but they involved the largest **of** latitudinarian doctrines, — namely, that the powers granted **by** the Constitution must grow with the size of the country. The bill passed the House by a handsome majority ; **it** passed the Senate too, and Monroe signed it **on** the ground that **it** provided merely for the collection **of** information. It resulted in nothing beyond the making of surveys for some roads and canals. However, Clay had on the occasion of this debate not only put the internal-improvement part of his programme once more **in the** strongest form before Congress and the people, but he had also managed to revive the memory of his opposition to the Monroe administration.

Next came a plunge into the domain of foreign politics. The rising **of** the Greeks against the Turks was at that time occupying the attention of civilized mankind. The Philhellenic fever, fed partly by a genuine sympathy with a nation fighting for its freedom, partly by **a** classical interest in the country **of** Leonidas, Phidias, and Plato, swept over all Europe and America alike. In the United States meetings were held, speeches made, and resolutions passed, boiling over with enthusiasm for the struggling Greeks. It is curious to find even the cool-headed Gallatin, **at** that period

Minister of the United States in Paris, proposing in a despatch ("as if he was serious," writes Adams) that the government of the United States should assist the Greeks with its naval force then in the Mediterranean. Monroe expressed his sympathy with the Greeks in his message; and Daniel Webster, in January, 1824, in the House of Representatives presented a resolution to provide for the sending of an agent or commissioner to Greece, whenever the President should find it expedient. This resolution he introduced by a speech not only eulogizing the Greek cause, but also gravely and elaborately arraigning the "Holy Alliance" as a league of despotic governments against all popular aspirations towards constitutional liberty.

A nation fighting for its freedom naturally called Clay to the front. He not only supported Webster's motion, but remembering that the "Holy Alliance," while it hung like a dark cloud over Europe, also threatened to cast its shadow upon these shores, he flung down the gauntlet by offering a resolution of his own to be called up at some future time. It declared that the American people "would not see without serious inquietude any forcible interposition of the allied powers of Europe in behalf of Spain, to reduce to their former subjection those parts of America which have proclaimed and established for themselves, respectively, independent governments, and which have been solemnly recognized by the United States."

This was essentially in the spirit of the utterances which **had** appeared at the opening of **the** session **in** Monroe's message to Congress, and which have since become celebrated as the Monroe doctrine. The message had been even a little stronger in language. Referring to the difference existing between the political system of the "allied powers" **in** Europe, and that of the American republics, it declared that " we should consider any attempt **on** their part to extend their system to any portion of this hemisphere as dangerous to our peace and safety." Further, with regard to schemes supposed to be contemplated by the allied powers, for interfering with the independence of the newly established Spanish American republics, it said that the American people could not view such interposition "in any other light than as the manifestation **of an** unfriendly disposition toward the United States." Here, **then,** Clay found himself in thorough accord with the Monroe administration, whose master spirit in **all** that concerned foreign affairs was John Quincy Adams. Moreover, although his resolution did not touch it, Clay certainly agreed with the other point of the Monroe doctrine, " that **the** American continents, by the free and independent condition which they have assumed and maintain, are henceforth not to be considered as subjects for future colonization by any European power."

But when he thrust his resolution into the debate **on** the Greek question, though with no intention **of** having it discussed immediately, there was an evident flutter in the House. It was darkly, shyly hinted at in several speeches as something "extraordinary," something peculiarly calculated to involve the United States in dangerous complications with foreign powers. The consequence was that Clay, irritated, broke out with a speech full of fire but rather loose in argument. He predicted that a "tremendous storm was ready to burst upon our happy country," meaning a design on the part of the "Holy Alliance" to subvert free institutions in America; he denounced as "low and debased" those who did not "dare" to express their sympathies with suffering Greece; and finally he defied them to go home, if they "dared," to their constituents, to tell them that their representatives had "shrunk from the declaration of their own sentiments," just as he had been "dared" when opposing the pension to Commodore Perry's mother.

Some members of the House resented such language, and a bitter altercation followed, especially undesirable in the case of a candidate for the presidency. Indeed, ambitious statesmen gifted with oratorical temperaments, whose perorations are apt to run away with their judgment, may study this debate with profit, to observe some things which it is well to avoid. Richard M. Johnson of Kentucky, at the time one of Clay's most ardent friends and backers for the presidency, dolefully remarked after this debate that "Clay was the most imprudent man in the world."

The resolution on the Greek cause was never

acted upon, and Clay's resolution concerning the Spanish American republics never called up. We shall see him return to that subject as the head of the department of foreign affairs in the government of the United States.

Clay's most important oratorical effort at this session, and indeed one of the most important of his life, was brought forth by a debate on the tariff. The country had gone through trying experiences during the last eight years. As we remember, the tariff of 1816 had been enacted to ward off the flood of cheap English goods which, immediately after the close of the war of 1812, were pouring into the country and underselling American fabrics. That object, however, was not accomplished, except in the case of cheap cotton goods, which had the advantage of a " minimum " provision : that all cotton fabrics invoiced at less than twenty-five cents should be taken to have cost that price at the place of exportation, and should be taxed accordingly. The tariff did not prevent the reaction naturally following the abnormally stimulated business and the inflated values of war times. When prices rose, people ran into debt in the hope of a still greater rise. Those who made money became accustomed to more expensive living. With the return of peace, the expenditures of the government were contracted. There was less demand for breadstuffs. Then came currency troubles. The return to specie payments in England, and the raising of the

French indemnity, created an unusual demand for
the precious metals in Europe, which rendered
more difficult the reëstablishment of specie payments in America. The notes of the state banks
outside of New England were depreciated, and
these banks resisted the efforts of the Bank of the
United States toward general resumption. A
great tightness of money ensued. Times became
pinching. Prices went down. A crisis broke out
in 1819. Many business failures followed. The
necessity of returning to more frugal ways of living was painfully felt. "Cheap money" theories
sprung up. The distress was greatest where the
local bank currency was most uncertain in its
value. The manufacturing interest suffered heavily, but the difficulties under which it labored were
only a part of those troubles always occurring when
the business enterprise of a country has, by abnormal circumstances or artificial means, been over-
stimulated in certain directions, and then has to
accommodate itself to entirely different conditions.
The process of natural recuperation had, however,
already begun, and that too on a solid basis, after
the elimination of the unsound elements of business. But the cry for " relief " was still kept up,
and a demand for "more protection " arose.

In 1818 the duty on iron was raised. In 1820
an attempt was made, and supported by Clay in
an eloquent speech, for a general revision of the
tariff, with a view to higher rates. The bill passed
the House, but failed in the Senate. Now, in

January, 1824, the Committee on Manufactures reported to the House a bill which, in the way of protecting the manufacturing industries, was to accomplish what the tariff of 1816 had so signally failed to do. The duties proposed were: 1, on articles the importation of which would not interfere with home manufactures, such as silks, linens, cutlery, spices, and some others, these being mere revenue duties; and 2, on iron, hemp, glass, lead, wool and woolen goods, cotton goods, etc., these being high protective duties.

Clay soon assumed the championship of the bill in committee of the whole. The debate began with a skirmish on details; but then the friends of the bill forced a discussion on its general principles, which lasted two months. This gave Clay one of his great opportunities. He was now no longer the Kentucky farmer pleading for hemp and homespun, nor the cautious citizen anxious to have his country make its own clothes and blankets in time of war. He had developed into the full-blown protectionist, intent upon using the power of the government, so far as it would go, to multiply and foster manufactures, not with commerce, but rather in preference to commerce. His speech, one of the most elaborate and effective he ever made, presented in brilliant array the arguments which were current among high-tariff men then, and which remain so still. He opened with a harrowing description of the prevailing distress, and among the most significant symptoms of the dreadful condition

of things he counted " the ravenous pursuit after
public situations, not for the sake of their honors
and the performance of their public duties, but as
a means of private subsistence." "The pulse of in-
cumbents," he said in his picturesque style, " who
happen to be taken ill, is not marked with more
anxiety by the attending physicians than by those
who desire to succeed them, though with very
opposite feelings." (To "make room" for one
man simply by removing another was at that time
not yet readily thought of.) The cause of the
prevailing distress he found in the dependence of
this country on the foreign market, which was at
the mercy of foreign interests, and which might
for an indefinite time be unable to absorb our
surplus of agricultural products; and in too great
a dependence on foreign sources of supply. It
seemed to him necessary to provide a home market for our products, the superiority of which
would consist in its greater steadiness, in the creation of reciprocal interests, in greater security,
and in an ultimate increase of consumption, and
consequently of comfort, owing to an increased
quantity of the product, and a reduction of prices
by home competition. To this end the development of manufacturing industries was required,
which could not be accomplished without high
protective, in some cases not without prohibitory,
tariff duties. No country had ever flourished without such a policy, and England especially was a
shining example of its wisdom. British statesman-

ship had therefore strictly adhered to it. A member of Parliament remonstrating against the passage of the corn-laws in favor of foreign production would, he thought, make a poor figure.

This policy Clay now christened "the American system." The opposite policy he denounced as "the foreign policy." He then reviewed elaborately one after another the objections urged against the "American system," and closed with a glowing appeal to the people of the planting states to submit to the temporary loss which this policy would bring upon them, since that loss would be small in comparison with the distress which the rest of the country would suffer without it.

This speech on the "American system" exhibited conspicuously Clay's strong as well as his weak points: his skill of statement; his ingenuity in the grouping of facts and principles; his plausibility of reasoning; his brilliant imagination; the fervor of his diction; the warm patriotic tone of his appeals: and on the other hand, his superficial research; his habit of satisfying himself with half-knowledge; his disinclination to reason out propositions logically in all their consequences. We find there statements like this : —

"The measure of the wealth of a nation is indicated by the measure of its protection of its industry. Great Britain most protects her industry, and the wealth of Great Britain is consequently the greatest. France is next in the degree of protection, and France is next in the order of wealth. Spain most neglects the duty of protecting the industry of her subjects, and Spain is one of the poorest of European nations. Unfortunate Ireland, disinherited, or rendered in her industry subservient to England, is exactly in the same state of poverty with Spain, measured by the rule of taxation. And the United States are still poorer than either."

And this still more startling remark : —

" No man pays the duty assessed on the foreign article by compulsion, but voluntarily ; and this voluntary duty, if paid, goes into the common exchequer, for the common benefit of all. Consumption has four objects of choice : First, it may abstain from the use of the foreign article, and thus avoid the payment of the tax ; second, it may employ the rival American fabric ; third, it may engage in the business of manufacturing, which this bill is designed to foster ; fourth, it may supply itself from the household manufactures."

By the side of this amazing revelation of the means by which the consumer can for himself neutralize the effects of a high tariff, we find strikingly wise sayings, which, however, sometimes fit economic theories different from his own. He observed, for instance, that : —

" The great desideratum in political economy is the same as in private pursuits ; that is, what is the best application of the aggregate industry of a nation that can be made honestly to produce the largest sum of national wealth ? "

Notwithstanding its weak points the speech made a great impression. The immediate effect may be judged from the extent to which it monopolized the attention of speakers on the other side. Among these stood forth as the strongest Daniel Webster. A remarkable contrast it was when, against the flashing oratory of the gay, spirited Kentuckian, there rose up the dark-browed New Englander with his slow, well-measured, massive utterances. These two speeches together are as interesting an economic study as can be found in our parliamentary history. The student can scarcely fail to be struck with Webster's superiority in keenness of analysis, in logical reasoning, in extent and accuracy of knowledge, in reach of thought and mastery of fundamental principles. Not only the calm precision with which Webster's speech exposed some of Clay's reckless statements and conclusions, but the bright flashes of light which it threw upon a variety of important economic questions, — such as the relation of currency to the production of wealth, the balance of trade, the principles of exchange, the necessary limits of protection, — give it a high and lasting value in our literature. It is a remarkable fact that Webster — although four years afterwards he became an advocate of high tariffs on the ground that New England had taken protection as the settled policy of the country, had therefore engaged its capital in manufactures, and should not be left in the lurch — never could deny or reason away the principles laid down in his great argument of 1824. It stands to-day as his strongest utterance upon economic subjects.

But Clay carried the day. After a long strug-

gle the tariff bill passed the House by a majority
of five, and after being slightly amended was also
passed in the Senate by a majority of four. **The**
vote in the House was significant in its geographical distribution. It was thus classed **by Niles:**
The "navigating **and fishing** states" of New England — Massachusetts, New Hampshire, and Maine
— gave twenty-two votes against and only three
for **the** bill. Of the "manufacturing states,"
Rhode Island and Connecticut, seven votes went for
and one against it. Of the "grain-growing states,"
Vermont, New York, New Jersey, Pennsylvania,
Delaware, Kentucky, Ohio, Indiana, Illinois, and
Missouri, ninety-two votes were given for and nine
against it. The "tobacco-planting and grain-growing state" of Maryland gave six against and three
for it. The "cotton and grain growing state,"
Tennessee, gave seven against and two for it.
The "tobacco and cotton planting states," Virginia, North Carolina, South Carolina, Georgia,
Mississippi and Alabama, threw fifty-four votes
against and one for it. All the three votes of the
"sugar and cotton planting state," Louisiana, went
against it. Since the time when Calhoun had elo-
quently argued for the fostering of manufacturing
industries and internal improvements, a significant
change had taken place in the current of Southern
sentiment. The planting interest, most closely
identified with slavery, began to present an almost
solid front not only against the tariff, but against
everything not in harmony with its system of labor.

Massachusetts, Maine, and New Hampshire opposed the tariff because it would be injurious to
commerce. But they soon accommodated themselves to **it**. It was a combination of the grain-
growing **with** the manufacturing interest, the **idea**
of the " home market," that carried the day.

Clay achieved a great triumph for himself. **He**
had not only far outshone all others by his championship of the successful measure, but he **had**
given to the protective policy a new name, the
" American system," which became inseparably
identified with **his own**. This appellation was indeed not without its ludicrous side, which Webster
did not fail promptly to perceive **and** to exhibit
with keen sarcasm. " If names are thought necessary," said he, " it would be well enough, **one**
would think, that the **name** should **be** in some
measure descriptive of the thing: and since Mr.
Speaker denominates the policy which he recom-
mends, ' a new policy in this country ; ' since he
speaks of the present measure **as** a new era in our
legislation; since he professes to invite us to depart
from our accustomed course, to instruct ourselves
by the wisdom of others, and to adopt the policy
of the most distinguished foreign states, — one is a
little curious to know with what propriety of speech
this imitation of other nations is denominated an
' American policy,' while, on the contrary, a preference for our own established system, as it now
actually exists and always has existed, is called a
'foreign policy.' This favorite American policy

is what America has never tried ; and this odious foreign policy is what, as we are told, foreign states have never pursued." But although the " American system " had nothing peculiarly American about it, the name was adroitly chosen and served its purpose. It proved a well-sounding cry which to many minds was as good as an argument.

Thus Clay had put his opinions on internal improvements, on the tariff, and on the foreign policy of the country, as conspicuously as possible before the people; his platform left nothing to desire as to completeness and precision. He was ready for the presidential campaign.

The " era of good feeling " under Monroe left the country without national parties ; for when there is only one, there is practically none. The Federal party had disappeared as a national organization ; it had only a local existence. There were differences of opinion on matters of public interest within the Republican party — about the tariff, for instance, and about internal improvements, which had some effect in the campaign, but which did not yet produce well-defined and lasting divisions. The violent and threatening excitement on slavery called forth by the Missouri trouble had come and gone like a thunderstorm. In the planting states the question was sometimes quietly asked, when a public man was discussed, whether he had been for or against " slavery restriction ; " but in the rest of the country the antagonists of an hour had, after the compromise was passed, silently agreed to say no more about it, — at least for the time being. Under these circumstances the personal question became the most important one. Hitherto candidates for the presidency had been formally nominated by the party caucus of members of Congress. But in the course of time the Congressional caucus **had** become odious, there being **a** popular impression that it was too much subject to intrigue. Recommendations of candidates had always been made by state legislatures, or even by meetings of **citizens**, but they had been looked **upon** merely as more or less respectable demonstrations of public sentiment. These, however, as the Congressional caucus fell into discredit, **gained in** importance. National conventions of political parties had not yet been invented. A suggestion to call **one was** made in Pennsylvania, but **it** remained unheeded. In the breaking up of old political habits, the traditional notion that the secretaryship of state should be regarded as the stepping stone to the presidency, had also become very much weakened. There opened itself, then, a free field for what might irreverently be called a " scramble."

The consequence was that no less than six candidates for the presidency presented themselves to the people: Crawford **of** Georgia, Jackson of Tennessee, Adams of Massachusetts, Clay of Kentucky, Calhoun **of** South Carolina, and Clinton of New **York**. The **two** last named **were soon** withdrawn. All belonged to **the** ruling **party.** **Crawford** was Secretary **of** the Treasury. He was a man of imposing presence. He had filled several public stations of importance creditably enough, but in none of them had he rendered services so eminent as to entitle him to rank among the first order of statesmen. Still he had managed to pass in those days as a great man. His was that temporary sort of greatness which appears in history as the reputation of a reputation. He had much of the intriguing politician in him. He was strongly and not unjustly suspected of manipulating the patronage of his department for his own political benefit. It was he who in 1820 had caused the four-years'-term law to be enacted, — that law which has done so much to develop the " spoils system." He insisted upon holding a " regular " Congressional caucus, having made his arrangements to control it. It was accordingly called to meet on February 14, 1824 ; but of two hundred and sixteen Republicans, only sixty-six appeared, and two more sent their proxies. Of these sixty-eight votes, Crawford received sixty-four. Thus he had the " regular " nomination ; but as it had been made only by a majority of a minority, all but his friends having refused to attend the caucus, it lacked authoritative weight. Moreover, his health was seriously impaired by a paralytic attack, which naturally injured him much as a candidate.

The candidacy of General Andrew Jackson was an innovation in American politics. From Washington down, no man had been elected to the presidency, nor indeed been a candidate for **it, who had not** grown up to eminence in civil station. Every President had been known as a statesman. Now, for the first time, a candidate was presented for the highest office whose reputation had been won **entirely** on a different field. General Jackson had indeed held civil positions. As a young man of thirty, he had for **a** short time represented Tennessee in Congress. But there he had shown no sign **of** capacity as **a** legislator, and had attracted **attention** in debate, as Jefferson said, only because " he could never speak on account of the rashness of his feelings," for as often **as he** attempted it he would " choke with rage." Next he had become a judge, but nothing was heard of his decisions. It was only as a soldier that he won brilliant successes, and in the field indeed achieved great renown by his energy, his intrepid spirit, and the natural gift of command. But whenever the general had to exercise any function of authority beyond the handling of troops on the march or in action, he distinguished himself by an impatience of restraint, a reckless disregard **of the** laws, an uncontrollable violence of temper, and a daring assumption of power, not seldom seriously compromising the character as well as the peace of the country. His private life **too,** while it was that of **a** man of integrity and generous impulses, abounded in tumultuous broils and bloody encounters. Thus his military achievements had **given** him his only prestige, while at the same time he **had** shown in their strong est development those qualities sometimes found in the successful man of war, which render him peculiarly unfit for responsible position and the delicate tasks of statesmanship in time of peace.

But his candidacy, although a complete abandonment of the good old tradition and made possible only by the battle of New Orleans, was " worked up " with consummate skill by one of his friends in Tennessee, Major Lewis, who thus earned a place in the very front rank of political managers. Some letters deprecating the spirit of partisan proscription in filling public offices, which General Jackson had written to Monroe years before, were brought before the public to propitiate the remnants of the Federal party. He was made to write another letter, to Dr. L. H. Coleman, pronouncing in a vague way in favor of a protective tariff. In order to keep a man of ability and character, but unfriendly to him, out of the Senate of the United States, and also to give the General an opportunity to renew friendly relations with public men with whom he had quarreled, Jackson himself was elected a senator from Tennessee, and took his seat in December, 1823. The Tennessee legislature had expressed its preference for him as a candidate for the presidency in 1822. A convention of Federalists at Harrisburg in Pennsylvania, a state in which the Federalists still maintained an organization, likewise nominated him in February, 1824, and a month later a Democratic convention at the same place followed their example. Thus Jackson was fairly started as a "man of the people," and presently many began to see in him not only the greatest military hero in history, but also a political sage.

The candidate who most completely answered the traditional requirements was unquestionably John Quincy Adams, the candidate of New England. He had been longest in public duty. He had won eminence by conspicuous service. His experience and knowledge as a statesman were unexcelled by any American of his time. His private life was spotless, and his public character above reproach. Austere, cold and distant in his manners, he lacked altogether those qualities which "make friends." He was the embodied sense of duty, commanding respect but not kindling affection. Although full of ambition to be President, he would owe his elevation solely to the recognition of his merits. His election was to signify the popular approval of his public conduct. He would not "work" to obtain it, nor countenance his friends in "working" for him. He would gratefully and proudly take the presidency from the hands of the people, but not be obliged to any person for procuring it. A letter which he wrote in reply to a suggestion that he should ask and encourage others to promote his interests as a candidate, portrays his ideal of public virtue : —

"*Detur digniori* is the inscription upon the prize. The principle of the Constitution in its purity is, that the duty shall be assigned to the most able and the most worthy. Politicians and newspapers may bestir themselves to point out who that is; and the only question between us is, whether it be consistent with the duties of a citizen, who is supposed to desire that the choice should fall upon himself, to assist, countenance, and encourage those who are disposed to befriend him in the pursuit. The law of friendship is a reciprocation of good offices. He who asks or accepts the offer of friendly service contracts the obligation of meeting it with a suitable return. If he seeks or accepts the aid of one, he must ask or accept the aid of multitudes. Between the principle of which much has been said in the newspapers, that a President of the United States must remember those to whom he owes his elevation, and the principle of accepting no aid on the score of friendship or personal kindness to him, there is no alternative. The former, as it has been announced and urged, I deem to be essentially and vitally corrupt. The latter is the only principle to which no exception can be taken."

This principle he not only professed, but he acted upon it. Compared with what the political usages of our days have accustomed us to consider admissible, such a principle may appear to be an exaggerated refinement of feeling, fitted only for an ideal state of society. It may be said that a statesman so conscientious will throw away his chance of rising into power, and thus set narrow limits to his own usefulness. But, after all, a conscientious public man, in order to remain perfectly true to his public duty, will either have to accept the principle insisted upon by John Quincy Adams, or at least he must make the friends, who promote his interests, clearly understand that there may be circumstances under which he will consider it a virtue to forget the obligations of friendship, and that, whenever the public interest demands it, he will always have the courage of ingratitude.

Clay was first nominated as a candidate for the presidency by the members of the Kentucky legislature in November, 1822. Similar demonstrations followed in Louisiana, Missouri, and Ohio. Of his anxiety to be elected President he made no secret. He conducted a large correspondence with friends all over the country, from whom he received reports, and to whom he sent his suggestions in return. One of his most active canvassers was Thomas H. Benton, who represented the young State of Missouri in the Senate. Benton travelled through Tennessee, Ohio, and Missouri advocating Clay's interest and reporting progress from time to time. Before long we shall find these two men engaged in a very different sort of conversation. A part of Clay's correspondence about the canvass with General Peter B. Porter and W. B. Rochester of New York, Senator J. S. Johnston of Louisiana, and his old friend Francis Brooke of Virginia, is still preserved. It reveals a very warm and active interest on his part in the conduct of his campaign — sometimes quite urgent as to things to be done. He was very much chagrined not to see a vigorous movement in his favor in Virginia, his native state, and he pressed his friends repeatedly, with evident impatience, to take some demonstrative step.

Thus he did not, as a candidate for the presidency, adopt the lofty standard of John Quincy Adams's principles for the guidance of his conduct. He did accept and encourage the aid of friends, and was quite active in spurring and directing their zeal. But beyond that he did not go. He kept rigidly clear of promises and bargains. As early as January 31, 1823, he wrote to Francis Brooke : —

"On one resolution my friends may rest assured I will firmly rely, and that is, to participate in no intrigues, to enter into no arrangements, to make no promises or pledges ; but that, whether I am elected or not, I will have nothing to reproach myself with. If elected I will go into the office with a pure conscience, to promote with my utmost exertions the common good of our country, and free to select the most able and faithful public servants. If not elected, acquiescing most cheerfully in the better selection which will thus have been made, I will at least have the satisfaction of preserving my honor unsullied and my heart uncorrupted."

And when in the heat of the canvass a proposition was made to him which looked like a bargain, he wrote (to J. S. Johnston, June 15, 1824) : —

"If the communication from Mr. —— is to be considered in the nature of an overture, there can be but one answer given. I can make no promises of office of any sort, to any one, upon any condition whatever. Whatever support shall be given to me must be spontaneous and unsought."

When in the course of the campaign Martin Van

Buren, then a leading manager for Crawford, becoming alarmed at the unexpected strength of the Jackson movement, caused Clay to be approached with the suggestion of a coalition between the Crawford and Clay forces to make Crawford **President and Clay Vice-President, Clay replied that he was resolved neither to offer nor to accept any arrangement with regard to** himself or to office for others, and that he would not decline the Vice-Presidency, provided it were offered to him " by the public having the right to tender it."   Neither can it be said that Clay, in the House of Representatives or in his public utterances elsewhere, had tried, as a candidate for the presidency, to trim his sail to the wind, to truckle to the opinions of others, to carry water on both shoulders. In the advocacy of his principles and policies he was as outspoken and straightforward as he ever had been, perhaps even more dashing and combative than he had occasion to be. It would hardly have been predicted then that twenty years later he would lose the presidency by an equivocation.

In the course of the canvass it became obvious that no one of the four candidates could obtain a majority of the electoral vote, and that the election would devolve upon the House of Representatives. This, however, did not prevent the campaign from becoming very animated. There being no marked difference of principle or opinion between the competitors, the effusions of stump orators and of newspapers turned mainly on personalities. **Adams**

wrote in August: " The bitterness and violence
of presidential electioneering increase **as** the time
advances. It seems as if every liar and calumniator in the country was at **work** day **and night
to** destroy **my character.** It **is** impossible to be
wholly insensible to this process while it is in operation. It distracts my attention from public business and consumes precious time." But the other
candidates fared no better than **he.** Against
Crawford charges **of** corruption were brought.
Jackson was denounced as a murderer; and Clay's
well known fondness for the card-table came home
to him in giving him the name of a gambler. His
adherents in Ohio resolved at a meeting that, as
" all the gentlemen named as candidates for the
presidency were honorable and intelligent men,
and to degrade and vilify them was discreditable
to the moral sense and **sound** judgment of the
country," the friends of Mr. Clay would **" not in-**
dulge in the unworthy practice of vilifying the
candidates whom they did not support." This,
however, did not have the effect of improving the
temper of his opponents. As the day of **election**
approached, the Jackson managers started a report
that Clay, seeing **no** chance **for** himself, would
withdraw from the contest and throw his influence
for Crawford; whereupon his friends issued another proclamation, declaring **that Clay "** would
not be withdrawn from the contest except by the
fiat of his Maker." **There** were demonstrations
of enthusiasm, too, — **not,** indeed, by uniformed

campaign organizations and great torchlight parades; but splendors of a different kind were not lacking. Niles records, for instance: "Presidential vests! A large parcel of silk vestings have been received at New York, from France, stamped with pretty good likenesses of Washington and of the presidential candidates, Adams, Clay, and Jackson." There was great confusion at the beginning of the campaign as to the vice-presidency. The Jackson men rallied on Calhoun. The friends of Adams tried to " run " Jackson for the second office. Indeed, such a combination had long been in the mind of Adams himself. Gallatin was at first on the Crawford ticket, but then withdrew entirely from the contest. The Clay men selected Sanford of New York.

The result of the election did not become fully known before December. It turned out that Jackson had won ninety-nine electoral votes, Adams eighty-four, Crawford forty-one and Clay thirty-seven. No one having received a clear majority, the election devolved upon the House of Representatives; and as, according to the Constitution, the choice by the House was confined to the three candidates having the highest number of votes, Clay's chance was gone. He received the whole electoral vote of only three states, Kentucky, Ohio, and Missouri, and four votes from New York. For the vice-presidency, Calhoun had a decided majority, one hundred and eighty-two out of two hundred and sixty one.

Clay was deeply disappointed. He had hoped to be at least among the three eligible by the House of Representatives. He had counted upon a majority of the electoral vote of Illinois; he had not despaired of Virginia, his native state. It was said that the five votes of Louisiana had been taken from Clay by a trick in the legislature, and that if he had received them, which would have put him ahead of Crawford, his personal popularity in the House would have given him the presidency. What "might have been" only sharpened the sting of the disappointment he suffered. In his letters he spoke philosophically enough: "As it is, I shall yield a cheerful acquiescence in the public decision. We must not despair of the Republic. Our institutions, if they have the value which we believe them to possess and are worth preserving, will sustain themselves, and will yet do well." But Martin Van Buren wrote on December 31, 1824, to a friend: " He (Clay) appears to me not to sustain his defeat with as much composure and fortitude as I should have expected, and evinces a degree of despondency not called for by the actual state of things." This is not improbable, for a man of Clay's sanguine, impulsive temperament feels misfortune as keenly as he enjoys success.

His greatest trial, however, was still to come. But before it came, he had as Speaker of the House a ceremonial act to perform, which at the same time was an act of friendship, and which, by the emotions it awakened, may for a moment have made him forget the humiliation of defeat and the anxieties besetting him. Lafayette was visiting the United States, and wherever he went, all the bitter quarrels of the presidential struggle were silenced by the transports of enthusiasm with which he was received. He appeared among the American people as the impersonation of their heroic ancestry to whom they owed everything they were proudest of. Only Washington himself, had he risen from the grave, could have called **forth** deeper feelings of reverence and affection. **As the** guest of the nation, he was invited to the Capitol, and Clay had to welcome him in the House of Representatives. It was a solemn **and** touching scene. **Clay** delivered an address full of feeling. With delicate instinct, **the orator** seized **upon** the poetic **side** of Lafayette's visit. **"The vain** wish has been sometimes indulged," said **he, "**that Providence would allow the patriot, **after** death, to return to his country, and to contemplate the intermediate changes which had taken place, to view the forests felled, the cities built, the mountains leveled, the canals **cut,** the highways constructed, the progress of the arts, the advancement of learning, and the increase of population. General, your present visit to the United States is a realization **of** the consoling object of that wish. You **are in the** midst **of** posterity."

The relations between Clay and Lafayette were of the friendliest character. They had long been in correspondence, which continued for years after this meeting at Washington. Lafayette's letters to Clay, many of which have been preserved, abound in expressions not only of regard, but of affection. It seems that the heart of the old patriot was completely captured by the brilliant, frank, and generous American, and he was repeatedly heard to speak of Clay as the man he wished to see made President of the United States.

CHAPTER X.

INSTEAD of being made President, Clay found himself invested with the dangerous power of choosing one among his rivals for the great office. It was generally admitted that his influence commanded in the House of Representatives a sufficient number of votes to decide the contest between Adams, Jackson, and Crawford. He was, therefore, so long as his preference remained unknown, a much-sought, much-courted man. In a letter written on January 8 to Francis P. Blair, whom he then counted among his friends in Kentucky, he humorously described the situation: " I am sometimes touched gently on the shoulder by a friend, for example, of General Jackson, who will thus address me: 'My dear sir, all my dependence is upon you; don't disappoint us; you know our partiality was for you next to the hero, and how much we want a Western President.' Immediately after a friend of Mr. Crawford will accost me: 'The hopes of the Republican party are concentrated on you; for God's sake preserve it. If you had been returned instead of Mr. Crawford, every man of us would have supported you to the last hour. We consider you and **him** as the only genuine Republican candidates.' Next a friend of Mr. Adams comes with tears in his eyes [an allusion to Adams's watering eyes]: 'Sir, Mr. Adams has always had **the** greatest respect for **you, and** admiration **of** your talents. There is no station to which you are not equal. **Most** undoubtedly you are the second choice of New England, and I pray you to consider seriously whether the public good and your own future interests do not point most distinctly to the choice which you ought to make?' How can one withstand all this disinterested homage and kindness?"

General Jackson himself thought it good policy now to be on pleasant terms with Clay. There had been "non-intercourse" between **them ever** since that memorable debate in which Clay found fault with the General's conduct in the Florida war. Jackson had left Clay's visit of courtesy unreturned, and when accidentally meeting **Clay at a** Kentucky village **inn, in the** summer of **1819,** he had hardly deigned to notice Clay's polite salutation. But now, having become an anxious candidate **for** the presidency while Clay was believed to control the decisive vote in the House of Representatives, Jackson took a less haughty view of things. Several members of Congress from Tennessee approached Clay to bring about an accommodation. They declared in General Jackson's behalf, that when treating Clay's courtesy with apparent contempt, he was "laboring under some indisposition," **and meant no** offence. Clay in response said that in censuring General Jackson's official conduct he had merely "expressed opinions in respect to public acts," without any feeling **of** personal enmity. The Tennessee delegation then arranged a dinner to which both Clay and Jackson were invited, and at which both appeared. **They** exchanged salutations and dined together. When Clay retired from the table, Jackson and his friend Eaton followed him to the door and insisted **that** he should take a seat with them in their carriage. Clay, dismissing his own coach, rode with them **and** was set **down** at his door. **Jackson** then invited him to dinner and he accepted. Soon afterwards Jackson with several members of Congress dined at Clay's lodgings, and then they " frequently met in the course of the winter, always respectfully addressing each other." Thus the " non-intercourse " was laboriously raised.

But all the while Clay was firmly resolved to give his **vote** and influence to Adams. He had made this declaration to J. J. Crittenden before he left Kentucky for Washington, and he informed Benton of **his** determination early **in** December. The legislature of Kentucky passed **a** resolution requesting the members of Congress from that state **to** vote for Jackson, but even that could not swerve Clay from his purpose. His conclusion was, for him, the only possible one. Crawford was a paralytic. For months he had been unable, as Secretary of the Treasury, to sign his official papers with his **own** hand. **It was** extremely doubtful whether, if elected President, he would ever be able to discharge the duties of the office. For this reason, aside **from** other considerations, **Clay** could **not** vote for him. Could **he** vote **for** Jackson? We remember Clay's speech **on Jack**son's **lawless** conduct in **the** Seminole **War.** He **had not since** changed **his** opinion. **"As a** friend **of** liberty, **and to the** permanence of our institutions," **he wrote** to Francis Brooke, **"** I cannot consent, in this early stage of their existence, by contributing **to** the election of a military chieftain, to give **the** strongest guaranty that the Republic will march **in** the fatal road which has conducted every **other** republic to ruin." So again he wrote to **Blair :** " Mr. Adams, you know well, I should never have selected, if at liberty to draw from the whole **mass of** our citizens, for a President. **But** there is no danger in his elevation now, or in time to **come. Not so of** his competitor, **of whom I** cannot believe that killing two thousand five **hun**dred Englishmen **at New** Orleans qualifies for **the** various **difficult and complicated** duties **of the** chief **magistracy." These were his honest** opinions. **How could** he vote to make Jackson President?

It was indeed argued that, as Jackson had received, not a majority of the electoral votes (for he had only ninety-nine out of **two** hundred and sixty one), but more votes than any one of his competitors, the members of the House of Representatives were bound, in obedience to the popular will, to ratify that verdict. **Not** to do so was, as Benton expressed it with a desperate plunge into **Greek,** "**a** violation of the *demos krateo* principle." This was equivalent to saying that a **mere** plurality **of the** electoral vote should be sufficient to elect a President; for **if** the **House of Representatives** were in duty bound to ratify that plurality **as if** it were a majority, then the plurality would practically elect. But **the** Constitution expressly provides that a President shall not be elected by a plurality **of** the electoral votes, and that, when no clear majority is obtained, the House **of** Representatives shall freely choose from those three candidates who shall have received the highest numbers. Moreover, the electors having in six states been appointed **by** the legislatures, it was a mere matter of conjecture whether General Jackson would have had **a** plurality of the popular vote, had the electors in all the states been chosen by the people. Finally, there was nothing to prove that Adams would not have been the second choice of the friends of Crawford and Clay, in a sufficient number of cases to insure him a clear majority in **an** election confined to him and Jackson. The presumption may **be said** to have been in favor of this, **if,** as proved to be the fact, the House of Representatives was inclined to give him that majority. There was, therefore, nothing in such an argument to limit the freedom of Clay's choice.

Benton himself admitted that his "demos krateo principle" **was in** conflict with the theory of the Constitution. Indeed, if carried to its logical consequences, it would have demanded that a candidate receiving an absolute majority of the electoral vote, but a smaller popular vote than another candidate, could not legitimately be President. Nobody could have gone this length. But in 1825 a great cry was **raised** because a mere plurality was not regarded as a majority, and it had much effect.

When the friends of Jackson and of Crawford began **to** suspect that Clay favored Adams, their conduct towards him changed abruptly. As they could not persuade him, they sought to drive and **even** to frighten him. He received anonymous **letters** full of abuse and menace. Some of them contained threats **of** personal violence. In others he was informed that, unless Jackson were elected, there would be insurrection and bloodshed. A peculiar kind of fanaticism seems to have been blazing **up among** Jackson's friends. Their newspapers opened furiously on Clay, and denounced his unwillingness **to vote** for Jackson as a sort of high treason. **But Clay could not** be moved. " I shall risk," **he said in a** letter **to his** friend Brooke, " I **shall risk without emotion these** effusions of malice, and remain unshaken **in my** purpose. What **is a** public man worth if **he** will not expose himself, on fit occasions, for **the** good of the country?"

At last the Jackson party resorted to a desperate expedient. The election in the House was to take place on February 9. On January 28 a letter dated at Washington appeared in a Philadelphia newspaper pointedly accusing Clay of having struck a corrupt bargain with Adams. Clay, the writer said, was to transfer his friends to Adams for the purpose of making Adams President, **and** Adams **was** then **to** make Clay Secretary of State. " And **the** friends of Mr. Clay," so the letter continued, " gave the information to the friends of Jackson that, if the friends of Jackson would offer the same price, they would close with them. But none of the friends of Jackson would descend to such mean barter and sale." The letter pretended to come from a member of Congress, who, however, did not give his name. A copy of the paper was mailed to Clay. This stung him to the quick. **On** February 1 he published " a card " in the " National Intelligencer," in which he expressed his belief that the letter purporting to come from a member of the House was a forgery ; " but," he added, " if **it be** genuine, I pronounce the member, whoever he may be, a base and infamous calumniator, a dastard and liar ; and if he dare unveil himself and avow his name, I will hold him responsible, as I **here admit** myself to be, to all the **laws** which govern and regulate men of honor." Clay's hot blood had run away with his judgment. He himself felt **it** as soon as he saw his " card " in print. But a high-spirited man, conscious of his rectitude, should not be judged too harshly if the first charge of corruption publicly brought against him does not find him cool enough to determine whether the silence of contempt or the angry cry of insulted honor will better comport with his dignity.

Unfortunately, the threat of a challenge, which would have been wrong under any circumstances, in this case turned out to be even ludicrous. Two days afterwards another "card" appeared in the "National Intelligencer," in which George Kremer, a Representative from Pennsylvania, avowed himself as the author of the letter. George Kremer was one of those men in high political station of whom people wonder "how they ever got there;" an insignificant, ordinarily inoffensive, simple soul, uneducated, ignorant, and eccentric, attracting attention in Washington mainly by a leopard-skin overcoat of curious cut which he was in the habit of wearing. This man now revealed himself as the great Henry Clay's antagonist, declaring himself "ready to prove, to the satisfaction of unprejudiced minds, enough to satisfy them of the accuracy of the statements which were contained in that letter." The thought of a duel with George Kremer in his leopard-skin overcoat appeared at once so farcical that the most passionate duelist would not have seriously entertained it. As Daniel Webster wrote to his excellent brother Ezekiel, who lived on a farm in New Hampshire, "Mr. Kremer is a man with whom one would think of having a shot about as soon as with your neighbor, Mr. Simeon Atkinson, whom he somewhat resembles."

The rashness of Clay's fierce proclamation was

thus well punished. He had now to retrieve the dignity of his character. On the day of the appearance of Kremer's card, Clay rose solemnly in the House to ask for a special committee to inquire **into** the charges made by that gentleman, "in order that if he [Clay] were guilty, here the proper punishment might be applied, or, if innocent, here his character and conduct might be vindicated." He expressed the anxious hope that his request for an investigation of the charges would be granted. " Emanating from such a source," **he** said, " this was the only notice he could take of them." The challenge to mortal combat, Henry Clay against George Kremer, was thus withdrawn. **A** motion was made by Forsyth of Georgia that the committee asked for be appointed. This unexpected turn of affairs threw poor Kremer into a great flutter. He followed Forsyth, saying that, if it should appear that he had not sufficient reason to justify his statements, he trusted he should receive proper reprobation. He was willing to meet the inquiry and abide the result, but he desired to have **the** honorable Speaker's " card " referred to the committee too. He was restless and bustled about, saying to one member that the letter in question was not really of his own making ; to others, that he had not intended at all to make any charge against Mr. Clay. Then he put a sort of disclaimer **on** a piece of paper and sent it to Clay, asking whether this would be satisfactory ; but he received **the** answer that the matter was now in the hands of the House. After two days' debate the committee was elected by ballot, not one member being on it who had supported Clay for the presidency.

On February 9, the very day when the electoral vote was to be counted and the election by the House was to take place, the committee reported. And what was the report? George Kremer, who at first had promised to "meet the inquiry and abide the result," had reconsidered over night; instead of giving the testimony the committee asked of him, he sent to that tribunal a long letter, refusing to testify. He would not, he wrote, appear before the committee either as an accuser or a witness, as there was no constitutional authority by which the House could assume jurisdiction over the case; such an assumption would threaten a dangerous invasion of the liberty of speech and of the press; he therefore protested against the whole proceeding, and preferred to communicate to his constituents the proofs of his statements with regard to the corrupt bargain charged.

This letter the committee laid before the House, and that was all the report they made. In the course of time, much light has been thrown upon this remarkable transaction. It has now become clear that, instead of a bargain being struck between Adams and Clay, overtures were made by Jackson's friends to Clay's friends; that George Kremer, a simple-minded man and a fanatical adherent of Jackson, was used as a tool by the Jackson managers, especially Senator Eaton from Tennessee; that they were the real authors of Kremer's first letter to the Philadelphia newspaper; that Clay's demand for an inquiry by the House into the charge made by Kremer was an unwelcome surprise to them; that Kremer, having been told by them that the charge would be substantiated, blunderingly assented to the inquiry when the motion was made; that they, knowing the charge **to** be false, wanted to avoid an investigation of it by the House; that, when the committee called upon Kremer for proofs, he was taken in hand by the Jackson managers, who wrote for him the letter protesting against the Congressional proceeding; that, in avoiding an investigation by the House and a report on the merits of the case, their purpose was to keep the charge without any authoritative refutation before the people; **that** they first hoped to terrorize Clay into supporting Jackson, or at least to separate his friends from him, while, in the event of Jackson's defeat, the cry of his having been defrauded of his rights by a corrupt bargain would help in securing his election the next time. This was the famous "bargain and corruption" affair, which during a long period excited the **minds of** men all over the United States. **It** was an infamous intrigue against the good name of two honorable men, designed to promote the political fortunes of a third.

The "inside view" of **the** relations between Adams and Clay came, long after this period, to public knowledge through the publication **of**

Adams's Diary. The most unfavorable inference which can be drawn from the revelations therein made is, that some of Clay's friends very urgently desired his appointment as Secretary of State; and that one of them, Letcher of Kentucky, a good-natured but not very strong-headed man, had said to Adams that Clay's friends, in supporting Adams, would expect Clay to have an influential place in the administration, disclaiming, however, all authority from Clay, and receiving no assurance from Adams. Those who have any experience of public life know that the adherents of a prominent public man are almost always extremely anxious to see him in positions of power, and very apt to go ahead of his wishes in endeavoring to put him there, thus not seldom compromising him without his fault. Adams received a good many visits of men who wished to sound his disposition, among them Webster, who desired to obtain a promise that the Federalists would not be excluded from office, and who himself hoped to be appointed minister to England, though he did not express such a wish at the time. Clay too visited Adams, to tell him that he would have the vote of Kentucky, and to converse with him upon the general situation. It would be absurd to see in these occurrences anything to support the charge that Clay's vote and influence were thrown for Adams in execution of a bargain securing him a place in the Cabinet; for by the testimony of Crittenden and Benton, the fact stands conclusively proven that, before all these conver sations with Adams happened, Clay had already declared his firm determination to vote for Adams, upon the grounds then and afterwards avowed. The "bargain and corruption" charge remains, therefore, simply a calumny.

The effect produced at the time upon Clay's mind by these things appears in his correspondence. They aroused in him the indignant pride of one who feels himself high above the venal crowd. Just before the appearance of Kremer's letter he wrote to Blair: "The knaves cannot comprehend how a man can be honest. They cannot conceive that I should have solemnly interrogated my conscience, and asked it to tell me seriously what I ought to do." And to Francis Brooke on February 4: "The object now is, on the part of Mr. Crawford and General Jackson, to drive me from the course which my deliberate judgment points out. They all have yet to learn my character if they suppose it possible to make me swerve from my duty by any species of intimidation or denunciation." When the election came on, Clay's whole influence went in favor of Adams, who, on the first ballot in the House of Representatives, received the votes of a majority of the states, and was declared to be elected President.

But Clay's trials were not over. When Adams began to make up his Cabinet, he actually did offer to Clay the secretaryship of state. After what had happened, should Adams have made the offer, and should Clay have accepted it? These questions have been discussed probably with more interest than anything connected with a cabinet appointment in our political history.

Under ordinary circumstances, the offer would have been regarded as a perfectly proper and even natural one. Clay was by far the most brilliant leader of the ruling party. His influence was large and his ability equal to his influence. It was desirable to have a Western man in the Cabinet. Clay towered so high above all the public characters in that region that it would have looked almost grotesque to pass him by, exalting somebody else. It is true that Adams had differed from Clay on important things, and had expressed some unfavorable opinions of him, as, indeed, he had of almost all other public men of note. But the subjects on which they had differed were disposed of ; and as to personal feelings, it was one of the remarkable features of Adams's character that, strong as his prejudices and resentments were, he put them resolutely aside when they stood in the way of the fulfillment of a public duty. So, to the end of conciliating the Crawford element, he sufficiently overcame a feeling of strong personal dislike to offer to Crawford himself, in spite of that gentleman's physical disabilities, to continue him as the head of the Treasury Department, — an offer which Crawford promptly declined. Adams had even conceived the idea of tendering the War Department to General Jackson, but learned that Jackson would take such an

offer "in ill part." In an administration thus designed to be constructed upon the principle that
the leaders of the ruling party should form part
of it, Clay was of course a necessary man ; and
to offer him a place in the Cabinet appeared not
only in itself proper, but unavoidable. Clay would
therefore undoubtedly have been invited into the
Cabinet whether he had or had not exercised any
influence favorable to Mr. Adams's election.

Neither would there have been any question as
to the propriety of Clay's accepting any place in
the new administration under ordinary circumstances. But that the actual circumstances were
not of the ordinary kind, Clay himself felt. When
Adams, a few days after the election by the House,
offered him at a personal interview the secretaryship of state, he replied that he " would take it
into consideration," and answer " as soon as he
should have time to consult his friends." It was
an anxious consultation. At first some of his
friends were opposed to acceptance. Would not
his taking the secretaryship of state be treated as
conclusive evidence proving the justice of the im-
putations which had been made against him ? It
was known that Clay and Adams had not been on
terms of cordial friendship. They had seriously
differed on important points at Ghent. Clay had
made opposition to Monroe's administration, and
especially had criticised Adams as Secretary of
State. Less than two years before, Adams had
been attacked by one of the Ghent Commissioners,

Jonathan Russell; he had published an elaborate defense, in which he referred, with regard to some points of fact, to Clay as a witness, and Clay had, in a public and somewhat uncalled-for letter, questioned the correctness of Adams's recollections, — an act which was generally looked upon as an indication of an unfriendly spirit. Would not this sudden reconciliation, accompanied with an exchange of political favors, look suspicious, and render much more plausible the charge of a corrupt bargain? Besides, was not the House of Representatives Clay's true field? Would not the administration want his support there more than in the Cabinet? Would not the Western people rather see him there than in an executive department?

These were weighty questions. On the other hand, it was urged, whether he accepted or not, he would be subject to animadversion. If he declined, it would be said that the patriotic Kremer, by bravely exposing the corrupt bargain, had actually succeeded in preventing its consummation. Conscious of his own rectitude, should he attach such importance to an accusation coming from so insignificant a person? Indeed, would not either of the other candidates, had he been elected, have made him the same offer? Moreover, there was a consideration of duty. It might be difficult to form the administration without him. Could he permit it to be said or suspected that, after having contributed so much to the election of Adams as

President, he thought too ill of him to accept the first place in his Cabinet? As Adams was now **the** constitutional head of the government, ought not Clay to regard him as such, dismissing any personal objections which he might have had **to** him? These arguments, as we know from Clay's correspondence, finally changed the opinions of those of his friends who had at first been averse to his taking office. The friends of Adams in New England were especially urgent. Some of Crawford's adherents too, and even some of those of General Jackson, expressed to Clay their conviction that he should accept. He had declared that he would follow the advice of his friends, **and** so he did. To Brooke he wrote: "I have an unaffected repugnance to any executive employment, and my rejection of the offer, if **it** were **in** conformity to their deliberate judgment, would have **been** more compatible with my feelings than its acceptance."

In spite of that "repugnance," it is not probable that much persuasion was required to make him accept. He was a high-spirited, proud **man.** When George Kremer made a charge, should Henry Clay run away? Not he. He would not appear to be afraid. This may not have been all. Clay's ambition for the presidency was ardent and impatient. He would forget it for a moment when discussing public questions. But it was not likely to be absent from his mind when considering whether he should not take the place offered him.

He had looked upon the secretaryship of state as the stepping-stone to the presidency before; he probably continued to do so. **The** presidential fever is a merciless disease. **It** renders its victims blind and deaf. **So** now Clay misjudged the **situation** altogether. **"An** opposition **is talked of** here," he wrote to Brooke; " but I regard that as the ebullition of the moment. **There are** elements for faction, none for opposition. Opposition to **what**? To measures and principles which are yet to be developed!" He believed the new administration would be judged on its merits. He did not know the spirit it was to meet. **When he declared** himself resolved to accept the secretaryship of state, six days after the offer had been made, he was very far from having counted the cost.

Immediately before the final adjournment **of the** Eighteenth Congress, on March 3, 1825, the **House** of Representatives passed a resolution thanking " the Honorable Henry Clay for the able, impartial, and dignified manner in which he had presided over its deliberations," etc. In response, " retiring, perhaps forever," from the office of Speaker, Clay was able to say that, in the fourteen years during which he had, with short intervals, occupied that difficult and responsible position, not one **of his** decisions had ever been reversed by the House. Indeed, Henry Clay stands in the traditions of the House of Representatives as the greatest of its Speakers. His perfect mastery of parliamentary **law, his** quickness of decision in applying it, his unfailing presence of mind and power of command in moments of excitement and confusion, the courteous dignity of his bearing, are remembered as unequaled by any one of those who had preceded or who have followed him. The thanks of the House were voted to him with zest. Yet many of those who felt themselves obliged to assent to this vote were then already his bitter enemies.

The next day John Quincy Adams was inaugurated as President of the United States. As soon as the nomination of Henry Clay for the office of Secretary of State came before the Senate, the war against him began in due form. An address by George Kremer to his constituents, in which all conceivable gossip was retailed to give color to the " bargain and corruption " cry, was freely used in Washington to prevent Clay's nomination from being confirmed. General Jackson himself expressed his hope of its rejection. A letter written, evidently for publication, by Jackson to his friend Samuel Swartwout, in New York, which bristled with insidious insinuations against Clay, was circulated in Washington on the eve of the day when Clay's nomination was to be acted upon.

Still trying to obtain an authoritative investigation of his conduct, Clay asked a Senator to move a formal inquiry by a senate committee, if any charge should be made against him in that body. But no tangible charge was brought forward ; only one Senator indulged in some vague animadversions, presenting no ground for an inquiry. General

Jackson, then still a member of the Senate, said nothing; but he, together with fourteen other Senators, among them the leading Southerners, voted against consenting to the nomination. It was, however, confirmed by a majority of twelve, seven Senators being absent.

On the day of the inauguration, General Jackson had been one of the earliest of those who "took the hand" of President Adams, congratulating him upon his accession to power. The newspapers highly praised the magnanimity of the defeated candidate. But after the adjournment of the Senate, when Jackson was on his way to his home in Tennessee, his tone changed. Everywhere he was cordially received; and to every one willing to hear it, at public receptions, in hotels, on steamboats, he was ready to say that the will of the people had been fraudulently defeated, and that the presidential office had virtually been stolen from its rightful owner by a corrupt combination. This foreshadowed the presidential campaign of 1828. The cry was to be: "The rights of the people against bargain and corruption."

Not having had the benefit of an official inquiry, Clay now tried to put down the calumny once and forever by an explicit statement of the case over his own signature. On March 26, not many days after he had become a member of the new administration, he published an address to his old constituents in Kentucky, in which he elaborately reviewed the whole story, conclusively refuted the charges brought against him, and fully explained and defended his conduct. It was an exceedingly able document, temperate in tone, complete and **lucid** in the presentation **of** facts, and unanswerable in argument. One of its notable passages may be mentioned as characteristic. Clay was very much ashamed of having threatened to challenge George Kremer. Expressing his regret therefor, he added : " I owe it to the community to say that, whatever I may have done, or by inevitable circumstances might be forced to do, no man **in it holds in** deeper abhorrence than I do that pernicious practice [of dueling]. Condemned **as** it must be by the judgment and the philosophy, to say nothing of the religion, of every thinking man, it is an affair of feeling, about which we cannot, although we should, reason. Its true correction will be found when all shall unite, as all ought to unite, in its unqualified proscription." But until that comes to pass, shall we go on challenging and fighting, the slaves of false notions of honor? **At** any rate, we shall soon see the Honorable Henry Clay again with pistol in hand.

Clay may have thought that his address would **make** an end of the " bargain and corruption " charge for all **time,** and so it should have done. Indeed, he received letters from such men as Chief Justice Marshall, John Tyler, Justice Story, Daniel Webster, Lewis Cass, and others, congratulating him upon the completeness of his vindication and triumph. But he lived to appreciate the wonderful vitality of a well - managed political lie. Nobody believes that lie now. But it defeated his dearest ambitions, and darkened the rest of his public life. It kept him refuting and explaining, explaining and refuting, year after year; yet still thousands of simple-minded citizens would continue honestly to believe that Henry Clay was a great knave, who had defeated the will of the people by bargain and corruption, and cheated the old hero of New Orleans out of his rights.

17

CHAPTER XI.

THE administration of John Quincy Adams was the last one in which the conduct of the government accorded strictly with the best traditions of the Republic. Nothing was farther from his mind than to use the power of appointment and removal for political ends. At that time the notion that the accession of a new President must necessarily involve a thorough reconstruction of the Cabinet, was not yet invented. Following the example of most of his predecessors, he applied the rule that no unnecessary changes should be made, even in the heads of the executive departments. His election to the presidency and Calhoun's to the vice-presidency had vacated the secretaryships of state and of war, and these vacancies he filled with Henry Clay, and James Barbour of Virginia. As we have seen, he offered to continue Crawford at the head of the Treasury Department, and only after Crawford had declined he summoned to that place Richard Rush of Pennsylvania. Southard of New Jersey remained Secretary of the Navy, and William Wirt of Virginia, Attorney General. The Postmaster General, McLean, was also left in his

place, but that officer did not at that time occupy
a seat in the Cabinet; and there **was** no Department **of** the Interior. The members of the Cabinet **all** passed as Republicans. **But the** Federalists, of whom **there were** scattered **remnants** here
and there, — **some of** them looked up to as venerable **relics, — were by no** means excluded from
place. **When De** Witt Clinton had declined the
mission to England, Adams urged it upon Rufus
King of New York, who then stood in the politics
of the country as a fine and reverend monument of
ancient Federalism.

The new administration had hardly taken the
reins in hand, when that spirit of hostility to **it**
which prevailed among the following **of** Jackson,
Crawford, and Calhoun appeared even among per-
sons in federal office; **and** the question whether
it would not **be well** to fill the service with friends,
or at least **to** clear it of enemies, presented itself
in a very pointed form. Then Adams proved the
quality of his principles, as witness, by way of example, this case : The member of the House of
Representatives from Louisiana denounced Sterret,
the Naval Officer at New Orleans, as **a** noisy and
clamorous **reviler of** the administration, who had
even gone so far as to get up a public demonstration to **insult** the member of Congress for having
voted **to make Mr.** Adams President. The member
of Congress, therefore, demanded Sterret's removal.
There seemed to be no doubt about the facts. The
insulting demonstration had not actually come off,

but Sterret had been active in making preparations
for it.

Clay agreed with the member. During the pendency of an election, said he, every man in the
service should feel free to " indulge his preference ; " **but no** officer should, after election, **" be**
permitted to hold a conduct in open and continual
disparagement of the administration and its head."
In the treatment of persons in the service, he
thought, the administration " should avoid, on the
one hand, political persecution, and on the other
an appearance of pusillanimity." Adams came to
a different conclusion. He looked upon this as a
test case, and it is wholesome to remember what a
President of the United States thought upon such
a question in the year 1825. He asked Clay in
reply why he should remove this man. The insulting demonstration, of which **the** member of
Congress complained, **had** only been intended, but
not practically carried out. Would a mere " intention never carried into effect " justify the removal of a man from **office ?** " Besides," he continued, " should I remove this man for this cause,
it must be upon some fixed principle, which would
apply to others as well as to him. And where was
it possible to draw the line ? Of the custom house
officers throughout the Union four fifths, in all
probability, were opposed to **my** election. They
were all now in my power, and I had been urged
very earnestly to sweep away my opponents and
provide, with their places, for my friends. I can

justify the refusal to adopt this policy only by the steadiness and consistency of my adhesion to my own. If I depart from this in one instance, I shall be called upon by my friends to do the same thing in many. An insidious and inquisitorial scrutiny into the personal dispositions of public officers will creep through the whole Union, and the most selfish and sordid passions will be kindled into activity to distort the conduct and misrepresent the feelings of men whose places may become the prize of slander upon them." This was the President's answer to Clay's suggestions, and, as the Diary tells us, " Mr. Clay did not press the subject any farther." It would have been useless.

What moved Adams, in laying down this rule of action, was not faint-heartedness He was one of the most courageous of men; he never shrank from a responsibility. He even enjoyed a conflict when he found one necessary to enforce his sense of right. Here he made his stand for the principles upon which the government in its early days had been conducted, and his decision in the Sterret case became the rule by which his administration was governed from beginning to end. He made only two removals during the four years, and these were for bad official conduct. With unbending firmness he resisted every attempt to make him dismiss officers who intrigued against his reëlection, or openly embraced the cause of his opponents. The reappointment of worthy officers upon the expiration of their terms, without regard to politics, was a matter of course.

Clay continued to think, not without reason, that the President carried his toleration to a dangerous extreme. He would not **have** permitted men in office to make their hostility **to** the administration conspicuous and defiant. But he was far from favoring the use of the appointing and removing power **as** a political engine. He was opposed to arbitrary removals, **as** to everything that would give the public offices the character of spoils.

While these were the principles upon which **the** administration was conducted, the virulent hostility of its opponents continued to crop out in a ceaseless repetition, in speech and press, **of** the assaults **upon** its members, which had begun with the election. In May Clay went to Kentucky to meet his family and to take them **to** Washington. Wherever he passed, his friends greeted him with enthusiastic demonstrations. Public dinners crowded one another, not only in Kentucky, but in Virginia, Pennsylvania, and Ohio, along his route of travel; but everywhere, in response to expressions of **af**fection and confidence, he felt himself obliged to **say** something in explanation of his conduct in the last presidential election. The spectre of the " bargain and corruption " charge seemed to pursue him wherever he went.

When he returned to Washington, in August, he was in deep affliction, two of his daughters having died in one month, one of them on her way to the national capital. But as to the state of the public mind he felt somewhat encouraged. He

had found many friends to welcome him with great warmth. He had heard the President spoken of with high respect and confidence. Daniel Webster, too, sent him cheering reports as to " an entire and not uneasy acquiescence in the events of last winter," which he had found on his summer excursions. Clay almost persuaded himself that the storm had blown over. But then he was startled again by some stirring manifestation of the bitterness which the last presidential election had left behind it. One day he met a general of the regular army, with his aid-de-camp, in the President's ante-room. The aid-de-camp being introduced to him, Clay politely offered his hand, which the young man, drawing back, refused to take. It turned out that he was a connection of General Jackson. Clay was so shocked by this rude demonstration that he wrote the General a complaining letter about it.

Something far more serious happened in October. The legislature of Tennessee met, and proceeded forthwith to nominate General Jackson as a candidate for President to be elected in 1828. On October 13, more than three years before the period of the election, General Jackson addressed a letter to the legislature, accepting the nomination, and at the same time resigning his seat in the Senate. In this letter he laid down his " platform." He gave the world to understand that there was much corruption at Washington, and that, unless a certain remedy were applied, corruption would " become the order of the day there." The remedy was an amendment to the Constitution declaring " any member of Congress ineligible to office under the general government during the term for which he was elected, and for two years thereafter, except in cases of judicial office." This letter was generally understood. It was hardly taken as the promise of a valuable reform to be carried out if Jackson should become President. Nobody attached much importance to that; certainly Jackson did not, for when he did become President, he, as we shall see, appointed a much larger number of members of Congress to office than had been so appointed by any one of his predecessors. But it was taken as a proclamation by General Jackson that he had been defrauded of the presidency by a corrupt bargain between a sitting member of Congress and a presidential candidate, the member of Congress obtaining a cabinet office as a reward for seating the candidate in the presidential chair. It pointed directly at Adams and Clay. Thus—it being also understood that, according to custom, Adams would be supported by his followers as a candidate for a second term — the campaign of 1828 was opened, not only constructively, but in due form, with the cry of "bargain and corruption" sanctioned by the standard-bearer of the opposition. It became more lively with the opening of the Nineteenth Congress in December, 1825.

Under Monroe, during the " era of good feeling," there had been individual opposition to this or that measure, or to the administration generally, but there had been no opposition party. With the accession of Adams the era of good feeling was well over, and those new groupings began to appear which, in the course of time, developed into new party organizations. Men were driven apart or drawn together by different motives. Of these, the commotion caused by the last presidential election furnished the most potent at that time. A great many of the adherents of the defeated candidates, especially the Jackson men, were bound to make odious and to break down the Adams administration by any means and at any cost. This was a personal opposition, virulent and remorseless. There were rumors, too, of an opposition being systematically organized by Calhoun, who then began to identify his ambition exclusively with the cause of slavery. In the vote against Clay's confirmation Adams saw " the rallying of the South and of Southern interests and prejudices to the men of the South." Not a few Southern men began to feel an instinctive dread of the spirit represented by Adams.

But the hostility to the administration was soon furnished with an opportunity to rally on a question of constitutional principle. Already in his inaugural address, President Adams had brought forth something vigorous on internal improvements. But in his first message to Congress he went beyond what had ever been uttered upon that subject before. After having laid down the far-reaching doctrine that " the great object of the institution of civil government is the improvement of those who are parties to the social compact," he enumerated a vast array of powers granted in the Constitution, and added that, " if these powers may be effectually brought into action by laws promoting the improvement of agriculture, commerce, and manufactures, the cultivation of the mechanic and of the elegant arts, the advancement of literature, and the progress of the sciences, ornamental and profound, to refrain from exercising them for the benefit of the people themselves would be to hide in the earth the talent committed to our charge, — would be treachery to the most sacred of trusts." He spoke of the establishment of a national university, astronomical observatories, and scientific enterprises, and suggested that, while European nations advanced with such rapid strides, it would be casting away the bounties of Providence if we stood still, confessing that we were " palsied by the will of our constituents." This was opening a perspective of governmental functions much larger than the American mind was accustomed to contemplate. There had been some serious shaking of heads when this part of the message was discussed in the Cabinet, especially on the part of Barbour and Clay. This went a long way beyond the building of roads and the digging of canals, upon which Clay had been so fond of discoursing. But Adams, who was always inclined to express his opinions in the most uncompromising form, insisted upon doing so this time. The doctrine that the Constitution conferred by implication upon the government powers of almost unlimited extent, and also imposed upon it the duty of keeping those powers in constant activity, not only disturbed the political thinkers of the Democratic school, but it was especially apt to alarm the slaveholding interest, which at that period began to see in the strictest construction, and in the maintenance of the extremest states' rights principles, its citadel of safety.

The first actual collision between the administration and its opponents occurred upon another question. The President announced in his message that the Spanish-American republics had resolved upon a congress to meet on the Isthmus of Panama, in which they should all be represented; that they had also invited the United States to send plenipotentiaries; that this invitation had been accepted, and that ministers on the part of the United States would be commissioned to " attend at those deliberations." This was the famous Panama mission.

A grand council of the South and Central American republics was planned as early as 1821, Bolivar favoring it, and a series of treaties with regard to it was concluded between them. In April, 1825, Clay was approached by the Mexican and Colombian ministers with the inquiry whether an invitation to the United States to be represented in the Panama Congress would be favorably considered. Nothing could be more apt to strike Clay's fancy than such an undertaking. The Holy Alliance darkly plotting at its conferences and congresses in Europe to reëstablish the odious despotism of Spain over South and Central America, and thus to gain **a** basis of operations for interference with the North American Republic, had frequently disturbed his dreams. To form against this league of despotism in the **old** world a league of republics in the new, and thus to make this great continent the ark of human liberty and a higher civilization, **was** one of those large, generous conceptions well calculated to fascinate his ardent mind. He succeeded even in infusing some of **his** enthusiasm **into Adams's** colder nature. The **invitation** was promptly accepted. But the definition of the objects of the Congress, filtered through Adams's sober mind, appeared somewhat tame by the side of the original South American scheme, and probably of Clay's desires, too. The South Americans had thought of a league for resistance against a common enemy; of a combination of forces, among themselves at least, to be favored by the United States, for the liberation **of** Cuba **and Porto Rico** from Spanish power; of some concert of action for the general enforcement of the principles of the American policy proclaimed by President Monroe, and so on. **It is** very probable that Clay, although not going quite so far, had in his mind some permanent concert among American states looking to expressions of a common will, and to united action when emergency should require.

But the purposes of our participation in the
Panama Congress, as they appeared in the President's messages to the Senate and the House, and
later in Clay's instructions to the American envoys, were cautiously limited. The Congress was
to be looked upon as a good opportunity for giving
to the Spanish-American brethren kindly advice,
even if it were only as to their own interests ; also
for ascertaining in what direction their policy was
likely to run. Advantageous arrangements of
commercial reciprocity might be made ; proper
definitions of blockade and neutral rights might
be agreed upon. The "perpetual abolition of private war on the ocean," as well as a "concert of
measures having reference to the more effectual
abolition of the slave - trade," should be aimed at.
The Congress should also be used as "a fair occasion for urging upon all the new nations of the
South the just and liberal principles of religious
liberty," not by interference with their concerns,
but by claiming for citizens of the United States
sojourning in those republics the right of free
worship. The Monroe doctrine should be inter-
preted to them as meaning only that each American
nation should resist foreign interference, or attempts
to establish new colonies upon its soil, with its own
means. The recognition of Hayti as an independent state was to be deprecated, — this against
Clay's first impulse, — on the ostensible ground
that Hayti, by yielding exclusive commercial advantages to France, had returned to a semi-de-

pendent condition. All enterprises upon **Cuba** and Porto Rico, such as had been planned by Mexico and Colombia, **were by all means** to be discouraged.

This, **by** the way, **was an** exceedingly ticklish subject. **If Cuba and** Porto **Rico** were to **be revo**lutionized, slave insurrections would follow, **and** the insurrectionary spirit would be likely to **com**municate itself **to** the slave population of **the** Southern States. Cuba and Porto Rico would hardly be able to maintain their independence, and if they should fall into the **hands of a great** naval power, that power would command **the** Mexican Gulf and the mouth of the Mississippi. The slaveholding influence, therefore, demanded that **Cuba** and Porto Rico should **not be** revolutionized. **The** general interests of the United States **demanded that** the two islands should **not** pass into the **hands** of a great naval power. It was, **therefore,** thought best that they should quietly remain in the possession of Spain. **That** possession was threatened **so** long as peace was not **declared** between Spain and her former colonies. **It** seemed, therefore, **espe**cially desirable that the **war** should come **to a** final **close.** To this end the Emperor **of** Russia, whom American diplomacy had fallen **into the habit** of regarding as a sort of benevolent **uncle, was to be** pressed into service. He was **asked to** persuade Spain, in view of the utter hopelessness of **further** war, to yield to necessity and recognize the **inde**pendence **of** her former colonies **on** the American continent. Clay's instructions to Middleton, the American Minister at St. Petersburg, setting forth the arguments to be submitted to the Emperor, were, in this respect, a remarkable piece of reasoning and persuasiveness.

At the Panama Congress all was then to be done to prevent the designs of Mexico and Colombia upon Cuba and Porto Rico from being executed. On the whole, that Congress was to be regarded only as a consultative assembly, a mere diplomatic conference, leaving the respective powers represented there perfectly free to accept and act upon the conclusions arrived at, or not, as they might choose. There was to be no alliance of any kind, no entangling engagement, on the part of the United States. This was the character in which the Panama mission was presented to Congress.

The first thing at which the Senate took offence was that the President in his message had spoken of " commissioning " ministers at his own pleasure. A practical issue on this point was avoided when Adams sent to the Senate the nominations of the ministers to be appointed. Then the policy of the mission itself became the subject of most virulent attack. The opposition was composed of two distinct elements. One consisted of the slave-holding interest, which feared every contact with the new republics that had abolished slavery; which scorned the thought of envoys of the United States sitting in the same assembly with the representatives of republics that had negroes

and mulattoes among their generals and legislators;
which dreaded the possible recognition of the independence of Hayti as a demonstration showing the
negro slaves in the Union what they might gain
by rising in insurrection and killing their masters.
This element of opposition was thoroughly in earnest. **It had an** unbending logic on its side. **If
slavery** was to exist in the United States, it had to
demand that not only the home policy, but also **the**
foreign policy, **of** the Republic must be accommo-
dated to the conditions of its existence.

The other element of the opposition consisted
mainly of those who were determined to break
down the administration **in any event** and at **any**
cost. Their principal argument was that, notwithstanding the assurances given by the President,
participation in the Panama Congress would lead
the United States into entangling alliances; and
if it did not do so at first, it would do so in its consequences. In the country, however, the Panama
mission was popular. **A grand** Amphictyonic council **of** the American republics, held on the great
isthmus of the continent, to proclaim the glories
of free government to the world, pleased the fancy
of the people. When **public** opinion seemed to
become impatient at the interminable wrangle in
Congress, the Senate voted down an adverse report
of its Committee on Foreign Relations by twenty-
four to nineteen, and confirmed the nominations
for the Panama mission. In the House of Representatives another debate sprang up on the bill

making the necessary appropriation, which **passed** by more than two to one. The spirit of the "opposition in any event" betrayed itself **in** unguarded utterances, such as the following, ascribed to Van Buren, the anti-administration leader **in** the Senate: " Yes, they have beaten **us** by a few votes, after a hard battle; but if they had only taken the **other side and** refused the mission, we should have **had** them."

But that was **not the end of** the debate **in the** Senate. **The attack on** the administration was continued in the discussion on a resolution offered by Branch, of North Carolina, denying the competency of the President to send ministers to the Panama Congress without the previous advice **and** consent of the Senate, which competency the President had originally claimed in his message to Congress. This presented to John Randolph an opportunity for **a** display of his peculiar power of vituperation. **In a** long, rambling harangue he insinuated that the invitations to the Panama Congress addressed by the ministers of the Southern republics **to the** government of the United States had **been written,** or at least inspired, by the State Department, and were therefore fraudulent. **It** was in this speech that he characterized the administration, alluding to Adams and Clay, as " the coalition of Blifil and Black George, — the combination, unheard **of** till **then,** of the Puritan with the blackleg."

When Clay heard **of** this, **he** boiled over with

rage. Only a few months **before** he had, in the
address to his constituents, spoken of the duel as
a relic of barbarism, much to be discountenanced.
The same Clay now promptly sent a challenge to
Randolph. The explanation, which might **have**
averted the duel, Randolph refused to give. **On**
April **8 they** "met," Randolph not intending to
harm Clay, but Clay in terrible earnest. They exchanged shots, and both missed ; only Randolph's
coat was touched. At the second fire Clay put another bullet through Randolph's coat, but Randolph
emptied his pistol into the air, and said : "I do not
fire at you, Mr. Clay." Thereupon they shook
hands, and all was over. Randolph's pistol had
failed to prove that Clay was a "blackleg," and
Clay's pistol had also failed to prove that Randolph was a calumniator ; but, according to the
mysterious process of reasoning which makes the
pistol the arbiter of honor, the honor of each was
satisfied. Webster wrote to Judge Story : "You
will have heard of the bloodless duel. I regret it
very much, **but** the conduct **of** Mr. Randolph has
been such that I suppose it was thought that it
could no longer be tolerated." Benton looked at
the matter from a different point of **view.** With
the keen relish of a *connoisseur,* **he** describes the
whole affair down **to** the minutest detail in his
" Thirty Years' View," devoting nearly eight of its
large pages to it, and **sums up :** " It was about the
last high-toned duel **that I** have witnessed, and
among the highest toned I have ever witnessed,

and so happily conducted to a fortunate issue, — a result due to the noble character of the seconds, as well as to the generous and heroic spirit of the principals."

The net result was that Randolph's epigram about "the combination of the Puritan and the blackleg" received all the more currency, and that Clay, by his example, had given new sanction to the practice he had denounced as barbarous. He was by no means a professional duelist. His hand was in fact so unused to the pistol that on this occasion he feared he would not be able to fire it within the time given him. He simply did not possess that courage which is higher than the courage to face death.

The debates on the Panama mission served as a first general drill of the opposition. It went on harassing the Adams administration to its last hour, some of the most virulent attacks being directed against Clay. Every measure which was suspected of being specially favored by the administration had to meet bitter resistance. In the Senate an amendment to the Constitution was introduced, in accordance with Jackson's recommendation, to exclude members of Congress from executive appointments; another to circumscribe the power of the general government with regard to internal improvements; also a bill to limit the executive patronage. However much good there may have been in these propositions, it became apparent that they were brought forward mainly for the purpose of giving point to the opposition and to keep its spirit hot. Not one of them led to any practical result.

The confinement of office life, the anxieties of his position, and probably a feeling of regret that he had put himself into a situation in which he could only with difficulty defend himself against the virulent hostility assailing him without cessation, began to tell upon Clay's health. He felt weary and ill, so seriously sometimes that he thought of giving up his place in the administration. After the adjournment of Congress he visited his home in Kentucky. Again he was cheered and feasted on the way, as well as by his old constituents at home, and again he had, at dinners and receptions, to tell the story of the last presidential election over and over, in order to prove that the " bargain and corruption " charge was false. Again he returned to Washington, encouraged by the enthusiastic affection of his friends, and their assurance that there were large masses of people believing in the honorable character of the President and the Secretary of State.

The elections for the twentieth Congress which took place that summer and autumn began to show new lines of party division. In many districts the struggle was avowedly between those friendly and those hostile to the administration. The forming groups were not yet divided by clearly defined differences of principle or policy, but the air was full of charges, insinuations, and personal detraction.

General Jackson's voice, too, was heard again in characteristic tones. He took good care to keep his grievance before the people. Having been invited by some of his friends in Kentucky to visit that state "for the purpose of counteracting the intrigue and management of certain prominent individuals against him," he wrote a long letter declining the invitation.

"But [he added] if it be true that the administration have gone into power contrary to the voice of the nation, and are now expecting, by means of this power, thus acquired, to mould the public will into an acquiescence with their authority, then is the issue fairly made out — shall the government or the people rule? And it becomes the man whom the people shall indicate as their rightful representative in this solemn issue, so to have acquitted himself that, while he displaces these enemies of liberty, there will be nothing in his own example to operate against the strength and durability of the government."

No candidate for the presidency had ever held such language. Here he plainly denounced the constitutionally elected chief magistrate as a usurper, and arraigned him and the members of his administration as "these enemies of liberty" who were using the power of the government to dragoon the public will into acquiescence. This fierce denunciation was hurled against a President so conscientious in the exercise of his power that, among the public officers, his most virulent enemies and the most enthusiastic supporters of his opponent were as safe in their places as were his friends.

The last session of the Nineteenth Congress, which opened in December, 1826, passed over without any event of importance, but not without many demonstrations of " the bitter and rancorous spirit of the opposition," which, as Adams recorded, " produced during the late session of Congress four or five challenges to duels, all of which, however, happily ended in smoke ; " and, he added, " at a public dinner given last week to John Randolph of Roanoke, a toast was given directly instigating assassination." No opportunity was lost for defaming the administration. A fierce attack was made on Clay for having, in the exercise of his power as Secretary of State, made some changes in the selection of newspapers for the publication of the laws.

The clamor of the opposition grew, indeed, so loud that people not specially engaged in politics wondered in amazement whether the Republic really was on the brink of destruction. The sedate Niles, immediately after the adjournment of Congress, expressed in the " Register " his fear that the coming presidential election, which was still a year and a half ahead, would " cause as much heat, if not violence, as any other event that ever happened in this country ; that father would be arrayed against son, and son against father, old friends become enemies, and social intercourse be cruelly interrupted ; " and all this because " the resolution to put up or put down individuals swallowed up every consideration of right and of wrong."

The frenzy to which politicians wrought themselves up was sometimes grotesque in its manifestations. In Virginia it became known that John Tyler had written a letter to Clay approving his conduct in the last presidential election; whereupon the " Virginia Jackson Republican," a newspaper published at Richmond, broke out in these exclamations : " John Tyler identified with Henry Clay ! We are all amazement ! heartsick ! ! chopfallen ! ! dumb ! ! ! Mourn, Virginia, mourn ! ! for you, too, have your time-serving aspirants who press forward from round to round on the ladder of political promotion, under the disguises of republican orthodoxy, while they conceal in their bosoms the lurking dagger, with which, upon the mature conjuncture, to plunge the Goddess of Liberty to the heart." So John Tyler found himself obliged to explain, in a letter several columns long, that he might have approved of Clay's vote for Adams without supporting the Adams administration.

General Floyd, a member of Congress from Virginia, in a speech to his constituents, spoke of " times like these, when great political revolutions are in progress," and told his hearers that they were " now engaged in a great war, — a war of patronage and power against patriotism and the people." He fiercely denounced the " coalition " which had put Mr. Adams in power, and now made " the upper part of Virginia the great theatre of its intrigues;" but at the same time he informed

his friends that "the combinations for the elevation of General Jackson were nearly complete."
Martin Van Buren, who in the last presidential
election had been the great leader of the Crawford forces in New York, but now, discerning in
General Jackson the coming man, was traveling
through the Southern States in the interest of this
candidate, wrote mysteriously to some gentlemen
at Raleigh, who had invited him to a public dinner: "The spirit of encroachment has assumed a
new and far more seductive aspect, and can only
be resisted by the exercise of uncommon virtues."

Thus the leaders of the Jackson movement
worked busily to excite the popular mind with
spectral visions of unprecedented corruption prevailing, and of terrible dangers hanging over the
country ; and their newspapers, led by a central
organ which they had established at Washington,
the " Telegraph," edited by Duff Green, day after
day hurled the most reckless charges of profligacy
and abuse of power at the administration. They
also brought the organization of local committees
as electioneering machinery to a perfection never
known until then, and these committees were kept
constantly active in feeding the agitation. Repeating, by the press and in speech, without cessation,
the cry of bargain and corruption, and usurpation
of power; never withdrawing a charge, even if ever
so conclusively refuted, but answering only with
new accusations equally terrific, — they gradually
succeeded in making a great many well-meaning

people believe that the administration of John Quincy Adams, one of the purest and most conscientious this Republic has ever had, was really a sink of iniquity, and an abomination in the sight of all just men ; and that, if such a dreadful event as the reëlection of Adams should happen, it would inevitably be the end of liberty and republican institutions in America. Such a calamity could be prevented only by the election of the " old hero," who, having once been " cheated out of the presidency by bargain and corruption," was now "justly entitled to the office."

On the other hand, the friends of the administration were not entirely idle. The President did not, indeed, give them any encouragement in the way of opening places for them. While being constantly accused of employing the power and patronage of the government to corrupt public opinion, and to dragoon the people into " acquiescence," John Quincy Adams kept the even tenor of his way. The public service was full of his enemies, but he did not remove one of them. Even when well persuaded that McLean, the Postmaster-General, had been intriguing against him and using the patronage of his department in the interest of the opposition, and Clay with other members of the Cabinet urged McLean's dismissal, the President refused, because he thought the Post Office Department was on the whole well conducted. That he did not exclude his friends from place, was perhaps all that could be truthfully said. The administration had, however, some well - written newspapers and able speakers on its side. They vigorously denounced the recklessness of the attacks made upon the government, and spoke of General Jackson as an illiterate " military chieftain." But that phrase was a two-edged weapon ; for, while thinking men were moved to the reflection that military chieftains were not the safest chiefs of republics, the masses would see in the military chieftain only the " old hero " who had right gallantly " whipped the Britishers at New Orleans." The Jackson movement thus remained greatly superior in aggressive force and in unscrupulousness of denunciation.

On one occasion, however, this was carried to a very dangerous length by Jackson himself, and Clay apparently scored a great advantage. It is a strange story. In May, 1827, there appeared in a North Carolina newspaper a letter from Carter Beverly of Virginia, concerning a visit made by him to General Jackson at the Hermitage. The General had then said, before a large company, as the letter stated, that, before the election of Mr. Adams, " Mr. Clay's friends made a proposition to Jackson's friends that, if they would promise on his behalf not to put Mr. Adams in the seat of Secretary of State, Mr. Clay and his friends would in one hour make Jackson the President," but that General Jackson had indignantly repelled the proposition. Beverly's letter created much excitement. His veracity being challenged, he fell back upon **General Jackson, and** the General wrote **a** long reply, telling the story somewhat differently. According to his account, " a respectable member **of Congress** " **had told** him that, **as** he had **been informed** by Mr. Clay's friends, **Mr. Adams's** friends had held out the secretaryship **of** state **to Mr. Clay as a** price **for his** influence, saying that, **if General Jackson were** elected President, Adams would **be** continued **as Secretary of State,** that then " there would **be no room for** Kentucky," and that, if General **Jackson** would promise **not to continue Mr. Adams as** Secretary of State, they would **put** an **end to the** presidential contest in one hour. Then **he, General Jackson,** had contemptuously **repelled this** " bargain and corruption."

When this **letter of General Jackson** appeared in the newspapers, Clay thought **he had at** last what he **had long** been looking for, — a responsible **sponsor for the wretched gossip.** He forthwith, in **an** address **to the** public, made **an** unqualified and indignant denial of General Jackson's statements, **and called for** Jackson's **proof.** In **a very** spirited **speech** delivered at a dinner **given him by his old** constituents at Lexington, he **once more went** over **the** whole **dreary story,** and **in the most** pointed language he defied General Jackson **to** produce his " respectable member of Congress," or, in default thereof, to stand **before the** American people as **a** wilful defamer. The General could not evade this, **and named James Buchanan of Pennsylvania, as** his authority.　Now Buchanan had to rise and explain.　Accordingly, in a public letter, he denied having spoken to General Jackson on behalf of Mr. Clay or his friends ; he had said nothing that General Jackson could have so understood ; had he seen reason for suspecting that the General had so understood him at the time, he would have set himself right immediately.　He even suggested that the whole story of the attempted bargain might have been an afterthought on the part of the General.　Thus Jackson's only witness utterly failed him.　Not only that, but Buchanan's letter, together with the correspondence which followed, left ample room for the suspicion that, if bargaining was thought of and attempted, it was rather in the Jackson camp than among Clay's friends.

Clay now felt as if he had the slander under his heel.　To make its annihilation quite complete, he called all his friends upon the witness stand.　If their votes in Congress had been transferred to Mr. Adams by a corrupt bargain, many persons must have known of it.　One after another they came forward in public letters, declaring that, while the election was pending, they had never heard of any attempt at bargaining to control their votes in favor of Mr. Adams, and that, had the attempt been made, they would have refused to be controlled.　All these things were elaborately summed up and set forth in another address to the people published by Clay in December.

The case appeared perfect.　Clay and his friends

were jubilant. Letters of congratulation came pouring in upon him. Webster was lavish in his praise of Clay's dinner speech at Lexington, and thought General Jackson would never recover from the blow he had received. Was it possible that, in the face of this overwhelming evidence, General Jackson should refuse to retract his charges, or that anybody in the United States should still believe them to be true, and have the hardihood to repeat them? It was. General Jackson did not retract. His whole moral sense was subjugated by the dogged belief that a man who seriously disagreed with him must necessarily be a very bad man, capable of any villainy, and must be put down. He attempted no reply to Buchanan's letter and Clay's addresses, but, as we shall see, seventeen years later, at a most critical period in Clay's public life, when Carter Beverly, in a regretful letter to Clay, had retracted all aspersions upon him, Jackson repeated the slander and reaffirmed his belief in it. Neither did General Jackson's friends remain silent; on the contrary, they lustily proclaimed that Buchanan's letter had proved Jackson's charge, and that now there could be no further doubt about it. Among the masses of the people, too, who did not read long explanations and sift evidence, especially in Pennsylvania and in the West and South, the bargain and corruption cry remained as powerful as ever. It became with them a sort of religious belief that, in the year 1824, General Jackson, a guileless soldier, the hero of New Orleans, and the savior of his country, had been cheated out of his rights by two rascally politicians, Clay and Adams, who had corruptly usurped the highest offices of the government, and plotted to destroy the liberties of the American people.

The twentieth Congress, which had been elected while all this was going on, and which assembled in December, 1827, had a majority hostile to the administration in both branches, — a thing which, as Adams dolefully remarked, had never occurred during the existence of the government. Moreover, that opposition was determined, if it could, not only to harass the administration, but utterly to destroy it in the opinion of the country. The only important measure of general legislation passed at this session was the famous tariff of 1828, called the "tariff of abominations," on account of its peculiarly incongruous and monstrous provisions. Members of Congress from New England, where, since 1824, much capital had been turned into manufacturing industry, from the Middle States, and from the West, no matter whether Republicans or Federalists, Jackson men or Adams men, vied with one another in raising protective duties, by a wild log-rolling process, on the different articles in which their constituents were respectively interested. It created great dissatisfaction in the planting states, and more will be said of it when we reach the nullification movement.

The time not occupied by the tariff debate was

largely employed in defaming the administration. In the House of Representatives, the struggle between the Jackson men and the adherents of the administration grew almost ludicrously passionate. The opposition were agreed as to the general charge that the administration was most damnable, but they were somewhat embarrassed as to the specifications. One drag - net investigation after another was ordered to help them out. These inquiries brought forth nothing of consequence, but that circumstance served only as a reason for repeating the charges all the louder. The noise of the conflict was prodigious. It increased in volume, and the mutual criminations and recriminations grew in rancor and unscrupulousness as the presidential canvass proceeded after the adjournment of Congress.

Until then the friends of Adams and Clay had mostly contented themselves with the defense of the administration from the accusations which were hurled at it with bewildering violence and profusion. But gradually they, too, warmed up to their work, and it may be said that the campaign of 1828 became one of the most furious and disgusting which the American people has ever witnessed. The passions were excited to fever heat, and all the flood-gates of scurrility opened. The detractors of John Quincy Adams not only assailed his public acts, but they traduced this most scrupulously correct of men as the procurer to the Emperor of Russia of a beautiful American girl.

With frantic energy the speakers and newspapers of the Jackson party rang the changes upon the "bargain and corruption" charge, and Clay, although not himself a candidate, was glibly reviled as a professional gambler, a swindling bankrupt, an abandoned profligate, and an accomplice of Aaron Burr. On the other hand, not only the vulnerable points of Jackson's public career were denounced, but also his private character, and even the good name of his wife, were ruthlessly dragged in the dust. Such was the vile war of detraction which raged till the closing of the polls.

Some of Mr. Adams's friends, among them Webster, were hopeful to the last. But Adams himself, and with him the cooler heads on his side, did not delude themselves with flattering expectations. When the votes were counted, it turned out that Adams had carried all New England, with the exception of one electoral vote in Maine; also New Jersey, Delaware, four ninths of the vote of New York, and six of the eleven Maryland votes. South of the Potomac, and west of the Alleghanies, Jackson had swept everything before him. In Pennsylvania he had a popular majority of fifty thousand. The electoral vote for Jackson was one hundred and seventy-eight, that for Adams eighty-three. All the Clay states of 1824 had gone to Jackson. Calhoun was elected Vice-President.

The overwhelming defeat of John Quincy Adams has by some been attributed to the stubborn consistency with which he refused to build up a party

for himself by removing his enemies, and distributing the offices of the government among his political friends. This is a mistake. The civil service
reformer of our days would say that President
Adams did not act wisely, nor according to correct
principles, in permitting public servants to take
part in the warfare of political parties with as little
restraint as if they had been private citizens; for
whenever public officers do so, their official power
and opportunities are almost always taken advantage of for the benefit of the party, endangering
the freedom of elections as well as the integrity of
the service. But this is a conclusion formed in
our time, when the abuses growing out of a partisan service have fully developed themselves and
demand a remedy, which was not then the case.
Adams simply followed the traditions of the first
administrations. Had he silenced his enemies together with his friends in office, it would have
benefited him in the canvass very little. Neither
could the use of patronage as a weapon in the
struggle have saved him, had he been capable of
resorting to it. Patronage so used is always demoralizing, but it can have decisive effect only in
quiet times, while the popular mind is languid and
indifferent. When there are strong currents of
popular feeling and the passions are aroused, a
shrewd management of patronage, although it may
indeed control the nomination of candidates by
packing conventions, will not decide elections. In
1828 there were such elementary forces to encoun-

ter. Not only had the Jackson party the more efficient organization and the shrewder managers, but they were favored by a peculiar development in the condition of the popular mind.

In the early times of the Republic the masses of the American people were, owing to their circumstances, uneducated and ignorant, and, owing to traditional habit, they had a reverential respect for superiority of talent and breeding, and yielded readily to its leadership. Their growing prosperity, the material successes achieved by them in the development of the country, strengthened their confidence in themselves; and the result of this widening self-consciousness was the triumph of the democratic theory of government in the election of Jefferson. Still the old habit of readily accepting the leadership of superior intelligence and education remained sufficiently strong to permit the succession of several presidents taken from the ranks of professional statesmen. But there always comes a time in the life of a democracy — and it is a critical period — when the masses grow impatient of all pretensions or admissions of superiority; when a vague distrust of professional statesmanship, of trained skill in the conduct of the government, seizes upon them, and makes them easily believe that those who possess such trained skill will, if constantly intrusted with the management of public affairs, take some sort of advantage of those less trained; that, after all, the business of governing is no more difficult than other business;

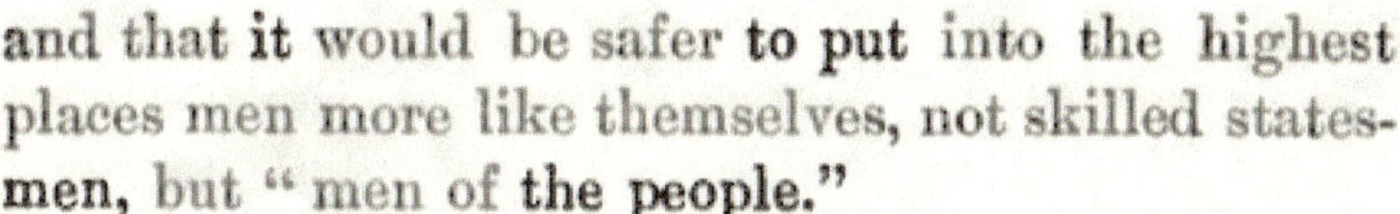

and that it would be safer to put into the highest places men more like themselves, not skilled statesmen, but " men of the people."

By the time the revolutionary generation of presidents had run out, — that is to say, with the close of Monroe's second administration, — large numbers of voters in the United States had reached that state of mind. Its development was wonderfully favored by the " bargain and corruption " cry, which, after the election of Adams in 1825, represented " the people's candidate " as cheated out of his right to the presidency by a conspiracy of selfish and tricky professional politicians. As this cry was kept resounding all over the country, accompanied with stories of other dreadful encroachments and intrigues, the masses were impressed with the feeling not only that a great wrong had been done, but that some darkly lurking danger was threatening their own rights and liberties, and that nothing but the election of a man of the people, such as " the old hero," could surely save the Republic. This was the real strength of the Jackson movement. It is a significant fact that it was weakest where there were the most schools, and that it gathered its greatest momentum where the people were least accustomed to reading and study, and therefore most apt to be swayed by unreasoning impressions.

No patronage, no machine work, could have stemmed this tide. No man endowed with all the charms of personal popularity could have turned it back. But of all men John Quincy Adams was the least fitted for such a task. We can learn from him how to act upon lofty principles, and also how to make their enforcement thoroughly disagreeable. He possessed in the highest degree that uprightness which leans backward. He had a horror of demagogy, and, lest he should render himself guilty of anything akin to it, he would but rarely condescend to those innocent amenities by which the good-will of others may be conciliated. His virtue was freezing cold of touch, and forbidding in its looks. Not only he did not court, but he repelled popularity. When convinced of being right in an opinion, he would make its expression as uncompromising and aggressive as if he desired rather to irritate than to persuade. His friends esteemed, and many of them admired him, but their devotion and zeal were measured by a cold sense of duty. To the eye of the people he seemed so distant that they were all the more willing to believe ill of him. With such a standard-bearer such a contest was lost as soon as it was begun.

Clay tried to bear the defeat with composure. " The inauspicious issue of the election," he wrote to Niles, " has shocked me less than I feared it would. My health and my spirits, too, have been better since the event was known than they were many weeks before." The hardest blow was that even his beloved Kentucky had refused to follow his leadership, and had joined the triumphal procession of the military chieftain.

On the day before General Jackson's inauguration Clay put his resignation into the hands of Mr. Adams, and thus ended his career as Secretary of State. It may, on the whole, be called a very creditable one, although its failures were more conspicuous than its successes. His greatest affair, that of the Panama Congress, had entirely miscarried. This, however, was not the fault of his management. He had desired to confide the mission to the best diplomatic mind in America, Albert Gallatin, but Gallatin, after some consideration, declined. John Sergeant of Pennsylvania, of whom we have already heard as an anti-slavery man in the Missouri struggle, and Richard C. Anderson of Kentucky, were then selected. Owing to the long delays in Congress, the envoys did not start on their mission until early in the summer of 1826. Anderson died on the way. In his place Joel R. Poinsett, American Minister in Mexico, was instructed to attend the Congress. When Sergeant arrived at Panama, the Congress had adjourned with a resolution to meet again at Tacubaya, in Mexico. But by the time that meeting was to be held, the attention of our southern sister republics was already fully engaged by internal discords and conflicts The meeting, therefore, never took place, and Sergeant returned without ever having seen the Congress. To Clay this was a deep disappointment. His zeal in behalf of the Spanish American republics had been generous and ardent. He had sincerely believed that national

independence and the practice of free institutions
would lift those populations out of their ignorance,
superstition, and sloth, **and** develop in them the
moral qualities of true freemen. He had battled
for their cause, **and** clung **to** his hopes even against
the light **of** better information. He had infused
some of his enthusiasm into Mr. Adams himself, although the cooler judgment of the President, even
in his warmest recommendations to Congress, always kept the contingency of failure in view. Clay
had **seen** his gorgeous conception of a grand broth-
erhood **of** free peoples on American soil almost
realized, as he thought, **by** the convocation of the
Panama Council. **Then the** pleasing picture **van**-
ished. He was obliged to admit to himself that in
the conversation **of** 1821, concerning the southern
republics, Adams, after **all, had been** right ; that
free government cannot be established by mere
revolutionary decrees; that written constitutions,
in order to last, must embody the ways of thinking
and the character of the people ; that the people of
the thirteen North American colonies (to whom revolution and national independence meant not the
creation of freedom, but the maintenance of liber-
ties already possessed, enjoyed, and practiced, the
defense of principles which had **been to** them like
mother's milk) were an essentially different people
from the Spanish Americans, who had grown up
under despotic **rule, to whom** liberty was a new
thing they did not know what to do with, and who
lived mostly in a tropical climate where the suste-

nance of animal man requires but little ingenuity
and exertion, and where all the influences of nature
favor the development of indolence and of the passions rather than the government of thrift, reason,
and law.

The disappointment was indeed painful, and he
could not refrain from expressing his feelings on a
notable occasion. In 1827 Bolivar wrote him a
formal letter complimenting him " upon his brilliant talents and ardent love of liberty," adding :
" All America, Colombia, and myself owe your
Excellency our purest gratitude for the incomparable services you have rendered to us by sustaining
our cause with a sublime enthusiasm." Clay answered, nearly a year later, in chilling phrase, that
the interest of the people of the United States in
the struggles of South America had been inspired
by the hope that " along with its independence would
be established free institutions, insuring all the
blessings of civil liberty," an object to the accomplishment of which the people of the United States
were still anxiously looking. But, lest Bolivar
might fail in making a practical application of these
words, Clay added : " I should be unworthy of
the consideration with which your Excellency honors me, if I did not on this occasion state that
ambitious designs have been attributed by your
enemies to your Excellency, which have created in
my mind great solicitude. They have cited late
events in Colombia as proofs of these designs.
But I cannot allow myself to believe that your Ex-

cellency will abandon the bright and glorious path which lies plainly before you, for the bloody road on which the vulgar crowd of tyrants and military despots have so often trodden. I will not doubt that your Excellency will in due time render a satisfactory explanation to Colombia and to the world of the parts of your public conduct which have excited any distrust," and so on. The lecture thus administered by the American statesman to the South American dictator was the voice of sadly disappointed expectations. Clay was probably aware that Bolivar's ambitions were by no means the greatest difficulty threatening the Spanish American republics.

Another disappointment he suffered in the failure of an effort to remedy what he considered the great defect in the Spanish treaty of 1819. In March, 1827, he instructed Poinsett, the American Minister to Mexico, to propose the purchase of Texas. But the attempt came to nothing.

In his commercial diplomacy Clay followed the ideas of reciprocity generally accepted at the time, which not only awarded favor for favor, but also set restriction against restriction. This practice of fighting restriction with equal or greater restriction was apt to work well enough when the opposite party was the one less able to endure the restriction, and therefore obliged by its necessities to give up the fight quickly. But when the restrictions were long maintained, the effect was simply that each party punished its own commerce in seeking to retaliate upon the **other**. **This** practice played a great part in the transactions taking place in and between Great Britain and the United States concerning **the** colonial trade. The traditional policy of Great Britain was **to** keep the trade with the colonies as exclusively as possible in the hands **of** the mother country. The United States, **of course,** desired to have the greatest possible freedom of trade with the British colonies, especially those in America, including the West India islands. Various attempts were made in that direction, but without success. The commercial conventions of 1815 and 1818 between the United States and Great Britain had concluded nothing in this respect, leaving the matter to **be** regulated by legislation on either side. The result was a confusion of privileges, conditions, and **re-**strictions most perplexing and troublesome. The desirability of a clear mutual understanding being keenly felt, negotiations were resumed. In July, 1825, Parliament passed an act offering large privileges with regard to the colonial trade on condition of complete reciprocity, the acceptance of the conditional offer to be notified to the British government within one year. Congress neglected **to** take action on the offer. Meanwhile Gallatin, upon whom the government was apt to fall back for difficult diplomatic service, had been appointed Minister to England in the place of Rufus King, whose health had failed. When Gallatin arrived in London he was **met by an Order in**

Council issued on July 27, 1826, prohibiting all commercial intercourse between the United States and the British West Indies. At the same time Canning, the Foreign Secretary, who was fond of treating the United States cavalierly, informed him that all further negotiation upon this subject was declined. A lively exchange of notes followed, in which Gallatin and Clay not only had the best of the argument, but excelled by pointed retorts given in excellent temper. Another session of Congress having passed without action, the President, in accordance with an act passed in 1823, issued a proclamation on March 17, 1827, declaring, on the part of the United States, the prohibition of all trade and intercourse with the ports from which the commerce of the United States was excluded. Soon afterwards Canning died. Lord Goderich rose to the post of Prime Minister, and Gallatin succeeded in making a treaty keeping the convention of 1815 indefinitely in force subject to one year's notice. Thus, while the controversy had not been brought to the desired conclusion, at least nothing was lost; the dignity of the United States was maintained; more dangerous complications were avoided; and the way was prepared for more satisfactory arrangements in the future. But it was, in popular opinion, a failure after all, and, the temporary cutting off of the West India trade being severely felt, naturally told against the administration. It was with regard to this transaction that, as we shall see, Martin Van Buren, when

General Jackson's Secretary of State, gave those famous instructions which cost him the consent of the Senate to his nomination as Minister to England.

On the whole, there was evidence of a liberal, progressive spirit in Clay's diplomatic transactions; and it gave him much pleasure to say that, during the period when he was Secretary of State, " more treaties between the United States and foreign nations had been actually signed than had been during the thirty-six years of the existence of the present Constitution." He concluded treaties of amity, commerce, and navigation with Central America, Prussia, Denmark, the Hanseatic Republics, Sweden and Norway, and Brazil, and a boundary treaty with Mexico. With Great Britain he was least successful in bringing matters in controversy to a definite and quite satisfactory conclusion. So a treaty concerning the disputed territory on the northwest coast, the Columbia country, provided only for an extension of the joint occupation agreed upon in the treaty of 1818, thus merely adjourning a difficulty, while by another treaty the northeastern boundary question was referred to a friendly sovereign or state, to be agreed upon, for arbitration.

The one disputed question between Great Britain and the United States which he did bring to a conclusion was one left behind by the treaty of Ghent, — the indemnity for slaves carried off by the British forces in the war of 1812. After seven

years of fruitless negotiation, the matter had been referred to the Emperor Alexander of Russia. He decided in favor of the claim. But the British government raised new objections, and a second negotiation followed. Great Britain finally agreed to pay a lump sum for the value of the slaves, and payment was made in 1827. Thus the administration of John Quincy Adams achieved, diplomatically, **one of** its most decided successes in a matter in which its sympathies were least enlisted.

But a kindred question turned up in another form still more unsympathetic. **On** May 10, 1828, the House of Representatives **passed a** resolution asking the President to open negotiations with the British government concerning the surrender of slaves taking refuge in Canada. Clay accordingly instructed Gallatin to propose to the British government **a** stipulation, first, **" for** the mutual surrender of deserters from the military and naval service and from the merchant service of the two countries ; " and, second, " for a mutual surrender of all persons held to service or labor under the **laws of one** party who escape into the territories of the other." The first proposition was evidently to serve only as a prop to the second; for, as the instruction argued, while Great Britain had little interest **in** the mutual surrender of fugitive slaves, she had much **interest in** the mutual surrender of military or naval deserters. The British government, however, as was **to** be expected, replied promptly that it " was utterly impossible for them to agree to a stipulation for the surrender of fugitive slaves."

The negotiation presents a melancholy spectacle: a republic offering to surrender deserters from the army or navy of a monarchical power, if that power would agree to surrender slaves escaped from their owners in that republic! And this happened under the administration of John Quincy Adams; the instructions were signed by Henry Clay, and the proposition was laid before the British government by Albert Gallatin! It is true that in Clay's despatches on this subject we find nothing of his accustomed strength of statement and fervor of reasoning. Neither did there appear anything like zeal in Gallatin's presentation of the matter. It was a mere perfunctory "going through the motions," as if in expectation of a not unwelcome failure. But even as such, it is a sorry page of history which we should gladly miss. Slavery was a hard taskmaster to the government of this proud American Republic.

It would not be just to assume that a man who had grown up in the anti-slavery school of the revolutionary period, and whose first effort on the political field was made in behalf of emancipation, would lend himself without reluctance to such transactions, unless his conscience had become completely debauched or his opinions thoroughly changed. Clay had remained essentially different, in his ways of thinking and feeling, from the ordinary pro-slavery man. That nervous, sleepless, instinctive watchfulness for the safety of the peculiar institution, which characterized the orthodox slave-holder, was entirely foreign to him.   He had to be told what the interests of slavery demanded, in order to **see and feel its** needs.   The original anti-slavery spirit **would** again and again inspire his impulses and break out in his utterances.   We remember how he praised the Spanish American republics for having abolished slavery.   In his great " American System " speech he had argued for the superior claims of free labor **as** against those **of** " servile labor."   He was scarcely seated **in** the office of Secretary of State, when, in April, 1825, as Mr. Adams recorded, he expressed the opinion that " the independence of Hayti must shortly be recognized," — an idea most horrible to the American slave-holder.   When he eagerly accepted the invitation to the Panama Congress, the association with new states that had liberated their slaves, and counted negroes and mulattoes among their generals and legislators, had nothing alarming to him.   Little more than a year before he instructed Gallatin to ask of Great Britain the sur**render of** fugitive **slaves from Canada, he had** made one of the most striking demonstrations of his genuine feeling at a meeting of the African Colonization Society, which is worthy of special attention.

That society had been organized **in 1816,** with the object of transporting free negroes to Africa and **of** colonizing them there.   It was in **the** main com-

posed of **two** elements, — pro-slavery **men, even** of
the extreme type of John Randolph, **who** favored
the removal of free negroes from **this** country, because they considered them **a** dangerous element, **a**
" pest," in slave - holding communities ; **and phi-
lanthropists, some of** whom sincerely believed that
the exportation of **colored** people on a grand scale
was possible, **and would** ultimately result **in the**
extinguishment **of slavery, while others** contented
themselves with a vague **impression that some good**
might **be** done **by it, and** used **it as a** convenient
excuse for not doing anything more efficacious.

Clay was one of the sincere believers in **the colonization** scheme **as** practicable **on a grand** scale,
and **as an aid to** gradual emancipation. In his
speech before the Colonization Society **in January,**
1827, he **tried to** prove — and **he** had armed himself for the **task** with **an arsenal** of figures — that
it was **" not beyond the** ability **of** the country " **to**
export and **colonize a** sufficient number of negroes
to effect a gradual reduction of the colored population in this country, **and thus by degrees to** eradicate slavery, or at least to neutralize **its** dangerous
effects. **We know now that** these sanguine calcu-
lations **were** entirely delusive ; **neither did his** prediction **come true, that** the **free negro " pests,"**
when colonized **in** Africa, **would prove** the most
effective missionaries of civilization **on that** conti-
nent. But he believed **in all this ; to his mind the**
colonization scheme was an anti-slavery agency, **and**
it was characteristic of his feelings when **he ex-**
claimed : —

"If I could be instrumental in eradicating this deepest stain upon the character of our country, and removing all cause of reproach on account of it by foreign nations; if I could only be instrumental in ridding of this foul blot that revered state which gave me birth, or that not less beloved state which kindly adopted me as her son, I would not exchange the proud satisfaction which I should enjoy for the honor of all the triumphs ever decreed to the most successful conqueror."

We might almost imagine we heard the voice of an apostle of " abolition " in his reply to the charge that the Colonization Society was " doing mischief by the agitation of this question." These were his words, spoken in his most solemn tone : —

" What would they who thus reproach us have done? If they would repress all tendency toward liberty and ultimate emancipation, they must do more than put down the benevolent efforts of this society. They must go back to the era of *our* liberty and independence, and muzzle the cannon which thunder its annual joyous return. They must revive the slave - trade with all its train of atrocities. They must suppress the workings of British philanthropy, seeking to meliorate the condition of the unfortunate West Indian slaves. They must arrest the career of South American deliverance from thraldom. They must blow out the moral lights around us, and extinguish that greatest torch of all, which America presents to a benighted world, pointing the way to their rights, their liberties, and their happiness. And when they have achieved all these purposes, the work will yet be incomplete. They must penetrate the human soul, and eradicate the light of reason and the love of liberty

Then, and not till then, when universal darkness and despair prevail, can you perpetuate slavery, and repress all sympathies, and all human and benevolent efforts among freemen, in behalf of the unhappy portion of our race doomed to bondage."

This, no doubt, was Henry Clay the man, speaking the language of his heart, and he spoke it, too, at a time when he must have known that the slaveholding interest was growing very sensitive, and that its distrust and disfavor might become fatal to all his ambitions as a candidate for the presidency. Knowing this, he said things which might have come from the most uncompromising and defiant enemy of slavery. Yet this was the same man who had helped to strengthen the law for the recovery of fugitive slaves; who had opposed the exclusion of slavery from new states; who at the beginning of the Adams administration had given the British government to understand that further negotiations for common action for the suppression of the slave-trade would be useless, as the Senate would not confirm such treaties; who, after having made that anti-slavery speech, would lend himself to a negotiation with a foreign government for the mutual surrender of fugitive slaves and military and naval deserters; who would, at a later period, vehemently denounce the abolitionists, again oppose the exclusion of slavery from new territories, again strengthen the fugitive-slave law, while in the intervals repeating his denunciations of slavery, and again declaring himself in favor of gradual emancipation.

This contrast between expression of feeling on the one side, and action on the other, was incomprehensible to the abolitionists, who, after **the** Missouri struggle, began to make themselves felt **by** agitating, with constantly increasing **zeal,** the duty of instantly overthrowing slavery on moral grounds. It is not easily understood by our generation, who **look back** upon slavery as a moral abnormity in this age, and as the easily discernible cause of great conflicts and calamities, which it would have been best to attack and extinguish, **the** earlier the better. We can only with difficulty imagine the thoughts and emotions of men of that period, who, while at heart recognizing slavery **as** a wrong and a curse, yet had **some** of that feeling expressed by Patrick Henry, in his remarkable letter of 1773, — who thought **that** the abolition of the great evil, while sure finally to come, would still be impossible for **a** considerable period, and that in the mean time, while slavery legally existed, it must be protected in its rights and interests against outside interference, and especially against all commotions which might disturb the peace of the community. We can now scarcely appreciate the dread of **the** consequences of sudden emancipation, the constitutional scruples, the nervous anxiety about the threatened Union, and the vague belief in the efficacy of compromises and palliatives, which animated statesmen of Clay's way of thinking and feeling. It is characteristic of that period, that even **a** man of John **Quincy** Adams's stamp, who was not under any pro-slavery influence at home, and all whose instincts and impulses were against slavery, permitted that negotiation with Great Britain about the surrender of fugitive slaves to go on under his presidential responsibility, without mentioning it by a single word in his journal as a matter of importance. Less surprising appears such conduct in Clay, who was constantly worked upon by the interests and anxieties of the slave-holding community in which he had his home, and who was a natural compromiser, because his very nature was a compromise.

His four years' service as Secretary of State formed on the whole an unhappy period in Clay's life. Although many of his state papers testify by their vigor and brilliancy to the zest with which they were worked out, — even the cool-headed Gallatin recognized that Clay had " vastly improved since 1814," — yet the office labor, with its constant confinement, grew irksome to him. Here was a lion in a cage. His health suffered seriously. He seemed to be in danger of paralysis, and several times he himself became so alarmed that he could only with difficulty be persuaded by President Adams to remain in office. It was believed by his friends, and it is very probable, that the war of vilification waged against him had something to do with his physical ailment. There is abundance of evidence to prove that he felt deeply the assaults upon his character. The mere fact that anybody will dare to represent him as capable of dishonor-

able practices is a stinging humiliation to a proud
man. There is refuge in contempt, but also the
necessity of despising any one is painful to a generous nature.

Moreover the feeling grew upon him that he had
after all made a great mistake in accepting the
secretaryship of state in the Adams administration. He became painfully aware that this acceptance had given color to the " bargain and corruption " charge. It kept him busy year after year,
in dreary iteration, at the humiliating task of proving that he was an honest man ; while, had he not
accepted, he might have remained in Congress, the
most formidable power in debate, leading a host
of enthusiastic friends, and defying his enemies to
meet him face to face. Thus for the secretaryship
of state he felt that he had given up his active
leadership on the field where he was strongest ;
and that secretaryship, far from being to him a
stepping-stone to the presidency, had become the
most serious stumbling-block in his way.

The most agreeable feature of Clay's official
life, aside from his uncommon popularity with the
diplomatic corps, consisted in his personal relations
with Mr. Adams. Their daily intercourse supplanted the prejudices, which formerly had prevailed between them, with a constantly growing
esteem and something like friendship. In 1828
Clay said of Adams, in a letter to Crawford : " I
had fears of Mr. Adams's temper and disposition,
but I must say that they have not been realized,

and I have found in him, since I have been associated with him in the executive government, as little to censure or condemn as I could have expected in any man." With chivalrous loyalty Clay stood by his chief, and Adams gave him his full confidence. Adams's Diary does not mention a single serious difference of opinion as having in any manner clouded his relationship with the Secretary during the four years of their official connection. On several occasions, when Clay's ill health seemed to make his resignation necessary, Adams with unusal warmth of feeling expressed the high value he put upon Clay's services, assuring him that it would be extremely difficult to fill his place, and earnestly trying to dissuade him from his purpose. Toward the close of his presidential term, Adams offered Clay a place on the bench of the Supreme Court, which Clay declined. John Quincy Adams probably never spoke with more fervor of any public man than he spoke of Clay shortly after the close of his administration, in answer to an address of a committee of citizens of New Jersey : —

" Upon him the foulest slanders have been showered. The department of state itself was a station which, by its bestowal, could confer neither profit nor honor upon him, but upon which he has shed unfading honor by the manner in which he has discharged its duties. Prejudice and passion have charged him with obtaining that office by bargain and corruption. Before you. my fellow-citizens, in the presence of our country and Heaven,

I pronounce that charge totally unfounded. As to my motives for tendering him the Department of State when I did, let the man who questions them come forward. Let him look around among the statesmen and legislators of the nation and of that day. Let him then select and name the man whom, by his preëminent talents, by his splendid services, by his ardent patriotism, by his all-embracing public spirit, by his fervid eloquence in behalf of the rights and liberties of mankind, by his long experience in the affairs of the Union, foreign and domestic, a President of the United States, intent only upon the honor and welfare of his country, ought to have preferred to Henry Clay."

These warm words did honor to the man who spoke them, but the " bargain and corruption " cry went on nevertheless.

John Quincy Adams, after his crushing defeat, took leave of the presidency with the feeling that " the sun of his public life had set in the deepest gloom." He thought of nothing but final retirement, not anticipating that the most glorious part of his career was still in store for him. Clay, too, spoke of retirement. But at the same time he asked Edward Everett, of Massachusetts, whether he thought that, at the next presidential election, in 1832, the Eastern States could be counted upon for him, Henry Clay; he would then feel sure of the Western. Here was the old ambition, ever dominant and restless, bound to drive him into new struggles, and to bring upon him new disappointments.

CHAPTER XII.

THE PARTY CHIEFS.

UNDER Monroe's presidency the old Federal party had indeed maintained a local organization here and there, and filled a few seats in Congress, but it had even then become extinct as a national organization. The Republicans were in virtually undisputed possession of the government. The "era of good feeling" abounded in personal bickerings, jealousies of cliques, conflicts of ambition, and also controversies on matters of public interest, but there was no gathering of forces in opposite camps on a great scale. In the presidential canvass of 1824 all the candidates were recognized as Republicans. It was the election of John Quincy Adams in the House of Representatives that brought about the first lasting schism in the Republican ranks. In its beginning this schism appeared to bear an essentially personal character. The friends of the defeated candidates, of Jackson and Crawford, with the following of Calhoun, banded together against the friends of Adams and Clay. Their original rallying cry was that Jackson had been wronged, and that the Adams-Clay administration must be broken down in any event, whatever policy it might follow. The division was simply between Jackson men on one side, and Adams and Clay men on the other.

The two prominent questions of the time, that of the tariff and that of internal improvements, were not then in issue between them. There were strenuous advocates of a high tariff and of internal improvements on both sides. Jackson himself had in his Coleman letter spoken the language of a protectionist, and he had voted for several internal improvement bills while he was in the Senate. In several states he had been voted for as a firm friend of those two policies. Even during the whole of Adams's administration, while a furious opposition was carried on against it, there continued to be much diversity of opinion among its assailants on these subjects. In fact the tariff of 1828, the " tariff of abominations," was passed by Congress, and the strict construction principles maintained by Madison and Monroe concerning internal improvements suffered one defeat after another, while both Houses were controlled by majorities hostile to Adams and Clay. The question of the National Bank was not touched in the campaign of 1824, nor while Adams was President; nor was there, at the time the opposition started, any other defined principle or public interest conspicuously at issue between him and his opponents; for the inaugural address, and the messages in which Adams took such advanced positions in the direction of paternal government, did not precede but followed, the break destined to become a lasting one.

But it is also true that, while the Jackson party taken as a whole was, at the beginning, in a chaotic state as to political principles and aims, a large and important Southern fraction of it gradually rallied upon something like a fixed programme. At a former period Southern men had been among the foremost advocates of a protective tariff and internal improvements. We have seen Calhoun almost contesting Clay's leadership as to those objects. The governmental power required, Southerners could at that time contemplate without terror. But a great change of feeling came over many of them. The struggle about the admission of Missouri had produced no open and lasting party divisions, but it had left in the Southern mind a lurking sense of danger. The slave-holding interest gradually came to understand that the whole drift of sentiment outside of the slave-holding communities was decidedly hostile to the peculiar institution; that a wall must be built around slavery for its protection; that state sovereignty and the strictest construction of the Constitution concerning the functions and powers of the general government were the bulwark of its safety; that any sort of interference with the home affairs of the Slave States, even in the way of internal improvement, would tend to undermine that bulwark; that the Slave States, owing to their system of labor, must remain purely agricultural communities; that

anything enhancing the price of those things which
the agriculturists had to buy would be injurious
to the planter, and that, therefore, a protective
tariff raising the prices of manufactured goods
must be rejected as hostile to the interests of **the**
South.

This was **a** tangible and consistent policy. The
spirit animating it early found an opportunity for
asserting itself by a partisan demonstration in the
extreme position taken by President Adams in his
first official utterances concerning the necessary
functions of the national government. These utterances, which gave the Jackson men a welcome
occasion **for** raising against Adams the cry of
Federalism, startled many old Republicans of the
Jeffersonian school. This was especially the case
in the South. The reason was not that the North
had been less attached than the South to the cause
of local self-government. **On** the contrary, home
rule in its democratic form was more perfectly developed and more heartily cherished in **New** England, with her town-meeting system, than in the
South, where not only a large part of the population, the negroes, were absolutely excluded from
all participation in self-government, but where **the**
aristocratic class of slave-holders enjoyed immense
advantages of political influence over the rest of
the whites. But **in** New England, and in **the**
North generally, local self-government was felt to
be perfectly compatible **with a** vigorous national
authority, while at the South there was constant

fear of encroachment, **and the** assertion **of the** home rule principle **was,** therefore, mainly directed against the national power. That **the** national government had a natural tendency hostile **to local** self-government **was** mainly a Southern idea.

The Southern interest, knowing what **it wanted,** compact, vigilant, **and** represented by able politicians, **was** naturally destined to **become the leading force** in that aggregation of political elements which, beginning in a **mere wild** opposition to **the** Adams administration, **hardened** into **a** political party. An extensive electioneering machinery, which was skillfully organized, **and** used **with great** effect in the four years' campaign, beginning with the election **of** John Quincy Adams **and** ending with Jackson's election in 1828, continued to form one of its distinguishing features.

The followers **of** Adams **and** Clay were, by the necessities **of** their situation, driven to organize on their side. **Having** been the regular administration party during Adams's presidency, **they became** the regular opposition **after** Jackson's inauguration. A **majority of** those who favored a liberal construction **of** the constitutional powers **of the** general government gathered on that **side,** interspersed, however, with not a few state-rights men. Among them **the** protective tariff and the **policy of** internal improvements **found most of** their advocates.

Each of these new parties claimed at **first to be** the genuine, orthodox Republican party, but, by way of distinction, **the Jackson men called them-** selves Democratic Republicans, and the followers of Clay and Adams National Republicans, — appellations which a few years later gave room to the shorter names of Democrats and Whigs.

These two new political organizations **are commonly** assumed to have been mere revivals of the old Federal and Republican parties. This they **were,** however, only in a limited sense. It certainly cannot be **said that the** Democrats were all old Republicans, and the Nationals all, or nearly **all, old** Federalists. John Quincy **Adams** himself **had** indeed been **a** Federalist; but **he had** joined the Republicans during Jefferson's presidency, when the conflict with England was approaching. **Clay** had been a Republican leader from the **start,** and **most** of his followers came from the same ranks. **On** the other hand many old Federalists, who hated Adams on account of what they called **his** desertion, joined the opposition to his administration, and then remained with the Democratic party, in which some of them rose to high places. **As to** the antecedents of their members, both new parties were, therefore, composed of mixed elements.

They did, indeed, represent **two** different political tendencies, somewhat corresponding with those which had divided their predecessors, — one favoring a more strict, the other **a more** latitudinarian, **construction of** constitutional powers. But this, too, must be taken with a qualification. The old Republican party, before Jefferson's election to the presidency, had been terribly excited **at the assumptions** of power by the Federalists, **such as the** alien and sedition **laws. But** when in possession of the government, they went fully as far **in that** direction as the Federalists had done. Their leaders **admitted that they** had exceeded the warrant **of** the Constitution in the purchase of Louisiana ; **and** their embargoes, and the **laws** and executive **measures** enforcing **them,** were, **as** encroachments upon **local** self-government and individual rights, hardly less objectionable in principle than the alien and sedition laws had been. But it must be admitted that these things were not done for the **purpose** of enlarging the power of the government, and **of** encroaching upon home rule **and** individual rights. It was therefore with a self-satisfied sense **of** consistency that they continued to preach, as **a** matter of doctrine, the **most careful limitation of the central power and the** largest scope **of** local self-government. **In** this respect the new Democratic party followed **in their footsteps.**

The **old** Federalists, on the other hand, **had** openly declared themselves **in favor of a** government strong enough to curb the unruly **democracy.** The National Republicans, or Whigs, **having in** great part themselves been Jeffersonian Republicans, mostly favored a liberal construction of constitutional powers, not with a **view to curbing** the unruly democracy, but to other objects, such **as** internal improvements, a protective tariff, **and a** national bank.

In practice, indeed, the lines thus more or less distinctly dividing the two new parties were not as strictly observed by the members of each as might have been inferred from the fierce fights occasionally raging between them. Strict constructionists, when in power, would sometimes yield to the temptation of stretching the Constitution freely; while latitudinarians in opposition would, when convenient to themselves, insist upon the narrowest interpretation of the fundamental law. On the whole, however, the new Democratic party, by its advocacy of the largest local self-government and a strict limitation of the central authority, secured to itself the prestige of the apostolic succession to Jefferson. It placed itself before the people as the true representative of the genuine old theory of democratic government, as the popular party, and as the legitimate possessor of power in the nation. This position it maintained until thirty years later, when its entanglement with slavery caused its downfall.

The National Republican, or Whig party, was led by men who recognized the elevated character of John Quincy Adams's administration, and who sustained it against partisan assaults and popular clamor. They dreaded the rule of an ignorant and violent military chieftain such as Jackson was thought to be. They took a lively interest in the industrial developments of the times, and thought that the government, or rather themselves in possession of the government, could give those developments more intelligent impulse, aid, **and** direction than the people would do if let alone. **They** felt themselves called upon to take **care** of **the** people in a larger sense, in a greater variety of ways, than did statesmen of the Democratic creed. Thus, **while** the Democratic party found its principal constituency among the agricultural population, **including the** planters **in** the Southern States, with all that depended upon them, **and** among the poorer and more ignorant people of the cities, the National Republicans, or Whigs, recruited themselves — **of** course **not** exclusively, but to a conspicuous extent — among the mercantile and industrial classes, and generally among the more educated and stirring in other walks **of** life. The Democratic party successfully asserting itself as the legitimate administrator **of the** national power, the Nationals found themselves consigned, **for the larger** part of the time, **to** the rôle of **a critical** opposition, always striving **to** get into power, but succeeding only occasionally **as a** temporary **corrective.** Whenever **any members of the** majority **party** were driven into opposition **by** its fierce discipline, they found **a ready** welcome among **the** Nationals, who could offer **them** brilliant **company in** an uncommon array of men of talent. **The Whig** party was thus admirably fitted for the business **of** criticism, and that criticism was directed not only against the enemy, **but not seldom** against itself, at the expense **of** harmonious coöperation. Its victories were **mostly fruitless.** In point of drill and discipline it was greatly the inferior of its antagonist; nor could it under ordinary circumstances make up for that deficiency by superior enthusiasm. It had a tendency in the direction of selectness, which gave it a distinguished character, challenging the admiration of others as well as exciting its own, but also calculated to limit its popularity.

There were, then, two political parties again, and at the same time two party leaders whose equals — it may be said without exaggeration — the American people had never seen before, and have never seen since, excepting Abraham Lincoln, who, however, was something more than a party leader. They were, indeed, greatly inferior to Hamilton in creative statesmanship, and to Jefferson in the faculty of disseminating ideas, and of organizing, stimulating, and guiding an agitation from the closet. But they were much stronger than either in the power of inspiring great masses of followers with enthusiastic personal devotion, of inflaming them for an idea or a public measure, of marshaling them for a conflict, of leading them to victory, or rallying them after defeat. But while each of them possessed the magic of leadership in the highest degree, it would be difficult to find two men more different in almost all other respects.

Andrew Jackson, when he became President, was a man of sixty-two. A life of much exposure, hardship, and excitement, and also ill-health, had made him appear older than he was. His great military achievement lay fifteen years back in the past, and made him the " old hero." He was very ignorant. In his youth he had mastered scarcely the rudiments of education, and he did not possess that acquisitive intellectuality which impels men, with or without preparation, to search for knowledge and to store it up. While he had keen intuitions, he never thoroughly understood the merits of any question of politics or economics. But his was in the highest degree the instinct of a superior will, the genius of command. If he had been on board a vessel in extreme danger, he would have thundered out his orders without knowing anything of seamanship, and been indignantly surprised if captain and crew had not obeyed him. At a fire, his voice would have made by-standers as well as firemen promptly do his will. In war, he was of course made a general, and without any knowledge of military science he went out to meet the enemy, made raw militia fight like veterans, and won the most brilliant victory in the war of 1812. He was not only brave himself; his mere presence infused bravery into others.

To his military heroship he owed that popularity which lifted him into the presidential chair, and he carried the spirit of the warrior into the business of the government. His party was to him his army; those who opposed him, the enemy. He knew not how to argue, but how to command; not how to deliberate, but how to act. He had that impulsive energy which always creates dramatic conflicts, and the power of passion he put into them made all his conflicts look tremendous. When he had been defeated in 1825 by the influence of Clay, he made it appear as if he were battling against all the powers of corruption which were threatening the life of the Republic. We shall see him fight Nicholas Biddle, of the United States Bank, as if he had to defend the American people against the combined money power of the world seeking to enslave them. In rising up against nullification, and in threatening France with war to make her pay a debt, we shall see him saving the Union from deadly peril, and humiliating to the dust the insolence of the old world. Thus he appeared like an invincible Hercules constantly meeting terrible monsters dangerous to the American people, and slaying them all with his mighty club.

This fierce energy was his nature. It had a wonderful fascination for the popular fancy, which is fond of strong and bold acts. He became the idol of a large portion of the people to a degree never known before or since. Their belief was that with him defeat was impossible; that all the legions of darkness could not prevail against him; and that, whatever arbitrary powers he might assume, and whatever way he might use them, it would always be for the good of the country, — a belief which he sincerely shared. His ignorance of the science of statesmanship, and the rough manner in which he crossed its rules, seemed to endear him all the more to the great mass of his followers. Innumerable anecdotes about his homely and robust sayings and doings were going from mouth to mouth, and with delight the common man felt that this potent ruler was " **one** of us."

This popularity gave him **an** immense authority over the politicians of his party. He was a warm friend and a tremendous foe. By a faithful friend he would stand **to** the last extremity. But one who seriously differed from him on any matter that was **near his** heart, was in great danger of becoming **an object of** his wrath. The ordinary patriot is apt **to** regard the enemies of his country as his per**sonal enemies.** But Andrew Jackson was always inclined, with entire sincerity, to regard his personal opponents as the enemies of his country. He honestly believed them capable **of** any baseness, **and it** was his solemn conviction that such nuisances must be abated by any power available for that purpose. The statesmen of his party frequently differed from him on matters **of** public importance ; **but** they knew that they had to choose between submission and his disfavor. His friends would sometimes exercise much influence upon him in starting his mind **in a** certain direction; but **when once** started, that mind was beyond their control. His personal integrity was above the reach of corruption. He always meant to do right; indeed, he was always firmly convinced **of** being right. His idea of right was **not** seldom obscured by ignorance and prejudice, and in following **it he** would sometimes do the most unjust or dangerous things. **But his friends, and the statesmen of his** party, knowing that, when he had made up his mind, especially on a matter that had become a subject of conflict between him and his "enemies," it was absolutely useless to reason with him, accustomed themselves to obeying **orders,** unless they were prepared to go to the rear or into opposition. It was, therefore, not **a** mere invention of the enemy, but **sober** truth, that, when Jackson's administration was attacked, sometimes the only answer left to its defenders, as well as the all-sufficient one with the Democratic masses, was simply a " Hurrah for Jackson ! "

Henry Clay was, although in retirement, the recognized chief of the National Republicans. **He** was then fifty-two years old, and **in** the full maturity of his powers. He had never been an arduous student ; but his uncommonly vivacious and receptive mind had learned much **in** the practical school of affairs. He possessed that magnificent confidence in himself which extorts confidence from others. **He** had a full measure of the temper necessary for leadership : the spirit of initiative ; but not always **the** discretion that should accompany **it.** His leadership was not of that mean order which merely contrives to organize a personal **fol**lowing ; it was the leadership of a statesman zealously striving to promote great public interests. Whenever he appeared in a deliberative assembly, or in the councils of **his party,** he would, as a matter of course, take **in his** hands what important business was pending, and determine the policy to be followed. His friends, and some even among his opponents, were so accustomed to yield to him, that nothing seemed to them concluded without the mark of his assent ; and they involuntarily looked to him for the decisive word as to what was to be done. Thus he grew into a habit of dictation, which occasionally displayed itself in a manner of peremptory command, and an intolerance of adverse opinion apt to provoke resentment.

It was his eloquence that had first made him famous, and that throughout his career mainly sustained his leadership. His speeches were not masterpieces of literary art, nor exhaustive dissertations. They do not offer to the student any profound theories of government or expositions of economic science. They will not be quoted as authorities on disputed points. Neither were they strings of witty epigrams. They were the impassioned reasoning of a statesman intensely devoted to his country and to the cause he thought right. There was no appearance of artifice in them. They made every listener feel that the man who uttered them was tremendously in earnest, and that the thoughts he expressed had not only passed through his brain, but also through his heart. They were the speeches of a great debater, and, as may be said of those of Charles James Fox, cold print could never do them justice. To be fully appreciated they had to be heard on the theatre of action, in the hushed senate chamber, or before the eagerly upturned faces of assembled multitudes.

To feel the full charm of his lucid explanations, and his winning persuasiveness, or the thrill which was flashed through the nerves of his hearers by the magnificent sunbursts of his enthusiasm, or the fierce thunderstorms of his anger and scorn, one had to hear that musical voice cajoling, flattering, inspiring, overawing, terrifying in turn, — a voice to the cadences of which it was a physical delight to listen; one had to see that face, not handsome, but glowing with the fire of inspiration; that lofty mien, that commanding stature constantly growing under his words, and the grand sweep of his gesture, majestic in its dignity, and full of grace and strength, — the whole man a superior being while he spoke.

Survivors of his time, who heard him at his best, tell us of the effects produced by his great appeals in the House of Representatives or the Senate, the galleries trembling with excitement, and even the members unable to contain themselves ; or, in popular assemblies, the multitudes breathlessly listening, and then breaking out in unearthly shouts of enthusiasm and delight, weeping and laughing, and rushing up to him with overwhelming demonstrations of admiring and affectionate rapture.

Clay's oratory sometimes fairly paralyzed his opponents. A story is told that Tom Marshall, himself a speaker of uncommon power, was once selected to answer Clay at a mass meeting, but that he was observed, while Clay was proceeding, slowly to make his way back through the listening crowd, apparently anxious to escape. Some of his friends tried to hold him, saying: " Why, Mr. Marshall, where are you going? You must reply to Mr. Clay. You can easily answer all he has said." " Of course, I can answer every point," said Marshall, " but you must excuse me, gentlemen; I cannot go up there and do it just now, after his speech."

There was a manly, fearless frankness in the avowal of his opinions, and a knightly spirit in his defense of them, as well as in his attacks on his opponents. He was indeed, on the political field, the *preux chevalier*, marshaling his hosts, sounding his bugle blasts, and plunging first into the fight; and with proud admiration his followers called him " the gallant Harry of the West."

No less brilliant and attractive was he in his social intercourse with men; thoroughly human in his whole being; full of high spirits; fond of enjoying life and of seeing others happy; generous and hearty in his sympathies; always courteous, sometimes studiously and elaborately so, perhaps beyond what the occasion seemed to call for, but never wounding the most sensitive by demonstrative condescension, because there was a truly kind heart behind his courtesy; possessing a natural charm of conversation and manner so captivating that neither scholar nor backwoodsman could withstand its fascination; making friends wherever he appeared, and holding them — and surely to no public man did friends ever cling with more affec-

tionate attachment. It was not a mere political,
it was a sentimental devotion, — a devotion aban-
doning even that criticism which is the duty of
friendship, and forgetting or excusing all his weak-
nesses and faults, intellectual and moral, — more
than was good for him.

Behind him he had also the powerful support of
the industrial interests of the country, which saw
in him their champion, while the perfect integrity
of his character forbade the suspicion that this
championship was serving his private gain.

Such were the leaders of the two parties as they
then stood before the country, — individualities
so pronounced and conspicuous, commanders so
faithfully sustained by their followers, that, while
they were facing each other, the contests of parties
appeared almost like a protracted political duel
between two men. It was a struggle of singular
dramatic interest.

There was no fiercer hater than Andrew Jackson,
and no man whom he hated so fiercely as he did
Henry Clay. That hatred was the passion of the
last twenty years of his life. He sincerely deemed
Clay capable of any villainy, and no sooner had he
the executive power in his hands than he used it
to open hostilities. His cabinet appointments
were determined upon several days before his inauguration as President. Five of the places were
filled with men who had made their mark as enemies of Clay. Among these were two Senators,
who in 1825 had voted against the nomination of

Clay for the secretaryship of state, — Branch of North Carolina, whom Jackson made Secretary of the Navy, and Berrien, who became Attorney General. Eaton of Tennessee, whom Jackson selected as his Secretary of War, was the principal author of the " bargain and corruption " story ; and Ingham of Pennsylvania, the elect for the Treasury Department, had distinguished himself in his state by the most zealous propagation of the slander. Barry of Kentucky, chosen for the postmaster generalship, possessed the merit of having turned against Clay in 1825, on account of the "bargain and corruption," and of having contested Kentucky in 1828 as the anti-Clay candidate for Governor.

But the most striking exhibition of animosity took place in the State Department, at the head of which had stood Clay himself so long as John Quincy Adams was President. General Jackson had selected Martin Van Buren for that office; but Van Buren, being then Governor of New York, could not at once come to Washington to enter upon his new position. Jackson was determined that the State Department should not remain in any sense under the Clay influence for so much as an hour after he became President. On March 4, just before he went to the Capitol to take the oath of office, he put into the hands of Colonel James A. Hamilton of New York, his trusted adherent, a letter running thus: "Sir,— You are appointed to take charge of the Department of State, and to perform the duties of that office until Governor Van Buren arrives in this city. Your obedient servant, Andrew Jackson." A strange proceeding! Colonel Hamilton's account of what then took place is characteristic: "He (General Jackson) said, 'Colonel, you don't care to see me inaugurated?' 'Yes, General, I do; I came here for that purpose.' 'No; go to the State House, and as soon as you hear the gun fired, I am President and you are Secretary. Go and take charge of the department.' I do not state the reason he gave for this haste." Colonel Hamilton did as directed, and the moment the gun was fired, the danger that Clay might still exercise any influence in the State Department was averted from the country. The removal of Clay's friends, who were in the public service, began at once.

Three days after Jackson's inauguration Clay addressed his friends at a dinner given in his honor by citizens of Washington. He deplored the election to the presidency of a military hero, entirely devoid of the elements of fitness for so difficult a civil position. He beheld in it "an awful foreboding of the fate which, at some future day, was to befall this infant Republic." He recounted the military usurpations which had recently taken place in South and Central America, and said: "The thunders from the surrounding forts and the acclamations of the multitude on the Fourth, told us what general was at the head of *our* affairs." And he added, sadly: "A majority of my fellow-citizens, it would seem, do not perceive the dangers which I apprehend from the example." He also mentioned the " wanton, unprovoked, and unatoned injustice " which General Jackson had done him. Nevertheless, Jackson was now **President, and his** acts **were to be** discussed with **decorum, and judged with candor.**

Clay **was** mistaken if **he thought that the well- used refrain about the military** chieftain raised **to the** presidency without any **of** the statesman's qualifications, would still produce any effect **upon** the masses of the American people. They felt, at that period, exceedingly prosperous and hopeful. The improved means of communication — all **the** accessible inland waters being covered with steam- boats — had greatly promoted the material progress of the country. Railroad building had **just** begun, and opened **a vast** prospect of further develop- **ment. In the** public mind there **was** little anxiety and plenty of gorgeous expectation. **Under** such circumstances the generality of **people did not feel the** necessity **of** being taken care **of by trained** statesmanship. **On** the contrary, **the** only alarm of the time — and that an artificial **and** groundless one — had been that the trained statesmen **were** in corrupt combination **to** curtail in some way **the** people's rights, from which danger the election **of** General Jackson was supposed to have saved them. The masses saw in him a man who thought **as they** thought, who talked as they talked, who **was** be- lieved to be rather fond of treading **on the toes of** aristocratic pretensions, who was a living proof of the fact that it did not require much learning to make a famous general or to be elected President, and whose example, therefore, assured them that every one of them had a chance at high distinction for himself.

But President Jackson soon furnished a new point of attack. For the first time in the history of the Republic, the accession of a new President was followed by a systematic proscription for opinion's sake in the public service. What we understand by " spoils politics " had, indeed, not been unknown before. It had been practiced largely and with demoralizing effect in the state politics of New York and Pennsylvania. But by the patriotic statesmen who filled the presidential chair from the establishment of the Constitution down to the close of the term of John Quincy Adams, public office had been scrupulously re-garded as a public trust. Removals by wholesale for political reasons, or the turning over of the public service to the members of one party as a reward for partisan services rendered, or as an inducement for partisan services to be rendered, would have been thought, during the first half century of the Republic, not only a scandal and a disgrace, but little less than a criminal attempt to overthrow free institutions. Even when, after a fierce struggle, the government passed, by the election of Jefferson, from the Federalists to the Republicans, and the new President found the bulk of the offices in the hands of men whom the victors considered inimical to all they held dear, — even at that period of intense party feeling, Jefferson made only thirty-nine removals in the eight years during which he occupied the presidential chair. Some of these were made for cause ; others he justified upon the ground, not that the offices were patronage which the victors could rightly claim, but that there should be members of each party in the service, to show that neither had, even temporarily, a monopoly right to them, and that, this fair distribution being accomplished, appointments should thereafter, regardless of party connection, depend exclusively on the candidate's integrity, business fitness, and fidelity to the Constitution. This sentiment was so firmly rooted in the public mind that even Jackson, at the beginning of Monroe's administration, advised the President against excluding from office members of the opposite party.

When he himself became President he announced in his inaugural address that the popular will had imposed upon him " the task of reform," which would require " particularly the correction of those abuses that have brought the patronage of the federal government into conflict with the freedom of elections." Never was the word " reform " uttered with a more sinister meaning. An immense multitude had assembled in Washington to see their party chief invested with the executive power, and to claim their rewards for the services they had rendered him. It was as if a victorious army had come to take possession of a conquered country, expecting their general to distribute among them the spoil of the land. A spectacle was enacted never before known in the capital of the Republic.

Jackson had not that reason for making partisan changes which had existed in Jefferson's days. For when Jackson became President the civil service was teeming with his adherents, whom John Quincy Adams's scrupulous observance of the traditional principle had left undisturbed in their places. There was, therefore, no party monopoly in the public service to be broken up. Yet now removals and appointments were made with the avowed object of rewarding friends and punishing opponents, to the end of establishing, as to the offices of the government, a monopoly in favor of the President's partisans. Washington, John Adams, Jefferson, Madison, Monroe, John Quincy Adams had made in all seventy-four removals, all but a few for cause, during the forty years of their aggregate presidential terms. In one year, the first of his administration, Jackson removed four hundred and ninety-one postmasters and two hundred and thirty-nine other officers, and, since the new men appointed new clerks and other subordinates, the sum total of changes in that year was reckoned at more than two thousand. The first arbitrary dismissals of meritorious men indicated what was to come, and threw the service into the utmost consternation. "Among the official corps here," wrote Clay on **March 12, the** day before his departure from Washington, **"there is** the greatest solicitude and apprehension. **The** members **of it** feel something like the inhabitants of Cairo when the plague breaks out : **no one** knows who is next to encounter the stroke **of** death, or, which with many of them **is** the same thing, **to** be dismissed **from** office. You have no conception of the moral **tyranny** which prevails here over those in employment." Bad as this appeared, **it was** not the worst **of it. The** "spoils system," **full** fledged, had taken possession of the national government, and, as we shall see, **its most** baneful effects **were soon** to appear.

Clay foresaw the consequences clearly, and, at **a** great public feast given **to** him **by** his neighbors upon his arrival at his home, **he** promptly raised his voice against the noxious **innovation. This** principle he **laid down as his** starting-point : " Government is **a trust, and** the officers **of the** government are trustees ; and **both the trust and** the trustees **are created** for the benefit **of** the people." **In solemn** words of prophecy **he painted** the effects which the systematic violation **of this** principle, inaugurated by Jackson, must inevitably bring about : political contests turned into scrambles for plunder; **a** " system of universal rapacity " substituted **for a** system **of** responsibility ; favoritism for fitness ; " Congress corrupted, the **press** corrupted, general corruption ; until, the substance of free government having disappeared, some pretorian **band** would arise, **and,** with the general concurrence of a distracted people, put an **end to** useless **forms.**" This was the protest of the good old order of things **against** the new dis**order.** **Such** warnings, however, were in vain. They might move impartially thinking men to serious reflections. **But** Jackson was convinced that the political opponents he dismissed from office were really very dangerous persons, whom it was a patriotic duty to render harmless ; and the Democratic masses thought **that** Jackson could do no wrong. Many of them found something peculiarly flattering **in this** new conception of democratic government, that neither high character nor special ability, but only political opinions **of** the right kind, should be required to fit an American citizen for the service of his country ; that, while none but **a good** accountant would be accepted to keep the books of a dry-goods shop, anybody might keep the books **of** the United States Treasury ; that, while nobody would think of taking as manager of an importing business a man who did not know something **of** merchandise, anybody was good enough **to be an** appraiser in a custom-house.

Indeed, the manner in which Jackson selected his cabinet was characteristic of the ruling idea. Colonel James A. Hamilton, one of his confidential advisers at that time, tells us in his " Reminiscences " : " **In** this important work by President Jackson, no thought appeared **to** be given as to the fitness of the persons for their places. I am sure I never heard one word in relation thereto, and I certainly had repeated conversations with him in regard to these appointments." **To be a** good hater of Henry Clay **was** considered **a greater** requisite for a cabinet place than statesmanlike ability and experience. In this way Jackson collected in his executive council, with the exception of one or **two, a** rare assortment of mediocrities; and nothing could have been more characteristic than that **the** matter which most distracted this **high council of** statesmen was a difference **of** opinion concerning — not some important public question, **but** the virtue **of** Secretary Eaton's **wife.** The principle **that the** fitness of a man for a place, in point of character and acquirements, had nothing to **do** with his appointment to that place, was at once recognized and exemplified above and below ; and thus a virus was infused into the politics of **the** nation, destined to test to **the** utmost the native robustness of the American character.

Clay was nominally **in** retirement. When, after his return from Washington, the representative **of** his district in Congress offered **to vacate the seat in order** that he might succeed **to it, he** declined. Neither would he accept a place in the legislature of Kentucky. For a while he heartily enjoyed the quiet life of the farmer. He delighted in raising fine animals, — horses, blood cattle, mules, pigs, and **sheep. He** corresponded with **his** friends about **a lot of** " fifty full-blooded merino ewes," which **he** had bought in Pennsylvania. His dairy was profitably managed by his excellent wife. He raised good crops of hemp and corn. But, after all, the larger part of his correspondence ran on congressional elections, the prospects of his party, and the doings of President Jackson. He thought that Jackson could not possibly hold his following together. Jackson's friends in Congress "must decide on certain leading measures of policy;" if he came out for the tariff, the South would leave him; if against the tariff, there would be "such an opposition to him in the tariff states as must prevent his reëlection," — in all which prophesyings the prophet proved mistaken. He also believed that the great majority at the last election was directed rather against Mr. Adams than against himself, and that his own public position was improving from day to day.

After the great defeat of 1828 the plaudits of the multitude were especially sweet to him. On his way from Washington to Lexington in March, he had been received everywhere by crowds of enthusiastic admirers. With profound complacency he wrote to a friend: "My journey has been marked by every token of attachment and heartfelt demonstrations. I never experienced more testimonies of respect and confidence, nor more enthusiasm, — dinners, suppers, balls, etc. I have had literally a free passage. Taverns, stages, tollgates, have been generally thrown open to me, free from all charge. Monarchs might be proud of the reception with which I have everywhere been honored."

After a short period of rest at Ashland, he could not withhold himself from fresh contact with the people. During the autumn of 1829 he visited several places in Kentucky; and in January, 1830, he went to New Orleans and the principal towns on the Mississippi, where he had one ovation after another. In the spring he wrote to his friends again about the delights of his rural occupations, — how he was almost " prepared to renounce forever the strifes of public life," and how he thought he would make " a better farmer than statesman." But in the summer of the same year we find him at Columbus, Cincinnati, and other places in Ohio, being " received " and feasted, and speaking as he went. It was " private business " that led him there, but private business well seasoned with politics, and accompanied with brass bands and thundering cannon. In an elaborate speech on the questions of the day, which he delivered at Cincinnati in August, 1830, he could not refrain from describing his experiences.

"Throughout my journey (he said), undertaken solely for private purposes, there has been a constant effort on my side to repress, and on that of my fellow-citizens of Ohio to exhibit, public manifestations of their affection and confidence. It has been marked by a succession of civil triumphs. I have been escorted from village to village, and have everywhere found myself surrounded by large concourses of my fellow-citizens, often of both sexes, greeting and welcoming me.'

No wonder that his sanguine nature was inspired with **new** hope, **and that** he felt himself to be the man who could rally the defeated hosts, and overthrow the " military chieftain " **with all his** " pretorian bands."

He was certainly not alone in thinking so. **It** began **to be** looked upon **as a matter** of course among **the National** Republicans that Clay would be their candidate against Jackson in 1832. **On** May 29, **1830,** Daniel Webster **wrote to** him : " You are necessarily at the head of **one** party, and **General Jackson will be, if he is not** already, identified **with the** other. **The** question will **be put to** the **country. Let** the country decide **it.**" **But in the mean time a** curious movement **had** sprung up, dividing the opposition of which Clay **was the head.** It was the Anti-Masonic movement. In 1826 **one** Captain William Morgan, **a** bricklayer **living at** Batavia, **in western** New York, undertook to write a book revealing the secrets of Freemasonry. Some Freemasons of the neighborhood sought to persuade and then to force him, **by all sorts of** chicanery, to give up his design, but without success. **He was** then abducted, and, **as** was widely **believed, murdered.** The crime was charged **upon some** fanatical Freemasons ; but the whole order **was accused of** countenancing **it, and was held** responsible for obstructing **the** course **of** justice **on** the occasion of the investigations and trials which followed. The excitement springing from these occurrences, **at first** confined to one or two counties in western New York, gradually spread, and grew into a crusade against secret societies bound together by oaths. In spite of the efforts of leading politicians to restrain it — for they feared its disorganizing influence — it soon assumed a political character, and then some of them vigorously turned it to their advantage. Beginning with a few country towns where the citizens organized for the exclusion of all Freemasons from office, the " Anti-Masons " rapidly extended their organizations over the western half of the state. Committees were formed, conventions were held, and not a few men of standing and influence took an active part in the movement. In 1828, when Adams and Jackson were the presidential candidates, the Anti-Masons were mostly on the side of Adams; while the Masons generally rallied under Jackson's flag, who was himself a Mason. The Anti-Masons, however, refusing to support the candidate of the National Republicans for the governorship of New York, made a nomination of their own for that office. The result was the election of the Jackson candidate, Martin Van Buren. But from the large vote polled by the Anti-Masons it appeared that in the state election the balance of power had been in their hands. They also elected many members of the legislature, and secured a representation in Congress. Thus encouraged, the movement invaded the Western Reserve of Ohio, and won many adherents in Vermont, Pennsylvania, Massachusetts, Connecticut,

and Indiana. It had its newspaper organs and a
" Review," and presently it was prepared to contest a presidential election as a " party."

Clay had many friends among the Anti-Masons
who would have been glad to obtain from him
some declaration of sentiment favorable to their
cause, in order to make possible a union of forces.
But he gave them no encouragement. To the
many private entreaties addressed to him he uni-
formly replied that he did not desire to make himself a party to that dispute ; that, although he had
been initiated in the order, he had long ceased to
be a member of any lodge ; that he had never acted,
either in private or in public life, under any Masonic influence, but that Masonry or Anti-Masonry
had in his opinion nothing to do with politics.

He believed that, if the Anti-Masons were seriously thinking of nominating a candidate of their
own for the presidency, they would not find a man
of weight willing to stand, and that the bulk of the
Anti-Masonic forces would drift over to himself.
In this expectation he was disappointed. The
Anti-Masons held a national convention at Baltimore in September, 1831, which nominated for the
presidency William Wirt, late Attorney General
under Monroe and John Quincy Adams; and for
the vice-presidency, Amos Ellmaker of Pennsylvania. Wirt was at heart in favor of Clay's election, but, having once accepted the Anti-Masonic
nomination, he found it impossible to withdraw
from the field. Some of the leading Anti-Masons

indulged in the hope that Clay himself might be prevailed upon to give **up** his candidacy, and permit the whole opposition to the Jackson régime to be united under Anti-Masonic auspices. Far from entertaining such **a** proposition, he declared, **with** sharp emphasis, **in a** public letter to **a** committee of citizens of Indiana, that the Constitution **did** not give the general government **the** slightest **power to** interfere **with** the subject **of** Freemasonry, and that he thought the presidential office should **be** filled **by one who was** capable, " **unswayed** by sectarian feelings or passions, **of** administering its high duties impartially **towards the** whole people, however divided into religious, social, benevolent, or literary associations."

He felt so strongly on this point that **he wrote to** his friend Brooke : " If the alternative **be between** Andrew Jackson **and an** Anti-Masonic candidate, with his exclusive proscriptive principles, I should be embarrassed **in the** choice. I am not sure that the **old** tyranny **is not** better than **the new.**" It is not surprising that he, with many others, should have under-estimated the strength of **the movement.** We find **it now** hard to **believe** that **men of** good sense should have seriously thought of making the question **of** Freemasonry the principal issue of **a** national contest upon which the **American** people **were to** divide. But we meet **among** those who were prominently engaged in that enterprise such **names** as William H. Seward, Thurlow **Weed,** Francis Granger, Thaddeus Stevens, Richard **Rush** and William Wirt, two of Clay's colleagues in Adams's Cabinet, and even John Quincy Adams himself. Indeed, while Clay would have been loath to choose between Jackson and an Anti-Masonic candidate, Adams gravely wrote in his Diary: " The dissolution of the Masonic institution in the United States I believe to be really more important to us and our posterity than the question whether Mr. Clay or General Jackson shall be the President chosen at the next election." The Anti-Masonic movement furnished a curious example of mental contagion. But odd as it was, it kept the opposition to Jackson divided.

Many things had in the mean time occurred which created a loud demand for Clay's personal presence and leadership on the theatre of action at the national capital. President Jackson, treating the members of his Cabinet more as executive clerks than as political advisers, and dispensing with regular cabinet meetings, had surrounded himself with the famous " Kitchen Cabinet," a little coterie of intimates, from whom he largely received his political inspirations and advice, — a secret council of state, withdrawn entirely from public responsibility, consisting of able, crafty, personally honest men, skillful politicians, courageous to audacity, and thoroughly devoted to General Jackson. The members of this secret council were William B. Lewis from Tennessee, one of Jackson's warmest home friends ; Isaac Hill of New Hampshire ; Amos Kendall, who was employed in the Treasury ; and

Duff Green, the editor of Jackson's first newspaper organ. He fell from grace as being a friend of Calhoun, and was supplanted by Francis P. Blair. Kendall and Blair had been journalists in Kentucky, and near friends of Henry Clay, but had turned against him mainly in consequence of the so-called "relief" movement in that state, which, as already mentioned, was one of those epidemic infatuations which make people believe that they can get rid of their debts and become rich by legislative tricks and the issue of promises to pay. The movement developed intense hostility to the Bank of the United States. There had been personal disputes, too, between Clay and Kendall, engendering much ill feeling. The existence and known influence of the Kitchen Cabinet kept the political world in constantly strained expectation as to what would turn up next.

The "Globe" newspaper had been established, with Francis P. Blair in the editorial chair, as President Jackson's organ, to direct and discipline his own party, and to castigate its opponents.

In his first message to Congress, in December, 1829, President Jackson had thrown out threatening hints as to the policy of rechartering the Bank of the United States, the charter of which would expire in 1836; and in the message of 1830 those threats were repeated. The approaching extinction of the national debt rendering a reduction of the revenue necessary, there was much apprehension as to what the fate of the protective tariff would **be.**   Large meetings of free-traders as well **as of** protectionists were held to influence legislation.

President Jackson had vetoed the " Marysville Road Bill," and thereby declared his hostility to the **policy of** internal improvements. With regard to the proceedings of the State of Georgia against the Cherokees, President Jackson had submitted to the extreme state-sovereignty pretensions of the state, in disregard — it might **be** said, in defiance — **of** the decisions of the Supreme Court of **the United** States.

A great commotion had arisen in South Carolina against the tariff laws, leading to the promulgation **of** the doctrine that any single state had the power to declare a law **of** the United States unconstitutional, void, and not binding, — the so-called nullification theory. Webster had thrilled the country with his celebrated plea for Liberty and Union in his reply to Hayne, winning a " noble triumph," as Clay called it in a letter. Jackson had, at a banquet on Jefferson's birthday, in April, 1830, given an indication of the spirit aroused in him, **by** offering the famous toast, " Our Federal Union : it must be preserved."

Jackson had declared hostilities against Vice-President Calhoun in consequence of the discovery that Calhoun, as a member of Monroe's Cabinet, had condemned Jackson's proceedings in the Seminole war of 1818. In June, 1831, the whole Cabinet had resigned, or rather been compelled to resign, mainly for the purpose of eliminating from the administration Calhoun's friends, and a new Cabinet had been appointed, in which Edward Livingston was Secretary of State; Louis McLane of Delaware, Secretary of the Treasury; Roger B. Taney, Attorney General; and Levi Woodbury, Secretary of the Navy; the Post Office Department remaining in Barry's hands.

The Kitchen Cabinet had elicited demonstrations from the legislature of Pennsylvania, subsequently indorsed by that of New York, calling upon General Jackson to stand for a second term, notwithstanding his previous declarations in favor of the one-term principle, and it was generally understood that he would do so.

All these occurrences, added to the impression that in the President and his confidential advisers there was to be dealt with a force yet undefined and beyond the ordinary rules of calculation, produced among the opposition party a singular feeling of insecurity. They looked for a strong man to lead them; they wanted to hear Clay's voice in Congress; and it is characteristic that Daniel Webster, who had just then reached the zenith of his glory, and was by far the first man in the Senate, should have given the most emphatic expression to that anxiety for energetic leadership. " You must be aware," he wrote to Clay from Boston on October 5, 1831, " of the strong desire manifested in many parts of the country that you should come into the Senate: the wish is entertained here as earnestly as anywhere. We are to have an interesting **and** arduous session. Everything is to be attacked. An array is preparing much more **formidable** than has ever yet assaulted what we think the leading and important public interests. Not only the tariff, but the Constitution itself, in its elementary and fundamental provisions, will be assailed with talent, vigor, and union. Everything is to be debated as if nothing had ever been settled. It would be an infinite gratification to me **to** have your aid, or rather your lead. I know nothing so likely to be useful. Everything valuable in the government is to be fought for, and we need your arm in the fight."

Clay was reluctant to yield to these entreaties. His instinct probably **told** him that for a presidential candidate the Senate is not a safe place, especially while the canvass is going on. But he obeyed the call **of** his friends, which at the same time **appeared** to be the call of the public interest. When it became known that he would be a candidate for the Senate **of** the United States before the Kentucky legislature, the Washington "Globe," President Jackson's organ, opened its batteries **with** characteristic fury. Commenting upon **the** fact that Clay attended the legislature in person, and forgetting that his competitor, Richard M. Johnson, **the** Jackson candidate, did the same, the " Globe " spoke thus : —

"If under these circumstances Mr. Clay should come **to** the Senate, he **will** but consummate his ruin. He will stand in that body, not as the representative of Kentucky, but of a few base men rendered infamous in electing him. He will no longer represent his countrymen, but, like an Irish patriot become an English pensioner, he will represent an odious oligarchy, and, owing his station altogether to artisans and management, he will be stripped of the dignity of his character, and gradually sink into insignificance."

Nevertheless Clay was elected, but only by a small majority. Thus he entered upon his senatorial career, more heartily welcomed by his friends, and more bitterly hated by his enemies, than ever before.

CHAPTER XIII.

THE CAMPAIGN OF 1832.

HENRY CLAY appeared in Washington at the opening of Congress in December, 1831, in the double character of Senator and candidate for the presidency. It was at that period that the method of putting presidential candidates in the field by national conventions of party delegates found general adoption. The Anti-Masons had held their national convention in September. The National Republicans were to follow on December 12. That Henry Clay would be their candidate for the presidency was a foregone conclusion. Nobody appeared as a competitor for the honor. But it remained still to be determined what issues should be put prominently forward in the canvass. On this point the opinion of the recognized leader was naturally decisive. As a matter of course, a protective tariff and internal improvements, and an emphatic condemnation of the " spoils system," would form important parts of his programme. But a grave question turned up, on the treatment of which his friends seriously differed in opinion. It was that of the National Bank. The existing Bank of the United States had been created, with

Clay's help, in 1816. Its charter was to run for twenty years, and would therefore expire in 1836. In order to understand how the rechartering of that bank became a burning question in 1831, a short retrospect is necessary.

When President Jackson came into office the country was in a prosperous condition. There was little speculation, but business in all directions showed a healthy activity, and yielded good returns. The currency troubles, which had long been disturbing the country, especially the South and West, were over. The "circulating medium" was more uniform and trustworthy, and, on the whole, in a more satisfactory condition than it ever had been before. The agency of the Bank of the United States in bringing about these results was generally recognized. In the first two years after its establishment the bank had been badly managed. But Langdon Cheves, appointed its president in 1819, put the conduct of its business upon a solid footing, and thereafter it continued steadily to grow in the confidence of the business community. No serious difficulty was therefore anticipated as to the rechartering; and as there would be no necessity for final action on that matter until 1836, three years after the expiration of General Jackson's first presidential term, the public generally expected that any question about it would be permitted to rest at least until after the election of 1832.

Great was therefore the surprise when, in his

very first message to Congress, in **December, 1829,**
President Jackson said that, although the charter
of the Bank of the United States would not **ex-**
pire until 1836, it was time to take up that subject
for grave consideration ; that " both the constitu-
;ionality and the expediency of the law creating
the bank were well questioned by **a** large number
of our fellow-citizens ; and that it must be admitted
by all to have failed in the great **end** of establishing **a** uniform and sound currency." Then he
submitted to the wisdom of the legislature whether
a " national bank, founded upon the credit of the
government and its revenue, might not be devised."
What did all this mean? People asked themselves
whether the President knew something about the
condition **of** the **bank** that the public did not
know, and the bank shares suffered at once a serious decline at the Exchange.

The true reasons for this hostile demonstration
became known afterwards. Benton's assertion to
the contrary notwithstanding, Jackson had no intention to overthrow the United States Bank when
he came **to** Washington. His Secretary **of** the
Treasury, Ingham, complimented the bank **on** the
valuable services it rendered, several months **after**
the beginning **of** the administration. The origin
of the trouble was characteristic. Complaint came
from New Hampshire, through Levi Woodbury, **a**
Senator from that state and **a zealous** Jackson
Democrat, and through **Isaac Hill,** a member of the
" Kitchen Cabinet," that Jeremiah Mason, a Fed-

eralist **and a** friend of Daniel Webster, had been made president of the branch of **the United States** Bank at Portsmouth, and that **he was an unaccommodating** person very objectionable **to the people.** A correspondence concerning this case sprang **up** between Secretary Ingham and Nicholas Biddle, the President of **the** Bank of **the** United States, a **man of much literary** ability, **who** was rather **fond of** an argument, and liked **to say** clever things. No impartial man can read the letters which passed to and fro without coming **to the** conclusion that influential men in the Jackson party desired to use the bank **and its** branches **for** political purposes ; **that** Biddle wished to maintain the political independence of the institution, and that his **refusal to** do the bidding of politicians with **regard to Jeremiah** Mason was **bitterly** resented. **It** appears, also, from an **abundance** of testimony, of which Ingham's confession, published after he had ceased **to be** Secretary of the Treasury, forms **part, that** the members of **the** "Kitchen Cabinet" told **Jackson all** sorts **of** stories about efforts of the bank **to** use its power in controlling elections in a manner hostile **to him ; that** he trustingly **listened to all** the allegations against **it** which reached his ears, and that **he at** last honestly believed the bank **to** be a power of evil, **corrupt** and corrupting, dangerous to **the** liberties **of the** people and to **the existence** of the Republic.

The first message did not produce on Congress **the** desired **effect.** The President's **own** party failed to stand by him. In the House of Representatives the Committee of Ways and Means made a report, affirming, what was well known, that the constitutionality of the bank had been recognized by the Supreme Court, that it was a useful institution, and that the establishment of a bank such as that suggested in the message would be a dangerous experiment. A similar report was made in the Senate. In the House, resolutions against rechartering the bank, and calling for a comprehensive report upon its doings, were defeated by considerable majorities. Bank stock went up again.

In his second message, in December, 1830, President Jackson said that nothing had occurred " to lessen in any degree the dangers " which many citizens apprehended from the United States Bank as actually organized. He then suggested the organization of " a bank, with the necessary officers, as a branch of the Treasury Department." Congress did not take action on the matter, but Benton made his first attack in the Senate on the United States Bank, not to produce any immediate effect in Congress, but to stir up the people.

In his third message, in December, 1831, President Jackson simply said that on previous occasions he had performed his duty of bringing the bank question to the attention of the people, and that there he would " for the present " leave it. At the same time the Secretary of the Treasury, McLane, submitted in his report to Congress an

elaborate argument in favor of the United States
Bank. There is much reason for believing that
Jackson at that period was inclined to accept some
accommodation or compromise concerning the bank
question, or at least not to force a fight just then.
Thurlow Weed, in his " Autobiography," gives
an account of a conference between the Secretary
of the Treasury and the president of the bank, in
which the assent of the administration to the re-
charter was offered on condition of certain modifications of the charter. It is further reported that
the officers of the bank were strongly in favor of
accepting the proposition, but that, when they consulted Clay and Webster on the matter, they found
determined resistance, to which they yielded.

The officers and the most discreet friends of the
United States Bank felt keenly that a great financial institution, whose operations and interests
were closely interwoven with the general business
of the country, should not become identified with
a political party in all the vicissitudes of fortune,
and should never permit itself to be made the foot-
ball of political ambitions. They were strongly
inclined not to press the rechartering of the bank
until it should be necessary, and thus to keep the
question out of the presidential campaign.

Clay thought otherwise. As to the time when
the renewal of the charter should be asked for, he
maintained that the present time was the best.
There were undoubted majorities favorable to the
bank in both houses. If the President should de-

feat the renewal with his **veto**, he would only ruin himself. He **had** already greatly weakened **his** popularity by attacking the bank. It had many friends in the Jackson party who would stand by it rather **than** by the President. Being located in Philadelphia, the **bank** wielded great power and enjoyed great popularity in Pennsylvania, the hot-bed of Jacksonism. Losing that state, Jackson would lose the election. Moreover, the bank had **a** strong hold upon the business interests of **the** country everywhere, and everywhere those inter-ests would support the bank in a decisive struggle. **The bank** issue **was** therefore **the** strongest which the National Republicans could put forward. That issue should **be made** as sharp as possible, and to **give** it a practical shape, the renewal **of** the char-ter should be applied for **at** the present session of Congress. Such was Clay's reasoning and advice, or **rather** his command; **and** both the bank and the party obeyed.

On December 12, 1831, **the** convention of the National Republicans was held at Baltimore. Clay was nominated unanimously, and with the greatest enthusiasm, for the presidency. The nomination for the vice-presidency fell **to John** Sergeant of Penn-sylvania, **a** man of excellent character, whom we remember to have met, at the time of the struggle about the admission **of** Missouri, as **one of** the strongest advocates **of the** exclusion of slavery. The convention also issued an address to the peo-**ple,** which eulogized the Bank of the United States, denounced the attack made upon it by President Jackson in his messages, and declared that, "if the President be reëlected, it may be considered certain that the bank will be abolished." Thus the issue was made up: Jackson must be defeated if the Bank of the United States was to be saved. The memorial of the bank, praying for a renewal of its charter, was presented in the Senate early in January, 1832, to the end of forcing Congress and the President to act without delay. If it was Clay's object to make the bank question the most prominent one in the canvass, he succeeded beyond expectation; and if he had cast about for the greatest blunder possible under the circumstances, he could not have found a more brilliant one. This we shall appreciate when, at a later period of the session, we hear both sides speak.

The first subject which Clay took up for discussion in the Senate was the tariff. Two circumstances of unusual moment had brought this topic into the foreground: one was the excitement produced by the tariff of 1828, " the tariff of abominations," in the planting states, and especially in South Carolina, where it had assumed the threatening form of the nullification movement; and the other was the fact that the revenue furnished by the existing tariff largely exceeded the current expenditures, and would, after the extinguishment of the national debt, which was rapidly going forward, bring on that bane of good government in a free country, a heavy surplus in the treasury, without legitimate **employment.** A reduction of **the** revenue **was** therefore necessary, and lively discussions were going on among the people as to how it should be effected. In September and October large popular conventions **of free** traders had been held. One of their principal spokesmen was the venerable Albert Gallatin, who insisted on lower rates of duties throughout. The protectionists, fearing **lest the** reduction of the revenue should injure the protective system, were equally vigorous in their demonstrations.

Jackson's views with regard to **the** tariff had undergone progressive changes. When first a candidate **for the** presidency, in 1824, he had pronounced himself substantially a protectionist. In his first message **to** Congress, **in** 1829, **he** recommended duties which would place our own manufactures " in fair competition with those of foreign countries, while, with regard **to** those of prime necessity in time of war," **we** might even "advance a step beyond that point." He also advocated the distribution **of** the surplus revenue among the states " according to **the** ratio of representation " in Congress, and a reduction of duties **on** articles " which cannot come **into** competition with our **own** production." This meant a protective tariff. **In** his second message, December, 1830, he **ex-**pressed the opinion that " objects of national importance alone **ought to be** protected ; of these the productions of **our soil, our mines, and** our work-**shops,** essential to national defense, occupy the first rank." In his third message, December, 1831, he invited attention to the fact that the public debt would be extinguished before the expiration of his term, **and** that, therefore, "a modification of the tariff, which **shall** produce a reduction of the revenue **to the wants of the** government," **was very** advisable. He added that, in justice to the interests of the merchant as well as the manufacturer, the reduction **should be** prospective, and **that the** duties should be adjusted with a **view "to** the counteraction of foreign policy, **so far as it may be** injurious to our national interests." **This meant** a revenue tariff with incidental **retaliation.** He had thus arrived **at** a sensible plan **to avoid** the accumulation of a surplus.

Clay took the matter **in hand in the Senate,** or rather in Congress, for he held **a** meeting **of** friends of protection **among Senators** and Representatives to bring about harmony of action **in the** two houses. At that meeting he laid down the law for **his** party **in a** manner, as John Quincy Adams records, courteous, but "exceedingly peremptory and dogmatical." He recognized the necessity **of** reducing the revenue, **but he would** reduce the revenue without reducing protective duties. The "American system" should **not** suffer. It must, therefore, not **be done in** the manner proposed by Jackson. He insisted **upon confining the** reduction **to** duties **on articles not** coming into competition with American products. He **would not** make the **reductions prospective, to** begin after

the public debt was extinguished, but immediate,
as he was not in favor of a rapid extinguishment
of the debt. Instead of abolishing protective duties he would rather reduce the revenue by making
some of them prohibitory. He also insisted upon
" home valuation " — *i. e.,* valuation at the port of
entry — of goods subject to ad valorem duties, and
upon reducing the credits allowed for their payment. When objection was made that this would
be a defiance of the South, of the President, and
of the whole administration party, he replied, as
Adams reports, that " to preserve, maintain, and
strengthen the American system, he would defy
the South, the President, and the devil."

He introduced a resolution in the Senate " that
the existing duties upon articles imported from
foreign countries, and not coming into competition
with similar articles made or produced within the
United States, ought to be forthwith abolished, except the duties upon wines and silks, and that those
ought to be reduced ; and that the Committee on
Finance be instructed to report a bill accordingly."
On this resolution, which led to a general debate
upon the tariff, he made two speeches, one of
which took rank among his greatest efforts. Its
eloquent presentation of the well known arguments
in favor of protection excited great admiration
at the time, and served the protectionists as a text-
book for many years. He declared himself strongly
against the preservation of existing duties " in
order to accumulate a surplus in the treasury, for

the purpose of subsequent distribution among the several states." To collect revenue " from one portion of the people and give it to another " he pronounced unjust. If the revenue were to be distributed for use by the states in their public expenditure, he knew of no principle in the Constitution " that authorized the federal government to become such a collector for the states, nor of any principle of safety or propriety which admitted of the states becoming such recipients of gratuity from the general government." He thought, however, that the proceeds of the sales of public lands should be devoted to internal improvements. He called free trade the " British colonial system " in contradistinction to the protective " American system," two names which themselves did the duty of arguments. He contrasted the effects of the two systems, using as an illustration the seven years of distress preceding, and the seven years of prosperity following, the enactment of the tariff of 1824, — which drew from Southern Senators the answer that the picture of prosperity fitted the North, but by no means the South. He discussed the effect of the tariff on the South in a kindlier tone than that in which he had spoken in the meeting of his friends, but he denounced in strong terms the threats of nullification and disunion. He said:

"The great principle, which lies at the foundation of all free government, is that the majority must govern, from which there can be no appeal but the sword. That majority ought to govern wisely, equitably, moderately, and constitutionally; but govern it must, subject only to that terrible appeal. If ever one or several states, being a minority, can, by menacing a dissolution of the Union, succeed in forcing an abandonment of great measures deemed essential to the interests and prosperity of the whole, the Union from that moment is practically gone. It may linger on in form and name, but its vital spirit has fled forever."

This seemed to exclude every thought of compromise.

The efforts of the free traders to discredit the " American system," by resolutions, addresses, and pamphlets against the tariff, annoyed him greatly; and nothing seems to have stung him more than a calmly argumentative memorial from the pen of Albert Gallatin. Only the deepest irritation can explain the most ungenerous attack he made upon that venerable statesman in his great speech. This is the language he applied to him : —

"The gentleman to whom I am about to allude, although long a resident in this country, has no feelings, no attachments, no sympathies, no principles, in common with our people. Nearly fifty years ago Pennsylvania took him to her bosom, and warmed, and cherished, and honored him ; and how does he manifest his gratitude? By aiming a vital blow at a system endeared to her by a thorough conviction that it is indispensable to her prosperity. He has filled, at home and abroad, some of the highest offices under this government, during thirty years, and he is still at heart an alien. The authority of his name has been invoked, and the labors of his pen, in the form of a memorial to Congress, have been engaged, to overthrow the American system, and to substitute the foreign. Go home to your native Europe, and there inculcate upon her sovereigns your Utopian doctrines of free trade; and when you have prevailed upon them to unseal their ports, and freely to admit the produce of Pennsylvania and other states, come back, and we shall be prepared to become converts and to adopt your faith."

This assault was an astonishing performance. Gallatin had come to America a very young man. Under the presidency of the first Adams he had been intellectually the leader of the Republicans in the House of Representatives. He had been a member of that famous triumvirate, Jefferson, Madison, Gallatin. Jefferson had made him Secretary of the Treasury; and Madison, equally sensible of his merits, had kept him in that most important position. His services had put his name in the first line of the great American finance ministers. Clay had met him as one of his colleagues at Ghent, and he would hardly have denied that the conclusion of the treaty of peace was owing more to Gallatin's prudence, skill, and good temper, than to his own efforts. As Minister to France under Monroe, Gallatin had added to his distinguished services by his patriotism and rare diplomatic ability. When Clay, as Secretary of State, needed a man of peculiar wisdom and trustworthiness to whom to confide the interests of this Republic, he had thought first of Gallatin. It was Gallatin whom he had selected first for the most

American of American missions, that to the Panama Congress. It was Gallatin whom **he** had sent **to** England after the retirement of Rufus King, **to** protect American interests amid uncommonly tangled circumstances. But now, suddenly, the same American statesman, **not** present and unable **to answer, was** denounced by him **in** the Senate **as** one **who had** " **no** feelings, **no** sympathies, **no** principles, **in** common with **our** people," **as** " an alien at heart," who should "go home to Europe;" and **all** this because Clay found **it** troublesome to answer Gallatin's arguments on the tariff.

Gallatin, **during his long** career, **had** much **to** suffer on account **of his** foreign birth. The same **persons who had** praised him **as a great** statesman **and a** profound thinker, when he happened to agree with their views and **to** serve their purposes, had **not** unfrequently, so soon as **he** expressed opinions they disliked, denounced **him as an** impertinent foreigner who should " go home." **He** was accustomed **to** such treatment **from** small politicians. But **to see one of the** great men of the Republic, and **an old** friend **too, descend so** far, could not fail to pain **the** septuagenarian deeply.

But the irony of fate furnished a **biting commentary** on Clay's conduct. Scarcely a year after he had so fiercely denounced Gallatin **as " an alien at heart "** for having recommended a gradual reduction of tariff duties to **a** level of about twenty-five per cent, Clay himself, as **we** shall see, proposed and carried **a** gradual reduction of duties to a maximum **of twenty per** cent, all the while feeling himself to be a thorough American "at heart."

After a long debate Clay's tariff resolution was adopted, and in June, 1832, **a** bill substantially **in** accord with it passed both houses, known as the tariff act of 1832. It reduced or abolished **the** duties on many of the unprotected articles, **but** left the protective system without material change. As **a** reduction of **the** revenue it effected very little. The income of the government for the year was about thirty millions ; its expenditures, exclusive of the public debt, somewhat over thirteen millions ; the prospective surplus, after the payment of the debt, **more** than sixteen millions. The reduction proposed by Clay, according to his **own** estimate, was not over seven millions ; the reduction really effected by **the** new tariff law scarcely exceeded three millions. Clay had saved the American system at the expense of the very object contemplated by the measure. It was extremely short-sighted statesmanship. The surplus was as threatening as ever, and the dissatisfaction in **the** South grew from day to day.

One of the important incidents of the session was the rejection by the Senate of **the** nomination of Martin Van Buren as Minister to England. Van Buren **was** one of Jackson's favorites. He had stood by Jackson when other members of **the** cabinet refused to take the presidential view **of** Mrs. Eaton's virtue. He had greatly facilitated **that** dissolution of **the** Cabinet which Jackson **had** much at heart. When he ceased to be Secretary of State, Jackson gave him the mission to England, holding in reserve higher honors for him. In the Senate, however, the nomination encountered strong opposition. With many Senators it was a matter of party politics. The strongest reason avowed was that, as Secretary of State, Van Buren had instructed the American Minister to England to abandon the claim, urged by the late administration, of a right to the colonial trade, on the express ground that those who had asserted that right had been condemned at the last presidential election by the popular judgment. The opponents of Van Buren denounced his conduct as a wanton humiliation of this Republic, and a violation of the principle that, in its foreign relations, the vicissitudes of party contests should not be paraded as reasons for a change of policy.

Clay, leading the opposition to Van Buren, found it not difficult to show that the policy followed by the administration of John Quincy Adams in this respect was substantially identical with that of Madison and Monroe, and that, by officially representing that policy as condemned by the people, Van Buren had cast discredit upon the conduct of this Republic in its intercourse with a foreign power. But he had still another objection to Van Buren's appointment. He said : —

"I believe, upon circumstances which satisfy my mind, that to this gentleman is principally to be ascribed the introduction of the odious system of proscription for the

exercise of the elective franchise in the government of
the United States. I understand that it is the system
upon which the party in his own state, of which he is
the reputed head, constantly acts. It is a detestable
system, drawn from the worst periods of the Roman
Republic; and if it were to be perpetuated, — if the
offices, honors, and dignities of the people were to be
put up to a scramble, and to be decided by the result of
every presidential election, — our government and institutions would finally end in a despotism as inexorable
as that at Constantinople."

That Van Buren was a " spoils politician " is
undoubtedly true. But that to him " the introduction of the odious system " in the general government was " principally to be ascribed," is not
correct. Jackson was already vigorously at work
" rewarding his friends and punishing his enemies," when, a few weeks after the beginning of
the administration, Van Buren arrived at Washington. Jackson would doubtless have introduced
the "spoils system," with all its characteristic features, had Van Buren never been a member of his
Cabinet. In the Senate, however, Van Buren's
friends did not defend him on that ground. It
was in reply to Clay's speech that Marcy, speaking for the politicians of New York, proclaimed
that they saw "nothing wrong in the rule that to
the victors belong the spoils of the enemy."

The rejection of Van Buren's nomination was
accomplished by the casting vote of the Vice-President, Calhoun, who thought that after such a de-

feat Van Buren would " never kick again."   Clay
wrote to his friend Brooke : " The attempt to excite public sympathy in behalf of the ' little ma-
gician ' has totally failed; and I sincerely wish
that he may be nominated as Vice-President. That
is exactly the point to which I wish to see matters
brought."   Clay's wish was to be gratified. The
rejection of Van Buren made it one of the darling
objects of Jackson's heart to revenge him upon his
enemies.   He employed his whole power to secure
Van Buren's election to the vice-presidency first,
and to the presidency four years later.   Both Clay
and Calhoun had yet to learn what that power was.

The dangers to which a candidate for the presidency is exposed when a member of the Senate,
were strikingly exemplified by a curious trick resorted to by Clay's opponents.   They managed to
refer the question of reducing the price of the
public lands to the Committee on Manufactures, of
which Clay was the leading member, an arrangement on its very face unnatural. Clay understood
at once the object of this unusual proceeding.
" Whatever emanated from the committee," he
said, in a speech on the subject, " was likely to be
ascribed to me. If the committee should propose
a measure of great liberality toward the new states,
the old states might complain. If the measure
should lean toward the old states, the new might
be dissatisfied. And if it inclined to neither class,
but recommended a plan according to which there
would be distributed impartial justice among all

the states, it was far from certain that any would be pleased." However, he undertook the task, and the result was his report on the public lands, **the** principles of which became for many years a part of the Whig platform.

In 1820 the price **of** public lands, which **had** been $2.00 an acre on credit and $1.64 for cash, was fixed at $1.25 in cash. The settlement of the new states and territories had indeed been rapid, but various plans were devised **to** accelerate it still more. One was, that **the** public lands **should be** given to the states ; another, that they should **be** sold to the states at a price merely nominal ; **another**, that they should be sold to settlers at graduated prices, — those which had been in the market a certain time without finding a purchaser to be considered " refuse " lands, and to be sold **at** greatly reduced rates. These propositions were advanced by some in good faith for the benefit of the settlers, but by others **for** speculative ends. Benton was the principal advocate of cheap lands, for reasons no doubt honest. Jackson had never put forth any definite scheme of land policy ; but McLane, his Secretary of the Treasury, recommended in his report of December, 1831, that the public lands should be turned over at fair rates to the several states in which they were situated, **the** proceeds to be distributed among all the states.

Under such circumstances, the subject was referred to Clay's Committee on Manufactures. He reported that the general government should not give up its control **of** the public lands ; that **it** would be unjust to the old states if the public **lands were** disposed of exclusively for the benefit **of the** new states ; that the price should not be reduced; and that the proceeds of the sales, excepting ten per cent set apart for the new states, should be distributed among all the states according to their federal representative population, to be applied to the promotion of education, to internal improvements, or to the redemption of any debt contracted for internal improvements, **or** to the colonization of **free** negroes, as each state might see fit, — such distribution to take place only in time of peace, while in time of war the public land should again **become a** source of revenue to the general government. While condemning the principle of the distribution of surplus revenue arising from taxation, he defended the distribution of the proceeds of public land sales, **on the** ground that Congress had authority to stop revenue from taxation, but not, without the exercise of arbitrary power, the revenue from the public lands.

No sooner **had** Clay submitted his report than it was referred to the Committee on Public Lands, where the whole subject should have gone origi nally. That committee, under the inspiration of Benton, made a counter-report, setting forth that the net proceeds of the land sales could be arrived at only by deducting from the gross proceeds the whole cost of the administration of the land department, inclusive of surveying ; that such a deduction would leave little to be distributed ; and that, if distribution were made of the gross proceeds, it would be equivalent to taking so much from the customs revenue to divide among the states under the name of proceeds of land sales, — a scheme against which Clay himself had loudly protested as utterly unwarranted by the Constitution. This criticism was undoubtedly correct, and Clay could not controvert it. The Land Committee further recommended a reduction of the price of land from $1.25 to $1.00 per acre ; the offering of lands remaining unsold for five years after having been offered once, at fifty cents per acre ; fifteen per cent of the proceeds of land sales to be set apart for the benefit of the new states.

A debate followed, in the course of which Clay made some predictions proving how little a mind even so large as his, and so intent upon grasping the proportions of the rapid growth of this Republic, was able to form a just estimate of future developments. He said : " Long after we shall cease to be agitated by the tariff, ages after our manufactures shall have acquired a stability and perfection which will enable them successfully to cope with the manufactures of any other country, the public lands will remain a subject of deep and enduring interest. We may safely anticipate that long, if not centuries, after the present day, the representatives of our children's children may be deliberating in the halls of Congress on laws relating to the public lands." He did not foresee — as probably nobody did at that period — that, fifty-five years after he spoke thus, the protected industries, having for twenty-five consecutive years enjoyed an " American system " far more protective than his, would still be demanding more, and bidding fair to continue doing so for an indefinite time; while, on the other hand, the public lands still **under** the control of the government would have shrunk to a comparatively poor remnant in quantity and quality, likely to be in private hands **in** another generation, except perhaps some deserts, and some forest reserves in mountainous regions.

His bill passed the Senate, but failed to be acted upon in the House **of** Representatives. It did, however, not fail, as some of those who forced the subject upon him had foreseen, seriously to injure **the** candidate for the **presidency in** the Western States, as being an opponent of " cheap lands."

But the principal, and the most ominous, struggle of the session was still to come — the struggle concerning the Bank of the United States. As we have seen, the memorial **of the** bank praying for a renewal **of** its charter was presented to Congress **in** January. The committees in the two houses, to which the memorial was referred, reported favorably, recommending the renewal **of** the charter with some modifications. It was well known that good majorities in both houses were ready to vote for the renewal.

The enemies of the bank, or rather President Jackson's nearest friends, under Benton's leadership, then rushed to the attack. Several serious charges against the Bank of the United States, drawn up by Benton, were made in the House, with a demand for an investigation by committee. The majority of the committee was composed of known opponents of the bank ; among the minority, probably the most conscientiously impartial man of all, was John Quincy Adams, then in the first year of his distinguished career as a member of the House of Representatives. An exposition of the charges and specifications, and of the findings of the committee in detail, will not be undertaken here. The reader will find an eminently clear and complete presentation of the case in Professor W. G. Sumner's " Andrew Jackson." John Quincy Adams made a separate report, which was of especial value. The majority of the committee declared that the bank was unsound, and recommended that it should not be rechartered ; the minority said that it was safe and useful, and ought to be rechartered ; in this latter view John Quincy Adams substantially concurred. One member of the majority declared that he had seen nothing in the conduct of the president and directors " inconsistent with the purest honor and integrity ;" but, being a warm friend of General Jackson, he consented to sign the majority report. Jackson himself honestly believed all the charges, whether proved or disproved. On the whole, the result of the investigation was regarded as favorable to the bank. The bill to renew the charter passed the Senate June 11, 1832, by 28 to 20, and the House July 3, by 109 to 76. It looked like a great victory; it was only the prelude to a crushing defeat.

If Jackson had ever been inclined to drop his attack on the bank, that inclination vanished the moment the National Republican Convention made the bank question an issue in the presidential canvass. From that hour he saw in the bank his personal enemy — that is to say, an enemy of the country, whose destruction was one of the duties he had to perform. His combativeness became aroused to its highest energy. But there was his Cabinet divided, the Secretary of the Treasury having in his official report made an elaborate argument in favor of the bank; there was his party divided, some of its leading men in and out of Congress being warm friends of the bank; there was his faithful Pennsylvania, the seat of the bank, and more than any other state under its influence, likely to be turned away from him by that influence; there was Congress, with Democratic majorities in both houses, yet both houses having emphatically declared for rechartering the bank. Could he, in the face of these facts, continue the fight? He did not hesitate a moment. The bill to renew the bank charter, as passed by both houses, was presented to him on July 4, 1832, and on July 10 came his veto.

As a legal, financial, and historical argument, that veto presented many vulnerable points; but as a campaign document it was a masterpiece. **No** more powerful stump speech was ever delivered. In ingenious variations of light **and** color, it exhibited the bank before the eyes of the people as an odious monopoly ; a monopoly granted **to** favored individuals without any fair equivalent ; **a** monopoly that exercised a despotic sway over the business of the country ; a monopoly itself controlled by **a few** persons ; a monopoly giving **dangerous** advantages to foreigners as stockholders ; **a** monopoly the renewal of which would put millions into the pockets of a few men ; a monopoly **in** its very nature unconstitutional, the decision of the Supreme Court notwithstanding ; a monopoly mismanaging its business to the detriment of the people, and using its power for corrupt purposes ; a monopoly tending to make the rich richer **and the poor** poorer.

This was in substance Jackson's veto message. **There** was one bitter pill in it intended for Clay's special enjoyment. As to the constitutionality of the bank, Jackson simply repeated the argument which Clay had used in 1811, when opposing the rechartering of the first Bank of the United States. The Supreme Court, Jackson argued, had decided the charter to be constitutional on the ground that the Constitution gave Congress power " to pass all laws which shall be necessary and proper for carrying these powers [the granted powers] into execution." Chartering a bank might have been necessary and proper then, but the President was sure that **it** was not **at all** necessary and proper now. Just so Clay had reasoned in 1811. It was in overruling the Supreme Court that Jackson in the veto uttered the famous sentence: " Each public officer who takes an oath to support the Constitution swears that he will support it as he understands **it, and** not as it is understood by others."

The arrival of the veto in the Senate was the signal for a grand explosion of oratory. Webster opened the debate with his heaviest artillery of argument; Clay, Ewing, and Clayton spoke, thundering magnificently against the veto and its author. With great force it was argued that **the** bank denounced by Jackson as an unconstitutional and tyrannical monopoly was, in all essential features, the bank established under Washington and sanctioned by him; that the privileges it enjoyed were far outweighed by the services it rendered to the country; that the holding of bank stock by foreigners, **who** were excluded from taking part in its management, was **as** little dangerous to the country as **the** holding **by** foreigners of United States bonds; that, according to the doctrine of President Jackson, a law held **to** be constitutional by the Supreme Court was not binding upon him if he saw fit **to** deny its constitutionality; that, if such a doctrine prevailed, there was an end of all law and judicial authority, and the President was an autocrat like Louis XIV.; and finally, that the overthrow of the bank would plunge all business interests into confusion, and the **whole** country into disaster and distress. Clay urged with especial warmth a proposition, which thenceforward formed part of his political programme, — that the veto power, "though tolerated by the Constitution, was not expected by the Convention to be used in ordinary cases;" that it was designed for "instances of precipitate legislation in unguarded moments;" that the principle upon which it rested was "hardly reconcilable with the genius of representative government," and, indeed, "totally irreconcilable with it, if it was to be frequently employed in respect to the expediency of measures as well as their constitutionality."

Nothing could have been more characteristic and significant than the manner in which Jackson's spokesman, Benton, defended the veto and raised the war-cry against the opposition. "The bank is in the field as a combatant," he said, "and a fearful and tremendous one, in the presidential election. If she succeeds, there is an end of American liberty, — an end of the Republic." He described how the bank, by increasing and by withdrawing its loans and accommodations, sought alternately to bribe and to coerce the people to support it. Then he whipped the Democrats into line, exclaiming : —

"You may continue to be for *a* bank and for Jackson, but you cannot be for *this* bank and for Jackson. The bank is now the open, as it has long been the secret, enemy of Jackson. The war is now upon Jackson, and if he is defeated all the rest will fall an easy prey.

What individual **could** stand in the states against the **power of** that bank, **and** that bank flushed with a victory over the conqueror of the conquerors of Bonaparte? The whole government would fall into the hands of the moneyed power. An oligarchy would be immediately established, **and** that oligarchy in **a few** generations would ripen into a monarchy."

He declared that this Republic deserved a more glorious death, and **he** preferred that she should end in " a great immortal battle, where heroes and patriots could die **with the liberty** they scorned to survive."

After a wild wrangle between Benton and Clay about a street fight between the Benton brothers and Jackson, which had occurred years ago, — for the debate degenerated into bitter personalities, — the vote was taken, and the bill, the President's objections notwithstanding, received 22 against 19 votes, not the necessary two thirds. Thus the veto was sustained.

Clay and his friends were still in good spirits. The veto, they thought, would severely shock the sober sense of **the** people, and, in effect, be **Jack-son's** death-warrant. Nicholas Biddle wrote to Clay that he was "delighted with it." Anti-Jack-**son** newspapers found the veto-message " beneath contempt," and advised that it be given the widest possible publicity. **So** it was, and with a startling **result.**

The Democratic **National** Convention had been **held in** May, while the struggle in Congress was still going on. That Jackson would be a candidate for reëlection had been taken for granted since the first year of his administration. He had no competitor. The formality of a nomination was therefore in his case deemed unnecessary. The Convention was called merely to designate a candidate for the vice - presidency. That candidate, too, had been selected by Jackson, — Van Buren, endeared to him by the enmity of his own enemies. The National Convention had only to ratify the decree. Eaton, Jackson's first Secretary of War, was inclined, as a member of the Convention, to vote against Van Buren. But he received a warning not to do so, " unless he was prepared to quarrel with the general."

The National Republicans hoped that the veto would disgust the many supporters of the bank among the Democrats, and thus demoralize and scatter Jackson's following. It had the opposite effect. The bank Democrats found that there was a man at the head of their party whose resolution no opposition could stagger, and who had a will much stronger than theirs ; to that will they bowed. The Secretary of the Treasury, who had made a report in favor of the bank, did not resign. The Democratic politicians, who had been at the same time friends of the bank and friends of Jackson, soon discovered that the cry against the great monopoly was the popular cry and would win. Many of them had to " turn very sharp corners," but they turned them with alacrity. Members of

Congress, **who had voted** for the renewal of the bank charter, took part **in the** anti-bank meetings, apologized for what they had done, and then lustily joined in the outcry against the " monster." Having once changed their position on a question they had considered highly important, simply because Jackson would have it so, they found no further difficulty in surrendering their will completely to **him.** The effect of the veto had therefore been, not **to** scatter Jackson's following, but actually to consolidate his party, giving it more cohesion and discipline than it had ever had before, **and** strengthening **it** numerically **too,** for, although there were **a few** defections, **the** war against **the** bank drew crowds **of** recruits to its ranks.

The cholera appeared that summer in the United States, but it checked only **for** a moment **the** animation of the campaign. The Clay party remained hopeful to the end. In **May** a convention **of** " young men " had met **at** Washington, representing almost every state, to ratify Clay's nomination for the presidency. William Pitt Fessenden of Maine was one of its vice-presidents, and there were not a few among **its** members who became distinguished men in later days. **The Demo-**crats dubbed the meeting " Clay's infant school," but it encouraged him in the belief that he had the youth of the **country on his** side. The **Na-**tional Republicans, having **great** strength among the merchants, manufacturers, and professional men, and commanding a large proportion of the talent of the country, sought to make a campaign of argument, and flooded the country with addresses, pamphlets, and printed campaign matter of all kinds. The United States Bank itself did its share of the work. But this kind of effort failed to reach the large class of voters, then much larger than now, who were not " reading people." The Jackson party trusted more to speeches, meetings, and processions. The figure of the " old hero," grown to greater proportions than ever since he was engaged in his struggle against the "monster monopoly," exercised a wonderful charm over the popular imagination, — a charm against which all the learned arguments about the usefulness of the Bank of the United States and its constitutionality, and the abuse of the veto power, availed nothing. Before the eyes of the masses Jackson appeared as a St. George killing the dragon, and as the invincible champion of " hard cash," of the " yellow boys," driving out " Old Nick's money " and " Clay's rags." Further, the country was made to ring with the old " bargain and corruption " charge, revived to do new service.

At a late period of the campaign the hopes of the Clay party were highly excited by the defection of the New York " Courier and Enquirer," under James Watson Webb, and of several other newspapers which turned from Jackson to Clay. The National Republicans became extremely sanguine of success. So much the more terrible was their disappointment when the returns of the election came in. Of the 288 electoral votes Jackson had won 219, Clay only 49, those of Massachusetts, Rhode Island, Maryland, Delaware, and Kentucky. Wirt, the candidate of the Anti-Masons, had carried Vermont ; South Carolina gave her vote to John Floyd of Virginia. It was a stunning defeat. Clay and his friends stood wondering how it could have happened.

Clay had committed two grave blunders in statesmanship, and one equally grave in political tactics.

The South was in a dangerous ferment against the tariff. The impending extinguishment of the public debt made a large reduction of the revenue necessary. Clay might, therefore, in recognition of the necessity for reducing the revenue, have proposed a reduction of tariff duties sufficient to take off the edge of the Southern discontent, without the least appearance of yielding to Southern threats. The measure he did propose reduced the revenue very little, and, by maintaining the high protective duties, exasperated the South still more. This was the first blunder in statesmanship.

The other was that, instead of advising the United States Bank to keep clear of politics and to accede to any reasonable modification of its charter that might avert the opposition of Jackson, he forced the fight, and made the question of the bank a party question; thus involving in the changing fortunes of party warfare the most important financial institution of the country, whose solvency,

credit, **and** political impartiality were of **the** highest concern to the business community.

The blunder **in political tactics** was that **he be-**
lieved **he** could **excite** the enthusiasm of the masses
for a great moneyed corporation **in its** contest
against **a** popular **hero** like Jackson, — a most
amazing infatuation ; and **thus he made** the bank
question the leading **issue in the** presidential campaign.

Without these blunders **he would,** probably, not
have been victorious; but with them **his** defeat became certain **and** overwhelming.